The Extra-Ordinary Lives of Blue Haven

Sylvia Kim

The Extra-Ordinary Lives of Blue Haven

Copyright © 2020 by Sylvia Kim

All rights reserved. No part of this publication may be reproduced, distributed, stored in a retrieval system, or transmitted in any form or by any means, including electronic, mechanical, photocopying, recording, or otherwise, without the prior written permission of the copyright holder except for the use of brief quotations in a book review or scholarly journal permitted by copyright law.

ISBN: 978-0-578-84324-7

First edition paperback, 2021.

Author: Sylvia Kim
Cover Design: Sylvia Kim

This book is a work of fiction. References to historical events, real people, or real places are used fictitiously. Other names, characters, places, and incidents either are the product of the author's imagination or are used fictitiously. Any resemblance to actual persons, living or dead, businesses, companies, events, or locations are entirely coincidental.

*Dedicated to God, the greatest love I'll ever know,
my mom, who taught me how to dream,
and to anyone who's ever battled depression and mental illness.*

*You are not alone and
you are deeply loved.*

"I have fought the good fight, I have finished the race, I have kept the faith."

2 Timothy: 4:7

Chapter 1

Grace

"Do you remember anything about that place?"

"I remember the smell. Lemon Clorox." I told my therapist, not wanting to go any further. I sat uncomfortably on a cushioned chair with harsh plastic armrests, staring at a motivational poster of a sunset. I swayed my weight to the left, then to the right, seeing whether my therapist – the woman I told my life story to within a matter of minutes, would now steer the conversation elsewhere. She waited.

"I guess that was the low point of my life." I said. "But when I was there, it didn't feel like a low point. I think it hadn't hit me yet."

She nodded and waited some more.

"Sometimes I'm reminded of that place. The people – I mean friends, that were there. I honestly don't remember how long we stayed there. It could've been a few weeks, maybe a month, maybe half a year."

"How old were you then?"

"16."

Austin, Texas
Spring of 2008

It was my sophomore year of high school. The days hovered between winter and spring, so that my body got confused by the warming sunlight and shivering wind. I took the bus back home on a normal day that was filled with laughter and friends. When I reached my apartment building, my steps stopped as I saw Umma and my older sister, Janice, move suitcases into our car.

"Oh. Hanul. Come, come! We going somewhere." Umma said as she waved her hand for me to come sit inside the car. At school, I was Grace. At home, my real name was Hanul, which means sky or heaven. It's the Korean name I grew up hearing. Outside, I referred to Umma as Mom. But "Mom" was still a foreign word to me, even after growing up through all my years in the states.

"Where are we going?" I asked as I sat in the backseat of our car, Janice in the passenger's side not saying a word.

"We going to great place – great place!" Umma said as I saw her eyes speaking back to me in the rear-view mirror. "We go to somewhere else, like a hotel! My lawyer said we can stay there *for free*!"

"Free? Where is it? What about my stuff?"

"It's in the back. I pack for you."

I sat in silence, knowing not to ask any more. Janice, the one who always had a plan didn't explain. If this really was a trip, she'd have handed out itineraries by now.

We took a few turns, and after 20 minutes ended farther up north in a different suburb of Austin. We parked in a non-existent parking lot made up of loose gravel. The place didn't look like a house or a store. It was something in between. No sign was placed above the single wooden door. The windows were concealed by plastic blinds from the inside and placed off center, as if they were two eyes peering suspiciously sideways at you.

We climbed through the gravel, our feet sinking quickly with each step as we tried to reach the front door. There was a tiny speaker with a row of numbers and a single red button placed purposefully at eye-level next to the door. Umma pressed the button as she took out a piece of paper from her pocket.

"Yes?" A woman's voice asked.

"Yes, hi! We are – I am Mrs. Park. My lawyer called you to say we come stay here."

"Yes, one moment please." I looked up to my left and saw a security camera staring back at me. I heard the shuffling and clinking of locks and the door opened. A black lady in her early 30s greeted us with a polite smile. We walked into an immediate office and were told to sit down.

"My name is Paula. We talked over the phone."

"Hi." Umma said with a forced smile that was echoed by a curt greeting from Janice. Paula had a soft, polite face. Her hair swooped outwards at the end, like a cartoon character, and she smelled like vanilla frosting. As she rummaged through a stack of papers, my family and I waited in the narrow, horizontal office. There was a large window opening up to a white open space with a white-tiled floor, white walls, and a white popcorn ceiling. It was like we were in one of those interrogation rooms with a one-way viewing window that people use to observe scientific experiments or criminals.

Paula handed Umma a series of papers and was asked to read all of the information. Janice took over and looked at each piece of paper, translating briskly to my mom on where to sign. Paula then redirected her speech to my sister. I picked up random words including, "secret," "chores," "lawyer," "husband," and "location." My mind started to float away. I had to work on my reading assignment for AP World History. I made plans to go to my friend's birthday party this weekend.

Suddenly, we were standing and walking. First the living room, a vast empty space with a bookcase shoved against the left wall, filled with kid's picture books and tween series like Goosebumps, The Baby-Sitters Club, and Magic Tree House. The buildup to some focal point of a room was anticlimactically unmet by three small brown faux suede couches surrounding a TV that was stuck in the '90s. To the right, a big kitchen, the kind with an island that I only saw on

TV. Paula opened and closed the refrigerator while saying more words.

We walked back through the lackluster "living room" and into a narrow hallway that diverged into two paths. One path led to the bathrooms. I heard the word "communal." Then the other hall was marked by a series of white doors. It looked like the kind you'd see in a cheap motel on your way to Disney World. Paula handed Umma a key to our room. The first on the right side, Room #2.

The room opened to a small space composing of one queen-sized bed, a single-person cot, a small TV, lamp, desk, and a tiny closet without a door. Umma and Janice began putting bags down on the beds as I stood amidst the entrance and slowly closed the door behind me.

"Is this a shelter?" I asked.

"Yes." Umma said, without looking back at me.

Chapter 2
Sarah

I fucking hate it when teachers ask what I want to be when I grow up. As if I'm not already grown. As if I have the time to daydream like a child about some magical future where I'm not weighed down by the responsibilities of having to support my mom and little brother. As if the future will be any easier than the present. Most of the time, I just reply to their question saying I want to be a teacher. Teachers love students who want to be teachers like them. It makes them feel important.

I used to dream of becoming an actress. When I was a kid and my mom and dad were still, Mom and Dad, I would perform plays for them. I'd be the princess and do a dance, then suddenly a bunch of stuffed animals would storm the castle. Luckily, I ninja-kicked their asses. Then I simultaneously played both the prince and princess being reunited at the top of a tower. My lack of casting availability was due to my lack of siblings, that is – until my brother arrived. But by the time he could act, both my dad and temporary stepfather were already gone.

As I listened to the conjugations of nosotros in Spanish class, I remembered what my stage name would've been. Silver DeSoto. Silver, like silver screen. DeSoto like the last name of a girl I once knew. But that's just a foolish daydream. Reality is, I'll probably never have the time to do anything.

Today's Tuesday. Last period on Tuesdays, Wednesdays, and Thursdays are followed by my evening shift at the Cold Stone across the street from school. A solid four hours of scooping cookie dough, gummy bears, brownies, and ice cream, then smashing them on a stone slab to eager children and sometimes eager parents. I don't mind working there. I get to snack on gummy bears and ice cream samples for free. And I like seeing the families. It's a precious stage for most of my customers, the stage when kids still get excited by treats and parents still find joy in their children's innocent smiles.

Friday nights and Saturdays are spent waiting tables at the 24-hour diner at the corner of my neighborhood. The crowds there are different. Broke teenagers treating their girlfriends to a date, and also broke middle-aged men wanting a comfortable place to eat alone. The food is average, as are the tips. But my co-workers are fantastic. Beck, who always gets mistaken for a waitress, is the owner. She has violently red, curly hair. She taught me a lot of new cuss words and doesn't ever take shit from anyone. Then there's my friend Tyler, who works the cashier and counters most nights.

Mondays I reserve for studying. I try to get ahead on homework so I don't have to worry about it during the rest of the week. But Sundays – Sundays are different. Sundays I make an effort to do absolutely nothing. No plans. Unless, I decide to go see my dad – my real dad. From the time he left when I was nine until I was 16, I thought he lived far away. That was what both he and my mom told me. Turns out, he lives about a half hour away with his replacement family. It's been over a year since I've known.

It was during one of my shifts scooping ice cream when I saw him. He walked in wearing an enormous grin, holding the hand of a young platinum blonde child. Trailing behind him was his new blonde wife and other blonde daughter, who looked just a few years my junior. Looking down at the display of ice cream flavors, he started ordering for everyone, but my hands didn't move. He looked up at me. The smile in his eyes disappeared. "S-S-Sarah?" He stuttered.

I dropped my metal scooper in the mint chocolate chip and ran back to the employee break room like a total loser. I paced around the carpeted floor with tears in my eyes. Questions frantically rushed through my mind. Why the hell was he here? He's not supposed to be living here. He's supposed to be living far away. Did he come back? Why hasn't he come to see me?

The confusion escalated into a heated rage. I stormed back out to ask him why he lied and where he lived. But he was already getting back in his car with his kids, who were holding fucking ice cream cones! I threw off my apron and got in my car. I followed him, always leaving a car between us so I wouldn't be seen. I could see the back of their shiny blonde heads as Dad drove completely normal – as if a momentous event hadn't just occurred!

They pulled into their three-car driveway. I watched Dad and his new family disappear behind a closing garage door. I'd been in this neighborhood before. I'd been to the outlet mall in this area before. He was barely in another city. All this time, he was right here.

His house was so much bigger than mine and Mom's. His was a surplus of floors and tall ceilings, a front garden with a stone walkway up to a home that I imagined to be owned by a dentist or lawyer. That evening, I planned on confronting him. I imagined myself pounding on the door and demanding an answer. But for some reason, I was glued to my car seat. A heavy stream of tears poured out of me as I tried to inhale a few breaths through my sobbing. The air around me turned to night. I cried through an entire rotation of my Alicia Keys album. He moved on. My dad wasn't my dad anymore. He was someone else's.

After the mountain of shock began to wear down, from time to time, I was reminded of the good moments we had. I remembered how he would throw stuffed animals at me when I cued him with my, "And they stormed the castle," line during my plays. I remembered how he would drive me to soccer and stay to cheer me on through every practice and every game. I remembered when he would read me a bedtime story using all his animated fairytale voices.

Every time I was reminded of the good times, my heart ached to see him. So occasionally, I drove back to his neighborhood on a Sunday, my only free time of the week. I never knock on the door. I never even get out of my car. I park a few houses away and wait to see him from afar. I try to catch a glimpse of him as he walks the dog (also a blonde golden retriever) or walks around his kitchen. Every once in a while, I see him step out onto his third-floor balcony. But when his new wife comes to join him, I leave. When I see one of his new daughters, I leave. When I see him too happy, I leave.

He told me once, that I reminded him so much of Mom. We would be having a great time together, during one of my visits with him right after the split. He rented a room at an extended-stay hotel where we got to build forts and swim in the pool. We would be having fun. But then he would look at me, and his face would turn sad. I guess he didn't want to be reminded of his old life. Sometimes I dreamed of leaving it all behind as well.

Chapter 3

Grace

I wish I had good memories of my father, my Appa. Just one I could look back on and smile. But I have none. The closest thing I have to a good memory is when we were living back on the East Coast. We were getting ready for church. Already finished, I sat and waited on my parents' bed. He came and sat next to me. He patted my head, touched my hair, then stuck my tag, that was sticking out and exposed, back into my shirt. We sat like that for a few minutes as we watched Umma frantically get ready for service.

That's all I have. Whenever I try to think of another memory, I am reminded of the preceding events. Him showing up to my piano recital and sitting in the back, after refusing to come beforehand. Our family trip to Korea, getting cut short after he mysteriously lost a large sum of our travel money. Him coming home one day, after months of being gone. Him eating dinner with me and my sister, after coming home to see Umma collapsed on the kitchen floor a few hours prior. I wish I loved my father.

Within the deepest beliefs of my heart, I never thought we'd leave him. Things had gotten so bad, but they were always bad. Inconsistency was the only consistent thing in our lives.

***

"What do you remember about your father, during that time in your life?"

"There's one memory, an image really, that I can't seem to forget…I think I was 15. It was when we were all still living together. I was hungry one night, so I went to the kitchen to make some mac and cheese. At this point, Appa was sleeping in the living room. I passed by the silhouette of him sitting on the floor, leaning up against the backside of our couch. I microwaved my Kraft mac and cheese and ignored him.

As I walked back to my room, I saw him. His legs were sprawled out beneath the kitchen table. He was sitting in his underwear. He had a belt around his arm and he was holding a syringe. His face was staring at the wall, completely dazed, his mouth was hanging open and his eyes were black and empty. It was a long time before I realized he was high. I finally understood during health class one day during my junior year. They had an informative video on drugs, and I recognized a lot of the objects in the lesson, they were the objects that used to sit on my kitchen table at home."

***

After we moved into Blue Haven, none of us acknowledged what happened. Our routine was the same. Janice still studied all day for her upcoming MCAT test. And Umma still dropped me off and picked me up after school where I'd rant about the day's events. I'd sprinkle in a little flair about the people I was mad at or amplify my wonderful new accomplishments. Then, she'd energetically rebuke my enemies and praise my talents. Umma always took my side. I loved that about her. I was always shocked at how little my friends talked to their moms. I thought everyone had the same familial closeness as I did with mine.

Sometimes at school, I wondered how much longer we had to stay at the shelter. But I never asked. I just waited to see where we'd end up on our drive after school.

The only thing that's actually changed since moving is the fear. Fear of everyone else. I had this spike stuck in my throat and this shouting thought that as soon as I stepped back into school – everyone would know. They'd see it on my face, they'd smell it on my clothes, they'd hear a difference in my voice. But nobody did. Nobody noticed anything. My teachers didn't know. As I talked to my friends, they didn't notice a single thing.

I turned in my AP World History assignment at school today. My teacher talked about our upcoming AP test and how helpful it was to test out of the required course so we wouldn't have to take it in college. College. I had the rest of the semester and all of junior year before I had to start applying to schools. In the meantime, I was relieved to see that no one knew about my sudden change in address.

"You're going to Rebecca's party this weekend, right?" Angela asked me.

"Of course, I am!" I responded enthusiastically. This would be the second house party I ever attended. The first was a Halloween party during the seventh grade, which I hated.

"What are you gonna get her as a gift?" Tabitha asked.

"I have no idea yet. I have to go shopping after school and find her something."

The idea of buying my friend a birthday gift suddenly weighed on me.

Chapter 4
Sarah

It was a Sunday when it happened. I was sitting in my car, two houses away from Dad's house. I smiled when I saw him smile in the kitchen. But then I got angry as I saw him sit down at the dinner table surrounded by his new family. The younger daughter was holding a stuffed tiger – seemingly refusing to take him off the dinner table. The new mom had a stern face, I imagined she was telling her to put it away. Dad waved his hand in the air laughing, as if he was saying it wasn't a big deal for Mr. Snuggles the tiger to join them for dinner.

For me it was a teddy bear. His name was Phil, like the boy I had a crush on from Disney channel's Phil of the Future. I brought Phil wherever I went, to the salon where my mom cut hair, to doctor check-ups, to the mall. Phil slept beside me to comfort me whenever Mom and Dad fought. Dad brought Phil to watch my soccer matches from the bleachers. The last time I saw Phil was when I slept over Dad's hotel room during one of my weekly visits. I left Phil with Dad, explaining it would make him feel better whenever he got sad again. I never got him back.

It made me angry, seeing Dad happy. But sometimes it gave me comfort – maybe leaving was worth it, for him. The older daughter appeared in the front yard to let the dog out. She glanced in my direction and I ducked down, hiding behind my steering wheel. Please don't see me. Please don't see me. Please don't see me. I waited three whole songs to come back up. She was nowhere to be seen. I got out of park and drove home.

I live with Mom and David in a small but cozy two-bedroom home. Since living here, my room has slowly transitioned from makeshift castles made of colorful scarves, to posters of Mia Hamm, to cutouts I found from old issues of Elle and Vogue. After David was born, my stepdad, Curt, painted my bedroom walls yellow. A cloud, moon, and star mobile used to hang above his crib.

One day, Curt left and David stayed. Now our walls are a mix of Sonic the Hedgehog posters, my weekly work schedule, and pamphlets of colleges I plan on applying to in the fall – UCLA, NYU, Georgetown, and Chicago. Anything outside of Texas near a big city I can get lost in.

I parked my car on the curb. Our lawn was overrun with weeds that wrapped around my tires. We don't have a garden, the only flowers we have are dandelions that breed like rabbits throughout our front and backyard. Despite the lack of golden retriever and perfectly placed stone pathway, I love our home.

I love our front porch. The one me and Mom relax on after David falls asleep. We rock back and forth on our swinging porch chair, each holding a condensating glass of sweet tea. We forget all the hard work we did that day and talk about trips we want to take one day – Hawaii, Bali, South Africa. Mom sometimes asks me what I want to be when I grow up. I tell her I don't know yet. I don't want her to worry about being alone before it happens.

As I stepped onto our sacred resting place, I was stopped by a crisp white piece of paper taped to our front door. In black, bolded capital letters was the phrase, **NOTICE OF EVICTION**. This couldn't be right. I gave Mom my paycheck for rent weeks ago.

"Mom! Mom! What is this?" I shouted as I looked for her inside. She was in the kitchen making dinner and David was playing video games in the living room, within earshot of us. He looked up at me worried.

"Mom! What the hell is this?"

Mom stopped chopping vegetables and squinted at the paper I was holding. Her face suddenly emptied of color as she grabbed the paper from my hand. Staring hard at the words as if the longer she looked at it, there was some chance the words would change.

"I gave you money for rent two weeks ago." I said absolutely frustrated. "You were supposed to mail the check! Did you mail the check? Did you forget? You should call them and tell them it was a mistake." I stated through a clenched jaw.

"It wasn't enough." She said calmly.

"What? What are you talking about? It was enough to cover the rent for this month!"

"No. It wasn't enough."

"What the fuck are you talking about?"

"I had to pay off the divorce lawyer. Curt stopped sending money after the divorce was finalized. I had to pay the electricity bill or we'd have no power for the month. And I had to pay for David's hospital bill after he sprained his ankle. We also needed groceries. We're four months behind on rent." Mom said quietly as she continued staring blindly at the notice.

I was stunned. With my money it should have been enough. Why the hell did Curt stop sending money? David was still his son.

"But don't you have any money saved? I have about $3,000 in my college savings account. We can use that."

"No, you keep your money."

"Then what the hell are we going to do? Don't you have any savings?"

"Curt."

"Curt what? What about fucking Curt!"

"He took it. Well, technically I gave it to him."

"What do you mean?"

"The money's gone." I stared at her incredulously, my eyes heavy with tears waiting to fall. "Curt wanted to start his own real estate company. He said we would be making much more money with his own business and I wouldn't have to work at the salon anymore. I could stay home and take care of David."

"How much?"

"About $30,000." I couldn't believe it. I was out of my mind. The sheer magnitude of my rage was so strong I could taste the bitter bile in the back of my throat. Mom gave Curt $30,000. $30,000! Her life's savings. Gone. To Curt, a man with his own business who no longer sent money for his son.

"You're so stupid." I muttered under my breath. Mom stared at
me, her eyes open wide.

"What did you say?"

"I said, you're so fucking stupid! How could you give away all your money! To Curt! What! Some man says he loves you so then you give him all your money? You're a fucking idiot!"

A harsh sting formed on my cheek. Mom slapped me. Mom never hit me before. The sound of David crying was suddenly ringing in my right ear.

"I hate you." I told Mom and left. I headed back towards my car.

"Where the hell do you think you're going?" Mom followed.

I kept on walking. My back turned to Mom as she continued yelling at me from the porch, the place we used to sip sweet tea.

"Fine! Go! What else are you good for? You'll leave just like the rest of them!" She spat the words and they pierced my back like arrows. No. I wasn't like them. This was her fault. All her fault. She did this to herself. She did this to all of us. I got in my car and started driving.

Chapter 5
Grace

On Friday after school, we returned to the shelter. Umma pressed a series of numbers then pressed the red button and the door magically opened. We went to the kitchen fridge to unload some food from the Korean grocery store. A middle-aged Hispanic woman was also in the kitchen. We locked eyes for a moment. I didn't say hi and escaped to my room.

I guess that answered my question. I wondered if anyone else was staying in the other rooms. Paula said the shelter was only allowed for women and their children. Sometimes I heard sounds across the hall, but I made sure to wait for the rustling to end before I went to the communal bathroom to brush my teeth.

Back in our room, I dug through my bag searching for something I could use for Rebecca's gift. Something that looked new, unworn, and trendy. I couldn't find a thing. I fell asleep with knots in my stomach. The next morning, the day of

Rebecca's party, I asked Umma if we could go back home so I could pack more things.

Walking into the apartment, I thought things would look different. But everything was exactly where it used to be. The remote control was still sitting at the same angle on top of the coffee table. The mail was still splattered in a semi-pile on the kitchen counter. I walked down the hall into my room as Umma turned the opposite way into hers. My guitar, which I named Molly Sue, had gathered dust as it stood in the corner of my room. My bedside table still held a half-filled cup of water, my clock that was shaped like a coffee mug, and a stack of books consisting of The Kite Runner, The House on Mango Street, and the Bible.

I searched my closet looking for some hidden gem that could pass as new. My handbags, Rebecca had seen me wear before. My candles, used. My books, worn from dog ears and underlining. I went to my jewelry box filled with $5 items I bought at Forever 21. Then I spotted it, a green and gold bangle bracelet. Not a scratch in sight. Next to my jewelry box was my limited line of make-up. A liquid eyeliner pen I was too scared to try and a Maybelline lipstick my sister got me for my birthday two years ago.

Then, I spotted a Clinique lip gloss I bought a week ago that was still in its packaging. Perfect! I packed it in my bag along with a stack of clothes and underwear. I stared back at Molly Sue and decided to leave her. Then I looked back at my book pile and decided to bring back the Bible and a notebook filled with poems I wrote.

That night, I asked Umma to drop me off at my friend's birthday party. She told me to text Janice for a ride instead. She had already taken the car to the library to study. Janice made it a point to tell me I was being annoying but eventually agreed to give me a ride.

We used to be super close, Janice and I. She was my person. But once she went off to college, we steadily drifted. I had to learn to take over the work of helping my parents. I'd text her while she was at MIT, asking her to do her usual work, but she told me I had to do it now. She was too busy living her new life. And I had to learn on my own – how to talk to credit card representatives over the phone, how to translate for Umma during doctor appointments, how to call AAA for car maintenance.

She was gone when things got really bad again with Appa. And I resented her for it. The night I saw Appa high in the living room, I never told her what I witnessed. I wondered if she knew already. I wondered if he was always like this and I was just the last to find out.

"Don't drink too much. And if someone offers you weed, don't smoke it." Janice told me bluntly as she parked outside Rebecca's house.

"Why? I saw you drinking and partying while you were in college. You were tagged on Facebook."

"That was different. I'm an adult now."

"Yeah? Well, so am I."

"No. You're not." Janice said facing me. I didn't know what to say to the words I knew to be true. "Don't screw up your life before you get to live it."

"…Whatever. I'm leaving." I got out of the car and slammed the door. I called up my friend, Tabitha, knowing that I needed to find my people fast to avoid the looming awkwardness. No answer. I hated big crowds, but Rebecca was an actual friend. She was the kind of person who was genuinely nice to all her friends – and she had a lot of them. I opened the door to the booming sound of Flo Rida and swam through the crowd of strangers to see my friends leaning over the dining table and pouring drinks. The sight of their faces quickly put me at ease.

"Are you guys drinking *alcohol*?" I said wagging my finger, impersonating a disapproving parent.

"Graaaaace!" I could tell Tabitha was already tipsy.

"Just Tabs here. I'm drinking coke." Angela said passing me a soda.

"Should I pour some alcohol in here?" I said, half joking and half serious. Before I could decide, Tabitha put her arm around my shoulder.

"You're heeeere!" Tabitha said. "We should go say hi to Rebecca!"

"Ok! Let's go! Where is she?" I asked as I put my arm around her shoulder. The three of us scouted the house. People were dancing on the first floor and groups of twos and threes were scattered on the staircase leading up to a crowded second floor as well. Who the hell were all these people? We pushed our way upstairs to get a better view. I spotted Rebecca outside talking to a group of people I vaguely recognized from school.

We walked back down the stairs, Angela and I supporting Tabitha from either side. As we made our way outside, I noticed a giant trampoline. Rebecca was talking to a group of people I always passed by in the halls. Jamal, DeShawn, Jamie, Abbey, and a couple other people I never thought I was cool enough to talk to. I waited awkwardly to the side of their circle waiting for them to finish.

"RE-BEH-CCAAAA! Ca-kaw! Ca-kaw!" Tabitha shouted and waved her arms like a bird, quickly breaking the ice.

"Heeyyy!" Rebecca responded with a smile, hugging each of us. "Looks like someone had her first experience with alcohol tonight." Rebecca laughed and patted Tabitha on the head.

"How's it going?" Angela asked.

"Yeah! Do you feel any different? You're *finally* 16 now!" I asked making firm eye contact with Rebecca, avoiding the popular people standing behind her. Jamie and Jamal were attractive. I always ran away and avoided contact with attractive boys – especially ones that weren't Asian. I knew Umma would freak out if she found out. Umma gave me a lecture any time she'd pick me up and a boy was even within a three-feet radius of me.

"Yes. I feel like a new woman." Rebecca replied dramatically, flipping her hair. "Hey! This is Jamie, Jamal, DeShawn, and Abbey."

"Hey. How's it going?" Angela asked for me. The four of them nodded at us in acknowledgement. It was moments like this when I was thankful Angela understood how uncomfortable I felt when meeting new people. Angela and I instantly became friends during freshmen year. We bonded over our similar sense of humor and love of K-pop. She introduced me to Tabitha, and it's been the three of us at the core of my friend group since the beginning of high school.

"I got you a present!" I said as I handed Rebecca a small gift bag which I had saved from my 16th birthday a few months prior."

"Thank yooouuu!" Rebecca said, giving me a squeeze.

"We're gonna jump on your trampoline!" I blurted, trying to escape her reaction of my second-hand gift.

"Ok, sure! Knock yourselves out."

I always envied families that had giant trampolines or pools in their backyards. I always wondered what it would be like. Angela, Tabitha, and I climbed up onto the trampoline. Each of us cautiously figuring out how to balance, like babies learning how to walk. Then we started jumping. First, a few inches up in the air. Then, higher and higher until I was laughing hysterically. I fell on my back and they continued bouncing – catapulting me into the starry night sky.

Laying on the giant laughter propeller, I felt alive. Tabitha and Angela joined me and we laid down together, staring at the stars. The steady hum of people chatting, bass booming, and bottles clinking surrounded us. It made me forget that I had moved into a shelter that same week. Just then, I heard a sniffle to my left. I turned my head to Tabitha thinking she was getting sick from the combination of jumping and beer. But she was crying. I didn't know what to do. I hated seeing people cry. And I hated crying in front of people.

"What's wrong?" I asked tentatively. Angela looked over to me and the three of us sat up, waiting for Tabitha to finish crying, unsure of how to comfort her.

"I just feel so stressed lately." Tabitha said in her boozed crying state.

"What's going on?" Angela asked.

"My parents have been pressuring me so much to get better grades. They're saying I should've studied harder in school and that I won't get into a good college unless I do better. I don't know what more I can do. I work hard. I'm in honor society. I got into our health studies club. But I still got a B+ in AP chemistry. And I feel so stupid."

"Yeah, I know the feeling." Angela chimed in. "My parents just tell me I should be more like my older brother. He's the golden child." Angela said rolling her eyes in distaste. "It's hard having Asian parents."

"It's so unfair!" Tabitha said as she wiped the remaining tears from her face. "White people, black people – they have it so much easier! But we're expected to do so much more. I can't keep up. What if I don't get into college!" Tabitha asked panicked.

"Of course, you're going to get in." I stated matter-of-factly. "You're so smart Tabs. This is just something we have to go through." The truth was, I didn't feel the immense pressure most of my Asian friends got from their parents. Umma congratulated me when I got an A- on a test. If anything, I put the pressure on myself to do well in school.

"It's just so hard." Tabitha said dejectedly.

"Yeah…life is hard." I said. I wondered if I should tell them what had happened to me over the past week. But instead, I placed my hand on Tabitha's shoulder and stayed silent.

Chapter 6
Jamie

"Hey, man."

"Hey, Jamal. What's going on?" I asked over the phone, hoping Jamal wasn't about to enlist me in Saturday night plans.

"Rebecca's having a party tonight, brother. To-Night!"

"That's cool."

"Cool? Nah, man. You gotta be there. Everyone is gon' be there. Rebecca is *fine*. You said you was digging her! And, she's got some hot friends too! You'll be there, right?"

"I don't know, man. I gotta watch my sisters tonight."

"Man, I thought they was full grown by now. Isn't Aisha 'bout ready to be drivin' cars now?"

"Nah, man. Aisha's only 12. And Quinn is...shit, how old is Quinn?"

"How the hell do I know? She's yo' sister!"

"Well, she still brings a lunchbox to school – so she's still a kid. Ma's got a late-night shift tonight." Ma worked as a nurse in the same hospital since I was a kid. People there called her Nurse Jackie. She still complained that she should've gotten compensation when they stole her name for the TV show.

"That's perfect! Just wait'll yo' ma leaves and Aisha and Quinn are sleeping. No one will know!"

"I dunno. I don't wanna get an ass whooping."

"Jamie! Imma whoop yo' ass if you don't come!"

"Ok man! Ok! I'll be there."

"Good. You better be. Aight. I'll see ya later."

"Yeah, see ya."

I knew better than to say no to Jamal. Every time I did, the situation would always escalate. It was better to agree near the beginning. Or else, the party would have been followed by a mandatory trip to a club or bar on Sixth Street and mission impossible scenario where we tried to get a homeless man to buy us cigarettes.

"Jamie! Jamie!" I heard Ma yelling my name.

"Yes, Ma?"

"Come over here!" I slunk out of my room, hands deep in my pockets hoping she didn't just hear my rendezvous plans with Jamal.

"What is it?"

"Now this here's the potato salad. For dinner, I want you to give everyone some of this." Ma said as she placed the glass tupperware in the fridge. "Then, now look here." Ma opened the oven door to show a glistening chicken. "I put the oven on a low heat. Now in one hour. Jamie, look at me." She held her index finger to my face. "In exactly one hour, you take out this chicken and turn the oven off. You hear me? I don't wanna come home to find the house burned down."

"Ok, Ma."

"Good. Then you guys gotta eat some veggies so I have another tupperware of spinach salad in the fridge." Ma said as she went back to open the fridge.

"Ugh." Aisha groaned from the living room.

"Aisha, ya better eat your vegetables or you'll stay the shortest girl in your class! Don't you wanna reach five feet one day?" Aisha rolled her eyes and proceeded to paint Quinn's tiny toenails.

"I got it, Ma. I got it! Go to work!"

"Repeat what I said to you."

"Ma!" I said exasperated. Ma still forgets that I'm 17 now. She treats me like I'm Aisha's age, and Aisha like she's Quinn's age. And Quinn, like she's still a baby.

"Just tell me or I'll be late!"

"Potato salad and regular salad in the fridge. Turn the oven off in one hour and give everybody chicken."

"Ok good!" Ma said as she placed a series of tiny items sprawled on the counter in her purse. "Now, don't you go running off with Jamal tonight. I need ya here! I swear, that boy needs to stop thinking about girls and basketball. He needs to start thinking about his future! Maybe, you should try tutoring him again Jamie-"

"-Ma you're gonna be late!"

"Ok! Ok! I'm leaving." Ma gave me a kiss on the cheek and headed for the door. "Y'all behave!" Ma shouted as she left the house.

"So, when are you leaving?" Aisha asked me.

"What?"

"I know you sneak out at night." Aisha said.

"I do not! Shut up Aisha!" Hoping that would be enough to cover my lie. How the hell did Aisha know?

"Ummmm hmmmm." Aisha hummed disapprovingly. I don't know when she became such a diva. I sat on the couch with Quinn and watched SpongeBob SquarePants, waiting for time to pass.

At midnight, I parked my car at the party and wondered if I should just drive back home. Weekends were the only time I got to rest. Most evenings I studied for the SATs and got ahead on assignments so I could watch Aisha and Quinn while Ma was at work. I also helped Aisha with her homework. She didn't know, because I acted like it was a pain, but I enjoyed going over multiplication tables and the solar system with her. Seeing her face light up when she understood something made me feel good.

But Jamal was one of the few people I could never say no to. He was my boy since the beginning. Defending my honor when I got bullied in the first grade. Teaching me how to talk to girls since we hit puberty – he hit puberty much earlier than I did, which is why he showed me the ropes from his years of failed attempts and growing wisdom on females.

Jamal was the only one who asked about Dad. He knew how much harder it was whenever he got stationed in another country with the Army and we could barely communicate. Ma thought it best for us to stop moving around every time he got stationed somewhere new after Aisha was born. Every time he got deployed, I felt myself go insane waiting to see him again. It's been 15 months since he's been somewhere in the Middle East, before that it was Germany, Florida, Virginia, Southeast Asia, and Fort Worth, Texas – where he and Ma met.

I started walking towards the front door of Rebecca's house when I got a text from Jamal saying he and the crew were in the backyard. I tried to slide through the crowd of grinding people, some I vaguely recognized from calculus class. Then I passed through the giant kitchen where some horny teens were making out. I wondered what Rebecca's parents did to afford this kind of house. It was like the ones I saw on MTV Cribs.

"Jamie's here!" Jamal shouted. I walked up to him and we completed our ceremonial handshake – the same one we made up in the fourth grade. "Becca, you remember Jamie. He's the genius in our little family."

"Of course, I know Jamie!" Rebecca said with a smile and leaned in for a hug. I always thought she was pretty. We worked on an assignment in AP Biology together once, and I corrected her about the location of mitochondria in a cell.

"Happy birthday." I said, not knowing what else to follow up with. She smiled graciously.

"Now, Jamie here, he's in the AP, IB, ABC, whatever the hell those classes are with all the extra letters in front of it. He's probably gon' be a doctor one day, or maybe an Airforce pilot – something big ya know."

"Nah, man." I said in feigned embarrassment. If you ever needed a hype man, Jamal was your boy.

"Is that so?" Rebecca asked amused. Jamal proceeded to talk about how he was destined to be famous after high school, whether that be through his looks or NBA career. The rest of the crew joined in and began to single out the other attractive people at the party as we collaboratively brainstormed each other's first moves and pick-up lines.

Amidst the chatter, I spotted three Asian girls quietly approaching our circle, the one in the middle obviously drunk out of her mind. The one on the right was pretty. She had long black hair. I liked the way she ran her fingers through it, nervously. I could feel her mixture of discomfort and excitement as she waited for a pause in Jamal's banter to speak. I looked at her and she turned away.

"Ca-kaw! Ca-kaw!" The drunk one said creating a window for her and her friends to swoop in and talk to Rebecca. The pretty one didn't say much. I've never seen her at a party before, only at school in passing. Halfway through their conversation, I wondered whether it was too late to ask her name, but then the three of them ran away to jump on the trampoline.

"Who's that girl?" I asked Rebecca.

"Who? The drunk one? That's Tabith-"

"Nah. The one on the right." Jamal and Rebecca looked at me with a playful grin.

"That's Grace." Her name is Grace.

"Come on man! Let's get some drinks in you." Jamal said with his arm around my shoulder, leading me to a bucket of ice filled with Mike's Hard Lemonade, Samuel Adams, and Smirnoff Ice. The following hours became a blur of glass bottles and a crowded dance floor. I checked my phone in the middle of a Chris Brown song and it said 3:13 a.m.

"Shit!" I pulled Jamal's sleeve and shouted that I was going home.

"Aight man, I'll hit you up tomorrow!" Jamal shouted as he continued grinding with one of Rebecca's friends.

I got home by 3:41 a.m., carefully stopping for at least 15 seconds at every stop sign so I wouldn't get pulled over by the cops and thrown in jail. I tried with all my might to silently park my car in the garage. Ma's car was already parallel parked on the front curb. Her shift ended at 2 a.m. I hoped for the life of me that she would assume my car was already in the garage and I was already fast asleep. I took out my keys from my pocket and unlocked the door, making sure there wasn't even the slightest jingle.

I tiptoed through the hallway, past the oven – which I double checked was turned off. I was nearly to the finish line, on the way to my bedroom, the place where I had *always* been tonight. But then I heard a faint whimper. I let my heels plant on the floor and turned around. It was Ma, sitting on the sofa, alone in the dark.

"Ma? I was uh, just checking a sound I heard, uh- outside…" I nervously turned on the light. It took me a minute to realize that Ma was crying.

"Ma?" I asked again, sitting next to her with great caution. She wouldn't have been this sad about me sneaking out. If anything, she would be taking off her shoe preparing to thrust it at my head. Why is Ma crying?

"Jamie. Oh, Jamie. I don't know what to do now." Ma said, still crying and wiping her nose and eyes. I handed her a tissue. "Thank you, baby."

"What happened?" Ma let out a deep, tear-filled sigh.

"I went into work today. Doctor Mark called me into his office." Doctor Mark was Ma's boss. He sounded like both a prophet and reliable physician to me. My mind wandered to my memories of him. Doctor Mark giving me a mini basketball out of a giant gift box reserved for pediatric patients when I was six. Doctor Mark showing me X-rays and later quizzing me on diagnoses. "It's a broken bone!" I'd say, and he'd give me a lollipop. I always liked Doctor Mark.

"Did you hear what I said?"

"Huh, what?" I said quickly awakening from my half-drunk, half-exhausted stupor.

"I got laid off." A long silence sat between us.

"...what?"

"Doctor Mark said they were doing staff cuts in every department. It's cause of the recession. Our hospital isn't doing so well."

"But you...but they can't. You've been there so long..."

"That don't matter now. It's all over. It's finished. I don't know what I'm gonna do now. Thirteen years I was working there. Now, it's over. And you'll be off to college soon. How am I gonna save money for you to go to college? And this house? Lord, yo' daddy and I have been trying to pay off this house since you was born."

"Don't worry about me or college. That's not gonna happen for a long time. Have you talked to Dad?"

"No son. I can't talk to him about this."

"Why not? I'm sure he'll know what to do." I asked with an increasing pain thumping in my chest. "I'll call him then. I'll talk to him."

"You can't, son."

"What? Why not?" I said, feeling angry and terrified.

"They said he's gone missing." I stared back at Ma, lifeless. "I didn't want you worrying Jamie. I never told you exactly where he was stationed this time. He's been in a tough part of Afghanistan. He was called out on a mission. It's been almost a month, they said he's been MIA – Missing In Action. They still looking for him." Ma said sobbing into a tissue.

    I waited for my mind to catch up with what I just heard. Ma lost her job. No she got fired. No wait, laid off. Dad's missing? Dad's missing. Dad is missing! I don't know what to do. I don't know what to do. I don't know what to do.

Chapter 7
Sarah

I drove away as quickly as I could, leaving my screaming mom behind me. Then I wondered where I could go. I couldn't go to Dad's house. He didn't even know that I knew where he lived. I couldn't go to work. I don't have a shift today. I don't have any friends either.

Friends are a scarcity in my life. I rarely hang out with people outside of class where we have nothing more than tepid conversations. Plus, I don't have the time. And they never understand why I have to work so much. Most of the time, the people I talked to smoked pot, drank, or went to go skateboard after school. The thought of confiding in someone at a skatepark made my stomach turn.

I thought about calling Tracey. She used to be my best friend, well, my only real friend. We met as kids. Her parents also divorced, earlier than mine did. She coached me through my parent's divorce. During the eighth grade, she moved to San

Francisco with her mom and new stepdad. We promised each other we'd stay best friends. We didn't.

After a while, I found myself calling Tyler. We've been working the same shift at the diner together for almost a year. Tyler was taking time off before going to college while sporadically appearing in bars and cafés for open mics. One night during a nocturnal shift many months ago, I felt so overwhelmed in the process of Mom and Curt's divorce that I spilled out my life story to him after the restaurant cleared out of customers. I remembered how good it felt to talk to someone.

"Hey. What's up?" Tyler answered nonchalantly.

"…Hey." I answered, unsure of what to say. After my breakdown, neither of us mentioned it again. A few moments of silence passed. What the hell was I thinking calling him?

"Are you ok?"

"I – I don't know. My mom and I got into a fight. I left the house."

"…Do you wanna come over?" Tyler asked gently.

"Ok."

I always wondered what kind of place Tyler lived in. I imagined a one-bedroom apartment in some trendy area further south, like near SoCo Avenue where the hipsters of Austin liked to congregate. But he lived in a residential neighborhood, six blocks from the diner. His lawn looked just like mine. I clumsily knocked on his front door, wondering if I should just go back home.

"Hey!" Tyler opened the door with a smile. I always thought Tyler was attractive in an easygoing way. He was tall but not towering, fit but not buff. He had the demeanor that made you feel at ease.

"Hi." I said, trying to hide the fact that my eyes were thoroughly swollen and my cheeks were stained with dried-up tears. He let me in and guided me towards the backyard. We were stopped by two kids sitting cross legged in the living room, surrounded by a sea of Legos.

"Hellloooooo! Are you Tyler's giiiiirlfriend?" One of the kids asked through a high-pitched giggle.

"Oh, you hush Daisy! Don't mind her." Tyler told me. "Mom! My friend is here! We're going outside!" He shouted into thin air.

"You live with your family?" I asked confused as we passed through the back door and into the backyard.

"Yeah. My mom and my younger brother Jeff. Daisy and Steph are my little cousins. Jeff's a freshman. Hey, you might know him!"

"Probably not. I'm a junior…For some reason I thought you lived on your own."

"Nope. Trying to save money, not spend it. At least until I can go back to Brown."

"Back?"

"Yeah, I was actually there for almost a semester. But then I had to come back." We sat on the steps of his patio overlooking a slightly overgrown green lawn.

"Why?"

"My dad passed away." Tyler stated as he started throwing a tennis ball to a black and white-spotted dog that appeared out of nowhere.

"I'm sorry." I said confused. I thought Tyler was one of the kids who chose to take a gap year to *find themselves*.

"It's alright." I peered at Tyler's face to see if I had stupidly brought up a horrible memory. But his demeanor didn't seem to change. Suddenly, all my problems seemed childish.

"So, what happened? You sounded upset on the phone."

"It's nothing." I said, lowering my head in shame.

"Obviously it's not nothing or you wouldn't be here." Tyler waited patiently and I felt new tears start to form.

"Everything is fucked up." I said through sharp inhales, trying to hold back the tears. "I thought all the shit with Curt was over after he left. But – Curt took Mom's savings! I had no idea. She didn't even tell me."

"She probably didn't want you to worry." Tyler answered calmly.

"But that doesn't even matter! We're all fucked now. I found an eviction notice on the front door when I got home today."

"Oh shit." Tyler looked back at me surprised.

"I don't even care that Curt left. I never considered him a part of my family. But he made another mess even after he left. I don't know what to do. I don't know what my family can do. We have no one else. All the friends we thought we had, left after my real dad or Curt stepped out of the picture. My aunts and uncles stopped sending us money a long time ago. We have no one else left."

Tyler put his hand on my shoulder and I let more tears fall. I was too sad to feel embarrassed in the moment. He wrapped his arm around me and rubbed my shoulder as I sobbed.

"It'll be ok." He whispered.

"How do you know? How do you know that it's gonna be ok?"

"Because of you." I stopped crying and stared at him confused. "Sarah you're stronger than you know…Do you know what my friends at Brown would do when they didn't have any more cash to blow?"

"What?"

"They would complain. They'd complain and complain. Then, they would call their parents and beg for more money. You know, there are so few people our age that actually work to provide for themselves. And there are even fewer that work to help their family. But you're one of those people. Jesus! You're in high school and working two jobs. You're a total badass!"

I stared at Tyler, blinking hard a few times to let his words sink in. All I could come up with was silence.

"I know you don't like talking about him. But have you tried reasoning with Curt?"

"No. We were never close. I don't think he'd change his mind about child support. When I read over the divorce papers, it wasn't part of the final agreement."

"Damn." Tyler said. We sat in silence. We stared as the dog rolled around the lawn. A soft spring breeze passed through us, gently caressing the trees. I let out a long sigh. Then Tyler started fidgeting, putting his hands underneath his thighs.

"…What about your real dad?" Tyler asked cautiously, avoiding my gaze.

"What about him?" I asked bluntly, reminding myself that I had told him during my venting session months ago, how much I missed my real dad.

"Do you think he would help if you asked?"

"No."

"Are you sure?"

"Yes. Because I'll never ask."

Chapter 8
Grace

A few things began to change after we moved into the shelter. I started getting my school lunch for free. Once I got to the cashier, I entered my student ID number and a new series of beeps would alert the lunch lady. Then they'd just let me walk away with my food. It was exhilarating! Another thing that was new, we got our groceries for free at H-E-B.

"Hanul! Guess what?" Umma asked in exaggerated excitement as we walked towards the supermarket with its three, red glistening letters shining as a beacon for mothers everywhere.

"O-M-G, what?" Asking with the same level of cartoonish enthusiasm.

"We get food for free now. For free!"

"Huh? How?" I asked.

"Janice, she sign us up for the food stamps. Now we get all the groceries for free. Except not for the alcohol or the stuff – like clothes, shampoo. But food – all free!"

"진짜? Really? That's amazing!"

"Yeah, today we buy all expensive, delicious food only."

"아싸! Let's do it!" I replied. To friends and outsiders, the way Umma and I talked to each other made no sense. Most of the time, Umma talked to me in Korean or if we were outdoors, in broken English. And I talked back to her in an amalgam of grammatically incorrect Korean and toned-down English. But to us, we understood each other almost completely. To us it wasn't a broken mix of two separate languages. It was a steady stream of conversation and fluid thoughts.

We approached the H-E-B. The automatic doors opened to us announcing our arrival and a sudden breeze of AC and newfound opportunity took over our bodies. We had a mission. To eat like kings. The fact is, most of the time, Umma, Janice, and I almost always ate well. Even when we didn't have enough money for health insurance or cellphone upgrades – we still delighted in Texas-style barbecue, sushi, and traditional Korean meals. I guess that's what comes from being raised by chefs. Umma and Appa used to run a restaurant when we lived in New Hampshire. Appa grilled on the hibachi and Umma helped cook the entrées, until it went bankrupt and they decided to open a dry-cleaning business instead.

We started scouring the supermarket, filling our cart with strawberries, lettuce, thick steaks, a giant bag of salmon, loaves of bread, a six back of Snapple, and chocolate-flavored cereal. We had to remind ourselves it was all free now. Prior to food stamps, we'd prioritize our search for the items with the yellow-tag sale prices. Now, we filled our cart in a frenzy with only our gluttony to drive us. We made it to the checkout aisle. I stared at a tube of mini M&M's and Umma told me to get it.

"That's ok." I quickly reacted.

"No, you get. It's ok. I have this." Umma said pulling out a white plastic card. It looked like a credit card.

"Oh, I thought it would be like little pieces of paper?" I asked confused. I imagined food stamps would be actual stamps, or like those token sheets you get at carnivals.

"No. It look like credit card, no?" Umma said skillfully flipping the card in between her fingers.

We creeped up in line and started placing our treasured items on the conveyer belt. I looked up at our cashier and felt a peculiar sense of déjà vu. I've seen this guy before. He was wearing an H-E-B apron but he looked like a guy in my statistics class. White, skinny, with a buzz cut. I think his name was Dylan. Oh no. Crap! It *was* the guy from my statistics class! Crap! I wasn't sure if he saw me standing behind Umma. My heart started to race and I felt a panic climb from my stomach up to my throat. Had he seen me? Umma slid her food stamp card in the card reader and chose the food stamp option with the plastic pen.

"I'm gonna wait over there." I whispered to her and quickly disappeared towards the exit doors.

"Ok." Umma said, slightly confused. God, I hope he didn't see me. Please God. Please. Don't let him recognize me. Why God? Why!

We drove back to the shelter in silence. I helped Umma carry our trunk load full of groceries back inside. As I passed the living room, I spotted a young boy crouched by the bookcase. He was flipping through one of the Goosebumps books. He whipped his head around and looked at me. Then he quickly got up and ran away to his room. Someone new had come to stay in one of the rooms.

That night, after Umma, Janice, and I had each devoured a steak, I lied utterly awake in bed. I wondered if Dylan saw me. And if he did, did he know Umma and I paid for our food with food stamps? Do cashiers see what customers select when they pay for things or does it just proceed to the next step? I never worked a cash register before so I had no idea. But then again, we never made eye contact. If anything, he just saw a middle-aged Asian lady that used food stamps. My mind repeated the same series of thoughts until I fell into an unfulfilling night of half sleep.

The next morning, I waited to take a shower. I waited for the sound of running water to disappear but I didn't want to be late for school. A woman was taking a shower in one of the stalls which closed with an opaque plastic door and lock – like the ones you used at the gym. Impatiently, I gave up on waiting and decided to take a shower next to the stall that was occupied by a stranger. I washed quickly, making sure to thoroughly cleanse my body so I didn't have that lingering smell of Lemon Clorox on my skin.

At school, all I could think about was going to statistics, my second to last period of the day. I walked through the crowded hallways with Angela, about to part ways. Me to dreaded statistics class, her to French. She nudged me with her shoulder and looked to her two o'clock. It was Jamie and Jamal, leaning effortlessly by the lockers. I looked away as fast as I could.

"I heard he asked about you?" Angela said with a sly smile.

"Oh." I said reactionless, continuing my march to statistics.

"Are you alright?" Angela asked. Usually, any mention of an attractive boy was followed by loud squeals and endless plotting of what we should do even though we usually never did anything.

"I'm fine."

Finally, I stepped into class and took my usual seat towards the back corner, where I liked to hide from the teacher's questions and attract as little attention as humanly possible. Math was never my gift – despite my prevailing genetics. I always tried to avoid participating in class instead of being outed as a non-stereotypical Asian.

The bell rang and I heaved a heavy sigh of relief as Dylan appeared to be absent. The teacher started roll call. "Adams. Bennet. Benson." But halfway through the B's, he rushed in.

"Sorry, I'm late!"

This must be the first circle of hell Dante was talking about. The teacher signaled a look of disapproval but then decided to be merciful today. Thankfully, Dylan took an empty seat in the front. For the first 15 minutes of class, I felt a burning sensation all over me. He must know. He must be waiting to shout to the class, "Grace and her mom use food stamps! They're poor!" I kept staring at the back of Dylan's head. But he was looking into his math book and scribbling numbers on a piece of paper. Maybe it was all in my head. Maybe he didn't care. He probably didn't even know. Just then, the teacher's voice shook me out of my stupor.

"Get into pairs with the people around you and do activity numbers 10 through 16." Everyone started to move and scratch their desks and chairs on the squeaky linoleum floor.

"You wanna be my partner?" The girl sitting next to me asked. I recognized her vaguely. White, tall, skinny to the bone with a pretty face. We might have gone to the same middle school. She looked kind but in a slightly intimidating 'I don't give a fuck' kind of way by the look of her gloriously long hair, simmering hazel eyes, baggy clothes, and bohemian crossbody bag.

"Uh, sure. Sorry, I wasn't paying attention at all. Where are we?" I laughed anxiously.

"Girl, me too. We're on page 87." I quickly flipped to the activity and stared blindly at the pile of numbers.

"So uhhhh." I sighed. "I don't get this." I said glancing at my new partner.

"Me either." She smiled. "You'd think they'd teach us something useful in school."

"I know right?! When are we ever gonna need to make a parabola in the real world?" She chuckled and proceeded to peek at the pair to our left for answers. I followed her lead and tried to scope the territory to our right. As I searched, I spotted her mint green iPod and headphones tangled up at the corner of her desk. The screen was still shining and I recognized a photo of the band Paramore.

"No way! Do you like Paramore?" I asked in excitement. Finding someone with the same taste in music during high school was like finding a secure place to stand amidst a field of land mines.

"I do! I've had their song, Misery Business, on repeat for the past week." She said with her eyes glistening in excitement.

"That song is the best! That whole album really – have you listened to their song, Born For This?"

"I have! It's a banger. Did you know they're playing at Warped Tour this year?"

"Oh yeah! I saw that on Myspace. I wish I could go." Umma would never let me go to a concert downtown, let alone one that included rock music and cost more than $15.

"Yeah, me too. I wish I could go this year but I'm working that weekend. By the way, I'm Sarah." She said offering her hand.

"I'm Grace."

Chapter 9
Sarah

After my talk with Tyler, I tried to figure out some options. I could empty out my bank account, visit my leasing office with a check, and beg them to give us more time and forgo the eviction. Or, I could try to find an apartment for us to live in. But with Mom's newly traumatized credit score, financial history, and limited income, I doubt we could get approved for a new place so soon. We could stay at a motel, one of the shady ones with neon signs off the side of the highway.

I needed more time. Not wanting to face Mom, I drove south on highway I-35. I ended up parking at Café Mozart, my favorite place in the whole world. It overlooked the lake and hung twinkle lights outdoors. Around Christmas time, Dad and I would come see the light show.

With the rapid progression of spring, the café was now filled with stressed out University of Texas students gearing up for midterms. They were all clothed in UT burnt orange hoodies, like an unofficial uniform. I liked pretending to be one of them, sipping cold brew with my face hidden behind my laptop, completely anonymous.

    I pulled up my email and searched for my leasing office's contact information from a maintenance request I put in months ago. Then I started typing out my desperation. How Mom had gone through a divorce and my stepdad stopped providing child support. How David had a $3,000 hospital bill simply from chipping his ankle bone. How I was working two jobs and would be able to pay the remaining balance once I asked my bosses for advances. I told Claudia, our housing lady, that I would pay everything that was owed.

    My email was nearly three pages long. I read over it for spelling errors before clicking send. Through the glass walls of the café, I saw the sun say goodbye for the night. Ducks started covering their faces with their wings in preparation for sleep. I wondered how they were able to stay in the same spot overnight, without floating somewhere far away while unconscious. A cashier announced they would be closing soon and students around me started slamming their laptops closed.

    I headed back home, driving as slowly as I could and stopping at a Whataburger drive-through for a late dinner. By the time I got back, it was past 11 p.m. I crept back into my room and saw David asleep. After getting in my bed, I checked my email inbox a few times for a reply from Claudia. Maybe she was the type to check her work email at home. No reply.

My eyes started to droop with heaviness. It had been one of the worst days, my body was trying to recuperate. As I let my mind drift away from the glaring problem of eviction, I heard my door creak open. Mom was walking towards my bed. She sat on the corner carefully and brushed my hair with her fingers. I pretended to be in deep sleep.

"I'm sorry honey." She said in a cracking whisper. "I'm so sorry…" I wondered if I should open my eyes, then decided not to. "None of this is your fault. I didn't mean what I said…" I sensed her hand flipping through the college pamphlets and printouts on my desk.

"…You're not like the rest of us Sarah. You're the best of us. You're going to do so much better than I ever could." She started crying. "It's ok for you to leave. It's ok for you to have dreams. I want you to have dreams and I want you follow them somewhere far away." She paused for a moment and I felt a flood of guilt wash over my body.

"After your dad left, I tried to make a family for you again. But I failed, again…I want you to know…" Her voice shook under a sadness so thick and heavy, it broke me. "I tried. I tried really hard for you." I sat up from my artificial sleep and hugged her. Mom's tears wet my shoulder as we held each other tightly.

"It's gonna be ok." I said feeling her fragile body shake. "I'm going to figure something out. We're going to be fine."

As soon as I woke up the next morning, I opened up my email. There was a reply from Claudia.

> Dear Sarah,
>
> I am sorry to hear about your situation. Unfortunately, with this being assisted housing we must follow the protocol. We have a strict policy against lack of payments. We have given your mother fair warning that if she did not pay the owed expenses by the given deadline (over two months ago) – we would have to terminate your housing agreement.
>
> We were also notified about your new family situation, which changes your status with us as a three-person household. We currently have a waiting list of over 20 families in need of assisted housing and have already lined up new residents to stay at your address at the beginning of next month. I am sorry, there is nothing I can do.
>
> Sincerely,
Claudia

Nothing I can do. Nothing I can do? There must be another way! There must be a way to fix this. I brushed my teeth and washed my face in a hurry and headed out the door. The leasing office opened at 7:30 a.m., which meant I had enough time to go and plead my family's case before school started.

I parked outside the dilapidated leasing office. It looked more like a run-down home than an office which rented out government-owned houses for a discounted price to the less than wealthy people of Austin. I was abruptly stopped in my mission when the receptionist told me to sign-in.

"I just need to talk to Claudia." I told her in annoyance.

"You need to sign-in and then take a seat. Your name will be called as soon as it's your turn."

I took a few deep breaths and succumbed to society's bureaucratic ways. I had never been more impatient in my life. I sat for 15 minutes with both my knees jumping violently and my restless heels tapping the cold tile floor incessantly. I stared at the middle-aged receptionist hoping my disapproving glare would speed up the process. She picked up the phone.

"There's a Ms. Sarah Miller waiting to see you…Yes…Ok." She put down the phone and looked back at me. "Claudia will be with you soon." This bitch waited 15 minutes to tell her I was even here. I waited another seven minutes.

"Sarah?" Claudia appeared holding a clipboard and wearing glasses that were also a necklace.

"Yes." I said, standing and heading her way. We walked into her office that was barely bigger than a closet. We sat down in unison and I prepared to unleash my passionate speech about the value of compassion and the government which had the sole responsibility to serve the people – and that we were those people in desperate need.

"Before you begin, I just want to reiterate a few things with you." Claudia stated calmly. I wasn't even able to begin what I thought would be the impetus to saving our future.

"Ok." I said in resignation.

"I want you to know that I understand what you and your family are going through." How the hell did she understand? "I've worked for this assisted housing metroplex for over 10 years. Unfortunately, all of our cases come from this similar type of background." My stomach dropped. "I just want you to know that I don't create the rules of assisted housing. None of us do." She said motioning around to the other tiny office rooms.

"This is a government-instituted program designed to help individuals and families who are unable to afford normal housing for a given period of time. Our prices are fixed and our regulations are incredibly rigid. With your stepfather leaving and his increase in income, your family no longer meet the standards for our program – in addition to the lack of payments."

"No! But he's not a part of our family anymore. So then that shouldn't affect us!" I exclaimed. Once again, Curt was the cause for all of our problems.

"Yes, but he is still David's father. And your mother did report that he has helped financially in the past on a few occasions."

"But he doesn't even pay child support!" I said, trying for the life of me not to cry. Claudia looked back at me with compassion and reached out to touch my hand, and I let her.

"Unfortunately, my bosses do not consider that enough for your family to keep living at your residence. Your mom still has her job. I have an incredibly long wait list for families right now that have gotten laid off from work, are unable to work at all due to sickness, and a whole host of other reasons…Your mom still has her job, yes?"

I stared at her completely helpless.

"But there are other things you could do."

"What?"

"I reviewed your case and I think you and your family are qualified to stay here." Claudia handed me a brochure entitled, "Blue Haven: A Shelter for Women and Children."

"A shelter?"

"Yes. But this is not the kind of place you see in movies, or like the shelters downtown. It's not located in a gym or a church. From the outside, Blue Haven looks like a regular home. It's tucked away in a residential area up north and is completely unknown by the outside world to protect many of the women who need to stay there, often due to domestic abuse. This shelter is specifically for moms and their children under the age of 18."

I was shocked. The thought of staying at a shelter never crossed my mind. Were we really that desperate? Was there really no other way?

"I talked to your mother about this already. She was hesitant. But I want to assure you that Blue Haven is a safe place. You and your family would be staying in your own room. The only shared aspects are the bathrooms, kitchen, and living space.

"The only people that stay at Blue Haven are the ones who are referred through agencies like ours, social workers, or family and divorce lawyers who come in contact with difficult family and financial situations. If you were to stay, no one would know except for myself and the staff that work there."

I hesitated. What would it mean for us to live at a shelter? What would that mean for David? Claudia sensed my apprehension. She looked back at me patiently and leaned forward.

"I'm telling you this as a human being, not as an employee. If I were in your mother's situation, I would choose this option."

Chapter 10
Jamie

The sound of cicadas buzzed in the damp night air. Ma had just dropped a bomb on our lives. In a single moment, I felt like I transformed into the mythological god, Atlas, holding up the world. Ma was now jobless. Come to think of it, I don't remember a time when she wasn't working. Ma wasn't the type to sit idly around, waiting for Dad to come home. Dad. Dad was missing. Afghanistan.

I took out my phone as I laid in bed, the bright light like a beacon to my worry. I Googled Afghanistan and found a horrifying list of articles on recent suicide bombings. I Googled Dad's name. Just a biography still published on his last station's website, First Lieutenant Richard Thomas Davis. Next to it, a photo of his face. The sight of it made my eyes water.

I've always loved my dad. But as I got older, I got used to not seeing him for years. Over time, I started to forget the details. I looked at his photo and tried to remember what he was like. Strict when he had to be, but mostly kind, easy going, and loving. His laugh always made others smile. He loved music, dancing, and food. Any fight he had with Ma could be cured by a delicious meal, which she often gave as a sort of peace offering.

    His favorite movie: Saving Private Ryan. He said it was the most realistic war movie he'd ever seen. Favorite singer: Stevie Wonder. He always said if his parents taught him the piano – he could've been just as good as Stevie. Favorite thing to do: barbecue in the backyard and dance with Ma. My favorite memory of Dad: playing football in the backyard during an outrageously hot summer day, then running through the sprinklers with Aisha and Quinn. And now, he's missing. Alive? Please God. Keep him alive. Let him be alive.

    I woke up the next morning, hoping it was all a dream. I walked out into the kitchen for our usual, loud and hectic morning. Ma was braiding Aisha's hair, and Aisha was braiding Quinn's like an assembly line.

    "G'morning!" Quinn greeted me with a sweet smile. Quinn was the angel of our family. She was still young enough to be obedient without question, but just about old enough to make microwavable meals for herself and comfort Ma when she was feeling down.

    "Morning, sis." I said, weary eyed. I looked at Ma. She seemed her normal self. Maybe it really was a dream.

"Jamie, Imma need you to make breakfast for everyone. I need some extra time to look presentable today for my interview."

"What interview?" Aisha asked. Seriously though, what interview?

"Your mama is gonna get a better job."

"Really?" Aisha asked, annoyed that she had not been consulted with this decision.

"Well, if I ace this interview. Then, yes."

"Ma…how did you?"

"Sheila called me early this morning, saying she had a friend at St. David's Hospital. Sheila set the whole thing up for me. Isn't she a sweet thing?"

"Yeah." I paused, wondering if this was legit or if Ma was just pretending for all of us. I went to the kitchen and started toasting bread and scrambling eggs. In the reflection on the toaster I saw Ma try on a black blazer. The interview must be real. We sat around our kitchen table and munched our toast as Ma and Aisha argued over dance team tryouts.

"Aisha! You're barely hanging on in your studies. I don't want you wasting all your free time shaking what God gave you. You gotta get ready for high school. Look at your brother. Jamie, tell her how much harder high school is…Jamie! Hey!" Ma snapped her fingers in my direction.

"What? Oh…yeah, Aisha you need to start getting serious." I said.

"Can *I* join the dance team when *I* go to middle school?" Quinn asked, lighting fire to the fuse.

"That's not fair! How come Quinn gets to?" Aisha whined.

"Who said I'm letting either of y'all join the dance team? Y'all know just how many after school practices that is? I can't keep up. Maybe when your daddy comes back."

"If he ever does come back." Aisha said.

"You shut your mouth Aisha!" I screamed, slamming my fists on the table. They all looked back at me horrified. Quinn started crying. I felt a wave of embarrassment.

"Come with me, Jamie." I followed Ma to her room. She sat on the bed and patted the empty spot next to her, signaling for me to sit.

"I-I'm sorry Ma. I don't know what came over me." She lifted her arm and I flinched, thinking I was about to get smacked on the head. But she hugged me. My eyes started to tear up and we rocked back and forth for a while.

"Jamie. It's ok for you to be sad. It's ok for you to be angry. But we have to be strong – for Aisha and Quinn. I was worried to tell you about Dad, cause I wasn't sure you were ready yet." I wasn't sure either. "But Jamie, you're a man now." I guess I was.

"I believe that your daddy's alive. I feel it. I feel it in my heart. I feel it in my bones. I feel it when I pray. He's alive."

"I think he's alive too." I said quietly. Ma smiled and brushed my cheek with her thumb.

"Until his unit can find him, I don't want Aisha and Quinn to hear about it. I don't want to give them any unnecessary worry. So you gotta be strong and keep this between us. You understand?" I nodded. "Well good. Now come back outside when you're ready. And apologize to Aisha. She's going through enough puberty as it is!"

Ma left the room and I stayed a while staring at Dad in his wedding photo. Then I started praying. Please God. I'm begging you, protect Dad. I don't have to get into my dream school. I just want Dad. Please. Protect my Dad. Keep him alive for me.

I came back into the kitchen to see Aisha's arms crossed in expectation. "I'm sorry Aisha." I said bluntly, then sat back down. Aisha shrugged. She never did stay mad for very long. We devoured our toast and eggs, then Ma, Aisha, and Quinn made their way to Ma's car for the daily school run. Ma gave me another hug and whispered to me.

"I'm gonna get this job, son. And everything is gonna be ok again."

I got in my car and started driving to school, listening to Tupac's All Eyez on Me. I used to worship Tupac. But suddenly his lyrics felt so foolish. *"Cause all I want is cash and thangs. A five-double-oh Benz, flauntin' flashy rings… Live the life of a thug…until the day I die. Live the life of a boss player…All eyes on me. All eyes on me."*

Was that it? Was that all there was to look forward to in life? Money, power, fame? If that's true then I guess I don't have much of a reason to live. I opened my glove compartment looking for another CD. Jay-Z. The Notorious B.I.G. Lauryn Hill. Stevie Wonder. None of it felt appealing right now.

I began saving up for this car, my pride and joy, when I was 14. I had my heart set on a vintage Mustang. The kind that reminded me of cars from the movie Grease or West Side Story. I mowed lawns for my neighbors, then my neighbors' neighbors, then to other neighborhoods as I became physically stronger and stronger willed each summer. I also occasionally tutored my cousins and the neighborhood kids. I gave away my flier after I finished each lawn mowing job. It said, "Is your child smarter than a 5th grader? I'll make sure they're smarter than Einstein." I tried to throw in the TV show reference to get parent's attention which seemed to work.

Dad taught me how to drive when I was 15. We got in his white Ford truck and practiced driving in empty parking lots on Saturday mornings. Turns out, nobody wakes up to shop at Big Lots or eat at Pluckers before 8 a.m. on the weekends. He was patient with me as I fumbled between driving in a straight line and figuring out how the hell to drive in reverse. He drilled me until I perfected parallel parking – which was a necessity if I ever wanted to drive downtown with Jamal.

"How far away are you from buying your beloved Mustang?" Dad asked as I carefully drove up and down the empty parking lanes.

"I think I'm about $1,500 away from making an offer. It's listed for a little over $10,000 on Craigslist. But I think I can knock him down to $9,500."

"My son, the negotiator. I'm impressed. But I think if you tell him you'll pay him in cash – you could get it for $9,000. Maybe even $8,500."

"You think so?" I asked excitedly.

"Yeah, I know so! Get your cash ready."

The next day, I spent the afternoon shooting hoops with Jamal. He was actually getting really good. Beat me almost every time, except when I could tell he let me win a round or two. I heard Ma shouting my name down the street. I ran back home thinking Ma wanted me for dinner. Then I saw it. My 1969 vintage Mustang. The one I bookmarked on my laptop and had been messaging the owner on Craigslist for the past two weeks. It was beautiful. Dark navy blue with two sharp white stripes down the hood. My jaw dropped as Dad motioned to the car like Vanna White.

"But Dad? I don't understand. I didn't give you the money for it yet, and I still haven't heard back from the Craigslist guy. How did you…"

"My gift to you son."

"Ooooh Lord, that is a beauty." Ma said standing on the front porch.

"Ma, you knew?"

"Of course, I knew. Yo' ma knows everything."

"Woooow! I wanna ride it!" Quinn said zooming past me, Aisha quickly following to inspect the new addition to our driveway.

"But Dad. I can pay for it. Are you sure?" I touched the slick blue paint, confirming that it was indeed real.

"Jamie. You worked so hard for that money. I want you to use it to pay for college. You're gonna get into Harvard or Yale. I just know it. You need all the money you can for those genius schools. You save your money for that. I'm your dad. I want to give you your first car."

I ran and hugged him, still in disbelief.

"Thanks Dad! Thank you! I love you!"

"Can we ride it? Can we ride it?" Quinn asked, jumping in excitement.

"You wanna take it for a spin, Jamie?"

"But I don't have my license yet." My 16th birthday wasn't for another two months.

"Yeah, but you got your permit. I'll sit on the passenger side with you. Jackie, you's coming?"

"I'm still cooking dinner. Y'all have a good time. Don't spoil your appetites though!"

We got in my new car and I slowly turned on the ignition. The sound of the quietly roaring engine was music to my ears.

"Where should we go?" I asked.

"Don't tell Ma, but I'm craving an Oreo Blast." Dad said sparkly eyed.

"Me too!" Aisha agreed.

"Me third!" Quinn shouted.

I parked in the Sonic drive-through and the four of us sipped on our Oreo Blasts with nothing but the sounds of guilty laughter and Stevie Wonder in the background.

Dad wasn't there to see me pass my driving test. He wasn't there to coach me for my first date (which went horribly wrong). And now, he wasn't here to figure out what we should do about Ma getting laid off and the lingering worry of mortgage payments.

After parking outside school, I ejected my Tupac CD and dug through my glove compartment to find the case. But then a white folded piece of paper fell out. I thought it was an old receipt. But then I noticed Dad's handwriting.

Jamie,

My dear son. I am so very proud of you. Jamie, you have grown into such a kindhearted and hardworking man. I want you to know that every time I have to leave, I miss you. I think about you always. It makes me sad to think how much you're growing up at home while I'm somewhere far away.

You've had to take on so much while I'm gone. But in a way, I am thankful that in my absence you have turned into a great leader. The way you help Ma, Aisha, and Quinn makes me proud that I'm your dad.

While I'm gone, I want you to put God first and your family second. Everything else in life comes after, got it? You are the man of the house. Be the man I know you are. If it's my time to meet God during my next mission, I want you to be the man our family can depend on. I love you son.

Love,
Dad

All the tears I'd been holding in released as I read the letter. Dad still thought of me. He was proud of me. He must love me still. But where was he now? He needs to be alive. He needs to live. I heard the warning bell and wiped away my tears. I needed to find Jamal.

I rushed through the halls, whizzed past the library, the cafeteria, trying to find Jamal by his locker. He wasn't there. I started running towards his second hangout spot – by Stacey's locker, the girl he was dating for the past month.

"Hey man! Why you running?" Jamal said coming out of the bathroom.

"I've been looking everywhere for you!"

"Well, I'm right here. You found me!" I stopped to catch my breath, heaving as I bent my head over my knees.

"Damn son. We need to get you back in shape. We should shoot some hoops or something cause you-"

"-Did you still wanna buy my car off me?"

"Huh? Yeah man. You got the sweetest ride I've ever seen. All the used car dealerships I've shopped at have dank-looking wheels. But your car is dope!"

"I'll sell it to you."

Chapter 11
Carlos

Tío and I had our heads under a Jeep. I stared at a mass of metal machinery with names I had already forgotten. Tío held his little flashlight and I helped him by passing him tools from a rusted, red metal toolbox.

A man named Tony came in earlier that day saying his engine was making a weird coughing noise. Tío promised to fix it and give the friends and family discount. Tío was always giving some sort of discount to all his customers, which made Tía Julia upset. She'd always ask my uncle, "What about *our* family?"

But I loved Tío and his business plan. Everyone in the neighborhood came to Juan's Car Shop because Tío didn't scam them. They all trusted him, including me.

"Carlos, pass me the wrench." I passed it dutifully as he continued teaching me about a car's anatomy. "See, one can know all about cars. But it's more than that. You have to really feel the car. Each one is different. Each has its own personality."

"I think you've been sniffing too much paint Tío." He laughed.

"Say, who's that girl you've been texting?" I paused. How did Tío know? Tío caught my silence and smirked. "I know you've been texting a girl. You don't smile as much when you're texting Benny or Luis."

"I'm not texting no girl."

"Sure you're not, eh? Haven't sealed the deal yet?" Tío said loudly so the other mechanics could here.

"Tío!" I said rolling him away.

"Whoa, hey! Don't be pushing me away from my patient. I'll have to charge you for the delay."

Tío was my mom's brother, but he was also my dad, and Tía Julia felt like my mom. When I was in Kindergarten, my real mom left me waiting in the car at an El Mercado parking lot. After two hours, I left the car and tried to find her inside. I heard a commotion in the back. I opened the employee exit door and watched her getting handcuffed with her face pushed up against a dumpster.

They took me to the station. She was arrested for buying coke. Back then, I wondered why she was getting in so much trouble for buying Coca-Cola. When the policeman asked me where my dad was, I told him I didn't know. That's when Tío and Tía came to get me. I was living in San Antonio, but that night they drove me to their house in Austin. I've been living with them and my cousin Benny ever since.

"Alright. Looks like this car no longer has the flu." We rolled out from underneath the Jeep and I got to press the button which descended the car back to earth. "Give it a whirl." Tío told me. I got in and turned on the ignition.

"She's healthy." I said with a thumbs-up diagnosis.

Friday night fiestas are my favorite part of the week. That's when everybody comes to party at our house. Abuelo and Abuela come to visit. Tía's friends come over with their kids. Tío's best friend, Alejandro – Ali for short, and his wife come with their kids. Our house is always packed come Friday. The sound of Tejano music fills all the rooms. Tía prepares a ginormous spread for everyone to fill their tortillas in the kitchen. My cousins chase our dog CeCe around. CeCe yaps incessantly at everyone – except for Abuela who swoops CeCe onto her lap and rocks on her rocking chair while Tío strums his guitar. I love it all.

I always invite Luis over for Friday fiesta. He's my best friend. We became friends after getting into a fist fight in the fifth grade. He asked me why I didn't live with my real parents then I punched him in the face. While we were in the principal's office, I saw him eyeing a comic book sticking out of my backpack. We started reading it together. His mom and my Tía walked into the principal's office confused.

Cousin Benny used to love Friday fiestas. He would sing loud and proud to Tío's guitar playing or even play along on his drums and everyone would applaud. But once he started high school, we ran in different circles. By the time I became a freshmen and he was a junior, he was already one of the popular kids. But I didn't mind. I had Luis. But Benny, his crew was wild. They talked super loud in the halls, smoked pot, and hit on the other Mexican girls at school. They knew everyone and did everything, except stay home on the weekends.

At first, Benny tried to get me in with his crew. But after I refused to smoke, I was quickly phased out. I hated drugs and I didn't want to end up like my mom. I told Benny about her but he shrugged, saying he only smoked pot at parties. He had it under control. Sometimes I thought about telling Tío or Tía. But then I worried they would choose Benny's word over mine – he was their real son.

Today's Friday fiesta was slowly winding down. Luis and I sat on my back porch to get some air. You could still hear the sound of laughter, barking, and music inside.

"You talk to Sabrina yet?" Luis asked, holding a bottle of ice-cold coke.

"Yeah man. But what the hell do you think this means?" I held out my phone to him. The last text she sent confused me. I asked her if she was free to hang some time. And she replied, *"Idk. Maybe. <3."*

"What's this 3 with an arrow next to it?"

"Ay, dios mío! Are you dumb? That's a heart! It means, she likes you." Luis said, fed up by my lack of game. I tilted my head sideways and saw more of an ice cream cone than a heart.

"She likes me? Then why did she say maybe instead of yes?" I asked, in over my head. The last girlfriend I had was in the eighth grade. Our love story lasted a tragic three weeks.

"I think she wants you to be her prince charming?" I stared at Luis, still confused. Luis sighed. "Girls want the guy to sweep them off their feet. You know, all that fairytale shit. With Jennifer, she wanted me to do all sorts of stuff in the beginning. Write her long love letters, take her to fancy restaurants, make her a mixed CD. Make sure you save up some money, cause dating is expensive." Luis has been dating Jennifer for almost two years after they first met at a Dave & Buster's.

"Man then, what should I say?" I asked desperately.

"We'll think of a game plan tomorrow. Man, I gotta go home soon or my mom will try to ground me again. She's been watching too much news. She always says I'll get kidnapped or worse – the cops will find me and try to deport me."

"Weren't you born in Texas?"

"Yeah man, but you know how it is with us."

"Yeah, I know." I saw the way policemen talked to Tío and how the security guard at school always *randomly* checked my backpack at school.

"Oh and Carlos…There's one more thing I need to tell you."

"What is it?"

"My mom…she uh…lost her job."

"Shit, when?"

"Almost three month ago."

"Three month ago! Why didn't you tell me sooner?" Luis and I always shared everything in our lives without judgement. One time, I even asked him to look at my dick thinking I got an STD (even though I never had sex). Turns out it was just a rash cause my underwear was too tight.

"Man, I didn't want to burden anyone…" Luis started twirling his coke nervously.

"What is it?" I asked.

"My mom, she's been trying to find somewhere new to work. But she still can't get a job anywhere. All her friends in town have been laid off too."

"Don't worry. She'll find something soon."

"Actually, she did."

"That's great! Problem solved!" I said clinking my bottle with his and taking a big gulp.

"But it's at my uncle's restaurant…He lives in Ohio."

I stared at Luis in shock. We sat, not saying a word. I began to hear the buzzing of bugs and felt the cold breath of night creep onto the back of my neck. My best friend is moving. My best friend, the one I rode bikes with every summer and waited in line with for the new Call of Duty release, the one who had dinner with my family almost every Friday, my Luis is moving…to Ohio. Where even is Ohio? I tried to come up with some comforting words to say, but when I opened my mouth, not a sound came out. I could tell Luis was sad. He wasn't making eye contact with me anymore.

"When are you leaving?" I finally asked.

"Next weekend."

Chapter 12

Grace

Spending spring break at a shelter was less than ideal. Before at least, I had school and friends as an escape. But now, all my friends were out of town skiing in Colorado or soaking in paradise in Hawaii. Now, I woke up at the shelter. Spent the majority of my days, at the shelter. And was in my bed every night, at the shelter. More specifically, our room. I still avoided entering shared areas at all costs.

Umma and I tried to eat out or go somewhere at least once a day. Sometimes Janice came with us. But she spent most of her days and nights at the library or one of those late-night boba cafés studying. Her MCAT test was less than one month away. She was in full-crazy mode now. Her hair was disheveled and she was so high on coffee that any time you tapped her she would freak out like a rabid animal.

As silly as it may seem, one of my favorite things to do is go to IHOP with Umma. Breakfast was and is our most important meal of the day. We sit in the same booth each time and order the same exact thing, Rooty Tooty Fresh n' Fruity. Despite over 30 years of age between us, sometimes it feels like we're the same person. Our sense of humor, the inflections in our speech, and our shared love of food, music, and Jesus. It was like looking at a before and after shot.

Watching movies is another favorite pastime of ours. I used to love coming home after school every day and go through the consistent TV scheduling of George Lopez and Everybody Loves Raymond, followed by our collaborative selection of an exciting movie. For Umma, the movie had to be a thriller. Deep, emotional dramas or noir films only confused Umma on top of her already limited understanding of the English language. So then came the classic options of Harrison Ford's The Fugitive, Bruce Willis' Die Hard, Tom Cruise's War of the Worlds, or Kathy Bates' Misery.

One late morning, after Umma and I resumed our IHOP scheduling, she told me we needed to go back home and start packing the rest of our things.

"Where are we going to put everything?" I asked.

"In storage unit. We put there for short time then bring it all back when we get new apartment." Umma said.

"So are we gonna move out of the shelter?"

"Shhhh!" Umma said, looking around her. "Don't tell anyone about shelter."

"I know! I didn't!" I replied, frustrated that she didn't trust me.

"Yeah, we trying to find new place. Lawyer help me find new apartment and find job."

We started driving back to our old apartment. We'd been living in the same one since moving to Austin over four years ago. It was the type of apartment where you didn't regret not living in a house. There was a pool where I once had my birthday party. A gym, which Umma and I swore to go to everyday but ended up visiting no more than once every six months. There was also a trail behind it which led to a park where I'd meet my friends.

Appa wasn't living at home the last couple of weeks we were there. Well, it was more like he'd come home drunk or high in the middle of the night and Umma wouldn't let him in. He'd bang on the door for at least an hour and I would stay in my room terrified that he would somehow get in.

Things were always better when Appa wasn't living with us. Looking back at our home in New Hampshire – we were all so much happier whenever he was gone for months at a time. I didn't have to hold my breath when I came home after school. But sooner or later, the same inevitable cycle would follow.

We'd be doing fine on our own. We'd laugh and Janice and I would roll snowmen outside or dig for colorful rocks in the garden. Then Umma would complain about money, cried to us saying we had no options and that none of her family in Korea would help us. As kids, Janice and I didn't know what to say or do. Then one day, Appa would be back. I'd have to pretend to be happy and act nice towards him. Then, within a matter of months, weeks, or even days, they would start fighting again. A strange woman would appear at our house uninvited or a large sum of money would turn up missing. Umma and Appa screaming in the kitchen. Crashing plates. Umma shouting into the telephone. Nights hiding under the covers in my room. Then Appa was gone.

The same cycle, over and over and over again. Like clockwork. Until we moved to Austin, thinking this would be a fresh start for all of us. Only the problems, Appa's problems, got worse. The drunken nights, the high nights. As soon as the sun set and light disappeared, Appa went back to being who he really was. Over the years he no longer tried to hide it. He'd shout at Umma after coming home at 4 a.m. "I went downtown to buy drugs. So what?"

I was in my old room. I started packing my clothes, my books. I threw my old stuffed animals in a plastic bag to toss in the garbage. I opened up an old box of mine, the one I bought at Ross that was covered with yellow sunflowers. My awards, Soprano 2 Texas All-Region Choir, Stony Brook High School Award in Poetry, Certificate of Excellence – English, Third Place Art Contest Award, Essay Contest Winner for the Austin Rotary Club. I used to be proud of these. But now they just felt like heavy pieces of paper and blocks of wood.

A bang on the door awakened me from my nostalgia. Bang Bang Bang! Bang Bang Bang! I knew in an instant, it was

Appa. He had come for us. He was living here while we were gone. I smelt his scent when I walked past the empty living room today.

"Janice's Umma! Open the door! Open the door!"

He continued banging on the front door and I didn't know what to do with myself. I rushed back out into the living room. Umma was there too, contemplating our next move. It's in these moments when I wish I didn't freeze. I wish I had the strength to fight back. But I never did, fight back. I just stood there, frozen.

Umma stepped up close to the front door and proceeded to cuss out Appa, telling him to 꺼져, or get the fuck out of here. She told him this was our home and that he had to leave. It wasn't enough. He kept banging on the door. I was afraid our neighbors would hear. Then Umma threatened to call the police.

"I dialing 911 now!" Appa went silent. Then I heard him step down the concrete stairway of our apartment. Umma was bluffing this time. But she called the police once before. It was after Janice came back from college.

Umma turned around towards me. I hadn't moved the entire time. Every time an emergency happened, I got stuck, like I was frozen inside my own skin. Umma had a steady face and looked back at me.

"You go back. Keep packing." She said.

We drove back to the shelter in silence. I came back to my cot and opened my laptop, trying to drown my mind with

YouTube vloggers I followed. Janice looked up at me from her tiny desk. We locked eyes for a moment, then went back to our individual screens. Umma sat back on the bigger bed and turned on the TV.

After a while, I started getting tired of watching "What I Eat in a Day" and "Get Ready With Me" videos on YouTube. It felt like an elephant was sitting on my chest and I couldn't get it off me. I got up to go outside.

"Where you go?" Umma asked me.

"I'm just gonna make a snack."

I left and stood in the middle of the vast living room. It seemed like the shelter was empty today. I felt safer going to the kitchen unnoticed. I opened the fridge but nothing interested me. Then I went to the cupboards, which revealed a depressing mix of oatmeal packets and easy mac. I stopped eating those Kraft mac and cheeses because it reminded me of seeing Appa on the living room floor. Now the sight of the blue and orange microwavable cups made me nauseous.

I spotted a sliding door to the backyard which I never noticed before. Most of the time, I waited for Umma to bring a tray of food for us back to our room. We never used the dining table or the kitchen for more than 10 minutes tops. The thought of eating dinner at the risk of seeing strangers in the same depressing situation was unappealing to all of us.

I slid the heavy glass door and stepped out into a gust of wind, the kind that made cedar and pollen infamous in Austin. There was a patchy green lawn behind the shelter about the size of a typical backyard for a single-story home. A rusty, metal swing set sat adjacent to a plastic playground which was really just a single, cherry red plastic slide.

    I sat on one of the middle swings and swayed up and down, hating the creepy, squeaking sound it made. I wondered if people could see me from the rooms. But the only visual into the shelter was a tiny window above the kitchen sink and the glass patio door. I was safe. Invisible.

    Up and down. Up and down. Higher and higher. Sometimes I hoped that God would take me. Not that I wanted to die, but I was filled with the thought that heaven would be a million times better than life on earth. Now seemed like a good time to go. My swings started to lessen as my body got tired from keeping up the momentum. I stared at the gravel floor waiting to cry. But there were no tears. It became harder to cry as I got older. I stopped crying after events like today's many years ago. It was like I became immune to it all.

    I stopped moving completely when I heard the sound of the porch door slide open. Janice must be coming to join me. I leaned my head to the side of one of the metal chains. But it wasn't Janice. Without my glasses on, her face was blurry. But as she walked closer, I thought she looked familiar. Was it one of the staff members telling me to go back to my room?

    "Grace?"

Chapter 13
Sarah

"Grace?...Is that you?" I said, walking up to a familiar face on the swings. It was Grace, the girl I had recently befriended in statistics class. She looked back at me surprised, not saying a word. We took in each other's presence silently. Maybe I shouldn't have approached her.

"S-Sarah?" She finally said. "What are you…Do you live here too?" I nodded and sat down slowly on the swing next to her.

"Well, temporarily. Until me, my mom, and brother can find a new place to stay." She was silent for a while, looking down at the gravely ocean beneath us.

"…Yeah me too. But we're moving out soon once we find a new apartment." I could tell she wasn't ready to share. We were barely friends. At least not the kind to reveal to each other that we were both temporarily homeless with nowhere else to stay but a secret shelter – hidden beneath the outside world.

"Are you here with your family then?" I asked tentatively.

"Yeah. My sister and my mom." Grace said quietly.

"Right. No fathers allowed here." I said comically, trying to relieve some of the tension. It didn't work. Grace was a shy yet exuberant girl. At school she was mostly smiling and laughing with her two friends. They looked like the three musketeers in the halls and at lunch. In stats, we gave each other answers sometimes by passing notes. Here, she looked sad. More than sad. She looked tired from being sad.

"It sucks…doesn't it? Having to stay here?" I asked.

"It's not so bad." Grace said in a fog.

"Seriously?" I asked her, ready to cut the bullshit. This was our rock bottom. Grace looked back at me for the first time, making eye contact.

"Well, I planned on staying at the Sheraton. But all the rooms were booked." Grace said with a deadpan look on her face. I stared at her for a couple of seconds. Then, I smiled. We both burst out into laughter. Louder and louder. We laughed until our stomachs hurt. We laughed until our eyes filled up with a different form of tears. We laughed so we wouldn't feel sad.

"So, is it your first day?" Grace asked, wiping a happy tear from her eye.

"Yeah it is. We completed our tour. I just had to help my mom lug all of our belongings out of the car. My arms are sore!"

"Yeah, I just spent the afternoon unloading boxes from my old apartment to put into storage." Grace responded. "But look – how come, when I try to flex my muscles nothing happens?" I spat out another round of laughter then flexed my biceps. "Ohhh dang! You've got better muscles than me. What's your secret?" Grace asked.

"You know, I just drink a dozen eggs each morning. Then I hunt for meat in the woods and roast it over a roaring fire I built with my bare hands." Grace chuckled.

"It really isn't that bad here though." She said. "It's not like the shelters you see in movies."

"Yeah, I was expecting a Pursuit of Happyness type of place." The shelter was truly different from what I imagined. Ny gymnasium with rows of endless beds, filled with people living off the street. The people here seemed…normal.

"Yeah. It's fine for a short time…" Grace started shuffling her feet on the gravel again. We let a few minutes pass in silence. I didn't mind. We both needed a little silence.

"So how did you end up here?" Grace asked. I looked at her surprised. I thought she didn't want to talk about the nitty gritty. I wondered if it was right to tell her the truth, all of the truth. Most people only end up leaving anyway. But as I looked at Grace's face, I didn't feel that fear. The fear that she would see me, decide it's too much, then walk away.

I told her my story, bits and pieces of it, as we sat and swayed gently on the swings. Starting with Curt, then Mom losing all her money, my argument with the housing lady, and the two weeks in between of convincing my mom that this was our only option.

Then she told some of her story. It was as broken and chaotic as mine. Grace, the girl from my statistics class had gone through hell and back. But she walked the halls like she didn't have a care in the world. She finished by telling me what happened earlier today.

"It's amazing." I said.

"What is?" Grace asked confused.

"The fact that you've been through all of this, but you seem like such a happy person still." She paused for a moment, looking down again.

"I don't know. People always tell me I'm such a happy person. That my laughter is contagious. And in those moments – I really am happy. But they don't see the in between…" I nodded slightly. "They don't see the thoughts in my mind at night. They don't see how tired I am whenever my dad comes back and we have to go through it all over again. They don't see how much I just want to leave it all behind sometimes." Her dark hair glided back gently with the evening breeze.

"But what can you do?" She asked, shrugging her shoulders. "You just have to keep living."

Two Weeks Earlier

After talking to Claudia, I felt even worse than when I saw the eviction notice. Was a shelter really our only option? Shelters are for homeless people or drug addicts. We weren't homeless. We weren't on the streets. We have a house. Mom has a job. David and I go to school. We weren't that desperate. Were we?

I went to school but all I could think about was how little time we had left. We had two weeks to make a choice. It was either the shelter, beg Curt for money, beg Dad for money, or stay at a motel. I felt an intense hatred and anger rise up within me when I thought of Curt and Dad. I would never ask for their help. Never.

So that left two options. Apply for a new apartment or stay at a motel. Maybe we could stay at an affordable extended-stay hotel like the one Dad stayed in. During my lunch break at school, I went to the library to do some research. I Googled, "extended-stay hotel in Austin."

Shit. A single night cost over $130. Why the hell would they charge that much? I reevaluated my options then searched for, "cheap motels Austin." Some rooms cost $40 a night. Better, but still more expensive than I thought. More than we can afford. That just left the shelter. Shit again.

After school, I went to my shift at Cold Stone. Against my initial apprehension, I thought about calling Curt and asking him for money. If anything, he was the one responsible for this mess. He needed to take responsibility. I took out my phone after a row of teenagers filtered out of the shop. I pressed Curt's name, then the call button. Fuck! Where is your integrity Sarah?

I rushed outside and waited for him to answer, hoping he wouldn't. But he did answer and he was…laughing. He was in the middle of talking to a woman. And he was laughing! I felt so disgusted. We were about to become homeless and Curt was laughing? He was living it up with some other woman?

"Hello?" He said. I felt ashamed of myself for even calling him and hung up the phone. He wasn't going to help. And I would only demean myself in the process by asking. I blocked Curt's number then felt an intense urge to throw my phone on the concrete pavement. But then I thought it would be wiser to keep it. I can't afford a new phone right now.

I got home and felt an enormous sense of relief after seeing Mom. She was the only good person left. She wasn't like Curt or Dad. Mom and David – they were the good ones. I ran and gave her a giant hug letting all of my weight fall on her.

"Woooaaa, there." Mom laughed. "Well, isn't this a nice surprise?" I looked at her face, still beautiful, and gave her a giant kiss on the cheek. Then I ran to David, sitting on the living room floor and gave him a giant, unwelcomed bear hug.

"Get off me!" David yelled.

"What, you're too cool for your sister now?" I asked as I slobbered his cheek with a kiss.

"What is going on with you Sarah?" Mom asked amused yet slightly concerned.

"Oh nothing. I'm just happy to be home." I said rolling over David and onto the couch. "What's for dinner?"

I devoured a meal of pasta, salad, and mashed potatoes. Then I went to my room to finish up my AP government, AP lit, and stats homework. I smiled at the memory of meeting Grace during class. She seemed cool.

After a few hours, I put my finished worksheets, textbooks, and piles of paper back into my bag. There was something caught on the zipper. I dug my hand in and pulled it out. It was the Blue Haven pamphlet. The pasta and mashed potatoes suddenly felt heavy and gross in my stomach. I would have to talk to her. I would have to tell Mom, this was truly our only option.

It was 1:30 a.m. but there was a chance Mom was still awake. We were both night owls that detested the sight of sunshine and sound of alarm clocks in the morning. I got up and left my room, holding the pamphlet in one hand, being careful not to wake up David. I made it down the hall and into the living room where Mom was already sitting on the sofa with her feet rested up on the coffee table. She was holding a glass of wine.

"Mom?" She looked up at me, alarmed.

"Sarah." She whipped her head around to check the clock. "You should be asleep right now."

"Mom. I have something to tell you." I said cautiously while taking a seat across from her. "I talked to Claudia today."

"Claudia? Who's…" Mom's eyes blinked with sudden understanding. "What did she say?"

"She said this is our only option." I placed the pamphlet on the table and slid it towards her. Mom's eyes looked panicked. She took a long sip of wine then set the glass on the table. She straightened out her shoulders and looked directly at me as if superior to the situation.

"No."

"But Mom!"

"I am your mother and I am saying no to this. I am not allowing my children to live in a shelter, like we're some helpless abused people on the run."

"But that's not what it's for."

"I don't care!" Mom said raising her voice.

"Mom. I've done the research. We can't afford the apartments in this area and all the hotels and motels are overpriced."

"I don't like the idea of motels." Frustration started getting the best of me.

"It's not about what you like Mom! We have to survive!" I shouted.

"Don't you raise your voice with me. *I* am in charge of this family and *I* will figure out another way." I sat there with tears starting to sting my eyes. Mom's face went soft and she took my hand. A lot of people were taking my hand lately.

"Listen Sarah. You don't have to worry about this. I'm going to call my friends and see if we can stay with them until we're back on our feet. I'll get us out of this."

I wanted to believe Mom. I wanted to believe her when we took tours of apartments I knew we wouldn't get approved for. I wanted to believe her during every visit she made to see a friend and ask for help, only to return home looking fatigued. I wanted to believe her after driving up to see a motel, until Mom and I stepped out of the car and both of us got catcalled by a sixty-year-old obese man in a baseball cap and jean vest. I wanted to believe that Mom would find a way out for us.

But as the date approached for us to move out and a new needier family to move in, I knew that we were out of options. And I could see the defeat in Mom. She walked in one day as David and I were packing our things into cardboard boxes, not knowing where we were going.

"Ok. Let's go to Blue Haven."

Chapter 14
Jamie

After school I went to Jamal's house to finalize the deal. Seven-grand for my mustang. Seven-grand to keep me, Ma, Aisha, and Quinn afloat for a while. Jamal handed me the cash made up of an unorganized mix of $20, $50, and $100 bills from tips he saved up while working at the country club. Turns out he was a hit with older white men, helping them perfect their golf swing and giving them advice on who to place bets on during games.

"Are you sure your parents are going to be ok with this?" I asked Jamal.

"Ok with this? Man, they just happy they don't have to pay for my new ride."

I counted all the crunched-up bills then started to recount them. Twenty. Seventy. One hundred and seventy. One hundred and ninety. Two hundred and ten.

"Man, you doing aight?" I stopped counting for a second. Jamal was sitting on his bed, looking up at me with a worried face.

"Everything is fine…" I said unconvincingly.

"…You don't have to lie to me Jamie. I knew something was up when you wanted to sell yo' car. Man, I begged you for your mustang last year and you said no before I could even make an offer. What's going on?"

I couldn't hide anything from Jamal. He knew me too well. Since we were kids, he could always tell when I was hiding something. I sighed and sat next to him. Jamal waited patiently as I began to purge the details of Dad gone missing and Ma losing her job. I got to the point of today's breakfast outburst and Ma's interview. Ma! Ma should be home now. Her interview! I stood up with a jolt and told Jamal I had to go home and see if Ma got the job.

"Hold on." Jamal grabbed my arm. He then lied down on the bed and threw his arms over his head to reach for something on the floor behind him. He sat back up with a shoebox. Inside was a neat wad of cash tied with a rubber band which he handed to me.

"What the hell is this?" I asked utterly confused.

"That's just my spending money. There should be about a thousand in there. I've been betting on my games. You know I never lose." Jamal said with a wink.

"I…I can't take this Jamal."

"Consider it a loan then. Just till yo' dad comes back home."

I had no idea what to say. What do you say to a friend who gives you $8,000 in one afternoon because you need it?

"I'll pay you back Jamal. I promise…Also you should really put your money in the bank."

"You know I don't trust banks! The only one to hold mah money, is me." Jamal said pointing to himself. I looked at him – unable to express the shock of gratitude. I hoped he didn't notice the tears weighing heavily on my eyes.

"You go on home Jamie. Text me when you find out 'bout yo' Ma."

"I will." I carefully placed both piles of cash deep into my backpack, then started running home. I blazed through the front door. Ma wasn't in the kitchen. Quinn and Aisha were in the living room. I checked the backyard, empty. I stepped back in the house.

"Ma's in her room." Aisha said, then continued coloring Quinn's face with Crayola markers. Ma only stayed in her room with the door closed when she was too angry, sad, or disappointed to face us. She never liked showing herself that way to us. I knocked on the door.

"Ma?" Silence. I knocked once more. "Ma?" I heard the sound of Ma blowing her nose. "It's Jamie."

"I know who my son is. You can come in."

With one look I knew Ma didn't get the job. Her shoulders were caved forward. Her eyes were bloated. Her face was sad.

"What happened Ma?" She let out a long exhale.

"Jamie hand me the trash can, will ya?" I handed her the bin and she started gathering tissues scattered all over the bed. "It wasn't even a real interview Jamie. I went in to meet Sheila's friend at St. David's. I gave my resume, said all the right answers, then he said he'd keep my resume on file for when a position opens up. They're not even hiring. I think he just owed Sheila a favor."

I started rubbing Ma's back as she sniffled through her words. "But you know, I didn't wanna waste a good hair day and I had on my power suit already. So, I started driving to hospitals all over Austin. Up north, all the way downtown. Nobody's hiring right now. I don't know what I can do. You'd think a nurse wouldn't have problems finding a job. People always get sick, even during a recession."

"Ma, I have something for you." I opened my backpack and took out the wads of cash. Ma gasped as if I committed a crime.

"Jamie, where the hell you get this money?"

"Ma! It's ok. I got it from Jamal."

"What the hell? Why'd Jamal give you all this?"

"I sold my car." Ma looked at me wide-eyed. Then she began sobbing loudly. The sight still felt unfamiliar to me.

"My baby! You didn't have to sell your car. You love that car!"

"Ma, it's alright! I don't even need it. I can just ride the bus to school."

"But baby! That car's yours! I don't want you to give it up. I remember when yo' daddy bought you that car. The look on your face." Ma rubbed my cheek and started squeezing my face.

"Ma, I can't breathe."

"Jamie. You gotta get it back. Give Jamal his money. We'll be alright. You love that car! Give Jamal back his money!"

"It's just a car, Ma." I smiled to lift some of the tension. Ma cried even harder, letting the tears fall down her face. "We already talked it over. Jamal's been eyeing my car since Dad gave it to me. He wants the car and I got a good price for it."

"How the hell did Jamal make this kinda money?" Ma asked, staring at the green wads in disbelief.

"Apparently, people at the country club are generous tippers." I decided to leave out the part about Jamal's basketball gambling wins.

"Jamie." Ma hugged me and we sat holding each other for a while. The last time I saw Ma cry like this was when I was in the seventh grade and Dad came home using crutches. Ma collapsed on the kitchen floor sobbing before Dad could explain he only sprained his knee during a practice drill.

"Shhhhh." I whispered into Ma's ear. "It's gonna be ok."

Chapter 15

Carlos

I lived through the following week in a daze. I tried to avoid Luis. He was my best friend. My only friend really. Sure, there were other people at school. People I said hi to. But Luis was the only one I could talk to about the real stuff. We understood each other. His dad left, and my mom left. Money was always tight. We had the same worries. The same fears. But now, he was leaving.

Luis tried to keep the conversation light at school when I inevitably sat with him in the cafeteria. He tried to keep things upbeat and happy for me. But as each day passed, I started getting angrier and angrier. How could he leave me like this? How can everyone I care about always leave me like this?

Today's Thursday. The week's almost over. Luis called and texted me but I ignored my phone. Maybe that was better. Everyone leaves one day. Better to just forget about him.

Instead of going home where I thought Luis might be waiting for me, I went to Tío's shop. Tío was changing tires and shouting in Spanish to Dave and Pedro who worked for Tío since I remember there being a Juan's Car Shop.

"Hola Carlos!"

"Hola." I replied flatly.

"What's with the voice mijo? You look like a hormonal teenager today." Tío slouched and frowned, impersonating me.

"Nothing."

"Ah, well. I can't help you if it's nothing." Tío stood up wiping a wrench with a towel, smiling at me.

"It's Luis." I looked at my phone as it flashed again with another missed call.

"I see. He's been calling you? Don't you want to answer? He's leaving this weekend, sí?"

"He is." I said, not wanting to hear whatever wise advice Tío was about to give me.

"How do you think he's feeling right now with you not answering his calls?"

"He doesn't care." I said, convinced that Luis had already forgotten about me, even as I held contrary evidence in my hand.

"Carlos. You know I love you right?"

"Yeah sure." I said confused.

"Well since I love you, I will tell you this. You're being kind of an asshole right now."

"What! Tío! How could you say that?"

"It's my job to tell you *because* I love you. Only family can tell this to family – when they are being an asshole."

"You're supposed to be on my side!" Tío smiled and put his hand on my shoulder. We leaned against his workstation and watched as Dave, Pedro, and a few more people worked their magic on a black sedan and dark green minivan.

"Do you think that Luis wants to leave Austin and move to Ohio?" Tío asked.

"Well…no."

"And do you think Luis's mom wanted to lose her job?"

"Of course not."

"I know it's hard losing Luis. He's your best friend. But you're also *his* best friend. He has to lose a best friend and a home. He also has to go to a new school in a new city. Maybe now's a chance for you to be there for him, sí?"

I didn't know how to respond. I knew Tío was right. But in the moment, I was too angry that he was leaving me. A picture of Mom came flooding into my mind. Tío waited for a response, but I kept silent.

"You know mijo. Sometimes in life, these things happen. Change happens all the time. Money comes and goes. Circumstances change. People come and go whether we like it or not."

"Like Mom?"

I regretted the words instantly as they came out of my mouth. Tío was taken aback. I hadn't mentioned my real Mom in years. I refused to see her years ago when Tío and I went to visit her in jail. I never replied to her letters. When she got out, I hid in my room when she came to the house. She came a couple more times after that, but I always ran. Last I heard from Benny, she was at a rehab center in Los Angeles after getting dumped by a new boyfriend.

"Your mom..." I felt guilty for reminding Tío of his sister. Tío tried to be there for her. But after getting back on drugs six days after being released from jail, he stopped giving her money hoping she would stop. But Mom found other ways to get money. "She became someone else after your papi left. The woman she is now, that's not her. But I know she loves you very very much." Tío turned away his face to wipe a tear from his eye.

"I'm sorry Tío." I said, feeling a flood of remorse.

"No, no. Carlos it's ok to talk about your mom if you want to."

"No. I shouldn't have said anything. I'm sorry."

Tío rubbed my shoulder assuring me he was fine despite the blanket of sadness that now wrapped around him. I hated seeing Tío sad.

"You know. We all get to write our own stories. But the ending – the *ending* is what's truly important." Tío said wagging his finger. "With you and Luis. You get a say as to how it ends. You get to write that ending yourself. Not many people get that chance."

Tío started rolling a fresh, new wheel towards a minivan. I looked at my phone feeling guilty. There was only one full day left before Luis was going to leave forever. Tomorrow was my last chance. Then the idea struck as the sound of buzzing metal surrounded me.

"Hey Tío?"

"Sí, Carlos?"

"Do you think there's time to turn tomorrow's fiesta into a going away party for Luis?"

Tío smiled.

Chapter 16

Grace

I feel like I'm living a double life. There's the part of me that lives in the shelter. The part of me that has befriended Sarah. The part of me that has come to terms that Appa is no longer a part of my life. Then there's the part of me that is still in absolute denial. The part of me that has refused to accept that words like "poor" and "homeless" could be in the same sentence as my name. The part of me that worries about school and grades and friends. The part of me that still gets excited about little things like going to the movies or getting boba after school. It's becoming confusing which life I'm supposed to live now that spring break is nearly over.

I can't tell how I feel about seeing Sarah at the shelter. The night after our mutual discovery on the swings, a sea of thoughts filled my mind. Fear, that I had been discovered. Relief, that someone was going through the same exact thing that I was. Comradery with Sarah, who understood this life of feeling like you're constantly hiding. Thankfulness, that for one evening I felt the freedom of not having to hide anymore.

It's hard to say if we're really friends. I lied and told Umma that she went to school all the way downtown so she wouldn't have to feel worried about me befriending someone precariously within the radius of my actual life. But Sarah and I have done a lot of "friend" things. She took me to Cold Stone and gave me a free cookie dough monster sundae. She even took me to her second job at the diner where I met Tyler. I immediately felt uncool in his presence, but he was actually nice. As soon as he talked to me, I felt relaxed, like I was talking to an old friend.

After I witnessed Sarah's relentless work ethic, I felt like I had to keep up and fill my free days with something productive. I signed up to volunteer at the library. First, because I had only one line of volunteer work for my college resume and needed some new experiences. And second, because I had this fantasy of taking care of books and then writing one someday. I also secretly wanted to live out the scenes of a Korean drama, where I look through an empty gap in one of the shelves, lock eyes with a handsome man, then fall madly in love.

I didn't know that volunteering at a library meant repeating the alphabet in your mind about a thousand times before your shift is over. Screw the alphabet and the Dewey Decimal System. I hope they burn and die. My Saturday morning surrounded by screaming children was instantly made easier by a visit from Sarah.

"Excuse me miss but I'd like to rent the Guide to World Domination. I heard it teaches you how to exile idiots and gain supreme wealth." I whipped my head around to see who would ask for such a book at a public library, where its main visitors were either children or elderly women. I laughed when it turned out to be Sarah.

"Hey! Oh, I already rented that book. Didn't help much." I laughed. Sarah started helping me shelve. I was only a tiny bit irked that she said the alphabet in her head faster than I did.

"It's alright. I got it." I told her. Sarah ignored me and continued shelving.

"Wouldn't it be great?"

"What?"

"If we could take over the world and get rid of all the ass suckers." Sarah said.

"Yeah, that would be nice." I whispered, not wanting the kids around us to hear any more words like ass suckers.

"But not everyone sucks…What about Tyler?" I asked with a smile.

"What about Tyler?" Sarah responded, raising her left eyebrow.

"He seems like a nice guy…a non ass-sucker." Sarah smiled. I hesitated but continued to poke at the subject. "You guys would be a cute couple." At first glance I thought Tyler and Sarah were already boyfriend and girlfriend. They seemed effortless the way they finished each other's train of thought. They were just in sync.

"Tyler and I are purely platonic."

"*Sure*, you guys are. He just happens to be one of the few people in the world that knows everything about you and one of the few people you can rely on when shit hits the fan." I responded, dissatisfied by Sarah's retreat.

"I don't want to lose him…" Sarah said, pausing in her tracks. She looked beautiful, her face lost in thought. The only reason I wasn't jealous of her appearance was the fact that she had a good heart and passionate soul. If Sarah and I met under other circumstances, I don't think we'd become good friends. Sometimes the very air around her made me feel intimidated.

"If we take a chance on each other, it could all end up fine." She continued. "But there's the much bigger chance that it will end, we'll get awkward, and I'll lose one of my only friends. I don't want to risk that."

"I get it." Sarah was right. Finding real friends during your teen years was a Godsend and risking that for a brief romance was a naïve pipe dream.

"Why'd you want to volunteer at a library?" Sarah said, going back to shelving.

"Well I already payed my dues at a homeless shelter." We both smiled. It was nice finding someone I could share my dark sense of humor with.

"But what about you?" Sarah asked with a mischievous grin.

"What about me?"

"There must be someone *you* like. You watch enough of those Korean soap operas."

"They're called Korean *dramas*! And once you start, you can't stop!" We laughed loudly but were interrupted by the subtle coughs of my supervisor. I then began vigorously stacking books regardless of their exact placement. Kids didn't know the difference anyways.

"Well, I wouldn't say I have a crush on anyone right now. But I guess there are people I find attractive."

"Who?" Sarah asked eagerly. For the first time, I felt like Sarah was acting her own age. By the way she lived and took care of her family, I could assume she was 35.

"Ok well, I kinda had a thing for this guy in my bio class. But then again, on some days he just seems ok."

"What's his name?"

"Jackson. He's Korean."

"Never heard of him." I didn't want to let the brief excitement die.

"But – there's this other guy I kinda had a crush on. Or do, I don't know anymore. But he must not even know who I am. It's totally ridiculous anyways…" Sarah was now in full anticipation mode, her arms resting on my book cart, her head resting on her clenched fists. I surrendered to the anticipation. "His name is Jamie…Jamie Davis."

Sarah's jaw dropped. "You like *Jamie*?!"

"Is that so hard to believe?" I asked defensively.

"No! It's just so unexpected! I would have never guessed that." Sarah said surprised.

"Are you friends with him?" I asked, genuinely curious. "Do you know any more about him? I've barely even talked to him. I just think he's cute and he seems like a nice guy. I also heard he's really smart."

"I don't know him all that well. But I remember having a few classes with him when we were in middle school. He's really nice. And he is super smart. I think we dissected frogs together once. He hangs with Jamal and his crew right?"

"Yeah, I saw him at a party once."

"Could I ask you a personal question?"

"Aren't all of our questions extremely personal?" I tilted my head to the side, smiling.

"Yeah, I guess they are." Sarah snickered. "But how would your mom feel about you dating someone who isn't Asian? Not that I have a problem with it, but Jamie's black. Would your mom freak? I know you told me before that she's really strict with boys."

"Yeah, she'd kill me. But then again, she'd kill me if I were dating literally anybody right now. Once my mom gave my sister a beating after she found out she had a secret boyfriend back in high school. And he was Asian! I think she just doesn't want us dating anyone at all. But still…it's nice to dream." I sighed.

Sarah nodded. She understood. Her mom also had a no boys allowed policy after she got burnt by Curt. But then again, Sarah seemed burnt as well. We all were.

We then proceeded upstairs to the tiny DVD section. It reminded me of my childhood. Umma and I would always go to our neighborhood library and rent the Titanic or Sound of Music on VHS back in New Hampshire. I started stacking movies Janice and I used to adore during our childhood: Back to the Future, The Neverending Story, and Honey, I Shrunk the Kids.

"Have you thought about what you want to do after graduation?" I asked. Talking about the future has been one of my all-time favorite topics of conversation since childhood. My vision changed a lot. Singer, president, fashion designer, lawyer, actress, weatherman, talk show host.

"I'm not really sure." Sarah said. "I mean, I definitely know I want to go to an out-of-state school. Somewhere nobody knows me, without having to worry about…everything. But lately, that seems impossible." I nodded. Sarah had helped her mom financially since she was 14. It seemed stupid to tell her she should forget about her family and "go for it."

"What's your dream school?"

"Anywhere in California." Sarah said instantly. "I want to live by the beach and be one of those people that ride their bike places and go hiking on the weekends. They seem so carefree. What about you? What do you want to do once you graduate?"

"Well, I also want to go to an out-of-state school. But the money…" Sarah and I exchanged looks of mutual understanding. "I just know I want to live a big life. I want to make a name for myself and do something great! But I change my dreams about what I'll actually be doing like all the time….But lately, I think I want to be a writer."

The truth was, it wasn't a recent discovery. I'd been writing poems and little stories since I was in elementary school. But after the past few weeks in the shelter, writing became a life source. It was a means of survival. I couldn't imagine my life without it now.

"Oh! That's awesome! What do you like to write?"

"Well, poems mostly, or short stories, or long streams of consciousness that nobody reads online."

"Could I read one?" I winced and let out a long ummmmm. "Come on! I won't judge you. I promise!"

"Ok fine." We sat down at a computer reserved for teens only. I logged into my Tumblr account where I posted most of my poems, weeded through my pages splattered with funny GIFs, nature photography, and food photos until I found a poem I was most proud of. I wrote it after moving into Blue Haven.

I watched Sarah read, trying to catch any glimpse of expression that would show I wasn't a fraud, but actually a good writer. Her eyes were scanning my words with rapid focus and her eyebrows furrowed a bit – which could either mean she was in love or in hate with my writing. She lifted her posture and leaned back on her chair. Her face looked light and relieved.

"Damn." Sarah said and smiled.

Chapter 17

Sarah

It was nice having a friend. Someone I could talk to. Sure, there was Tyler or Mom or David, but with Grace it was different. I could be myself with her. I didn't have to worry about appearing strong or supporting someone else's emotions. I could just relax. I forgot so many pieces of my personality existed until we talked. I forgot how good it felt to laugh.

Plus, Grace was a welcome distraction from our family's new dwelling place. We got a room at Blue Haven during the start of spring break. Our several suitcases left barely enough space to walk to our shared queen-size bed. David didn't ask where we were. He always had his headphones in or was playing a game on his Nintendo. I tried to believe he was fine with everything.

Mom hasn't said more than a few words since coming here. The very first night we fell asleep exhausted. I woke up at 4 a.m. to go to the bathroom, my bare feet on the cold tile floor sent chills through my entire body. After returning to our room, I tried to reposition myself between Mom and David on the bed, moving carefully so I wouldn't wake them.

David seemed fast asleep. But Mom's body seemed to shake. I tried to lay absolutely still. Her shakes continued, now trickled with suffocated sobs. Her body trembled with every muted cry. I put my hand on her back and rubbed it back and forth the way she used to do to me when I was a child and woke up in the middle of the night from a nightmare.

She stopped crying after a few minutes and we both drifted into a tumultuous sleep. In my dreams, I saw a cloaked darkened figure. It floated through every room of our old home. I tried to follow it, catch it. But by the time it made its way through our house, all the rooms disappeared and I was standing alone in a black space, everything empty, gone.

Since that night, Mom's been lying in bed all day, only getting up to go to the bathroom or fix me and David some food. I haven't tried to wake her up from her stupor. She needed a break. Time to mourn. We all did.

And so, I happily if not blindly began spending time with Grace as an escape from our shared address. But now the days are dwindling and reality is seeping in. Spring break is almost over and I need to figure out a more sustainable future. I haven't unpacked a thing. I don't want to get comfortable here.

I've started making lists in my mind of people who could help us. But then I end up crossing out each person. Mom's friends won't help us. Curt doesn't care where we are.

Mom and I are both still working, but it could be many months before we save up enough money and build better credit for an apartment. Hotels and motels were a no-go. Family hasn't been an option since Dad divorced Mom. Dad. I couldn't bare myself the humiliation of asking him for help. But I knew I was the only one who could ask him. Mom would never.

After my shift at the diner, I began killing time by driving all over Austin, traveling to every neighborhood except Dad's. But then I started circling closer. My hands took over, recognizing each right and left turn, instinctively driving closer and closer like a magnet. As I drove further north, the houses became bigger, cleaner. After driving aimlessly for an hour or so, I ended up on Dad's street but refused to park outside his house as my last act of defiance. I drove back and forth nine times before slowing down across the street from his picturesque three-story home.

I wondered if his replacement family was home. A room on the third floor was lit but there weren't any cars parked in the driveway. Now was the best chance I had to knock on the door without an answer. Then I could forget I ever came and regain some of the pride I lost by coming here.

For the first time over the past year of knowing where my dad was, I got out of my car and headed towards the front door. I stopped on the sidewalk. His house looked even bigger up close. The ivory-colored stone towered above me along with the carefully placed trees and green vines which climbed up the side. It was like a fairytale that I wasn't a character in.

I walked up the pathway and to the mahogany front door. There was a brass knocker in the shape of a lion that reminded me of Aslan, the character in The Lion, The Witch, and The Wardrobe that Dad used to read to me as a child. I stared at it for a while, wondering why I was even here. Since the unfortunate mishap at Cold Stone, I haven't spoken to Dad at all. He was a complete stranger now. What good was blood when you no longer knew each other? I took a step backwards, laughing in disgust at myself. How pitiful was I for even coming here?

"Sarah?" Shit. It was his voice. It was Dad's voice. The one I waited to hear from a phone call that never came. I turned to my left. It was him. "Sarah, is that you?" What the hell am I supposed to do now?

He looked the same. Only taller somehow. His hair had white streaks and his face was freckled with wrinkles and smile lines. There was a slowness to his steps. He smiled at me.

"Do you wanna come inside?" He asked. Despite my better judgement, I followed without a word. Upon entering, I was immediately confronted by a spiral staircase that made my stomach turn. No one else seemed to be home except for the Golden Retriever that sniffed me, then walked away uninterested. I guess it knew I wasn't one of them.

He walked into the kitchen that had marble countertops, a kitchen island, and a beautiful rustic, long dining table that had table settings already laid out, as if waiting for a beautiful meal to be served and cherished.

"Would you like coffee? Do you drink coffee now?" He asked. Maybe he'd know if he made any effort to remain a part of my life.

"Coffee's fine."

"Cream and sugar?"

"Black."

We sat on stools at the kitchen island rather than the dining table. I guess it seemed safer, for him, without the risk of me staying over for dinner. He looked at me waiting for the conversation to start. Before coming, I imagined thousands of scenarios where I would dramatically yell at him for leaving and splash a glass of water in his face. But now that it's happening, my mind is blank.

Dad's face was nearly the same. I hated that he still looked kind with the same clear blue eyes. His sideburns had grown out. He still had a tiny scar on his right temple from when I accidently kicked him while on the swings as a child.

"I'm glad you came in this time." He said.

"Huh?" Did he know?

"Yeah, I noticed you've started to drive by here. I've been waiting for you to knock on my door." Fuck. He knew. I looked away and let a heavy silence stand between us.

"Bethany saw your car one day and told me about it." She must be the daughter. I wondered if she knew about me. "How have you been?" Dad asked cautiously.

"Fine." I responded bluntly. Dad nervously tapped the side of his mug with his index finger. Tap. Tap. Tap.

"Listen, Sarah. I'm sorry." My eyes darted to his again. Sorry? He was sorry? After all the time he left us, after abandoning me and Mom to fend for ourselves, after not picking up my phone calls or responding to my emails. He's sorry? Ha! I started laughing. Slowly, then loudly. Dad looked alarmed.

"You're sorry? Oh, you're sorry?" I shouted. "That must make it all ok then, right? Oh sure, I'm fine. Yeah, I'm doing fucking fantastic! The past-oh what eight or nine years? They've been great without you!" My hands were shaking and I could feel the blood gathering in my heated face.

"I know I did a terrible thing." Dad reached out his hand for my shoulder and I jerked it away. "I'm so sorry I stopped contacting you after the divorce. I-I was in a bad place."

"*You* were in a bad place?"

"I know it must have been hard for you and your mom. I tried to be there. But after the split I got into such a bad place. I was seriously depressed. And you – I couldn't be there for you. My mind, I think I lost it for a while. I became somebody else. It felt like all of a sudden I lost everything." *You* lost everything?

"I started drinking. I lost my job. I hit the road for a while, running away to city after city. Gambling, losing money. Trying to make money doing odd jobs. But I couldn't stop thinking about you the whole time."

"Is that supposed to make me feel better?" I yelled standing up.

"No! I know it doesn't make up for any of it." Dad started to hide his face with his hands that looked weathered and old. My heart felt sorry for him for a second, but then I forced myself to stay angry. "I was in a very dark place. I was ashamed of myself. I didn't want you to see who I had become. But then I met Madeline. She helped me come back to life. We started a family in Seattle and then moved back over here."

I instantly hated the thought of Madeline. If anyone was to bring Dad back to life, it should have been me.

"We moved back to Austin and I vowed to earn a spot in your life again. I called your mom when I came back."

"What?" I asked, feeling my knees buckle.

"I contacted your mother. Did she tell you?"

"No." Mom never told me.

"I told her that I was sober again, that I wanted to see you. But she said no. She said she got remarried and that you all were a happy family. It seemed like you had moved on. I-I didn't want to mess up your new life by showing up..."

He called Mom? And I never knew. I fell back on the stool. My eyes were burning and my head ached. Everything was a mess. I let a few tears drop. Then a few more. Suddenly, I was sobbing. I felt Dad wrap his arms around me. Then I cried my eyes out as he hugged me like when I was a child.

"I missed you." I whispered. Maybe Dad wasn't a monster. He tried to get his life together again and come see me. He came back for me. He moved to Austin for me.

"I waited for you to come find me Sarah. When I found out it was your car parked down the street, I wanted to run to you. But you never got out of the car. Maybe it was selfish of me, but I wanted to wait until you wanted to see me too. I wanted to wait until you were ready."

I didn't realize just how much I missed him until I heard the soothing sound of his voice again. He told me about all the places he stayed while on the road. Oklahoma, New Mexico, Colorado, Oregon, then finally Washington where he met Madeline.

"What's your daughter's name?" I asked, wiping away my tears.

"There's Bethany, the older one and Ruth, our youngest. Sarah, you'll love them! Madeline too! They're all dying to meet you."

"They know about me?" I asked surprised. All this time, I thought I was Dad's dirty little secret from his forbidden past life.

"Of course, they do! And they want to meet you. Do you think you'd want to meet them?"

"Yeah, maybe not today though." I said laughing and pointing at the state of my face, now stained with snot and mascara tears. Dad smiled and nodded.

"So tell me, *really*. How are you? How have you been?" I wondered just how honest I should be, not only about the past week but about the past eight years.

"Things have been…ok. I have a brother! David. He's fucking great. I love him. But Curt, my stepdad, he's not a part of the picture anymore."

"Oh, I'm sorry." Dad said.

"It's fine. We were never really close. And Mom is – she's fine, I think. She'll be ok." I paused, wondering if I trusted Dad enough to ask for help. But over the past half hour I was reminded, he was my dad. He felt like my dad. He felt like home.

"Dad…I'm actually not doing fine."

"What's going on?" Dad's face looked genuinely concerned.

"When Curt left, he took all of Mom's money. Mom wasn't able to pay rent and they kicked us out."

"Kicked you out? What do you mean? Where are you staying now?" I paused in hesitation. "Sarah, it's ok. You can tell me."

"We're staying in a shelter." Dad's eyes widened in disbelief.

"A shelter? You're staying in a shelter?" I nodded with new tears forming. "No daughter of mine is staying in a shelter. You're coming to live with us."

"Really?"

"Absolutely. I'm only sorry you didn't come to me sooner. I'm so sorry you had to go through this. Listen, go pack your bags and come right back here." I stood up in excitement and relief.

"Thanks Dad! I'll tell Mom and David."

"Oh, is your mother coming too?"

"Of course!" Dad's expression changed.

"Listen Sarah…Your mother and I, we're not exactly on speaking terms."

"But…you can't really think it's ok to just leave her there…right Dad?" I waited for him to confirm my feelings.

"You are welcome to stay with us Sarah. I can clear out a room for you right now. But your mom…" Please no. Please stop. "I don't think *she'd* want to stay here."

"What do you mean? What about David?" This can't be real.

"David. He's not my son. I don't even know him. You're my daughter. You're my family Sarah." My stomach dropped. My body felt frozen in the middle of Dad's sterile, white kitchen.

"Sarah you are welcome to stay here – just you. Think about it as a new start! We could finally be a family again!" How could I have let my heart trust him so easily. He wasn't kind. He was a wolf in sheep's clothing. He took a step towards me.

"Don't you fucking touch me. Don't you ever come near me! I already have a family! How could you think I could just abandon my family? Why, because you think I'm like you? I'm nothing like you! You are a horrible person! I wish I never came to see you!" I yelled and thought about throwing my coffee in his face. Instead, I took the delicate porcelain teacup that had a painting of a butterfly on it and threw it against the kitchen wall before storming out.

I was an idiot for believing he'd help us. A fool for thinking he was any better than the stranger that left our house all those years ago. Tears started sliding down my face as I tried to drive back to the shelter. The tears kept pouring as I shouted at myself in fury and punched my steering wheel. Sarah! You fucking idiot!

It was dark outside. I tried to drive out of his neighborhood as fast as I could. I wanted to escape the artificial lawns and pretentious houses. I drove through a stop sign. I sped through another, and then another. Up ahead I saw a traffic light blinking yellow. I floored the accelerator. Halfway through, I screamed as a car appeared to my left just inches from hitting me. I swerved to the right then felt my body jerk up and down as I ran over a curb and slammed into a tree. I heard a horrible crushing sound from my front bumper.

"Fuuuuuuuuck!" I screamed in my car. My heart was pounding and I felt a pain in my neck and shoulder. The car that nearly hit me drove and fled the opposite way from my now thoroughly beaten car. I tried to steady my breath to a normal pace. But it wouldn't slow down. It was all a mess. Everything. Dad. The shelter. Mom. David. Curt. Everything was a mess. I felt blood in my mouth. It was all a lie.

Chapter 18
Carlos

I've never thrown anyone a going away party before. What do I need to buy? Balloons? Are we too old to wear party hats? Tío and Tía will already have plenty of food and drinks prepared. I could get some of that nasty Swedish Fish that Luis likes and those streamers that you pop in people's faces like at surprise parties. I wonder if Party City is still open right now.

I told Tío I was going to head out for supplies but just as I was about to pull out of the garage, a seriously beat-up car pulled in. There was a girl sitting in the front seat that looked my age. As she stepped out, I noticed scrapes on her forehead. Did she really just drive here right after a wreck?

"Miss, I think you need to go to the hospital first. Do you want me to call an ambulance?" I heard Tío say to her. She seemed confused. I took the keys out of my ignition and walked back into the shop. I stood behind Tío to watch the scene unfold. She was tall and thin with long, messy brownish-blonde hair. Her eyes flickered between green, brown, and gold. She was beautiful. The sight of her made my heart race.

"Are you ok?" I found myself asking. "I can give you a ride to the hospital." I said holding my car keys.

"I don't need a ride! I need someone to fix my car!" She shouted. All of a sudden, I wondered why I wasted my time with this privileged white girl.

"It's alright miss." Tío said gently. "Do you need me to call your parents?" The girl started crying and I had no idea what to do. I wanted to get back in my car.

"I'm sorry. I think I'm just a little…in shock." The girl started hyperventilating.

"Carlos, go get her some water." I ran to the breakroom to get a water bottle, then decided to grab a Gatorade and bag of salted peanuts with it. I went back outside and showed all three items to her. She took the Gatorade and gulped down the entire bottle while Tío brought over a chair.

"Thank you. I'm so sorry." She said teary eyed.

"You don't have to apologize." I said. "I've been in an accident before. It's scary." When I was a kid, Mom once drove me while she was still high. She had also been drinking. We hit a car as it was crossing an intersection and I was flung out of my car seat. I pulled up my left sleeve to show her the scar on my arm. She nodded. "I'm Carlos." I held out my hand.

"Sarah." She said weakly shaking my hand.

"Hey, do you go to East Elmwood High School?" I asked. She shook her head.

"Stony Brook."

"Oh, I see. You guys are our rivals." I smiled, trying to relieve the tension. Tío glared at me as if signaling, now was not the time to be hitting on her.

"Miss, do you have someone we can call?" Tío asked.

"No. No it's alright. I can call them. Listen, I just need to get my car fixed for now. Thank you for all of your help. But I'm really fine. Just a few scrapes and bruises."

"But Miss. If you've been an accident, you can file a claim and then insurance can help cover some of the costs of your repair." Tío said.

"I don't have any insurance. I don't have health insurance either so I can't afford to go to the ER. If you could please help me out…" Tío nodded. He's dealt with people's lack of car insurance since he opened Juan's Car Shop. Many people came to him without it.

I slipped out while Tío and Sarah talked some more. I sat back in my car and could still see them through my rear-view mirror. I looked around, rummaging through the cup holders and back seat. Then I found it. I had put in a few band aids for the times when my ankles started bleeding cause my shoes got too tight. I could have asked Tía for new ones, but I always felt guilty asking them for things. I got out of my car and headed back towards Sarah. She was in the reception area signing papers. I opened the door without completely entering and held out the two band-aids towards her. She looked up at me confused, then took the band aids.

"Thank you." She said. I nodded, then left to go to Party City.

The next morning, I made it a point to be good to Luis. I knew Tío was right when he said I was being an asshole. I had one last chance to make up for it. The school day started with me bringing him a milkshake from McDonald's. His face looked relieved. Things were back to normal.

We made paper airplanes in Spanish class and threw them at Sabrina, the girl who was playing hard to get. She didn't seem as pretty when I thought about Sarah. At lunch, we drove to Pizza Hut and devoured an extra-large supreme pizza within a matter of minutes. Afterwards, we decided to skip the second half of the day and drive to Game Stop where I bought him a new game. Then we went to the movie theater and watched The Strangers with that elf girl who was in Lord of the Rings. That shit was scary! It was fun screaming as loud as we could, no one else was in the theater.

I wanted Luis's party to be a surprise, so I invited him over as if it was an average Friday fiesta. I hoped Benny wasn't going to be an ass and mess everything up. I put him in charge of getting everybody hidden and jumping out at once to yell "Surprise!" while the people in front popped the streamers and my cousins threw confetti. I wanted it to be a moment Luis would always remember.

Luis and I headed to the front door and I texted Benny. The lights were off so it looked like nobody was inside. Things were going smoothly.

"Man, did your family even show up to this?" Luis asked.

"I think they're just out buying food." I said sneakily. "Hey, you go on in. I think I left something in the car." I took a step back and let him open the door. As soon as it opened, the lights turned on and a tornado of red streamers and confetti flew at Luis's face.

"Suuuurprrriiiiiiiisssse!" Everyone yelled. I could hear Benny, Tío, and Tía's voices. Luis's mom was here too.

"What is this?" Luis asked, his eyes as big as saucers. I started laughing and gave one of my little cousins a fist pump for her excellent confetti throwing.

"It's for you!" I said. "I wanted to give you a surprise party. Sort of a grand send-off to Ohio."

"Yeah! Our little man, Carlos, planned the whole thing." Tío said with a grin. Luis looked around the crowded room.

"Thank you." He said stunned.

"You're welcome man." I said giving him a nudge on the shoulder. "You…you my brother." Luis gave me a powerful hug that pushed me a few steps back.

"Enough of the love fest. Let's party!" Benny said raising a beer to the ceiling.

"Salud!" The crowd shouted.

This Friday fiesta was one we could never forget. Tío sang at the top of his lungs while jamming on the guitar. Benny even got out his drum set. He and his band performed. Our living room shook as people danced around us. The tíos and tías were eating and talking loudly over the music. My young cousins were jumping and even Abuelo and Abuela got up to dance. Luis's mom was talking to Tía, who was smiling. Luis and me jumped up and down amidst the crowd of family.

    Six hour later, people started to tire out. The cousins were the first to fall asleep. They had a sugar crash after feasting on Luis's cake that said "Good Luck" written in Swedish Fish. Abuelo and Abuela tuckered out soon after. Benny and his crew also bounced to go to another party.

    By 3 a.m., only a few remained. Luis's mom, Tío, Tía, and Uncle Ali were circled around the kitchen table, still drinking and laughing. Luis and I went to sit on the patio one last time.

    "Gracias, Carlos. Really. I don't think I'll ever forget it." Luis said as the warm night air floated around us.

    "That was my goal…I wanted to make this night memorable so that..."

    "So that what?" Luis asked looking at me, eyes somewhat delirious.

    "So you wouldn't forget me." Luis smiled and hit my shoulder with his fist.

    "Man, I'll never forget about you. Don't even think that shit." I smiled and we both took a swig from our beer. We snagged a six pack of Dos Equis from the kitchen, while the adults were preoccupied, and were on our last two bottles.

    "What time are you leaving tomorrow?" I asked.

"Early."

"I could go to your place to say goodbye before you go."

"Don't even sweat it. You've done more than enough…brother."

Chapter 19

Sarah

After the wreck, I couldn't go home – or rather, the shelter. I guess our old home wasn't ours anymore. I didn't want David to see me like this, or Mom – although I doubt she'd notice. She's just barely slipped out of her emotional coma after moving into the shelter.

Hopefully, Juan would give me a good deal on the car. He seemed like a trustworthy guy. Ugh. Now was not the time to get into a wreck! I have no home and now no car. All I have is the dried up blood on my forehead. Could I be any more pathetic?

I checked my phone standing outside of the auto shop. Just 23 percent battery left. I can't call Mom. Grace? No, she doesn't have a car. And her mom seems less than pleased that we've become friends. Dad was not an option – he'll never be an option now. The recollection of our last conversation sent a stabbing sensation in my heart. It was over. Time to move on.

Wake up Sarah! There's no one. Tyler? Fuck. I don't want to bother him again.

Night started to form in the sky. I watched as my phone slid into 17 percent. I had to make a decision. I pulled up Tyler's phone number.

"Hey! What's up!" Tyler's voice sounded chirpy.

"Hey…Nothing much." I said, kicking my sullied Vans in the pavement.

"Do you need me to cover your shift?" Tyler asked immediately. How could he sense whenever I needed something?

"No, no. It's not about work…" Maybe I made a mistake calling him. I didn't want to dampen Tyler's mood, again. Silence took over our phone call as I watched a plastic bag dance across the parking lot.

"I'm so sorry to be doing this again Tyler…"

"What happened?"

"I've been in a car wreck."

"A wreck? Sarah! Why didn't you say sooner? Where are you? I'll come now!"

Within 10 minutes, Tyler pulled up to the car shop that was now closing. He got out of his car and rushed towards me.

"Fuck, Sarah!" He whispered as he pushed the hair out of my face to inspect the damage. I didn't know what to say. I didn't think he would care this much.

"Can you walk?"

"Of course, I can walk. I'm not crippled." I got into Tyler's car and we drove in silence. I knew better than to say anything by the look on his face. Without a word, Tyler parked at a CVS, got out of his car and I followed. He went to the medicine aisle where he picked a box of bandages, Neosporin, and Aspirin.

"Tyler, you don't have to do this." Tyler shushed me at the checkout aisle and we walked back into his car. It was completely dark outside now. Tyler turned on the mini overhead light and started removing the packaging of his recent purchases.

"Really, you don't have to-" He shushed me again and applied some Neosporin on the cut on my forehead, then my left arm and hand.

"Anywhere else?" Tyler asked. I shook my head no. He then started whipping out bandages and placing them on every scrape.

"Here, eat one of these." I obediently took the Aspirin and swallowed it without water. "Jesus, here!" Tyler passed me a half-drunken can of Red Bull.

"Thanks…"

"So, what happened?" Tyler asked with a worried look on his face. I had never seen him like this before. Suddenly, I felt embarrassed. "Come on Sarah. You can talk to me."

"I-I was just driving and someone ran a red light and hit my car. Then they drove away."

"What! That mother fucker! We gotta find him. Did you get the license plate?"

"No…I don't want to find anyone. Tyler, I don't even have car insurance."

"But still! That bastard should pay for what he did to you. We should go to the hospital. What if you have – I dunno, internal injuries?" Tyler asked frantically.

"Internal what? You must be watching too much Grey's Anatomy." I said, trying to laugh it off.

"I'm serious, Sarah! Shouldn't you at least get a check-up? What about your mom? Did you call her?"

"No, she-uh. She's not really all there right now. Things have been tough since the eviction."

"Oh yeah. I meant to ask you about that. Did y'all work it out? Where are you staying?" Tyler asked concerned. He couldn't know. He shouldn't know.

"Yeah we figured it out. Curt…he decided to pay child support again so we had enough money to pay for the house."

"That's great!" Tyler said and finally smiled. I liked seeing him smile. "I'll drive you home!"

"No!" I shouted. Tyler looked surprised and I tried to regain some sort of calm demeanor. "I mean, if my mom sees me like this, this late at night – she'll freak. I can't deal with that right now. You can just drop me off at the Y."

"The YMCA? Hell no, Sarah. It's not like you're homeless." My stomach dropped. I felt queasy. I couldn't even look at Tyler anymore. "If you want, we can go back to my place. Everyone should be asleep by now so it won't be any trouble."

What would that mean, going over to his place? I didn't want to spend the night. I didn't want for his mom to see me, some beat-up girl in her home. She'd probably think I was trash. But I had no choice.

"Ok."

We stepped into a sleeping house. I tried not to make a sound. Tyler led me to his room and I glimpsed at the backyard where I last poured out my soul to him.

His room smelt of cinnamon and cigarettes. There was a half-burnt, burgundy Yankee Candle sitting on his desk. His bed was unmade and there was an autographed poster of John Mayer on his wall. On another wall was a calendar with almost every single day marked with a to-do list. His bedside table held a Brown University flag, guitar keychain, and a mug with a picture of Dwight from The Office on it.

Tyler went straight to his closet and picked up a stack of blankets and pillows.

"Thanks, I got it." I said as I tried to take it from him and head to the living room sofa.

"No, you can sleep here. I'll sleep in the living room." Tyler said and walked out. I followed him briskly to the living room to argue.

"No Tyler. I'll sleep here!" I whispered loudly and pointed to the sofa. Suddenly my stomach grumbled like a bear that just awoke from hibernation. We both paused and Tyler laughed quietly. He headed to the kitchen and motioned for me to wait in his room. I retreated obediently.

 Tyler returned balancing an assortment of pizza rolls, Oreos, and Sprite cans in his arms. I couldn't help but smile as we sat cross-legged on his floor. He played The Office at an almost muted volume from his laptop. We sat and watched while devouring everything together. As I started to relax and felt my hunger subside, a new pain started to settle in. My neck ached and I tried rolling my head in circles to release the tension. Tyler stepped into his bathroom and came back with Icy Hot patches.

 "Here. This will help."

 "Did you get these because Shaq was in the commercial?"

 "Maybe." Tyler said with a smirk. "Nah. I played basketball during school and have been buying these since then."

 "Since high school?"

 "Yeah and at Brown." Tyler sighed a little, then straightened out his legs, taking another Oreo. Shit. Was Tyler a big deal or something?

 "Oh yeah…Do you miss it?" I asked. Tyler sat staring at Michael Scott's Prison Mike bit and laughed to himself.

 "A little. But in my mind, Brown will always be there. Family…might not. My brother…he wasn't doing so well after Dad died. They need me for the time being."

"I know what you mean." We paused to watch a montage of Jim's pranks on Dwight and tried not to laugh too loudly.

"Is your mom ok?" Tyler asked quietly as the credits rolled and he closed his laptop.

"She's hanging in there." I said, my mind starting to wander. "I hope she gets better." Tyler nodded. "I hope this doesn't make you think I'm a terrible person. But sometimes – I think about leaving her, everything, everyone behind. My whole life…I fantasize about running away. To another state, maybe to another country. And just starting a new life somewhere completely on my own…Does that make me a terrible person?" I waited for Tyler to confirm to me, that I was indeed a terrible human being.

"No. It makes you human." Tyler said unfazed. "But I'd miss you…if you left."

I stared back at Tyler. We sat for a long time, not saying a word. Tyler's eyes were a beautiful shade of green. I don't think I noticed until now. His hair was a dusty mix of black and brunette. He still had remnants of when he dyed his hair dark months ago. We waited, looking at each other, a little while longer. Then, he leaned in towards me and I didn't move. He pressed his lips on mine and my heart started pounding. In the blink of an eye, my hands were on his chest and I pushed him away so hard he fell backwards on the floor.

"I'm sorry!" I squealed in utter embarrassment. Tyler tried to sit back up. He looked dizzy and confused. "I'm sorry." I said again. Fuck. Way to fuck that up Sarah!

"No. No. I shouldn't have. I'm sorry." Tyler said waving his hand in the air and avoiding eye contact. "You should get some sleep. I'm tired. I'm gonna go sleep in the living room." Tyler left in a hurry and I wanted to slap myself for being so stupid. Could I have reacted any worse? Tyler liked me. And I liked him. Why did I push him away? The kiss wasn't bad. It was just…Ugh! How could I react so stupidly?

I laid in Tyler's bed trying to forget what just happened. God, how was I supposed to face him in the morning? I drifted uncomfortably between sleep and restlessness that night. His bed smelt like him. What if I had just let him kiss me? Would that have been so bad? Oh, God. What am I going to say to him when he wakes up? I checked the clock. It was already 5 a.m. I waited, completely awake, until 6:30 and got up. I washed my face and lightly tiptoed out of Tyler's room. He was asleep on the couch with his arm hanging off the side. I slipped out of the front door unnoticed and started walking. School should be open by the time I got there.

At school, my mind kept on reliving the horrifying moment I pushed Tyler on the floor with my apparently superhuman strength. Fuck, fuck, fuck! I tried not to think about it. But without fail, at some moment during every class I pictured Tyler falling backwards and I'd groan out loud. Sometimes my classmates looked at me, weirded out, but I didn't care. I already maxed out my level of embarrassment for the day – or the month really. Maybe I should text him. And say what? Oh, fuck. What a disaster!

I caught Grace after school and asked her for a ride. She agreed happily saying that her sister was picking us up so it would be ok. I understood why her mom didn't like us spending time together. No mom wants their child to live in a shelter, let alone have someone else be a witness to that. But I couldn't help but feel a lot of comfort when I was around Grace. The three of us talked in the car about teenage things.

I decided to let them in on last night's horrific event. But Grace just laughed and clapped her hands hysterically. Janice joined in on the laughter. They both had a similar laugh – uncontained, loud, and brimming with joy. Against my initial reaction, I started laughing too.

Back at the shelter, I tried to avoid close contact with Mom at all costs. I rushed to the kitchen to make some sandwiches for dinner. Being here was like a covert mission. Most of us tried to avoid each other. I could hear sounds in some of the other rooms, but it changed frequently. In and out. Someone leaving. Another one coming in. I didn't know who else was staying here, when they left, when someone new came to stay. Nobody wanted to be seen and neither did I. Grace and I only saw each other at the odd chance we went to the bathroom at the same time to brush our teeth. Sometimes, we texted each other to meet at the swings when we couldn't sleep. I got back into our room with a stack of paper plates and sandwiches hoping Mom was asleep. But she was already laying out an entire pan of lasagna.

"Mom?"

"Come sit." Was Mom back to normal? She seemed alert as she set the table for me and David. Normal, even.

"We can have those for dessert, then." David said, pointing to my less appealing ham sandwiches. Mom took my plates and set them on the bedside table. I sat down confused.

"Eat." Mom said. I sat and watched as Mom cut up a square chunk of lasagna and placed it on David's plate. "How was school?" Mom asked.

"It was good! Mrs. Peterson said I did a great job on my book report!" David said eagerly.

"That's good." Mom said with a bit of lightness reappearing on her face. Maybe Mom really was back. The coma was over. Mom put a piece of lasagna on my plate and pushed it closer to me, motioning for me to eat. She sat down with us and it felt like a familiar sensation returned. However, her smile quickly disappeared when she reached for my face.

"Sarah. What the hell happened to you?"

Shit.

"Nothing." I said then stupidly looked down at one of my other new scars on my arm.

"Oh my God! Sarah!"

"It's nothing."

"Who did this to you!" Mom yelled.

"Nobody did this to me. It was my car. I-I hit a deer on the road." Deer, tree, that's basically the same thing.

"A deer! Why didn't you tell me?"

"Mom! I'm fine now. It's not a big deal." Mom stood up and headed for the door.

"Where are you going?" I asked hoping she would drop the issue.

"I'm getting ice."

"No Mom. Sit down. I'll get it." I rushed past her and firmly closed the door behind me. Before I could make a dash to the kitchen, I was blocked by someone entering the narrow hallway.

Chapter 20

Jamie

I believe that my dad is alive. Even when Ma said he went MIA, I imagined him hiding in a cave in the middle of the mountains. He's grown a beard now like Tom Hanks in Castaway, and he's got some bruises and scratches. But he's out there, waiting to be found. His unit just haven't found the right cave yet. But he's out there. My dad is alive.

This is all my mind goes through. When I wake up. Dad is alive. When I ride the bus to school. Dad is alive. During class. Dad is alive. It's repeated over and over and over again in my mind. At first, I told myself he was alive to calm down when it felt like my heart started pounding in my throat. But now I believe it.

I can't seem to think about anything else. Except occasionally, the fleeting thought of Ma as a widow. But then I repeat to myself once more. Dad is alive. Everything else seems like a faraway phantom floating in darkness. Almost nobody knows. Quinn and Aisha still don't know about Dad. Only me and Ma know, and Jamal. He's been trying to help. I can tell. But all I want lately is to be alone.

But Mr. McGrady was the first to notice, or maybe just the first to say something. My standard straight A's started to spill into B territory. I don't think I got a B since I was in the seventh grade and cried in my room because of it. Now I just stared at my mid-semester progress report. Math was an A-. History was a B. Science was a B+. English, C. I didn't have the capacity to read Shakespeare right now. I stopped participating in discussions and I plopped out a B.S. analysis for my essay test.

As soon as Mr. McGrady, my English and homeroom teacher, passed out mid-semester progress reports, I stared at it then crumpled it up into a tiny ball. As I left, I tossed it in the trash. Mr. McGrady stopped me.

"Jamie, come here a sec." Mr. McGrady was Irish Catholic and hated the fact that he was raised both extremely Irish and extremely Catholic. He made up for it now by letting out curse words as a way to prepare his students for the "real world." I liked Mr. McGrady. He's been a good teacher and throughout the year always encouraged me to think and come up with my own opinions, to pursue originality and authenticity over perfection.

"Take a seat." I sat down next to his chair, staring blankly at the black board. I didn't realize we were already onto

George Orwell's Animal Farm. I haven't even bought the book yet.

"You have this dazed look about you lately. You seem like a zombie. Is everything alright?" Mr. McGrady asked as his red hair flattened beneath the AC unit.

"Fine." I replied. Mr. McGrady slid over a quiz on his great, big wooden table that had the number 67 circled in the corner in red ink that matched his hair.

"This isn't like you Jamie. Did you forget to do the reading?" I stared at the vast amount of red x's.

"I…uh, yeah. I forgot." My mind began to float away again.

"Did you forget or did you choose not to do the assignment?"

"Both? I guess." It seemed as though Mr. McGrady was wavering in between good cop and bad cop, unsure of which route to take.

"What's going on Jamie? You used to be my star student. Your junior year is the most important, you know. I thought you wanted to go to Harvard?" I looked into my teacher's eyes and felt the warmth of his concern.

"I did – I mean I do. It's just been…rough. It's been a rough couple of weeks." I said sighing and rubbing my right temple. It feels like I've had a non-stop headache for the past four days.

"Did something happen?"

"…yeah…"

"Listen Jamie, you don't have to tell me if it makes you uncomfortable. I just think it could help, getting things off your chest. I know from experience, holding it all in will just make you explode one day. Or you'll try to do things to keep it all tucked away inside, bad things." Mr. McGrady's face, peppered with freckles, stared back at me.

"My dad, you know he's in the Army." Mr. McGrady nodded. "Well, he's…" Inhale. "He's gone missing." Exhale.

"Shit, Jamie." Mr. McGrady leaned backwards. "Missing In Action…That…That's fucking terrible, what you're going through. I had no idea."

"Yeah, I haven't really told anyone."

"Have they given you any updates on him? The Army, I mean."

"No. I've tried contacting them but no one will give me any information. They just keep telling me to wait."

"You know that might be a good sign." Mr. McGrady said, mustering up a smile. "It means they're busy looking for him." I nodded, hoping what he was saying, what I was telling myself, was true. We sat in silence for a moment. "Jamie do you know why I teach literature?"

"Why?" I asked, genuinely unsure of why a guy like Mr. McGrady would choose to teach teenagers about Shakespeare, Orwell, Austen, and Hemingway for a living.

"Because these books are the closest thing to real life." I looked back at him confused. Mr. McGrady leaned in excitedly. "Every story an author writes, is written through the lens of his or her life and experiences. Whether it's an autobiography or sci-fi novel, there's pieces of every writer in their work. Books are filled with the pages of someone's life which means that all stories are filled with some sort of truth. My job as a teacher, is to help my students find that truth." I nodded again, unsure of where this conversation was going.

"So…what is the truth?" I asked.

"Well see, that's up to you to find out." Mr. McGrady said. "Jamie. Do you believe your dad is alive?" I sat up straight and thought for a moment.

"Yes."

"Good." Mr. McGrady responded with a smile. "Then that is your truth and I believe it too. Your dad is alive."

It was nice to think that someone other than me was believing for me. As if the cosmic power of two people's faith gave Dad a better chance of living.

"Now, what the fuck is this Jamie?" Mr. McGrady pointed at my quiz. "Seriously, you wrote, 'Animal Farm is about a petting zoo.' I mean, come on! Orwell would smack you across the face for that. I might just have to do it for him. You nimwit!"

I burst out laughing. Mr. McGrady started laughing too.

"Listen, I'm gonna let this quiz slide. In extenuating circumstances, I give my students a free pass. But you only get one! By next week, I expect you to be up to date and give me a full report of what this book is about. Find the truth in it. I'm not gonna go easy on your ass anymore."

"Thank you, sir."

"Jesus. Just call me McGrady. Why not just wear a sign around your neck that says Army child."

"Ok, McGrady. And thanks."

"You already said thanks."

"The first one was for the quiz, the second one was for…treating me like I'm normal." McGrady smiled.

Truth was, I didn't want people to know that Dad was missing or Ma lost her job, not because I was ashamed. I wasn't. I'll never be ashamed of my parents. I just don't want people to look at me with a face of pity. As if Dad was already dead. Jamal interacted with me as if I lost him. His words were tinted with sympathy and he wasn't as loud or as rambunctious around me anymore. When I came to his locker or sat down at lunch, it's as if someone turned his volume down three notches. I knew it was because he cared. But I hated it.

After leaving McGrady's class, I headed towards the dreaded cafeteria. I could see Jamal shouting at our table and nearly standing on his seat from my spot in the lunch line. I decided to ditch being a laughter killer and sat outside. There were a handful of people scattered around. Some sitting on the grass, others on the bleachers. I picked a shaded spot just around the corner, so I wouldn't be seen.

I munched on a below average burger and soggy fries. McGrady's words still lingered in my mind. Maybe Dad really was alive. Maybe it was really true. I just had to will it into existence. Dad was – is a good man. And good men have happy endings. Dad deserves a happy ending. I wondered if it was a fairytale to believe something so aggressively hopeful. But my thoughts were interrupted by a low chatter nearby.

    I heard two girls talking. They were talking about their dads. I leaned in closer to hear. One of the girl's dad left and the other girl started talking about how her dad left too. Suddenly, I felt bad for listening. This conversation was far too personal to eavesdrop. I think they thought no one else was around. I started gathering up my trash to go back into the cafeteria. Maybe I'd sit by Jamal and witness laughter die again. As I stood up, a girl appeared in front of me. She smiled, somewhat strangely.

    "Hey." She said.

    "Hey…" Was this one of the girls with the missing dad? "Uh, I didn't hear anything!" Shoot. Nice cover Jamie. Real subtle.

    "You don't remember me, do you?" I stared at her face and tried to figure out how she knew me. She seemed familiar but then again, she didn't. She had a kind yet rebellious look in her eyes – like she could both help you with your schoolwork and shank you if she had to.

    "Sorry I don't know who..."

    "Well, I am greatly offended. It's only your buddy from middle school. Sarah! Remember, we dissected frogs together?"

    "Sarah! Oh yeah, I remember! Mrs. Henley's class?" She nodded and I forced out a bit of awkward laughter. Sarah, that's right. I remembered her. We used to be friendly. I think we had a conversation about pro-wrestling once.

"I remember you were so scared, I had to dissect that frog myself!"

"What? Noooo." She smiled and I felt more at ease. She then motioned to her side and waved for someone to step forward. Another girl appeared. This girl I remembered instantly.

"Hi!" I waved and wondered if I had any food stuck on my face.

"This is-"

"Grace!" I blurted. "Yeah we met…at Becca's party that one time."

Grace waved timidly. Becca's party seemed like a lifetime ago. But just like then, I felt at a loss for words. Thankfully, Sarah stepped in and we reminisced on our shared middle school days. Grace seemed to respond naturally with Sarah around. Her voice was clear and sweet. I liked seeing her smile. It was like seeing her entire face be overcome with joy.

"We have lunch out here sometimes if you wanna join us tomorrow?" Sarah asked.

"Yeah sure!" I said too loudly. "I mean, if you don't mind." I asked, glancing back at Grace.

"Not at all!" Grace said happily.

I thought about our first real conversation for the rest of the day. It was a welcome break from my worries. I'm going to eat lunch with them tomorrow. Wait, no. Maybe I shouldn't. Actually, I think she likes me. God! What the hell am I thinking? Grace would never go for me. But, maybe the feelings were mutual.

At home after school, I continued the internal dialogue. It was nice, talking to new people. People who didn't know anything about me. People who didn't have a reason to feel sorry for me. What should I wear tomorrow? Man, if I still had my car, I could arrive at school cruising down the road in my Mustang, take her out and impress her. How would I take her out now? The bus?

"What are you saying, Jamie? You's crazy! Maaaaaa! Jamie's crazy!" Aisha announced.

"I'm crazy too!" Quinn said jumping on her seat at the dinner table. I laughed at the sight of Quinn now waving her hands in the air back and forth like a football referee.

"Girl, sit yo' butt down!" Ma shouted.

"Quinn, we all know you're crazy." I said, patting her head.

"Well ain't that nice to see." I turned to Ma who was smiling.

"What?" I asked.

"I haven't seen you laugh in a while Jamie." I smiled some more. This must make Ma happy. As we ate dinner together, there was a knock at the door.

"I'll get it. Y'all keep eating." Ma said and got up. I put some carrots on Quinn and Aisha's plates. I felt good. Like I was awakened from a deep sleep. Outside I heard someone mutter something to Ma. Maybe it was Jamal asking to shoot some hoops. I walked towards the front door and saw Ma collapsed on the floor.

"Ma!" I shouted. I bent down to try and get her up, but she was hysterical. Crying and wailing, flailing her arms in the air. What just happened? I looked up to see two soldiers in full uniform. It couldn't be true. This wasn't supposed to happen.

Chapter 21

Grace

I've begun to get accustomed to the smell of Blue Haven. The once severe stench of disinfectant has become a faint scent nearly worn away over time. Spring break was over and we were still living here. No word from Umma. No word from Janice.

I just got a text from Appa. He does this sometimes. Leaves a long text or email about how he loves me whenever Umma kicks him out of the house. He tries to get me to take his side in the matter. But these were all empty words. The truth is, Appa doesn't even know me. He doesn't know how much I love to write. How much I love to sing. What my favorite subject is at school. Or even my favorite food. Appa doesn't know me. And I don't know him.

A long time ago, Umma told me that when he was young, he had to grow up on his own. His parents abandoned him and he was partly raised by his elderly grandpa. But a lot of the time, he had to fend for himself. I wish that made me feel some sort of compassion towards him. Usually, people's life stories always moved me – sometimes to the point of tears. But after 16 years, I don't feel anything towards Appa. No compassion, no anger, no hate. Nothing.

I put my phone away after glimpsing at the text. I continued working on my homework from my little cot, which I think was meant for a child. It was reasonably comfortable though. Umma was watching Die Hard 2, which I rented from the library. Janice was at the desk studying. I don't know why she's still studying if she already took her MCAT exam. What else was left to study?

Sometimes, I wished I was as smart as Janice. But at other times, I was grateful I was the creative type. I could write the hell out of any essay, but Janice pretty much sucked at writing. Then again, Janice could work the hell out of any equation. If we were born with the same skills, I think we would've been crazy competitive with each other. Thankfully, both of us were born with opposing strengths.

I looked back down at my chemistry conversion chart and wondered if I should ask Janice for the second time how this worked. But then Janice took off her headphones. Could she sense I was about to ask her to do my homework for me?

"I got in!" Janice shouted.

"오모, really?" Umma asked.

"Huh? Got into what?" I asked confused.

"I got into medical school!" Janice shouted, staring at her computer screen. Both Umma and I lunged towards her laptop to see the news. It was an email from Johns Hopkins Medical School. With a quick skim I saw the words "Dear Janice" and "Congratulations."

"Oh my God! You got in!" I shouted. The three of us stood up and started jumping up and down in unison.

"Aigoo, 수고했어!" Umma said.

"Yeah! Your hard work has paid off!"

"This is so exciting!" Janice squealed happily, like I hadn't seen in years.

"Yeah, now you can throw that darn book away and stop studying!" I said pointing at that devil textbook. "We should celebrate!"

"Yes! Let's go barbecue?" Umma asked. Janice and I nodded in excitement.

Austin only had one decent Korean barbecue restaurant. Most of the time, we bought the meat at the supermarket, Umma marinated it, and we grilled at home. But with our new address, we ventured outside. Homework could wait until tomorrow morning. My stomach was ready for some juicy beef and pork wrapped in lettuce to my heart's delight.

The restaurant was packed by the time we got there and the smell of grilled galbi welcomed us inside.

"Oh barbecue. You sweet sweet temptress. How you tempt my weak soul!" I said pretending to be Hamlet, one hand dramatically lifted into the air.

"What she saying?" Umma said amused.

"You're so weird." Janice said smiling.

"Oh thine scent. How it calls me. To griiiill! Or not to grill. That is the question." I said fainting, as we waited for our name to be called.

As soon as we sat at the table, Umma ordered three servings of chadolbaegi, followed by three servings of galbi, and finished with a heaping plate of samgyeopsal. And to pair with our meat, we got two boiling bowls of soup to share – soondubu and daengjang jigae.

"Oh yeah. That hits the spot." I said while slurping down another bite. Janice talked about finding a dorm. Umma followed, saying she should find a boyfriend at school.

"Doctor couple. Very good!" Umma said.

"Umma, I'm going to med school to be a doctor, not to find a boyfriend. I won't have time to date."

"Yeah, yeah. Ok! When you have time! You find nice boy!" Umma said. I laughed and Janice rolled her eyes. Food was always our family bonding time. Nothing could cure a sad mood or put a smile on your face quite like a freshly made bowl of rice and pile of meat.

Just as we were finishing the last scrapes of pork belly off the stone grill, a group of middle-aged ahjummas approached our table. Maybe it was Umma's friends? But that couldn't be. Umma didn't have any friends. She hated people.

"안녕하세요!" They said and bowed one by one.

"안녕하세요!" Umma replied as she stood up to bow. The ahjumma ladies motioned for her to stay seated. They asked if she remembered them from church. Oh crap. This wasn't gonna be good. Umma, Janice, and I left that church after Korean politics got the best of leadership and Appa liked to appear superiorly holy compared to the rest of the congregation. He wasn't even a real Christian. What kind of a Christian beats his wife? If anyone was the real Christian, it was Umma. But she was the one who had to leave. Apparently genuine faith was seen as threatening to the Korean pastor.

Umma had a polite look on her face, but I could tell by her body language she was uncomfortable. I heard Appa's name mentioned by one particular ahjumma. The leader of the pack with a standard middle-aged perm and designer-logo handbag in plain sight.

"Aigoo. Grace and Janice's Appa comes to church? How come you all not coming anymore?" I wanted to smack her in the face. After our falling out at the Korean Presbyterian church, we moved to a mostly white, mixed church. And now these ahjummas, who cared more about status than sincerity, were judging us.

"네 네. Yes yes. We just not going now. We go to different church." Umma said, then refocused the attention on Janice getting into med school. Janice and I sat silently, waiting for it to be over. My insides were fuming. These fakes were the majority at our old church. The Korean ahjummas and ahjussis that treated people based on their income and shuttered away from actually helping people in the community. Church, for a lot of middle-aged and elderly Koreans at my last church, was treated as a social event. You had to put your best, fake foot, forward.

As soon as we got back to the shelter, my belly began making gurgling noises and I started feeling indigestion. Freaking ugh! Those old ladies ruined a damn good meal for me. I laid in bed and tried to get back to finishing my homework. But my fingers started typing the website of my old church. On the homepage, was a picture of Appa. My Appa? I laid in bed, dumbfounded. He was shaking the pastor's hand and people around him were clapping. I clicked the photo and an elder spotlight article appeared. My dad, got promoted, as a church elder. Appa. I couldn't believe it. There were quotes of how kind he was, how holy, how he had a serving heart, and loved Jesus.

I wanted to throw my laptop on the ground. That fucking psycho! He was being praised by the church! Those imbeciles! They didn't even know! Nobody knew! Nobody knew that he beat and cheated on his wife. That he's a fucking drug addict. That he abandoned his kids. They didn't know he was a complete and utter fake! And now people were praising him and his kindness? What the fuck kind of a world is this!

So, this is how the world works. Stupid people praise evil people and the world keeps turning. They're all a bunch of phonies. A bunch of stupid phonies! I slammed my laptop and rushed to the bathroom to wash the angry tears in my eyes. I wanted to punch the wall. So stupid. They're all so stupid. Everything is stupid and the world is one big shit storm. Stupid. Stupid.

    I woke up the next morning feeling like I got beat up in a boxing ring. My shoulders ached. My neck hurt and my forehead stung. I wish there was someone I could talk to. But what good would it do? They're all fakes anyway. Nobody really cares. Nobody really wants to know.

    I wondered what it would feel like seeing Sarah and Jamie back at school. Suddenly, I regretted our plans to have lunch together today. But maybe, they'd forgotten. Thankfully, when I got to the cafeteria, Sarah and Jamie were nowhere in sight. I guess they really did forget.

    I saw Angela and Tabitha at our usual table and sat down. They did most of the talking. Angela talked about how she missed being on a boat with her family in Maui. Tabitha chatted about something that happened in physics class.

    "What's wrong, Grace?" Tabs asked me. It seems I just missed an entire conversation.

    "Huh? Oh, nothing. I'm just tired. I think I have insomnia." I replied.

    "Aw man. I had insomnia once-"

    "Hey guys. I gotta go. I uh-forgot I have to return something at the library." I stood up and neither of them said anything as I left abruptly. For the rest of lunch, I walked aimlessly around the empty hallways. The bell finally rang. Statistics. I was going to have to see Sarah.

Maybe, Sarah was sick today. God, I hope so. Shit, sorry God. I didn't mean to wish that on her. Sarah's a good person. That's right. Sarah is a good person, one of the few that I know to have a genuine and kind heart. But then again, a lot of people seemed good on the outside.

I was the first to get to stats class. Minutes passed. Dylan entered and I instinctively looked away. Kids started trickling in. I stared at the huge clock above the teacher, watching the seconds endlessly turn. Only one minute left. As soon as the bell rang, Sarah rushed inside and sat down. Shoot. She waved at me with a big smile.

"Hey! I'm so sorry about lunch. I had to talk to my teacher about an extra-credit assignment. Did you end up eating with Jamie?"

I looked at her and shook my head no. For the rest of class, I tried not to make full eye contact with her or make any small talk. This was the best option for me. I needed Blue Haven to remain hidden. No one could know. No one should know.

The bell rang once more. I sprinted out of class and down the hall until my feet started to slow down. I felt the urge to look back. I turned around and saw Sarah standing outside class with a confused look on her face. She was fumbling with her textbooks. She looked up and saw me, then looked away.

"Hey." I said walking back towards her.

"Hey…" Sarah said not making full eye contact.

"I'm sorry. My head is just…yesterday was not a good day and I'm still kinda shaken up by it."

"It's fine. I understand." Sarah said nodding. Her face still looked hurt. This wouldn't do. Time to relieve the tension.

"So, this morning my chair squeaked during class and made a farting sound. So I tried to move it again so people would know it was the chair and not me. But then I actually farted *and* squeaked my chair. So to everyone else, it sounded like I just farted three times in a row."

Sarah looked back at me and blinked a few times. Then she burst out laughing. I laughed too. It didn't hit me how ridiculous first period was until I said the story out loud.

"Oh Grace. That was spectacular." Sarah said smiling.

Chapter 22
Jamie

I never saw Grace and Sarah after that day at lunch. In fact, I haven't gone to school for an entire week. After Dad's comrades came to tell us the news, it's like our lives were put on pause. The world was spinning around me, but I was stuck in the same place. I was here. But I wasn't here. It was like I was floating outside of my body, watching everything unfold.

I saw myself opening the door to accept food from neighbors, from church friends. I saw myself talking to Jamal and I saw Jamal's parents talking to Ma. I saw our relatives come and fill up our living room. Grandpa. Grandma. Uncle Willy. Aunt Becky. I saw Quinn cry every day and Aisha with tear stains on her face that never seemed to dry.

"We are sorry Mrs. Davis. But your husband is dead." Your husband is dead. Your husband is dead. Dad is dead? It couldn't be. My Dad is alive. He's hiding in a cave in the mountains. Why would he say Dad died? They never found a body. At least not a whole one. Instead, they found body parts. A foot. A leg that was shattered and severed. But apparently it was Dad's. It was left burnt to a crisp in a car that had exploded during a suicide bombing. But it wasn't enough. Dad could still be alive. God was supposed to keep him alive. He promised.

Ma used the money I got from Jamal to help pay off some of Dad's debts and for his funeral. Why after someone died were we supposed to now feed everyone he ever knew? Who the hell were all these people? Our church was filled with over two hundred bodies. Most wearing black. Some wearing disgusting costumey hats. Today was supposedly a Sunday. That's what Jamal told me when I walked in and asked him what day it was. He looked worried. I put my hand on his shoulder to reassure him I was alright. But I'm not sure if I am alright. It feels like a part of me has died.

I sat in the front row of our church looking at a large photograph of Dad. He had on his uniform down to the hat and medallions. He wasn't smiling. His face looked stern. They picked the wrong photo. They should have picked a picture of him smiling. They should have picked a picture of him dancing with Ma or playing with me, Quinn, and Aisha outside during summertime. I wanted to rip up the photo and burn his old uniform.

"And now, we would like to open the floor to anyone who would like to pay their respects." Our pastor stepped down from his pulpit, leaving an empty space. Someone from Dad's platoon stepped onto the stage and said something in regard to

Dad's bravery and courage. Something about what he did for the nation. I wondered what the nation ever did for my dad.

Next was Grandpa. He fumbled and cleared his throat while taking out a lined piece of paper and reading glasses from his suit pocket.

"My son is…I mean, my son was…excuse me." Grandpa started coughing and pressed on the inner corners of his eyes to keep the tears from falling. It was no help. The tears fell. Grandpa was crying. I looked to my right, Ma was quietly sobbing. I looked to my left, Grandma was also quietly sobbing with her shoulders shaking up and down. "Our Richard…" Why wasn't anyone helping him?

I found myself standing up and walking towards the pulpit. I put my hand on Grandpa's broad back. He turned around and wrapped his arms around me. I whispered to him, "I got this." What was I doing? Grandpa sat back down and I looked at the many aisles of people. On any other Sunday, the sight wouldn't have frightened me. But today it terrified me. I looked at my sisters. Quinn had her head rested on Aisha's lap and was openly crying. Aisha was sitting straight with her arm gently stroking Quinn's face, trying not to cry. Trying to be strong for Quinn.

"My dad is the best man I know…" I looked around and spotted Jamal towards the back. He nodded at me. "He always taught me that doing what is right is better than taking the easy road…" A few people nodded in response. "That greatness isn't a given, it is worked for and earned. My dad is a great man. He worked for everything he has – had…"

I'm not sure what more I said after that. I talked about the time in second grade, when I came home with a bruise on my face after getting beat up at school, and he consoled me. The next day at school, I found out he went to the kid's house to defend my honor. I also told everyone the story of my car and later, how I'll always remember him dancing with Ma in the living room. "Dad would always sing Stevie Wonder's Isn't She Lovely to Ma when she was sad."

Ma wiped her tears and smiled a bit. She stood up and made her way to the pulpit, gave me a hug and took my place. "You did good, baby."

She talked about how they first met and how after she immediately rejected him for being a military man, he never stopped pursuing her.

"He called me every day without fail. Whenever he was stationed in a different city, he took every chance he got to come visit me instead of asking me to visit him. Richard sent me letters, poems. Don't let the uniform fool you, Richard was a romantic. An idealist. He believed in love and goodness and hope. Doing good purely because it was the right thing and because that's what Jesus would do, he'd say. He never gave up on us, even until the end…" Ma looked up.

I wondered if he was really there. If Dad was truly gone. If heaven was actually real or just a made-up place people believed in to make themselves feel better after someone died.

But if heaven was real, I knew without a doubt that Dad was there.

After Ma finished speaking, a line started to form and we walked outside. Ma, Quinn, Aisha, and I stood outside staring at an empty hole in the ground. I held Aisha's hand which felt cold. They lowered a wooden casket into the empty hole. I wondered what was inside. Did they leave it empty? Or did they gather the broken limbs that were found and put them in the box? Our pastor quoted Revelation 21, "He will wipe away every tear from their eyes," as people threw dirt on Dad. He then proceeded to let everyone know dinner would be served at the Davis residence.

I walked into our house and found it overstuffed with people. People talking, some smiling sympathetically, some still crying. Our kitchen table was now covered with containers wrapped in silver tinfoil. Ma and Grandma were holding spatulas, serving each person in the assembly line. Jamal's mom ran over to her and took the spatula out of her hand, motioning for her to rest. I walked into the living room. All the cousins were sitting on the floor with Aisha and Quinn, who were now playing Go Fish together. I smiled a little. Jamal was on the couch. I took a seat next to him. He started telling me how sorry he was.

"Listen Jamal. I don't need another person in this room pitying me. I know you care. But please for the love of God could we talk about something else? I need to get my mind off of this. What's been going on at school? You still with that girl?"

Jamal's face stopped for a moment. Then a smile appeared. He talked about how Stacey had caught him texting another girl and accused him of cheating. He vehemently denied it but then cracked a smile saying how he actually started liking this other girl who was *fine as hell* and had just transferred here from Oklahoma. Her name was Melissa and they were now dating. He already confessed his love for her. He continued updating me on all the drama from our crew, who was fighting with who, who had starting dating, and his recent earnings from a basketball game where he played one against three and took home $500 in *cold hard cash*.

I smiled as my body began to melt into the couch cushions. Jamal's theatrical voice comforted me and I dozed off amidst the crowded room. I dreamt of Dad. He unlocked the front door of our home and walked in while I was sitting in the living room. He rummaged through the refrigerator and took out a bunch of food, balancing it all in his arms and dumping it on the kitchen table. He then started to cut up some vegetables and prepare a huge meal. I stood up in the living room and shouted at him, angry. I demanded to know where he'd been all this time. He smiled at me and said he never left.

A loud bang shook me awake. I was still on the living room couch in my black suit, but someone had taken off my shoes. The room was now empty of friends and relatives. I turned around to see where the noise came from, trying to shake the remnants of deep sleep away.

Ma was at the kitchen table wearing her reading glasses, staring seriously at a stack of papers. I walked up to her and saw messy piles of white envelopes with corners of checks and $50 bills peeking out. Ma looked up at me surprised.

"Oh, Jamie! Sorry honey, I thought you were still asleep." I took a seat across the table and scanned the tornado of documents. Ma was looking at a spreadsheet filled with numbers and dollar signs.

"Ma what's going on?"

"Oh, this is nothing baby. Don't you worry about this." Ma said, trying to stack and hide a few of the sheets beside her.

"Ma." I was shocked to see that her face had aged at least a decade. "You can tell me."

Ma slowly exhaled.

"Yo' daddy…he invested in stocks a few years ago before getting deployed. He hoped that it would create extra income for the family and take care of us in case anything ever…ever happened to him. But with the stock market crash…it didn't – it didn't do what yo' daddy thought it would."

"How much did we lose?" I asked.

"Don't you worry about this baby. I shouldn't have told you anything. You're too young. Go back to your room and go to sleep. I'll take care of this."

"Ma. How much?" I asked. Ma's face looked weak and tired. She stared at me, looking ready to collapse from exhaustion.

"About $45,000." I stared back at her incredulously. I couldn't wrap my head around it. $45,000? The most money I've ever touched in my life was what Jamal gave me.

"Can't we ask someone to borrow money? Grandma and Grandpa?" Ma sighed.

"Your grandma and grandpa, bless their heart, gave me this today. Here, take a look." I looked inside the envelope and counted $450. "Jamie, that's all your grandparents can afford. Your grandpa is still working even when he should be retired by now. Grandma's going in and out of the hospital for her dementia. They're already struggling. I can't ask for their help. This is all they can afford to give."

"What about Aunt Becky or Uncle Joe or Uncle Willy? Cousin Jeanette?" Ma pointed to the table of envelopes.

"Jamie they already tried to help. All of our family, the ones with money to spare gave us checks and cash to help out. But in total, it's not even a couple grand. I can't ask cousin Jeanette – she just started school. And all my friends are struggling already. I don't know a single couple with both people still at their job this year. This house has been bleeding me dry for years and I already had to take out a loan. This recession…it's made a mess of everything."

"I could get a job! I could go back to tutoring again. Maybe, Jamal could get me a job at the country club!"

"Thank you, baby. But you've done more than enough. I want you to stay focused on school. Don't you worry." Ma said flipping through the piles of paper.

I felt jittery and tense. My leg started hopping up and down and my arms started shaking. I crossed my arms to stop moving but my upper body started rocking back and forth. Ma punched some more numbers on her calculator when something caught my eye. I could see the big capital letters peeking out from beneath a few envelopes. I tugged on the corner gently without Ma noticing. The word FORECLOSURE appeared. I started to feel dizzy as the room spun around me.

"Ma...what's this?"

Chapter 23
Carlos

School was not as bad as I expected, even with Luis gone. I tried to make casual conversation with my classmates, the ones who looked like me. At lunch, I didn't know where to sit. Luis and I had our usual spot but I didn't want to sit there alone. I looked around the cafeteria and tried to find Benny.

He was sitting with his crew and I awkwardly approached his table. Benny stood up to make a seat for me and motioned for me to come over. "Hey everyone! Y'all know my brother, Carlos." A few of his bandmates greeted me, the ones who came over often. I was surprised he didn't call me his cousin. Maybe he really felt like we were brothers, or maybe it was easier to say rather than having to tell my backstory.

Benny was always cooler than me. The packed cafeteria table alone showed how many people liked him. I tried to make small talk with some of his friends, throwing in a reaction or two whenever somebody said something. But mostly, I just missed Luis.

After school I headed to Tío's shop. Most afternoons I either went to Luis's house or to help Tío. I didn't like being home alone. He was still working on that girl's car, Sarah, the one who came after being in an accident.

"Hola Carlos! Hey, hand me that screwdriver will ya?" I picked up Tío's toolbox and knelt down to inspect the damage alongside him. He put his arm around my shoulder.

"What do you think it needs mijo?" I stared at the bumper that was hanging off, the broken headlight and metal scraps dangling just inches above the ground.

"I think it needs…a lot of work." Tío laughed.

"I think so too!" He motioned to help lift the bumper as he unscrewed something behind it. "So how was school today?" I told Tío about lunch and how Benny introduced me as his brother.

"Man, that makes me feel good." Tío said with a big smile. "You know Benny loves you. You *are* a brother to him. He's just not good at talking about his feelings. Must be all that testosterone."

"Do you think Benny really thinks of me like that?"

"Of course! One day, when you take over this shop and if Benny ever needs a job – which he probably will one day since all he does is play that rock music. I swear, that music, it hurts my ears. Anyways, when you take over and he's ready to get a real job – I want you to give him a job here. Family is family. We must look after each other."

"When I take over?" I stood up and stared at Tío.

"Sí. Who else am I gonna leave this all to? I know it's not much. But I want you to have this…son." Tío kept working with a smile. I tried not to burst into tears.

That night, Tío and I came home while Tía was cooking tamales. We ate at the dinner table and Benny left with a plate to eat in his room, per usual.

Afterwards, Tío, Tía, and I sat in the living room watching an episode of Extreme Home Makeover. Tío sipped on a beer while I tried to finish some homework. Tía Julia seemed quieter than normal. She must have had a hard day working at the restaurant. Once Jay Leno came on the TV, I got ready for bed.

Benny was texting some girl on his phone from his bed across from mine. He started to put things in his backpack and sneak out our bedroom window. "If you tell Mom or Dad, you're dead meat."

"Leave me alone." I moaned, falling asleep already.

At 2:23 a.m. I woke up to go to the bathroom. Benny still wasn't home. As I stumbled back into our bedroom I heard a sound coming from the living room. I wondered if the TV was still on and went to check. It was Tío and Tía. I was about to go back to sleep, but something looked wrong. Tía had her hands on top of her eyes. She was crying and shaking her head. Tío wrapped his arms around her. I inched closer to hear what they were saying.

"It's gonna be ok, Julia. It's gonna be ok." Tío said quietly.

"No, it won't! You don't understand. My mom had it. That's how she died!" Tía said in a panic. She didn't look like herself. Her face was strained, her voice, desperate.

"But that's not gonna happen to you!" Tío said a little louder. "You're gonna be fine!"

"How do you know? What if I – what if…" Tío hugged Tía as she cried.

"It's only stage two right now. You'll be ok. I know it. Breast cancer is much easier to treat than other cancers. You're gonna be ok. We're gonna fight this together."

Breast cancer? Stage two? Tía. My mind started to race. This didn't make any sense. Tía Julia has cancer? Why didn't they tell me? Does Benny know? I don't think he does. Why didn't they tell us? Tía. My Tía.

I snuck back to my room and laid in bed. This couldn't be real. My body felt paralyzed but my mind was leaping and falling. This can't be. Not Tía. She's a good person. How could God do this to her? This isn't fair. Tío. What if…what if. No. Stop! I can't think like that. She's going to be ok. Tío was right. She's going to beat this. Because if she doesn't…God, please. I can't lose another one. Please save her.

My mind kept moving until it landed on a memory from many years ago when I was a kid. Things were still new then. I was still scared of Tío and Tía even though Benny and I quickly became friends. I didn't say much. I think the only things I said that first year were "thank you" and "I'm sorry." Most of the time I just nodded yes or no.

    Mom came to visit after being released from jail the first time. Tío and Tía had been telling me for weeks that she was coming to visit me and how excited she was to see me. I was getting a little excited too. I thought she was coming to take me home and I could leave these strangers. The day finally came.

    Mom walked through the front door and instead of hugging her, I immediately ran away into my room and hid in the closet. Mom knocked on the door. I could hear her voice, but for some reason I didn't want to see her. She knocked a couple more times and opened the door.

    She tried to give me a hug to quiet me down but I started kicking and screaming at the top of my lungs. I don't know what came over me. I thought I still loved my mom. But in that moment, I screamed like a possessed child. Mom stood up with a pained face and walked out of the room. I heard her talking to Tío and Tía back in the living room.

    A little while later, she came back and knocked on the closet door again. I shouted, "Get out! I hate you! Get out!" The sound of her footsteps pitter pattered away.

    That night I cried. I cried so much my shirt got wet. I stayed in the closet and wiped my tears with Benny's old stuffed animals. I tried to stop but I couldn't. Later that night, Tía Julia knocked gently on the closet door.

"You don't have to come out but I've left some food for you in case you're hungry." I waited for her to leave the room then snuck the plate of hot rice and chicken back into the closet where I ate in silence.

The tears kept falling. I'm not sure I've ever cried that much since. Hours passed and the loud sobs dwindled into silent tears. There was a soft knock at the door again. I pushed the door open a crack and saw Tía Julia sitting on the floor.

"Is it ok if I come in?" She asked in a hushed voice. I nodded and she came in and sat with me. It started off with me in one corner, her in the other. She didn't say anything. I tried to stop crying, but the tears kept on falling on my face as I wiped them away with a stuffed elephant. After a few minutes, she opened up her arms to me and I sat on her lap. She stroked my hair, kissed my head, and I kept crying until I fell asleep with her arms around me.

Tía can't die. Tía Julia is my real mom.

Chapter 24
Grace

Not seeing my dad wasn't hard. In fact, it made life easier. Umma didn't seem to understand that. She thought trying to fit Appa into our family was the best option. But whenever Appa was gone, I was happier. I didn't have to look over my shoulder and wait for the next disaster to strike. I could breathe. Even if the sadness made it hard sometimes.

School felt pretty much the same. It was all in my head. None of my teachers knew anything was going on still. Angela and Tabitha didn't know either. We carried on. But over time, our conversations didn't feel as urgent to me anymore. I used to think a pop quiz or finding a date to homecoming meant the end of the world. Now it felt like none of it really mattered.

I've been at Blue Haven for several weeks now, but sometimes I still don't realize where I am. I'm in a room, in a place, with many other rooms. But a shelter? As soon as I say the word in my mind, I push it away. We are fine. Everything is fine. As long as he's gone, we'll be fine.

"We should go!" Tabitha said excitedly.

"I don't know guys. I don't even know anything about basketball. Remember how boring the football game was last year?" I asked.

"I'm down with whatever." Angela said nonchalantly.

"Come on, Grace! We are in high school! We should get the full high school experience while we're here!"

"Ok fine!" I said. "But next time, I get to choose what we see at the movie theater."

"Deal!" Tabitha said happily as we shook hands.

That Friday night, we walked side by side up the bleachers to scope out our very first high school basketball game. We were never interested in going before. But lately, Tabitha wanted more out of her high school experience.

By the time we got there, our team was already getting annihilated. We sat and clapped when the people around us clapped and cheered when the people around us cheered. After 10 minutes, Angela asked if we should get some food. Tabitha and I nodded. Turns out none of us were basketball fans either. Maybe sports just wasn't in our DNA.

We stood in a long line for nachos and soda. A group of guys were standing in front of us like a giant cloud.

"Hi!" A voice shouted in front of me. Turns out it was Alex from my world history class.

"Oh, hi!" I said. Alex was a nice guy. He played soccer and liked to make small talk with almost everyone. I wondered how he did it. I always felt awkward starting conversations.

"Didn't think I'd see you here." He said.

"Yeah, me either." I said. Alex chuckled and started introducing us to his friends. They all kind of looked the same – thin, shaggy hair, unthreateningly attractive. I introduced Angela and Tabitha and we all ate our queso-drenched nachos together while semi-watching the game.

"We have no idea what's going on." I told Alex. He smiled.

"Our football team is good, but our basketball team, not so much." Alex proceeded to point at random players and explain the various rules of basketball. Angela, Tabitha, and I nodded our heads so it would stop. We didn't actually care about the rules. But I liked seeing Alex talk so passionately. It seemed, no matter who you were, everyone who was born and bred in Texas was a sports fan.

After parting ways, we walked back up to our spot on the bleachers, not paying much attention. Our school's basketball team sucked, but everyone seemed to make such a big deal about the game. There was one player who scored us a lot of points though, Jamal. I wondered if he remembered me from Becca's party. Suddenly, the thought of Jamie filled my mind and I scanned the gym to see if he was here to support his friend. No sign of him.

"Maybe we should just leave." I said, looking to Angela and Tabitha.

"Hey look!" Tabs said pointing back at the court. The marching band took over and I screamed my lungs out for my friend who played the trumpet. Finally, some real entertainment! This was way better. We shouted and cheered while people looked at the three of us as if we were crazy.

"Well *that* was fun!" I said. Angela and Tabitha agreed. The halftime performance was much more up our alley. We tried to stick it out for the second half. But we ended up crowding around Tabitha's Blackberry phone and watched YouTube videos of America's Best Dance Crew. Still, I was proud we stayed for an entire game, our first and last basketball experience.

The next morning, Umma and I took our weekly trip to IHOP. I decided to spice things up and ordered the International Crepe Passport while Umma ordered the tried and true Rooty Tooty Fresh n' Fruiti. We both eagerly waited for coffee, which we both loved. There was something about it. We knew it was bad. It was watered down and weakly caffeinated. But it never failed to warm our bodies and our minds, making us feel at ease with just a few sips. It tasted like home.

"Umma. What did you wanna be when you were my age?"

"Hmmm. Your age. How old you now?"

"I'm 16, Umma. You should know that." I said with a make-believe frown.

"When I was 16, I think I wanted to be nurse or teacher. Yeah, I used to like the teaching, I am good with little kids. They all love me." I laughed.

"Really? *All* the kids love you?"

"Oh yeah! I played with them, did all fun things. They all love me. I was good at it. I taught at church for Sunday School, many years."

"What else did you do? Did you ever have a job?" I asked. I couldn't imagine Umma working at an office or as a nurse. To me, she was always just my Umma.

"Of course, I work. After college, I worked in my uncle's big office. He had big company. He traded different machines with companies all over Asia. My uncle – your great uncle was very smart. He spoke Korean, Chinese, and Japanese! I do everything for him."

"Really? I didn't know that!"

"Yeah. I was a businesswoman. Your mom is smart!" Umma said tapping her head. "That's why you so smart."

"I guess so."

"Of course! You smart, because of me. But you know. After married, I quit job and had Janice." Umma's face darkened. "If it weren't for your Appa, I could have been boss one day I think." I didn't know what to say. I remembered, Umma mentioned to me stories of her youth. She had been well off. When she got engaged to Appa, her parents disapproved of him and told her to break it off. She didn't.

"You know Grace. When you go to college, you study hard and get good job. You make lots of money, ok? Even after marry, you keep working. You never know what can happen."

"I'm going to make lots of money!" I said. "I'm going to make money and then I'll buy you a house." Umma smiled.

"Really?"

"Yeah! I'm going to write a book and it'll be a best seller. I'll make a million dollars!"

"Ok! I like!" Umma said and clapped her hands together. The waitress came with our plates and we started eating our food as if we were in a rush. Umma and I shared the same trait of eating too quickly in fear that someone would take it from us.

"Umma." I said in between bites. "I feel like I really want to live a big life. Like a really big life." I stretched out my arms to represent just how big it was going to be. I dreamt of something big. A life where my writing could reach more than just my high school teacher. A life where I had a real impact on people, cities, states, countries, the world. I wanted to shake nations into change and people into understanding and compassion. A book, an article, a story, these things had the power to change the world. I wanted that. I wanted to create that.

"You will live big life! You know God put that dream in you, because one day you will do it. You do it!" Umma said enthusiastically in between bites of her pancakes. We finished our food in less than 15 minutes and waited for our check.

"Umma."

"What?"

"How much longer do we have to stay at the shelter?"

"Not too long now. Almost done. Just wait little longer, ok?"

"Ok."

Back in our room, Janice was on the phone talking to a friend that also got accepted into Johns Hopkins. They were going to be roommates. I was happy for Janice. But looking at her so happy also made me feel a tinge of sadness. She got to live her dream sooner than I could. What was I going to do without her?

Umma and I laid on the bed. I started flipping channels before landing on The Karate Kid, the Hilary Swank version.

"Aigoo. Why you like this?" Umma asked.

"I wanna watch!" I laid on my stomach while simultaneously scrolling on my Chocolate phone. A text message appeared from Sarah. *Meet me on the swings. I gotta tell you something ASAP!*

"I'm going to the bathroom." I said as I swiftly made my way down the hall, through the kitchen, and outside. Sarah was waiting for me on the swings.

"Hey! What's going on?" I asked.

"It's Jamie." Sarah said with a serious face.

"What about him?"

"He's here."

Chapter 25
Jamie

      I never thought it would come to this. It feels like I have a target on my back and God keeps shooting arrows at it. First Ma's laid off, then Dad's funeral, now we have to pack our things. I'm worried one of us might break soon. Maybe Ma or Aisha. Ma because she lost her husband or Aisha because she's stopped crying. Quinn cries all the time. That's how I know she'll be ok. But Aisha, she's not crying anymore. Her face has turned stone cold. She's too young to be this hard already.

      Maybe I'll be the one to lose my mind. Maybe, I'm already losing it. Sometimes it feels like my mind and body are moving separately, like a marionette and a puppeteer. I am packing. But I'm not really in control. My hands are moving. But it's like they've gone on autopilot. I watch as my hands pack my clothes. Throw away my old awards and certificates. Keep my baseball glove – the one I used when I played catch with Dad. My hands keep Dad's Medal of Honor, which he earned when I was a kid. Everything reminds me of Dad. Everything hurts.

I helped Quinn pack her things. She asked me when Daddy's coming back. I said, "You'll get to see him when you go to heaven." Aisha already finished packing and sat with a blank face at her old desk that's been wiped clean of belongings. It used to be littered with Polly Pockets, then Barbies, then copies of Cosmo Girl. The sight of it clean made me sad. Dad and Aisha used to be super close. He treated her like a princess and always gave her lots of attention. He never wanted her to feel left out, being the middle child. On any given day at home, I would walk in on them sitting in the living room brushing her Barbie's hair or Dad intently watching Aisha's doll fashion shows.

I moved all of our boxes to the living room. Ma was talking loudly on the phone. I haven't seen her shout in a long time. Ma's not one to show extreme emotions around us. She's level-headed. Dad was the more emotional one. Ma's dealt with dying people at her job. She's learned to detach herself from people emotionally. But Dad was different. She could never detach from him. Over the past few weeks, I've seen Ma weep and yell and scream. I've heard sobs I didn't know she was capable of. Ma's not the same. None of us are.

"Come on now. Let's get this in the car." Ma said, trying to reorder her face into a neutral position. It wasn't working. Ma and I started moving boxes to the trunk of her car.

Aisha and Quinn tried to help by carrying loose pillows and toys.

"Where are we going?" Quinn asked as I buckled her seat belt.

"To a hotel." Ma said.

"I thought we were going to Uncle Joe's house?" I asked confused.

"They said they still renovating their kitchen and living room."

"I thought they finished months ago?" Ma didn't respond and started driving. I liked Uncle Joe, but he wasn't always the most reliable guy. When Ma was pregnant and visiting Uncle Joe's house, her water broke. While she was about to go into labor with Aisha, he stopped at McDonald's on the way to the hospital and bought himself a Happy Meal.

We drove to the hotel in silence. Ma got the keys to our room from an Indian man wearing thick glasses and a gray hoodie.

"Just bring what you need for the night." Ma said. We opened the door to our room and were affronted by burgundy carpeting and an overpowering smell of eucalyptus. Something must have happened here for them to go bat-shit on the scented candles. Quinn ran to the bed and laid down. Aisha sat down beside her and started flipping through the TV channels like a zombie, eventually landing on Cartoon Network.

"Jamie." Quinn said as she tugged at my shirt sleeve. "I saw a pool. Can we go swimming?" Quinn looked at me hopefully. I smiled at the sight of her tiny eager face.

"Of course we can." I said. I looked back at Ma who was unpacking our bags.

"I found the swimsuits." Ma said holding them up in the air victoriously. "Let's go swimming."

Aisha and Quinn changed into their bathing suits and I kept on my sweatpants. We went to the ginormous pool that was positioned in the center of the hotel, so literally every guest could eavesdrop on us. Quinn jumped in and Aisha helped her swim back and forth, holding up her chest.

Ma and I sat on the foldable lounge chairs, each with a bottle of Nestle iced tea we got from the vending machine.

"Ma…I don't-"

"Look how much Quinn has grown." Ma interrupted. "And Aisha too. She's really become a big sister, hasn't she?" Ma asked me with a smile.

"…Yeah, she has Ma." We watched Quinn and Aisha swim back and forth. "Ma."

"Hmmm?"

"What happened with Uncle Joe?" Ma sighed.

"You know your uncle. He says one thing, then does another." Ma took a few gulps of her iced tea. "At first, when I asked for a place to stay, he said it was no problem. But as soon as I brought up the topic of money – he changed his mind. Typical." Ma sighed.

"Is there anyone else? What about Grandma and Grandpa?"

"Honey. They're hours away. I don't want you switching schools before your last year of high school."

"It's fine, Ma. Really." Ma stayed silent.

"I can't ask them baby. They just barely hanging on." I watched as Quinn and Aisha raced across the pool, bouncing on giant noodle floaties someone had left behind.

"What about Aunt Becky or Cousin Jeanette?" I asked.

"Yo' Aunt Becky has a different man over almost every night. I don't want Quinn or Aisha to see that. And Cousin Jeanette! Could you imagine us staying at her dorm?" Ma waved her arm in the air as if swatting away an invisible fly.

Ma seemed calmer than what the situation called for and I started getting angrier. Now was not the time for us to be swimming.

"You don't worry about a thing, Jamie." Ma said trying to placate my deteriorating mood. "I've set up an appointment to talk to someone tomorrow. She can help us. Don't you worry about a thing. Just keep doing well at school. I want you to go back starting tomorrow."

Ma pat my shoulder then covered her face with a towel. If anyone were to spot us, they would've thought we were on a family vacation.

The next morning, Ma nagged me to shower and change out of my sweatpants. I forget how long it's been since I've worn jeans. We all squeezed into the car, still packed with our belongings, and made our first school run since Dad died.

Before walking back into Stony Brook High School, I wondered how many people at school would know about Dad. Turns out, everyone. As soon as I walked through the doors and down the hallway, I caught people either turn and whisper to each other or give me a look of insincere sorrow. A girl from my science class stopped me and told me how sorry she was for my loss. One of my old teachers from last year did the same.

Fuck it. Today was gonna be a bad day. I rushed to my locker and tried to open it but failed three times in a row.

"Hey, asshole! You forget your locker combo?" It was Jamal. I looked at him and smiled in relief. He came over and opened my locker for me on the first try.

"How do you know my locker combo?"

"Man, I've been tying your shoes for you since the second grade." I smiled. Seeing an old friend put me at ease. Not somebody who saw me as the deceased hero's son who died in Afghanistan, but someone who saw me as the guy who couldn't tie his shoes. Jamal put his arm around me and we navigated the pitying crowd together back to our crew. I think Jamal warned them to act normal around me, and they listened. We all talked about the next basketball game – as if nothing major had happened to me, as if nothing changed.

The bell rang, herding us to first period. Each teacher had a similar way of being polite on all the assignments I missed. Most gave me a free pass. I tried to avoid talking to them as much as I could, especially Mr. McGrady. I knew he was the only teacher who actually cared, but I couldn't help hating him for some odd reason. During English class, I tried not to make eye contact or answer any questions. After the bell rang, I made a dash for it.

"Jamie, wait!" Mr. McGrady said. I stopped and turned around reluctantly. "Listen Jamie. I'm so sorry about your dad…He is…He was a great man." McGrady stood in the doorway with a pained look on his face.

"A hero, right?"

"Yes. Most definitely a hero." McGrady responded.

"That's right. That's what everyone said. That's what everyone's been telling me all day!" I yelled. "How would they know if my dad was a hero? He was found blown to bits! They don't know! You don't know! You don't know him!" My face was hot and I wanted to punch a hole in the wall.

"Listen Jamie. I know how you feel." McGrady stood up and reached out his hand.

"Don't touch me! You don't know how I feel! No one does!" I yelled as I threw my books on the floor.

McGrady kneeled down and started picking up my books. "My father died too." McGrady said quietly. "Not in a war…He had a problem with alcohol. They found him on the side of the road. He drove into a tree and ended up killing himself, drunk driving."

I stood frozen and watched as McGrady picked up my pile of belongings. Then without warning, I started to cry.

McGrady didn't seem shocked by my appearance. He leaned in and hugged me, patting me on the back a few times.

"It's gonna be ok. Not today, but one day. It'll start getting easier."

After school, I waited for Ma to pick me up. Things were harder without my car. I didn't realize how much freedom it bought me until I had to wait in front of school, dodging the crowd of people's sympathy. Whether it was genuine or fake didn't matter to me. I just wanted to escape being seen at all. Later that day I found out Dad was on the news. *"Local hero found dead after suicide bombing."* My dad, the hero.

Back at the hotel, Quinn, Aisha, and I ate Whataburger meals and watched a rerun of Spy Kids 2 on Disney Channel. I tried to catch up on schoolwork. It wasn't too hard. Once I saw a page, I could remember it clearly in my mind and save it for later. This was especially helpful for AP Chemistry. I could recall each element and its value on the periodic table.

By 9:30 p.m., I was caught up on schoolwork. Aisha and Quinn were already asleep. Ma had on her glasses and was looking at a bunch of pages on their shared bed.

"Ma, did you talk to the woman today?" Ma looked up at me. "The woman who was supposed to help us?"

"Oh yeah. Yes, I did Jamie." Ma said.

"And?" I asked impatiently.

"You don't have to worry about it, Jamie."

"Ma!" I raised my voice.

"Shhhhh. You'll wake them up." Ma whispered. I moved to the other side of her bed and sat on the edge of our exposed bathtub.

"I want to know. I-I need to know…" Ma took off her glasses.

"Ok look. I talked to a welfare representative today." I nodded, remembering that President Franklin D. Roosevelt enacted social welfare programs through his New Deal in 1935. "She said we wouldn't get approved."

"Why not?" I whispered.

"It's a lot of things. My car is worth too much. I haven't been unemployed long enough. Then there's our investments in stocks, savings I put away for your college fund. It's all put into account."

"But those stocks failed and you can use all the money in my college fund!"

"Either way, she said it was very unlikely for us to get approved."

"So, what did she say we should do?"

"We can apply for Temporary Assistance for Needy Families…but it's not much."

"Ok, but I think it's a good idea you still apply."

"I will, Jamie. Don't you worry. She also recommended something else…"

"What is it?"

"Well, she asked where we were staying now and I told her a hotel."

"What did she say?"

"She recommended a place we could stay for free instead. But it would only be temporary…just for a little while."

"Where?" I asked eagerly. Ma paused, then reluctantly took off her glasses.

"It's called Blue Haven. It's a place moms and their kids can stay when something drastic happens and they have no other options. But Jamie…it's technically a shelter." I stared at Ma not knowing what to say.

"Baby, it's not like one of those dingey places that you're thinking of. She says it's the equivalent of staying at an average hotel…kinda like this one. We would get our own room and everything would be confidential."

My mind started racing but there weren't any thoughts. Just black empty space waiting for some appearance of light. But there was nothing. No idea. No way out. No resemblance of another solution in my mind.

"Ma, how much money do we have left?" Ma sighed.

"Less than $200." I stared at Ma completely stunned. "Yo' daddy. He had some debts. We never told you because we didn't want you to worry. Nothing shady. He just invested in some real estate deals and stocks that didn't work out. I had to pay them back…after yo' daddy passed."

Come on, God. Give me an idea. Give me a sign. There must be another way. Something else? I waited. But nothing came. No divine intervention. No sign from Jesus. My mind was silent.

"Ma. Do you believe that this – Blue Haven, is the only way to get out of this?" Ma looked straight in my eyes and nodded. "Then, let's go."

We never told Quinn or Aisha it was a shelter. We were careful to make it a secret and told them we found a better hotel, one where we could cook our own food and that had a library. We make believed that the front office and security system was a fancy receptionist station. Quinn seemed to enjoy picking DVDs and books from the "library" which was really just a single bookcase of worn-out items. But Aisha caught on. Hotel rooms don't have communal bathrooms.

Everything would've been tolerable – if I hadn't seen her. Sarah. This can't be happening. The girl I dissected frogs with during middle school, is here too. I had no idea. I always thought Sarah came from money. I never thought I'd see her here or anyone I knew really.

I acted like a fool when I saw her earlier tonight. One look and I ran away into my room without a word. What was I supposed to say? "Long time, no see?" I didn't want anyone to know about this place, or that my family was here, or I was here. It was only temporary. We didn't truly belong here. Then again, I guess no one really belonged in a place like this. People are meant to live in homes. Not shelters.

I was too scared to even piss or drink water. I didn't want to cross paths with her on the way to the bathroom. Instead, I kept getting Quinn to do my errands for me. I asked her to bring a bottle of water from the kitchen. Then, another DVD to get my mind off of where we were. Then, again, a snack because I haven't had dinner yet and am now starving to the point I think my stomach is eating itself.

"Fool! Get your own snack and stop bossing your sister around!" Ma yelled at me.

"Yeah! You lazy bum." Aisha agreed. I didn't realize how much I missed the sound of Aisha's voice, or her sass.

"Fine. Aisha, you want anything?" I asked her smiling.

"I don't know. Something delicious."

"Me too!" Quinn agreed.

"Yeah, me three." Ma said.

"Ok. I'll see what the concierge has." I opened our door just a tiny sliver to see if anyone was in the hallway. No sign of movement. I slipped out and closed the door quickly behind me. Slowly, I stepped into the open living room, wading the waters. Empty. The kitchen lights were off. Now was my chance.

I dashed into the kitchen and tried to remember which areas Paula said were shared. The fridge was partly stocked but that was by individual guests. I refrained from swiping a plastic cup of sugar-soaked peaches.

Next, I moved to the pantry. There was a box of opened grits that looked about a year old. Pass. I spotted a box of Cinnamon Toast Crunch cereal. Aisha's favorite! I took it out along with a loaf of bread to the kitchen table. Score! There was a bottle of jam and peanut butter already sitting on the table. This would do.

I proceeded to unscrew the heavenly bottles of peanut butter and jam. But then I heard the sound of people talking. I turned around to check, but the coast was clear. No one. What the hell? I raced to get some paper plates and finished making my sandwiches as fast as I could but then the kitchen patio door opened. I turned around slowly, terrified of who I might encounter next. It was Sarah. My heart calmed down a bit. We already knew of each other's existence here. But there was someone standing beside her. It couldn't be.

"Well, this is awkward." Sarah said, standing a few feet in front of me. And there standing next to her, was Grace. She looked completely paralyzed. I blinked a few times feeling paralyzed as well.

"Yeah." I finally let out.

"You making pb and j's?" Sarah asked. I nodded silently. No one spoke again for what seemed like the longest minute of my entire life. We all looked at each other while simultaneously trying to avoid eye contact – like seeing a wreck on the road so bad but you can't seem to look away.

"I have some strawberries, if you want some?" Grace finally said, putting an end to her silence. Did she live here too? Or was she just visiting Sarah? I thought visits from the outside world weren't allowed. I didn't move as she walked up to the shared refrigerator.

"My mom bought them today. She said we can let other people take some." Grace went to the sink and started washing a bowl of bright red strawberries. She came back to the table and sat down. Sarah followed.

"Uh…th-thanks. Thank you. I uh…" I couldn't think of what to say so I sat down as well, not wanting to make any sudden movements, as if there were a bomb hidden somewhere and speaking or moving too suddenly would set it off. We all stared at each other again in silence. No one was eating or moving or making a sound.

"Well…fancy seeing you here." Grace said with a small smile.

"What the fuck, right?" Sarah whispered. She looked back at me about to laugh. I exhaled.

"Seriously. What the fuck." I said in disbelief. And in the strangest scenario imaginable, Sarah, Grace, and I ate strawberries together.

"You can't make this shit up!" Grace said with cheeks as bright as the strawberries.

Chapter 26
Carlos

There was no distinct moment, Tío or Tía told us the news. No sit-down talk. They just gradually stopped trying to hide things. Tío would ask me to help out at the shop so he could drive Tía Julia to treatments. Benny got to go with him. Tío said it was because I knew what I was doing and Benny didn't know anything about cars.

The house grew quieter. No more Friday fiestas. I missed the sound of Tía's voice. I missed Tío's singing and Benny's drumming. He didn't sneak out anymore. Benny started to help. He and Tío would cook healthy meals of green juice and quinoa for Tía. But from what I could see, the food wasn't helping, neither was the chemo. Benny told me, late one night, that the cancer was spreading and Tía had to stay at the hospital now – instead of going back and forth for treatments.

After Tía had left home for a few days, Tío finally asked if I wanted to go with him to the hospital while Benny stayed home to pack up more of Tía's things. I said yes without hesitation.

We walked down a stale, sad hallway with a harsh white light above us. Tío led me inside a room with six hospital beds separated only by white curtains. Tío stopped by a lady's bed and I wondered why we were visiting a stranger first before seeing Tía. It took me a few seconds to realize the lady was actually Tía. I couldn't believe it. She looked so thin. She was wearing a paisley bandana around her head that had uneven strands of hair poking out. She smiled at me weakly and lifted her frail arms. I wanted to cry.

"Give your Tía a hug, Carlos." Tío said mustering up a broken smile. I leaned in and lightly wrapped my arms around her. I didn't want to press down too hard because I was scared she would break. I looked into Tía's eyes trying to find her. Her eyes were deeply sunken in and surrounded by dark circles. Her usually rosy cheeks and tan, glowing skin had dulled into an inhumane beige color. My eyes filled up with tears.

"Oh mijo. Don't cry. Don't cry." Tía said. "I'm so glad I get to see you. I'm sorry it took so long. Your Tío says you've been helping out at the shop. I wanted to let you come visit. But I didn't want you to worry my love. I wanted to get better first."

I nodded, unsure of what to say. In that instant, I wanted to take away all her pain. I wanted to pick her up and carry her out of this sad place. I kept fighting back my tears.

"I thought it was only stage two? How come…"

"Your Tía is strong, eh Carlos? She's fighting through the chemo. Your Tía is a fighter." Tío said. Tía Julia tried to smile again for me.

"I'm sorry, Tía." I said timidly, tears beginning to fall.

"Oh, Carlos." Tía lifted her arm and placed it on my back. It felt like a feather, like barely anything was touching me. "I'm ok. I'll be ok."

"But what happened? How did it get so bad?" I asked confused. When I heard Tío and Tía discussing the cancer, it had been just a few weeks ago. Tío moved beside Tía and took her hand.

"We're sorry we didn't explain this to you or Benny." Tío said. "We thought that after a couple rounds of chemo that the cancer would be completely gone and we could move on." Tío tried hard not to cry. "Turns out, it spread more than we thought."

"We didn't want to worry you. I'm sorry." Tía said with glistening eyes.

A man in a white robe walked into our little corner of the room and started talking to Tío. He led him out of the room to talk in private and I was glad. I don't think I could handle any more news.

"I'm sorry I couldn't be there for you, Carlos." Tía said.

"Me?" How could Tía feel bad for me? I didn't understand.

"Listen, I don't want you to think that we don't care about you the same as Benny. It made me too sad thinking about you seeing me like this. Benny's older so we thought he could handle it better. Your uncle really did need help with the shop too. He's been trying to find a way to pay for all this…You know I have no health insurance. Please don't be angry with Tío if he's been distant lately." Tía never let go of my hand as she spoke.

I nodded in a daze.

"Listen. Before Tío comes back I need to ask a favor of you. Can you do that for me?" Tía asked lifting my chin with her thin fingers.

"Ok." I said beneath a layer of tears.

"Your Tío is a good man. He is trying to find a way to pay for the hospital bills and he's been scraping by. But now he says he's going to sell the shop. Honey, I want you to stop him. The shop is all we have. He needs to take care of you and Benny after I'm gone." Gone? I felt a heavy burning sensation in my chest and a fierce anger.

"How could you say that? You're not leaving!" I wanted to scream at her. "You can't go! You need to keep fighting." I started to hyperventilate. Tía rubbed my arm and tried to smile.

"I feel like my time is coming mijo. If God wants me now, I have to go to Him. Sí?"

"No! You can't! What about me? Don't you care about me? Don't you love me? What about Tío?"

"Of course, I love you. Mijo, you, Juan, Benny – you all are my whole life." Tía paused and sighed. "But sometimes honey, these things are out of our control." Tío's voice started to approach the room and Tía squeezed my arm a tiny bit harder. "Please Carlos." I looked at her unable to say a thing, then shook my head no as Tío and the man in the white robe walked back into the room.

 Tío and I drove back home in silence. I didn't repeat anything that Tía had said. How could I? How could I ask Tío to not do everything in his power to keep Tía alive? As he drove, Tío put his hand on my shoulder. He looked as if he wanted to say something. He opened his mouth a little but said nothing. Instead, he just looked at me before turning away again.

 A long time ago, Tío told me the story of how he met Julia back when they were living in Mexico. She was 16 and he was 18. Julia was the most sought-after girl in school with her beautiful looks and kind heart. But she always turned everyone down. She wasn't interested in dating because her parents had split up when she was a kid.

 "Julia didn't believe in love before I met her. But I changed her mind." Tío used to tell me with a wink. They met at a party and Tío knew instantly he had met his soulmate. "Like a lightning bolt." He used to say. Tía however, rejected his date offer. After that, Tío showed up almost every night knocking on her door, begging for a date. She finally caved in on his seventh try. They dated until she graduated high school, got married, and immigrated to the states together.

 It's hard to imagine Tío as a young man now. I've already forgotten his face when he smiles. When I see family photos mounted on our wall, Tío and Tía look like different people. Like those paid actors standing in as doubles for Tío and Tía.

At home, Benny was finishing up packing a bag of clothes for Tía.

"I'll deliver this and stay with your mom tonight. You both need some rest. I'll be back tomorrow morning." Tío said.

"No! I want to be with her!" Benny said angrily.

"Your mom needs her rest too. She needs to sleep. If she sees you, she'll want to take care of you. She needs to rest." Tío said.

"Fine. But I'm gonna go tomorrow." Benny said resigned. Tío nodded and left.

The house fell quiet. I stood in the living room without saying a thing. Benny went to the kitchen and stared at the refrigerator door that was covered with flyers and colorful magnets from our family trips back to Mexico.

"You want some pizza?" Benny asked.

"Sure." I said. We waited on the living room couch for the doorbell to ring. Then we ate a supreme extra-large pizza that reminded me of Luis. I wondered how Benny felt. I had already lost a mom, so the pain felt strangely familiar. This was Benny's first time.

"Do you think Tía will be ok?" I asked feeling the pizza grease swirl around in my stomach.

"She's gonna get better. She will." Benny said without looking at me.

"Did they tell you, when they found out?" I wondered how long Benny knew.

"No. But I found out before you did."

"Really? When?"

"A couple months ago." My jaw dropped. Months? No. It hasn't been that long. She still had time left.

"I thought they found out a few weeks ago…" Benny looked at me and shook his head.

"No. It's been much longer. I found out last winter break when I was sneaking back in one night.

"How could they have not told me…all this time?" I asked getting upset. I felt lied to, cheated out of time with Tía.

"Tía told me not to tell you." Benny said averting my gaze. "I wanted to tell you. But she made me promise."

"But why?" I asked unable to breathe again. Benny was silent. "Why!" I yelled.

"She said you experienced enough pain in life already. She said…she didn't want to give you any more. She thought she was gonna get better. She really did."

My mind started swimming. Tía has to survive. She has to. Tía Julia deserves to live. Benny and I lied in bed for a couple of hours. Neither of us sleeping. Memories of Tía Julia came swarming in my mind. Tía cooking me flautas in the kitchen. Tía singing along with Tío during Friday fiesta. Tía coming to my first soccer match, cheering me on even after I missed every goal. Tía buying me a new outfit for my very first date. Tía comforting me after I was stood up on my first date.

I wondered if I should tell Benny, what Tía asked of me. But I couldn't. What if Benny agreed? What if he tried to stop Tío from selling the shop? He couldn't. Tía was the most important thing right now. Nothing else mattered.

Chapter 27
Sarah

Living in the shelter with Jamie and Grace feels like living in our own separate world. There is school. Work. The outside world. But then there is this hidden world we share between the three of us. Not that we know everything about each other, like each other's favorite colors or grade point average, but we understand each other. There's this unspoken connection. I recognized that secret place inside each of us. A place that burned and felt pain and joy in a different way than most of the outside world. A hidden space that was deeper and felt the gravity of life more fully. It was a new territory, yet to be fully explored. But I saw that place in them – that dark, clear, unspoken place.

    I thought about asking Jamie how he ended up here, that evening when we sat at the dinner table sharing Grace's strawberries. But when I looked in his eyes, I realized I didn't need to know. The fact that he was here said enough. You only come to Blue Haven, because you have nowhere else to go.

At school, Jamie avoided contact with Grace and me. When we spotted each other in the hallways, he turned the other way. But I didn't blame him. It was already enough to have your dad die. That was the word around school. But to have people pull back that curtain and see inside your hurt, the deepest part of your pain – that was too much for any person to endure. We passed by each other sometimes at Blue Haven. He smiled and I smiled. It was enough. I didn't need any more.

It's been 15 days for me, three since I spotted Jamie, and 24 for Grace. I can tell she's getting restless. Her usual bright and natural smile feels coerced lately. I wanted to tell her, that she didn't have to act happy around me. That she could scream and get angry. But maybe pretending to be happy worked for her. As for me, I just keep telling myself that this place is temporary. This situation is temporary. We'll get out of here soon. We just need an escape plan. And I need my car to get back some freedom. I feel so trapped without it.

Walking to Cold Stone after school for my shift isn't too hard. Mom picks me up when I'm done. It's my late shifts at the diner I can't get to. I mean, I can go if I take the bus. But I've been avoiding Tyler ever since the incident at his house. He's called me a couple times, but I let the call go to voicemail. I can't face him right now. There's already too much to worry about. I can't worry about him too. It's best to cut ties early before you become too attached. I wish he could understand that.

It's been a particularly rough day. At school, I researched scholarships for college. Even if I did win a few, I'd be in debt for what seemed like the rest of my life. Another worry. Then there's the large chance I won't get into my dream school. UCLA. Worry after worry – the pile keeps getting bigger. I tried to refocus my mind by drowning myself in SAT vocabulary words. I went through the A's again. Abate. Abstract. Abysmal. Yes, that's the one. That's the word I felt today. Abysmal.

After school I walked to my shift at Cold Stone where an angry dad yelled at me for putting on peanut butter toppings and nearly killing his daughter. I told him he never told me to take that out, and he told me to go fuck myself. I am reaching my limit of bullshit today. My tolerance level has been sinking lower and lower with each passing day.

To put the cherry on top, Mom wasn't picking up her phone. She was supposed to pick me up after my shift today. But it's been nearly an hour and I've called her 14 times. Shit. I really need my car.

"Hey, do you need a ride?" It was Brad, the store manager. He was 25 and still battling adult acne. He also liked to smoke pot behind the store during his break.

"No. It's ok." I said curtly. Maybe there was a bus route. I started to research on my phone.

"Are you sure? It's no trouble."

Fuck. I would have to take three different bus routes to get remotely close enough to Blue Haven.

"Um. Actually, yeah. Thank you." I got into his car that smelt of sickly sugar. He immediately talked about his life and how he was just saving up some extra spending money while studying at the University of Texas. He was majoring in history for the last seven years but lately thinking about switching to economics. I wondered if he really was a college student or that was just his cover story for still working here.

"Gotta make that dough, you know?" He said. I nodded, forcing a smile. "So, what's your address? I can type it into my GPS." Shit. I can't tell him the address. It's confidential. Even if I told him and risked the embarrassment, his car wasn't authorized at the shelter. It would alert Pamela and havoc would erupt.

"I actually have to pick up some groceries. Could you just drop me off at the Target near my house?" I showed him my phone and he typed it into his car screen.

"You know, I actually have to do some grocery shopping myself. Maybe we could shop together?" You have got to be kidding me.

"Sorry. I have to shop quickly then meet up with my mom after…"

"Oh. Ok. No worries. Another time then."

Brad took the rejection well enough. There was an awkward silence, then he proceeded to tell me about all of his professors, one by one. The ratchet woman who cheated him out of a C. The old fart who couldn't talk loudly enough for him to hear at the back of the class. And so on. Finally, he pulled up to the Target entrance and I thanked him – one foot already escaping from his car.

    I rushed through the entrance, then turned around to make sure he left the parking lot. As soon as I walked in, I made a circle and left through the automatic exit doors. Blue Haven was just a mile away. I could make it in no time.

    Turns out that mile was littered with hills and the Texas heat was like a boulder that kept shoving me backwards. I couldn't believe Mom forgot about me. After 40 agonizing minutes, I made it back to Blue Haven. My hair stuck permanently to the sweat on my face and back. I was angry. Not just angry. I was furious. How could Mom forget about me? How could she just leave me like that? I'm her only daughter!

    I pressed in the code at the front door and marched straight to our room. I found Mom laying on the bed, sleeping. Sleeping! You have got to be fucking kidding me! My face was burning. I wanted to scream. I pushed her arm, forcefully shaking her awake.

    "What! What is it?" Mom sat up instantly and started looking frantically around the room.

    "Where were you?" I asked angrily.

    "Huh! What?" Mom asked confused.

    "You were supposed to pick me up! I called you! Why didn't you pick up your phone?" I pointed at her phone on the bedside table and noticed cracks all over her screen. Mom picked up her phone and turned it on. The light illuminated her worried face.

"Oh Sarah. I'm so sorry! I must have fallen asleep and my phone was turned off. I'm sorry honey-"

"Forget it." I said and looked around our room, which was becoming much too familiar for my liking. "Where's David?"

"Oh. He's sleeping over a friend's house tonight."

"On a school night? He should be here studying. He has a test this week."

"He's just a kid. It's alright, Sarah."

"I'm just a kid too." I muttered under my breath.

"Huh?"

"Nothing. Did you eat?"

"No. It's fine. I'm not hungry." Mom said trying to wake herself up by patting her cheeks with her hands.

"You have to eat." I said about to leave for the kitchen.

"Wait, Sarah. What day is it?" Mom asked.

"It's Thursday."

"I have to clean the bathroom today. It's our family's turn." Fuck. I forgot. This place had chores. Take out the trash. Do the dishes. Clean the bathroom. It was finally our turn for the shittiest option.

"I can do it." I said.

"No, honey. You rest. I'll do it."

"It's fine!" I said, raising my voice.

"We can do it together then." Mom said trying to appease me.

We walked to the women's bathroom in silence. Mom pulled out a bucket of cleaning supplies from underneath one of the sinks. She took the Clorox and went into one of the stalls. I started wiping the mirrors. After Mom was done with the toilets, she took out the mop, filled up the bucket with water and started mopping the floor. I could see her reflection in the mirror and it made me want to cry.

Mom used to be so free. She hated wearing shoes or tying up her hair. I remember her running around the yard with me as a kid, and then with David. She was always smiling or singing. After Curt came, things were different. She didn't sing anymore. Her smiles became rare and she turned into a woman who had to fight to be loved or even noticed by him. But my mom was a queen. She was beautiful and fierce. She shouldn't have done that – let Curt take that from her. She shouldn't have trusted him.

Mom's face is different now. It's older. I noticed a few gray hairs in her once unapologetically dirty blonde, shiny hair. I watched as Mom mopped the tiles back and forth, then in a circular motion. She's gotten so thin. Her arms are bonier and her legs look like sticks. From her reflection in the mirror, I spotted dark blue splotches on her knees.

"Mom." I turned around and pointed at her knees. They were covered with bruises. Mom tried to pull down her baggy gym shorts to cover them.

"It's nothing honey. Keep cleaning." She tried to continue mopping but I grabbed the handle from her.

"Mom what is that? Who did this to you?" Mom smiled and it infuriated me.

"No one *did* this to me honey." My mind traveled back to the time I saw Curt slap Mom in the face.

"Was it Curt? Did you go and see that asshole?" I asked accusatorily. How could Mom be so weak? Didn't she have any pride in herself?

"No. It wasn't Curt." Mom's face turned serious. "It's nothing you have to worry about."

"Tell me what happened!" I shouted.

"It's from my other job!" Mom said loudly then swiped the mop back from me.

"Your job? You mean at the salon?" I asked.

"No. I got another job."

"What other job? Mom where do you work?" Mom tried to ignore me. "Mom!"

"I got the night shift cleaning that office building down the road."

"What? Since when?"

"Since we came here. I didn't want to tell you because I didn't want you talking me out of it." I was speechless. How could I not have known?

"But why are your knees…what?"

"This is just cause they have a lot of tiled floors so I have to sit on my knees sometimes."

"They make you scrub the fucking floors? Mom, that's insane! Isn't there anyone else to help you?"

"Yeah, there's another lady. We divide up the floors and do it on our own."

"So you clean an entire building every night?" I wanted to cry.

"No! Me and the other lady."

"Mom!" I yelled. She paused from mopping then looked at my teary-eyed face. "You can't be a cleaning lady. You're already working at the salon. And I'm working. I can take more shifts. I can go back to the diner." I felt so stupid for being so selfish about the diner. I should have sucked it up and kept going. How could I have been so selfish and skip my shifts – while Mom was scrubbing floors!

"Sarah, it's alright. Really!" Mom said smiling. "The salon can't give me any more hours than they already have. We don't have that many customers right now. Business isn't too good nowadays. But this new job, it's good money. Just a few more weeks and I'll get my paycheck. Then I can get us out of here."

"But Mom…" Mom looked up at me and smiled again. Then she went back to cleaning.

"This is just the situation we're in Sarah. I'm working hard to get us out of it. It's all my fault we're here anyways. I should have done more for you and David. I should've been wiser with Curt." Mom turned away from me and wiped her eye. Then she left to clean the men's room.

As soon as she was gone, I let my tears fall. I wish I had known. All this time, I blamed her for laying in bed all the time. Meanwhile she was cleaning an entire building while David and I were fast asleep. How could I have been so blind? Just then, Janice walked into the bathroom and headed for a stall. I started wiping the sinks and turned away my face. Shit! I hope she didn't see me. Thankfully, my phone started ringing.

"Hello?"

"Hi, this is Juan's Car Shop. Are you Sarah with the Honda Civic?"

"Yes. That's my car."

"Yeah, your car is ready. You can pick it up today."

"Thank you! I'll be there soon to pick it up."

I looked at the mirror and tried to fix my haggard face. I blew my nose and washed my puffy eyes.

"Are you ok?" Janice asked, looking at me while washing her hands.

"Oh, hi Janice. Yeah, I'm fine."

"Do you need a ride to the shop?" I looked back at her surprised. Maybe Grace told her about the car accident.

"That would be super helpful. Thank you."

I didn't know much about Janice, other than what Grace told me. She was quiet, but not in a shy way. It was more like, she didn't feel the need to say unnecessary words. Her face looked young, but she held herself with maturity. At times, she seemed the exact opposite of Grace, who was more expressive and loved to talk and let out her thoughts openly. But by her small mannerisms, I could tell Janice and Grace were sisters. Their laughs sounded the same and they both had a quiet confidence to them.

"I heard you got into medical school. Congratulations!" I said, trying to fill the silence as I sat on the passenger side.

"Thanks." Janice said concisely. We drove for a few minutes without a word. I was surprised by her radio choice of heavy metal.

"You're a good daughter." She said with a relaxed demeanor. "Sorry, I don't mean to pry. I only heard a little bit of your conversation with your mom. She's lucky to have a daughter that cares so much."

I felt slightly unarmed. I guess she did hear our fight in the bathroom. I looked away from Janice, outside my window at the fading sky.

"I don't think I am…good. I should have known. I shouldn't have complained so much. And I shouldn't have slacked at my job at the diner. Then maybe, it wouldn't have to come to this."

"You can't fix everything." Janice said looking straight ahead. The sky had turned a pinkish hue as the sun set before us. "That's one thing I've learned, being the eldest child. You're expected to help out. Yes, it's your job, your role in the family. Take care of the younger sibling, help your parents, try to fix things. I've always accepted that. But, I used to think when things fell apart, that it was all my fault. I should've prevented it, as the eldest. I had to fix it, make things right again. But sometimes you can't. You can't fix everything. The most you can do is help."

Janice's words floated around in my mind. Did I really think this way? Did I think I had to fix everything – that it was all on me. I did. I do.

"Thanks, Janice."

"You're welcome."

We made it to the car shop and a familiar face greeted me. What was his name?

Chapter 28
Carlos

I'm getting tired of Tío sending me to the shop alone after school while Benny gets to visit Tía at the hospital. I understand why, but I can't help but feel like I'm no longer a part of the family. The past few days have been a whirlwind. After Tía Julia's cancer came out in the open, Tío has gone to the hospital every day and asked me to stay and check on things at the shop. I think Tío thinks I know much more about cars than I actually do. In reality, I just go to the shop and watch the others work. Sometimes I check out customers. I gave that girl Sarah her car back yesterday. I wished Tío didn't give her such a big discount. We could really use the money right now.

Maybe Tío really doesn't want me to see Tía sick. But I need to see her. It's just Benny and me at home now. I called Tía on the phone before getting ready for school. Her voice sounded so weak and tired. After hanging up, I wondered if I was only sucking the energy out of her. Benny looked at me, maybe he could see how depressed I felt.

"Come on. Let's go see her." I looked back at Benny confused. Turns out he had already planned on skipping school today to visit Tía at the hospital. Tío looked angry when he saw us walk in, but his face softened quickly.

"She's missed you guys." Tío said resigned and brought us into the shared hospital room.

I didn't think it was possible, but Tía Julia looked worse than before. Her lips looked purple and I could see her shoulder and collar bones so clearly, it frightened me.

"My boys!" Tía whispered. Her voice was crackly and sore. It was missing the sweetness from before the cancer. Benny and I carefully gave Tía a hug. I promised myself I wouldn't cry this time around. Benny asked Tía how she was feeling and Tía gave a weak thumbs up.

"You're gonna get better, Mom. I know it." Benny said. Tía smiled weakly. We watched Wheel of Fortune together and took turns helping her eat. She couldn't eat much though because the chemo made her nauseous. Benny tried to lighten the mood by telling her exciting tales of life at home and how much everyone was praying for her. I wished I could be like Benny and make Tía smile like he did.

Tío stood in the corner of the room talking to the doctor I recognized from before. I tried to listen to their conversation, but Tío caught me snooping and pulled back one of the divider curtains between us. I could still make out a few words: *surgery, time, chance.* My heart started to race.

"Carlos. You're quiet today. What's wrong?" Tía asked. I looked back at her fragile face and recognized a glimmer in her eyes. Tía is strong. Maybe she'll make it. She must.

"Nothing, Tía." I said.

"Are you still doing well with school. How did that history test go?"

"I don't know yet." I said, trying to hold back any show of emotion. I needed to be strong for her.

"Mijo. You are a smart boy. I want you to stay focused at school so you can go to college." I nodded dutifully. College. It seemed like a foreign word to me now. Tío always expected me to help out after graduation at the shop. I couldn't imagine a life anywhere else.

"I know your Tío wants you to stay at the shop. But I think there are bigger things out there for you mijo." Tía said. Benny looked at me a little annoyed.

"What about me, Mom? Do you think I can go to college?" Benny asked.

"Of course, mijo. If you stop skipping class." Tía said, giving him a nudge on the head. "If I wasn't here, I'd be giving you boys a beating for skipping school today." Benny smiled. The thought of Tía hitting us made me laugh.

Tío walked back in with the doctor. He was holding X-ray sheets and put them side by side on a light-up board.

"Mrs. Lopez. We've taken a look at your X-rays." The doctor pointed to the first X-ray. "This is the state of the cancer when you first came to us. As you know, we wanted to start chemo in the hopes that it would stop the cancer from spreading and shrink the tumor down as small as possible." Tía Julia nodded and Tío took her hand. "Unfortunately, the cancer has spread even after several rounds of chemo."

The doctor pointed to the second X-ray which showed small, lighter areas sprinkled around the largest light spot like its own solar system. I didn't understand. Wasn't the chemo supposed to get rid of the cancer? How could it have made things worse?

"So, what does this mean doctor?" Tía asked.

"It means, the best route to take now is surgery. We hope we can remove the tumors from inside. But there's no guarantee we will be able to remove everything or that the cancer hasn't already spread to other areas."

"He thinks this is the best option right now." Tío said to Tía.

"But surgery. Doctor, how much will that cost?" Tía asked.

"The sum is… sizeable unfortunately. Especially, without insurance. But your husband tells me he can come up with the money. You will need to speak to our financial advisor. I'll see if I can help trim some of the costs as well."

"Thank you, doctor." Tío said.

"No wait!" Tía reached out to the doctor as he turned to leave. "Even with the surgery, what are the chances I will completely recover?" Tía asked.

"Well, we can't know for sure until the surgery when I can see-"

"Just an estimate doctor?" Tía said trying to sit up. "What's my chance of being cured?"

"I'd say…" The doctor hesitated and looked at Tía and the rest of us. "About a 10% chance." Tía looked at Tío with a face of frustration. She started speaking fervently in Spanish to Tío.

"That's not enough. I don't want it. Doctor cancel it. I don't want the surgery." Tía said.

"No, doctor. She'll go through with it." Tío said talking over Tía.

"I'll give you two some time to discuss." The doctor finally left the room.

"How could you do this!" Tía said to Tío. "How could you agree to this? How could you sell the shop for me? And now you want to sell the house? For a surgery with not even a good chance I'll get better? You are ruining their lives!" Tía said pointing at me and Benny.

"How could I not?" Tío said in desperation. "How could I not even try? Do you want me to leave you here to die!" Tío's voice was filled with desperation. "Do you want your children to grow up without a mother? We can't…I can't." Tío started to cry. I had never seen him cry like this before. "I can't live without you."

Benny and I didn't move or make a sound. What was I supposed to do in a situation like this? Tía pulled Tío close to her. She rubbed his back and wiped the tears from his face. Benny was crying too now.

"Please, Julia." Tío said. "We have to at least try. What if by some miracle you are cured? There's still a chance. Please Julia. God has heard our prayers. You're going to get better. I can feel it."

"Yeah Mom. You're gonna get better!" Benny said. Tía looked at Tío for a long time. Then at Benny and me.

"Please Tía. You have to try." I said. Tía looked at me and we all stayed silent for a moment. This was Tía's choice now. She would have to agree to the surgery or go back home.

"Ok. I'll do it." Tía whispered. Tío smiled and gave her a huge hug, wiping away her tears. He brought the doctor back into our little corner of a room shared with other patients. There were only three other patients now. There were five others before.

"Doctor. We will go through with the surgery." Tía said. The doctor nodded.

"We will have the surgery the day after tomorrow." He said.

As soon as he left, a series of people came in and out of the room to talk to Tío and Tía. Tío went to talk to the financial advisor. Did he really agree to sell the shop? Was he going to sell the house too? Where would we stay? It didn't matter right now, as long as Tía survived. God, are you listening? Please. Please let Tía survive.

Today is surgery day. At the hospital, the doctor talked to Tío saying the procedure should take around four to five hours. Then he went into the operation room leaving us to wait in an artificially lit hallway. Before today, I've never felt time slow down so much in my entire life. Every time I look back at the clock, only minutes have passed. Tío has been pacing back and forth through the hallway. I sat next to Benny and tried to read Romeo and Juliet. After Tía told me she wanted me to go to college, I decided to try harder at school. Once the surgery was over and Tía was cured, I was going to show her the A- I got on my history test.

One hour passed. Two. Three. Benny got up to go the bathroom and came back with a cup of jello for Tío and me. Tío turned down his offer but pat Benny on the head. Four hours. The doctor should be coming out now. Five hours. I'm sure he's just being thorough. The longer it takes, the better right? Six hours. Is Tía ok? What happened? Six hours and five minutes. Six hours and eleven minutes. Seven hours and seventeen minutes. Tía's doctor finally came out and took off his white mask. The three of us got up to race toward him, but Tío motioned for us to stay put and approached the doctor alone.

I couldn't make out what they were saying. Tío dropped his head. No. It couldn't be! But then, Tío lifted up his head again and looked relieved. He was smiling. It must be good news! The doctor waved at us and smiled. We waved back. Tío rushed to me and Benny and hugged us – lifting us into the air.

"It's a miracle! Your mamá is gonna be ok! They got it. They got the cancer! The doctor says she should get better now!" Tío shouted.

I couldn't believe it! Our prayers were answered. Tía was going to be ok! We all started crying tears of joy. Tío was laughing and kissing Benny and me. It was all going to be ok! Everything was going to be ok!

We waited for Tía to be brought back to our room. She was still sleeping when she arrived. I saw a fresh scar on her chest. Tío started stroking her cheek up and down as Tía's eyes started to flutter.

"Am I alive?" Tía asked. Tío smiled.

"Yes, you are alive. The doctor says you're going to get better. They said they removed all the tumors. You're going to get better now!" Tía's eyes let out a steady river of tears. Tío kissed Tía on the forehead over and over again. Thank you, God! Thank you, God! It's all over. Benny and I moved in to hug Tía but Tío suddenly bent over.

"Juan, what is it?" Tía whispered. Tío was shaking and his hands were wrapped around his head. "Juan!" Tía shouted. Tío collapsed on the floor. His body was convulsing and his eyes turned backwards so that all I could see were the whites of his eyes. I heard screaming.

Benny ran out to get the doctor. Tía's doctor rushed in and pointed a small flashlight into Tío's eyes. I couldn't move. The room began to blur. Benny shouted something to me but I couldn't make out what he was saying. All I could see was Tío on the floor. His body twitched and convulsed as if he was mutating into some other-worldly creature. Then, Tío's body went still.

A nurse came in with one of those machines I'd seen on TV. The doctor rubbed two paddles together before shouting "Clear!" and putting them on Tío's chest. His body twitched. The doctor rubbed the paddles again. "Clear." Tío's body still wasn't moving. "Again! Clear!" Why wasn't Tío's body moving? A long high-pitched sound turned on. People were shouting. Benny was kneeling on the floor. Why was Benny on the floor?

Some people wearing teal uniforms brought a rolling bed and put Tío on it. Where were they taking him? I stopped the doctor wheeling him away. Tío's face looked like someone covered it with wax paper. I leaned down and looked at Tío sleeping on the bed.

"Where are you taking my uncle?" I asked as I stared at Tío sleeping. I shook Tío's shoulders. "Tío. Tío! Wake up Tío. Tía Julia's all better now. Why are you sleeping?" I leaned in closer and Tío's eyes were still closed.

"Tío? Wake up, Tío! Doctor how come he's still sleeping? Could you wake him up please?" The doctor wiped away something from his eye and turned away from me. I heard

Benny and Tía crying. Then I tapped Tío's forehead. He still wasn't moving. I put my hand under his nose. He wasn't breathing. I shook his shoulders again. He wasn't responding.

"Tío! Tío!" I screamed. "What happened! What's wrong with him! What did you do to him!" I yelled at the doctor. He tried to calm me down but I kept on shaking Tío. Why wasn't he moving? The doctor pulled me away from Tío and pressed his hands on my shoulders while the people in teal uniforms wheeled Tío out of the room.

"Son. Son. Your uncle has had a stroke. He's dead."

Chapter 29
Jamie

"Jamie. Get up, it's time for school." Ma said from across the room. It's the seventh day of our stay at Blue Haven. I've been on autopilot since the first. Seeing Grace and Sarah should have comforted me, but all it did was made me feel ashamed of myself and sorry for them. How could we all be here? How could God ruin so many lives at once? Do you enjoy doing this God? Do you like seeing us here? Is this fun for you?

"Jamie! Get up." Ma said a little louder.

"I'm not going." I said.

"Boy! You better get yo' ass up and ready for school. Do you think Harvard is going to accept someone who skips school?"

"I'm not going to Harvard." I said, feeling a hint of fear.

"What? Why aren't you going?" Ma asked, sitting on the edge of my bed.

"I'm not going to college!" I sat up and shouted. "Now leave me the fuck alone!" Ma took her pillow and started whacking me with it. I almost felt like laughing at how painless it was.

"Girls, wait outside for me." Ma said. Quinn and Aisha dutifully left the room. "Jamie. Do you know how much me and your daddy sacrificed for you – for you to be successful and go to college one day? I've worked extra shifts. Your daddy has taken on more missions than-"

"Yeah. And he's dead now." The regret was immediate as the words came out of my mouth. A heavy silence settled into the room. Ma leaned towards me. I flinched, thinking she would hit me. But instead, she hugged me. She held me, for a long time.

"Baby, I know this is hard." Ma said, her arms still wrapped around me. "You just lost your daddy. He loved you more than anything. And I know how much you loved him." Ma released me and looked into my eyes. "But I'm telling you from experience…If you sit in this pain, get comfortable in it, make a home in it – that sadness is gonna eat you up alive. I can see it taking over you, take over your spirit. Jamie you have to try and fight through it. I don't want to see you stop fighting."

Tears started to well up in my eyes and a deep sadness washed over me. I didn't feel the same after Dad died. How could I? It felt like someone had stolen my soul along with his. But I couldn't get out of it, no matter how hard I tried. I felt like a zombie – dead inside, but still moving.

"I don't know what to do." I said, letting the tears fall. Sometimes I didn't even notice the tears falling anymore. "I don't know how to stop feeling so sad all the time." Ma came in and hugged me harder.

"Oh baby. I'm so sorry. We're gonna get through this. I promise you. Look at me." Ma pulled back and looked straight into me. Her eyes, wide and determined. "We're gonna get through this. Because we are strong. You're strong! You hear me, Jamie! You are strong. You have more power inside of you than you know. Your daddy had it and you have it too." Ma said. I nodded.

"I'll call your school and tell them you're sick. You can stay here and rest today."

"Really?"

"Yeah! Just for today though, you hear me?"

I nodded, then laid back down as soon as she left. I fell asleep. Sleep came easily. Every time I woke up, I shut my eyes again and slept some more.

At around 2 p.m. I got up, went to the bathroom and then the kitchen. It felt necessary to eat something, even though I wasn't hungry. Food didn't taste the same. Even things that were sweet or bitter, all of it tasted bland to me. I took out a box of Goldfish from a cupboard and stuffed a handful of it in my mouth. Afterwards, I went back to bed.

I think Ma tried to wake me up for dinner but I nudged her away and kept sleeping. There was no use in being awake. Studying, working hard. It all seemed pointless now. Sleep is easy. Sleep is comforting. As soon as my head hits the pillow, sleep lands on me like a heavy blanket.

I used to get nightmares when I found out Dad went missing. Sometimes, I wished for another one just so I could see his face, hear his voice. I want to give him a hug and ask him why he had to leave so early. But lately, I've stopped dreaming.

I woke up at 3:14 a.m. Ma, Aisha, and Quinn were asleep on the bed next to me. On my bedside table sat a colored pencil drawing of our family signed, "To Jamie. From Quinn (Your sister)." The picture made me smile. Dad was still on it. He still made the cut for family drawings.

I've been asleep for too long. My neck hurts. My shoulders are sore. My legs feel restless. This bed is too small for me. This room is too small for the four of us. After lying in bed, awake in the dark for half an hour, I finally got up and went to the living room. The emptiness was haunting. The stale white walls and ceiling reminded me of a mental institution. I quickly traveled to the kitchen in the hopes that the ghost of a long lost psycho patient wouldn't catch me on the way.

I felt a faint sense of hunger and opened the refrigerator. The top row was filled with a glass jar of kimchi, a rectangle tupperware of rice, and metal pot of what appeared to be red soup with bits of tofu floating around. There were also three ginormous fruits that were larger than apples but smaller than cantaloupes. I wondered what it was. The middle row was also already filled with half a loaf of bread, a package of honey roasted turkey slices, and a glass tin of chicken parmesan. The bottom row seemed to be ours. Ma filled it with coleslaw, a box of seasoned raw drumsticks, and a bag of baby carrots. I took out the carrots, opened it and started to eat.

Then I opened the freezer and saw that Ma added a couple frozen pizzas I like. I took one out and put it in the oven. From the window above the sink, I saw the dimly lit silhouette of a playground. I never noticed it before. This shelter had a backyard – but who would play there? It made me sad to think of Quinn sliding down the single slide.

I set the oven timer to 15 minutes, sat down at the dinner table and waited. Time was taking too long. I moved to the sink and gulped down an entire glass of water. As I tilted my head back, I caught another glimpse of the backyard. There was a black lamp post standing in the back corner like a towering grim reaper, ready to take the souls of anyone who entered the forbidden ground. The light illuminated the outdoor area and danced on sparse patches of grass. I looked a bit closer and noticed a large swing set with four seats. The chains were rusted. In the stillness I heard a slow creaking sound. Maybe this place really did have ghosts. Maybe it was just the wind. I felt a sudden burst of fear. No, someone was actually outside.

I leaned in a bit closer but couldn't make out the person's face. All I saw were two feet hitting the ground as a shadow moved up and down. Crap! What should I do?

Like an idiot, I found myself opening the patio door and walking outside. The night air felt so drastically different from indoors. A crisp wind passed through me and goosebumps formed on my arms. My feet took me a bit closer. Step by step, I made my way to the small yard that was bordered by a gray chain fence. Trees and bushes intertwined with the fence that was either there to protect us or keep us from leaving. I could hear the steady sound of creaking in front of me.

I took a step forward, barely seeing what was ahead. I felt the presence of the plastic slide to my right. It must have been a nice shade of red in the morning. But now, it looked like a threatening blood stain. The rusty sound stopped abruptly and all I could hear was the crunching of my own two feet on the solid ground. I wish I had a weapon with me. I took a step closer and waited. Another. Again. I waited. The single shadow I saw from inside evolved into two separate shadows. I moved forward until the light illuminated the figures before me.

"Hi Jamie." It was Grace and Sarah! My tense heart loosened.

"Hi." I said, completely relieved I hadn't just walked into a murder scene. "I thought you were a ghost or a crazy person." Grace and Sarah laughed.

"Nope. Just us." Sarah said.

"Couldn't sleep?" Grace asked.

"Yeah…well actually I've been sleeping all day. I just woke up." I sat down on the empty swing next to them and shuffled my feet on the loose gravel.

"Man…I wish I could sleep all day." Sarah said. I looked to my left. Sarah was leaning her head on one of the chains and Grace was staring at the sky. I looked up.

"Wow. I never noticed that." I said, looking at a canvas of black lit up with what seemed like a million stars.

"It's beautiful, isn't it?" Grace asked.

"Yes." The backyard didn't seem scary anymore with the three of us sat on the swings.

"…I'm sorry about your dad." Grace said after a while.

"Thanks." I said reflexively. At this point, I've heard apologies from nearly everyone. People I'm close to and people I barely knew, like the school receptionist. Even the janitor apologized to me.

"We don't have to talk about it if you don't want to." Grace followed up carefully. I looked at her and smiled a bit.

"It's alright. I don't mind." I said swaying back and forth a bit. Strangely with them, I really didn't mind.

"Were you two close?" Grace asked.

"We were…I think. But he was gone for months or even years at a time – for work."

"He was in the Army, right?" Sarah asked.

"Yup. He was. The times he was at home with us, we were close. But…I changed so much during the times he left. I wonder if he really knew me by the time he…" The thought of Dad lingered in my mind. I tried to picture the way he smiled. The wrinkles that appeared around his eyes. His smile lines. I tried to imagine his scent.

"It's hard losing people." Grace said. I turned to look at her. She was staring at her shoes, digging them deeper into the tiny rocks piled beneath the swing set.

"Have you lost someone before?" I asked suddenly curious of how she ended up here. She looked at me briefly, then back down again.

"No. Sorry. I haven't. I just..."

"Sorry – I didn't mean to sound like I was accusing you or anything." Jamie, you idiot!

"No, no. You're fine." Grace said while moving her swing gently. A quietness drifted between each of us. It started at the top of our heads and moved down our bodies. I wondered if it was my turn to say something now.

"I haven't lost anyone...I mean, nobody close to me has died. But I guess I kinda know how it feels, to lose someone." Grace said staring in front of her, not really talking to anyone but the air. Sarah rubbed Grace's shoulder. They must be close already.

"I bet you're tired of answering questions about your dad, right Jamie?" Sarah asked.

"I'm not sure. I don't mind talking about my Dad. It's more...the look of pity I get from people. I mean, people I've never talked to at school come up to me and tell me how sorry they feel. But it's like – you don't even know me and you never even knew my dad! It all feels so phony to me."

"That fucking sucks." Sarah said.

"Yeah...thanks. It does fucking suck."

"It feels good to say, doesn't it?" Sarah asked with a lightness to her voice. She stepped forward on her swing and mouthed the word fuck to me before propelling backwards. I laughed. "Y'all can say it. Y'all are allowed. I give you permission." Sarah announced.

"Fuck." Grace whispered.

"Fuck!" I said a little louder. "Man, if my ma heard me. I'd be getting slapped right now."

"Me too. I only cuss when I'm around this one." Grace pointed to Sarah who gave her a salute. "Fuckity fuck fuck fuck!" Grace said between giggles and exhales.

"Mother fuckers! You don't know me!" I yelled, pointing my hand to an imaginary person in the sky.

"Whoa whoa! Ok, let's calm down now. Don't want to wake everyone up." Sarah said.

The three of us tried to hold back our laughter. I could see my breath in front of me. Grace and Sarah started swinging at full force.

Then I heard a crunching sound. Another shadow appeared before us. It was a boy. Well, a teenager. He looked around my age. Tan skin, probably 5'7 with short brown hair. His face looked pissed.

"Did one of you put a pizza in the oven because it nearly burned down this place!" He said angrily. I stood up from my swing instantly.

"Oh shoot. Sorry. I forgot I put that there."

"Yeah! Well, the beeping sound woke me up. That thing is completely burnt. You could've set this place on fire, dude!"

"Carlos?" Sarah whispered. The guy looked around confused.

"Do you know me?" He asked, leaning in closer towards Sarah's direction.

"I-I went to your shop. You're from Juan's Car Shop, right?"

Chapter 30
Carlos

"It's me S-Sarah. We met after my accident." She said. Holy shit! It was that girl! The girl from the wreck! My mind jumped to seeing her with cuts and bruises on her face. Sarah!

"Oh. Oh yeah. I remember you." I said, feeling like someone had just taken away my armor.

"Hey. Tell your dad thanks! He gave me a great deal on my car." Sarah said.

"I will. I mean…I can't…" I looked back at Sarah. Most of her scars had healed. There was still a faint blue hue on her left temple. "He died." All three of them stopped moving. Sarah's polite smile disappeared.

"I'm so sorry, Carlos." She said. I nodded. I had never said the words out loud before. Suddenly, it became real that Tío was gone. I tried to keep myself from crying in front of a group of strangers.

"That's...that's rough man. I'm sorry." The guy said.

"I-I know...how it feels. My dad...he died recently too." A sharp pain appeared in my chest and I started hyperventilating. It felt like I was gonna hurl but nothing came out. It was like a boulder just landed on my chest. "Hey man! Are you ok?" The guy moved towards me. I lifted up my hand to push him away.

"Fine." I wheezed.

"Here, why don't you sit." Sarah said and helped me to the ground.

"Try to steady your breathing." The other girl said.

"I don't know what's happening." I said.

"Here." The girl put her hand on my shoulder. "Follow me. Inhale and count to five. Hold it for five seconds. Now exhale and count to five." I looked back at her as she motioned with her hand how to inhale and exhale. She looked like a conductor as her hand moved gracefully up and down. Up and down. I started to catch my breath. Inhale, 2, 3, 4, 5. Hold it, 2, 3, 4, 5. Exhale, 2, 3, 4, 5.

"What just happened to me?" I asked, feeling my breath begin to steady.

"I think you had a panic attack." She said. "I had one once before...I'm Grace." She held out her hand and I shook it.

"I'm Jamie." The guy said.

"You guys...all stay here too?" The three of them nodded.

"Yup." Sarah said sitting cross-legged on the ground beside me. "Let's see the count. Grace has been here since before spring break. I got here during. And Jamie's been here…"

"About a week." Jamie said.

"Wow. I-I didn't know." I said confused that there were others. I noticed the hall of doors at the shelter when we got the initial tour, but I haven't seen anyone else besides Benny and Tía yet.

"When did you get here?" Sarah asked.

"Yesterday." I said. Grace and Jamie joined us, down on the patchy grass. If it had been any other setting, it looked like we were at summer camp getting ready for a bonfire. "So do y'all know each other from before?"

"Not exactly." Sarah said. "We all go to Stony Brook High, but we never really talked to each other before. Except for me and Grace. We're in the same math class." Grace nodded.

"I guess we kind of became friends afterwards though." Grace said shyly.

"That's interesting." I said. They all looked at me and I felt an urge to dodge the spotlight. "What grade are y'all in?" I asked.

"I'm a sophomore." Grace said.

"Me too." I muttered.

"These two are juniors." Grace said pointing to Sarah and Jamie.

"Yup! Jamie and I are just a bunch of old hicks." Sarah said in a gimmicky southern accent. I smiled. An awkward silence started to settle in, until Sarah started back up again. "Where did you say you went to school?"

"East Elmwood."

"Oh hey, I've been there a few times." Jamie said. "My best friend Jamal played there for a few basketball games." I nodded, hoping he wouldn't ask me about sports. "I'm not good enough to play on the team though. Do you play?"

"Nah. Sports aren't really…my thing. I guess I'm more into gaming and cars."

"That's cool man! I'm into cars too…or I was. I used to have a vintage Mustang. My dad and I worked on it together.

"No way! That's sick man." I said. "What year?"

"1969."

"Nice!" I said with a bit of a smile. "My uncle and I worked on a few Mustangs before. He always said it was a classic car…" I pictured Tío back at the shop with oil stains on his hands and a rag tied to one of his belt loops. He would've turned 46 next month.

"Are you here with your mom – if you don't mind me asking?" Grace asked after a while. I must have lost my train of thought.

"Oh…yeah. Well, she's technically my aunt. But she's like my mom. I'm with her and my cousin Benny. We're like brothers I guess…What about y'all?" I looked up at the three of them. Their faces seemed to glow in the moonlight.

"I'm with my mom and older sister." Grace said.

"Yeah, I got my mom and younger bro." Sarah responded.

"I've got my mom and two younger sisters." Jamie finished. Sarah looked at him surprised.

"Nice! Eldest child!" Sarah leaned in for a fist bump and Jamie obliged. It was funny seeing her here. I never imagined her in a place like this. I just assumed her family was well-off. Most of the white people at my school were.

"So uh…what were y'all talking about before I stormed out here?" I asked apologetically.

"Oh, I was just…telling them about my dad." Jamie said, folding his hands.

"Sorry. I can leave if y'all were talking about something personal." I started to push myself up to leave, feeling like I had barged in on their intimate moment.

"Nah man. Stay." Jamie motioned for me to stay seated. "I don't mind. Unless you do?"

"No…keep going." Jamie got ready to continue his story.

"I was just explaining to them how people have been treating me since…since my dad. He was found dead in Afghanistan. Then my mom got laid off from her job. Then…all this happened." Jamie said, pointing back to Blue Haven. "I'm just so tired of everyone acting sorry for me when they talk about him. I'm tired of people being so insincere about it. But mostly…I'm just tired. I'm so tired. Like literally all the time. I don't know man. Maybe, I'm just sad…still."

Grace turned to Jamie with eyes of concern. "I mean, it hasn't even been a month since you found out he died. Of course, you're still gonna feel sad." Grace said.

"I don't know. This feels worse than sadness." Jamie responded. "It feels like…like I'm laying at the bottom of an ocean. I can see the surface clearly. But the water is so heavy that I can't move. I don't have the strength to swim to the surface. People are shouting at me from above, but I can't hear them. Everything is cold and heavy and I'm just stuck there, at the bottom, too tired to move." Jamie looked up to the sky. "I guess it's normal right? To feel this way?"

"Yes. I know exactly how that feels." I found myself saying. "It feels like someone just ripped out your heart but you're still alive. And everyone around you is feeling sorry for you, but all you wanna do is see him again." Jamie nodded.

"Yes, that's it. That's exactly it. Like people are expecting that one day, I'll just get over it. But how can I?" Jamie replied.

"It's like…a piece of you is gone now and you can't ever go back to what life was like before…"

Jamie and I locked eyes for a moment. His dark eyes stared back at me. All of a sudden, he didn't feel like a stranger anymore.

"Shit. I don't even know what to say." Sarah said faintly.

"It's alright." Jamie said. I smiled at Sarah in agreement. "I remember my first day back at school. I-I was so nervous. People kept on staring at me. I just wanted to hide. But my boy, Jamal, he came up to me laughing and joking, acting normal around me. It felt so good."

"Man. I wish I had that. I had a best friend. His name was Luis but he moved away before it all happened." I wondered how Luis was doing now. He wasn't able to make it to the funeral.

"That must be hard." Grace said with a sweetness to her voice. With her, the words didn't sound fake to me.

"It's ok, I guess. Have you been able to sleep?" I turned to ask Jamie.

"Man, all I do is sleep! I wish I could stop sleeping."

"I haven't been able to sleep." I said.

"For how long?" Sarah asked.

"I think it's been three days now." Sarah gasped.

"Three days!" She exclaimed.

"Yeah. It's like my body won't calm down. I can't stop. My mind moves to different thoughts every few seconds. It feels like if I slow down, if I stop…I don't know, I might drop dead or something. Sorry. I know that sounds dramatic."

"No, it doesn't." Grace said. "I've felt like that before. Some nights I can't sleep. The nights I do…I get nightmares a lot. But you're not crazy. I thought I was going crazy when…everything happened. But then I looked it up online. You're just having anxiety. I guess it's kinda like stress only mixed with panic and worry. It feels more intense. I watched a

YouTube video for that breathing exercise. It helps me sometimes."

"Yeah. Thanks for that." I said. Grace nodded.

"How long have you felt like that, with the anxiety?" Sarah asked Grace.

"Oh. I don't know. Since forever, really. I never knew it had a name until recently…"

"Is it alright if I ask…how you ended up here?" Jamie asked her. I'm glad he asked before I did. The curiosity was already killing me. Grace's face and demeanor seemed so fragile to me at first glance. But by the way she spoke, she seemed kind of tough. Grace paused and looked at the ground. Sarah whispered something to her.

Chapter 31
Grace

"You don't have to tell them your story if you don't want to." Sarah whispered to me. I nodded at her gratefully. It was nice being seen by her. Sarah knew how private of a person I could be. But there was something about meeting Jamie and Carlos, I didn't feel the need to hide.

"Yeah, sure. I'll talk about it." I said. "It's not as bad as you guys…but basically we – me, my mom, and my sister, finally left my dad. He's not a good person. He's not really my dad either. I mean, he is my dad biologically. But he was never around. He keeps on leaving. He always leaves. But then he comes back and expects us to all act like a happy family again. As if he did nothing wrong."

"Why does he keep leaving – if you don't mind me asking." Jamie said.

"It could be because of anything. We could be having a hard time, financially. So he'd run away, leaving us with nothing. My mom could have caught him cheating, so he'd leave. Maybe to be with some other woman, I'm not actually sure where he goes. But most of the times it's cause of…the drugs."

I looked around me. Jamie. Sarah. Carlos, who I just met. They weren't saying a thing. I should have felt ashamed. But something inside of me wanted to keep going. Something inside of me was unraveling.

"My dad's a drug addict. I don't think I really knew or understood it until I got older. But that's where he squanders our money, most of the time. He keeps on messing everything up! We lost our family restaurant because he did something shady. Then we started a dry-cleaning business. And then he messed that up too! Wherever we go, whenever he's there, things turn into a disaster. It's all so tiring. Things always change, but it's the same cycle over and over and over again…Until we finally left him and came here."

"Damn. That must be tough." Jamie said. I nodded at him and smiled. I wondered how Jamie saw me now, after knowing everything.

"My mom was the same way." Carlos said. I looked up at him surprised.

"The mom you came with?" I asked.

"Oh, no. She's actually my aunt. They adopted me when I was a kid. My real mom is…somewhere. I don't actually know where she is now. She'd leave too, sometimes." Carlos explained. "When I was a kid, sometimes I'd be home alone for days. But she always came back to me. I tried to believe she would change for me, but she never did. It was the same type of deal you had. Things always changed. We'd move often. She always got fired and was changing jobs.

"Yeah…I'm past the point of believing my dad will change…Where's your real dad?" My arms started to tingle. My knee started to jump up and down. Suddenly, I felt a bit restless.

"I don't know where he is either. I actually don't even know his name. He left when I was a baby, apparently. That's what my mom told me." Carlos said.

"Oh. I see…"

"What was it – that made y'all finally leave your dad?" Sarah asked me.

"I'm not sure if there was one specific thing. I think Umma – I mean my mom, finally just decided it was enough. She started locking him out of our apartment, but he'd bang on the door for hours and wake up the neighbors. There was that one time…" I looked up to see if Jamie, Carlos, and Sarah were appalled by my story. But their faces looked patient, kind.

"There was one thing that happened." I said slowly, recalling a recent memory. "My dad hit my sister. He never did that before. He used to only hit my mom, but that stopped years ago after my mom started fighting back. But one day, my sister was just on the computer and my dad was saying something to her. I think he wanted to use the computer but my sister said no, because she needed to finish studying. So then my dad just hit her. And kept on hitting her. Like it was nothing. Like she was nothing. Like he could do anything he wanted. My mom got to her first and started screaming at him, blocking him from her and shoving him. And I just stood in the hall, not knowing what to do.

"Eventually, my sister dialed 911 after my mom told her to. And then my dad ran out of the house. The police came, like 10 minutes later and asked Janice questions. I hid in my room. They didn't even know I was there. I don't think the police even went looking for him. My dad came back at night and slept in the living room, like nothing even happened. Calling the police didn't do anything. Now that I think about it, that could've been why we left. I think it was a week before we moved out…"

I looked back at Sarah after staring into the distance. She looked like she was about to cry. Jamie and Carlos looked alarmed.

"You guys. It's ok." I said smiling, trying to break the tension.

"Grace. You're so brave." Sarah said. I looked back at her confused.

"I'm not really. I didn't do anything. I wish I could've done something. But in the moment, I just kinda…"

"Froze?" Carlos asked. I nodded.

"Does it feel like you're having an out of body experience?" Jamie asked.

"Yeah, kinda." I said. "It kind of feels like I'm watching the scenario from afar, even though I'm right there."

"I feel like that too sometimes." Jamie said. "I try to wake myself up from it, but I don't know how."

"Yeah!" I agreed. "I try to make myself move, or say something, yell. I want to do something. I want to push him away. But I'm just stuck. I wish I was a fighter, like Janice, my sister. Or like my mom."

"You are a fighter, Grace." Jamie said. I turned to look at him. He had his elbows rested on his knees and was leaning forward towards me.

"Really?"

"Absolutely. I mean look at you…" Jamie cleared his throat. "I mean, you just being here, and being able to talk about everything that's happened to you. You're a fighter."

"Yeah, you're one of the strong ones." Sarah said smiling. "And trust me, hitting someone back never feels as good as you think it would. I think you are brave."

"I think we all are." I said, not knowing how to take the compliment. I never found myself to be strong. If anything, I was just numb. I didn't feel the hurt of things like I used to. All the scars were closed and crusted over now.

"But truth is, I don't feel anything towards my dad anymore." I said. "I don't miss him at all. I try not to think about him because all the memories I have of him are bad ones." I looked back at Carlos who was listening intently.

"I feel the same way." He said.

"How long has it been, since you've seen your mom?" I asked. At this point, it seemed like no question was off limits.

"Oh God. It's been…I'd say, maybe 10 years." Carlos said. Jamie and Sarah's eyes widened a bit. Carlos laughed. "It's fine. I don't consider her my mom anymore. My aunt Julia, she feels like my real mom now."

"What's she like?" Sarah asked, resting her chin on her hand intently.

"Tía Julia is wonderful. She's super kind and gentle. She had cancer…My uncle, he gave away everything we had to pay for her hospital bills. He gave up the house, the car shop, so Tía Julia could get surgery. The surgery worked! She's all better now."

"That's great!" I said.

"Yeah…I thought if I was going to lose anyone, it was going to be her." Carlos said. "But as soon as she got out of surgery my uncle had a stroke."

"Damn. I'm sorry man." Jamie said. Carlos looked down.

"It's alright." I wondered if I should give him a hug, but decided to stay seated. Hugs always felt unnatural to me.

"Is that how you ended up here?" I asked, hoping he wouldn't cry.

"Kinda. After Tío passed away, we went to stay with my grandma and grandpa – my Tío's parents, for a few days. But after a while, they started hating Tía for some reason. I think they blamed her for Tío's death, saying that if she hadn't been sick, he wouldn't have been so stressed and had a stroke."

"That's fucked up." Sarah said.

"It really is." I said.

"I know. Eventually, Abuelo and Abuela told Tía to go somewhere else and that they would be the ones to raise me and Benny. He's my cousin. But then Benny told them to fuck off and we all left together. We slept in our car at first. But then when Tía went back to the hospital for an exam, she talked to someone at the hospital who told us about this place. That's how we ended up here. But looking back at it now, I wish I had said something to my abuelo and abuela. The things they said to Tía, I can't believe it. I didn't know they were capable of saying those things."

"You really can't trust family." Jamie agreed. "At least not the people outside your immediate family…A similar thing happened to me. My uncle, he said he'd give us a place to stay after my dad died and we lost the house. But then he didn't." Carlos nodded.

We took a break from telling our stories and listened to the crickets talk to each other. Even with the near arrival of summer, the night air felt brisk. I could smell the faint scent of lilacs from one of the bushes, beginning to bloom.

"All of your stories make mine seem like child's play." Sarah said, looking up at the night sky.

Chapter 32
Sarah

The night that surrounded us was disappearing. I began the evening hoping to have a venting session with Grace on the swings. But it quickly transformed into an outpouring with Jamie and Carlos. The four of us were stepping into the depths of each other's lives.

"I'm sure whatever you're going through is difficult enough for you to end up here." Jamie said. I liked Jamie. He had a wise presence about him that liked to teeter back and forth between man and teenager.

"If it's ok to ask, what led you here?" Carlos said.

"I'll tell you guys about it, another time. It looks like we should start getting ready for school." Morning seemed to rip night out of the sky within a matter of minutes.

"Oh my God. I didn't even notice." Grace said looking around her. "What time is it?" I checked my phone.

"6:15."

"Yeah, we should be heading back." Grace said. It was nice seeing Grace comfortable around all of us. When we first discovered each other at Blue Haven, Grace was heavily guarded. Now, she was joking around with all of us and sharing her most intimate secrets.

"Could we meet again tonight?" Carlos asked. The three of us looked back at him. I smiled, realizing how quickly we just became friends.

"Sure." I said with a smile. "Y'all wanna come back out here tonight? Maybe at 3 a.m.? That's usually when everyone is deep in their REM cycle." Everyone nodded.

All this time, I thought I was alone in this. Alone in suffering. Alone in being abandoned. But Jamie, Grace, Carlos – they've all lost someone.

I felt guilt churning in my stomach while I was at school. Today was the day I was supposed to meet with my guidance counselor to brainstorm ideas for college application essays.

"Tell them about *you*. What makes *you* special? What makes *you* stand out?" She said, beneath a blazer that was too warm to wear now with the blazing sun knocking on her window.

"I work two jobs…to help support my family…and…"

The guidance counselor nodded, getting excited. It seemed like sob stories were a turn on for admission departments and guidance counselors.

"My mom is also divorced..." She looked disappointed. Divorce didn't make the cut anymore. It was no longer special.

"Are there any other extenuating circumstances you've gone through? Any *unique* experience?" I looked back at her expectant eyes and felt the urge to walk out and leave.

"I'll have to think about it some more." I said.

"Yes. Well definitely talk about your two jobs. Colleges love applicants that seem hard working." *Seem?* "After you finish your essay, come and meet with me again and we can go over what you've written."

I nodded and got up in a hurry to leave. I drove to the diner and thought about last night. The way Grace's face looked while telling her story. It was as if she was talking about what she ate that day. As if the things she went through were totally normal. I wondered if she was really ok. Was I ok? How come I couldn't tell my story like everyone else? It's nothing I'm ashamed of. But maybe I was ashamed. Everyone shared their story so easily. How come I couldn't? A mix of nervousness and excitement for tonight's meet-up somersaulted in my chest.

At the diner, I tried to keep my cool. I decided, I was going to act like everything was totally normal between me and Tyler. He was my friend. He is my friend. I want to keep it that way. About 20 minutes passed. I took people's orders. A family. A double date of pre-teens. An older man that grabbed my ass as I walked away. I thought about smashing my coffee pot over his head but decided not to.

Another 30 minutes passed. Where the hell was he? In between refills and waiting for people to finish chewing and swallowing their food, I studied for my SATs. I only had two days left. I needed to score at least 50 points higher to give me a better chance of getting into my top-choice universities. After clearing a few tables, I hid my SAT practice book beneath the counter and started memorizing the V's of my vocab. Validate. Viability. Vital. Vow. Vow. Vows are always broken.

One hour later, Tyler was still a no-show. Halfway through my shift a confused teen came and worked the cash register. I wondered if I was ever that young. I decided to text Tyler. Maybe he changed his work schedule because of me. Was he avoiding me? I took out my phone and hid it beneath the counter. A text notification from Tyler appeared. *"I'm behind the diner. Could you come out for a sec?"*

What the hell? Tyler's here? I handed my coffee pot to the new kid without a word, took off my dirty apron, then checked my hair in the bathroom mirror before heading out.

"Hey." Tyler said. Damn, he looked good. Where did he get that leather jacket all of a sudden? Has he always worn that and I just never noticed? When did he become so attractive?

"Hi." I said nervously.

"I've been trying to reach you. Is everything ok?" Tyler asked. I nodded, not feeling the need to reveal more. "I went by your house." Fuck! "Did y'all move? Someone else was living there." I needed to come up with a lie quickly.

"Oh, uh. We moved to an apartment. It was cheaper and we didn't need all that space." I said. Tyler didn't seem convinced. God, I'm a terrible liar.

"You don't have to tell me the truth if you don't want to…"

"No, Tyler. It is the truth – really!"

"Listen. I'm going back to Brown."

"What? When?" My heart sank.

"Right now. I've packed all my things and I'm gonna drive there. They said I could start again during the summer semester." Tyler pointed at his car. I could see carboard boxes and his guitar case shoved up against the rear window. I didn't know what to say. I wanted to ask him to stay.

"Wow. I…good luck." I said weakly.

"Is that really all you have to say to me?" Tyler said, fully irritated.

"Well, what do you want me to say?"

"Fuck, Sarah. I don't know! More than good luck."

"What! Do you want me to tell you that I'm in love with you? Because I'm not! You're my friend. I've enjoyed our time together but now you have to leave. So good luck with everything at Brown." I shouted, regretting each word that came out of my mouth.

"You've enjoyed our time together? What am I – just a customer?" Tyler said with a look of disgust. He stepped away without another word and headed towards his car.

"No! Wait!" I rushed towards him and pulled him back.

"What! What the hell do you want from me?" Tyler shouted. I grabbed his neck, leaned forward and kissed him. My whole body pressed up against his. I had no idea what I was doing, but he kissed me back. Tyler wrapped his arms around me and I put my hands on his face. I opened my eyes and Tyler was smiling, beaming. I took a few steps back, surprised by my own actions.

"I love you, Tyler. If things were different than the way they are now…maybe we could…"

"But they can be!" Tyler said excitedly. "You can apply to Brown and we could be together again in a year!" I shook my head no and Tyler's great, big smile disappeared.

"In another life maybe. Goodbye, Tyler."

I walked away without looking back. I could feel his eyes stare back at me. In my chest, I felt a sharp pain I've never experienced before. I went into the employee bathroom and cried my eyes out. Tyler's leaving. Tyler's probably gone now. Now, I'm really alone.

Someone knocked on the bathroom door and I tried to stop crying, but I couldn't. I sobbed and the tears kept coming. Someone knocked on the door again.

"Someone's in here." I tried to say. The knocking continued. I quickly stood up and washed my face. I got out a few paper towels and tried to wipe away any evidence that I had just bawled my eyes out like a hurt child. I opened the door.

"Sarah, sweetie. Are you alright?" It was the owner, Beck. Her face looked concerned.

"I'm fine." I said and tried to walk back into the serving area. Beck gently held onto my arm.

"Listen, if you want, I can have Rob cover your tables and you can leave early tonight." I nodded gratefully.

I drove back to the shelter trying to leave the memory of Tyler behind me. But the wound was too fresh. Tyler was too present to even be a memory. I wondered if he left for Brown already. If he would call. I went into my room at Blue Haven and checked my phone a few more times. No call. No text. Shit. If I were Tyler, I wouldn't have called me either.

I tried to get my mind off of Tyler and started an SAT practice test. But every few seconds, I remembered our kiss. God! Everything was fucked up. You really fucked it all to shit, Sarah!

Mom put a plate of salmon on my desk before leaving for her night shift. I wish I could tell her not to go. I wish I could tell her that she didn't need to work anymore. I wished for a lot of things. But I learned to stop wishing and praying after Curt left. Wishing was for children who didn't know any better.

I finished my practice test and got a 1500. This was it. This was the answer. Don't worry Mom. I'm going to become so successful one day and make so much money, you'll never have to work another day in your life.

3 a.m. came quickly. I wondered if anyone else would come, or even remembered the promise we made while we deliriously shared our life stories last night. I took my time

making sure David was fast asleep. Mom wasn't coming back until at least 5 in the morning. I had time.

I stepped out into the backyard. To my surprise, I was the last one there. Grace, Carlos, and Jamie were already swinging on the swings like a bunch of innocent children. Grace saw me coming and waved. I couldn't help but smile back at them as I took the last swing.

"How was work?" Grace asked. I wondered if I should tell her.

"Work was crap." I said.

"Where do you work?" Jamie asked.

"At the diner off I-35. I also work at the Cold Stone across from school."

"Oh, so if I go there, can I get a free scoop?" Carlos asked.

"Sure! I'll give you a free scoop when my manager's not looking." I replied starting to swing, my body feeling lighter and lighter. What happened with Tyler was over. I needed to forget him. "So, where did we stop from last night's conversation?"

"Well, I think it's your turn." Grace said, turning to me.

"Right. Shit. What do y'all wanna know?" I asked. Grace, Jamie, and Carlos fell quiet. The tone was transitioning like the humming of a piano after it stopped playing.

"You don't have to share if you don't want to." Grace said.

"No…I want to." I said, still unsure whether I did or not.

I stared back at the familiar sky. It looked the same as yesterday. A towering black mass that felt so far away yet close. And then I told them. Three people I barely knew. I told them about my parent's divorce. What it felt like when Dad left. How much it hurt when he never answered my calls or replied to my emails. How much it sucked to see him again with his new family. How disappointed I was after our recent reunion. How much I didn't want to be like him and abandon my family. And yet how much, at times, I wanted to leave. Just like he did.

Then I told them about Curt. How nice he seemed at first. But after a year of settling in, how cruel he turned out to be. How much he hurt my mom. The time I saw him slap her. How he left. Finding out about the money he took – or rather Mom gave away. Being unable to pay for assisted housing, getting kicked out. And ending up here. Seeing my mom's bruised knees. Feeling like it was all my fault. Feeling like I was all alone in this world.

"But you're not alone." Grace whispered. I turned to look at her. She was barely visible underneath the lamp's shallow light, which immersed the four of us in a subtle haze.

"We're here." Grace whispered.

Carlos and Jamie nodded in agreement. I smiled back at them. Sure, I have them now. But for how long? All of us were going to leave this place. That was the goal.

"Anyways." I said, shaking my face and trying to bring my emotions back to a level place. "Let's talk about something fun." I said and started swinging up and down at a more forceful pace. Carlos followed.

"I put a frog on my teacher's desk today." Carlos said happily.

"What?" I laughed.

"Yeah. She was pissing me off. She was doing that thing – you know, what you said Jamie. Being all sorry for me but being a total phony about it. She announced to the entire class that my uncle died and how sorry she was for my loss."

"What? What the hell? People are so stupid." I said.

"Seriously!" Carlos said. "So I went to go to the bathroom, but really I went outside where there's this little pond. I found a frog and put it in my pocket. When I came back, I went up to her desk to talk about my *feelings* and put the frog on her desk. She practically screamed and ran to the corner of the classroom. Oh my God. I laughed so much! It was so funny."

"And then what happened?" Jamie asked.

"I picked up the frog again and put it in the teacher's water bottle. The other kids were laughing too. I don't think I laughed that much…in a long time." Carlos said with a face of pride. Carlos was an interesting guy. He was reserved but talkative. Shy but loud. His face looked happy but I could tell there was always a hint of sadness in him.

"That's incredible. What else? Come on! Give me the good stuff." I said, rubbing my hands expectantly.

"Let's talk about our dreams!" Grace said like a little child. We smiled at her. At times, Grace felt like my younger sister. At other times, she felt like my mom.

"Why don't you start?" I motioned to Grace.

"No, no. I don't want to start. One of you guys go." Grace said cheerfully as she swung up and down.

"I'll go." Jamie said. "I think I want to be a doctor."

"Really?" Carlos asked impressed.

"Yeah. My mom's a nurse and I've always admired her for it. But I want to work with low-income patients. I'm not sure how all that works logistically, but lately I've been thinking about…"

"Tell us!" Grace said excitedly. Jamie smiled at her enthusiasm.

"I've had this dream of working for Doctors Without Borders. It's this non-profit organization that travels to the toughest countries and doctors treat the people there for free." Jamie said in a measured voice. "I just think…it would be a great way to live, you know."

"That's amazing, Jamie." I said.

"It really is. You should do it Jamie. I believe in you." Grace said holding a thumbs up.

"Thanks." Jamie said, moving backwards, then lifting off with a full swing. "Someone else's turn. Carlos. Go!"

"I don't know. I don't know if I have a dream. I guess what I thought I'd do before was work at my uncle's shop. He said he would leave it to me. But now, somebody else owns it. I think they're turning it into a laundromat…I never thought about what else I wanted to do. Lately, I've been thinking I wanna go to college though."

"You should do it man." Jamie said mid-swing.

"I don't know. My grades aren't that great." Carlos said, shaking his head.

"There's still time, Carlos. There's plenty of time." I said.

"Really?"

"Yeah! You're only a sophomore. That means you have two years to raise your GPA." Carlos shrugged.

"Ok, one of you two. Your turn." Carlos pointed at Grace and me then started swinging alongside Jamie. Grace pointed back at me.

"I think…I just wanna be free. I want to make a lot of money so that I don't have to worry. And I don't want my family to worry. I want to make enough so that we'll be ok…happy."

"I don't know." Grace said. "People usually think they'll be happy when they have a lot of money. But I remember when my family was well off when I was super young. Nobody seemed all that happy."

"Hmmm." Carlos chimed in. "I know for me, I'd rather have problems with a lot of money, than problems without money. People always say, 'mo' money, mo' problems.' But I think life is still easier when you have money."

Chapter 33
Grace

I wondered if what Carlos said was right. All my life, money seemed like the root of my family's problems. But that's always because it seemed like we never had enough. Money was the tiny rock that our lives balanced on. I always thought, once someone kicked the rock out from under us, our lives would go plummeting off the cliff of stability. But we weren't plummeting. If anything, it felt like we were stuck, unable to move at all.

"What about you, Grace?" Sarah asked. "You're the last one. You gotta answer your own question."

"I'm not entirely sure…" I said. It was strange. I used to be so sure I wanted to pursue music. But lately, the feeling I got when I wrote, it felt glorious. Like I was finally free. The words just poured out of me. I felt alive.

"I've always known I want to live a really big life. But how I get there changes every couple of years. I love music but I don't know if I actually want to pursue it anymore…"

"Is there anything else you've thought about doing?" Jamie asked.

"Lately…I don't know. Maybe it's stupid." I said, afraid of what they'd think of me.

"It's not stupid." Sarah said shaking her head.

"Lately, I love writing. I think I always liked it as a kid. I always used to write poems or little stories. But since coming here, I've been writing almost every day. It just feels so good. When I'm writing and the words are just coming out of me, I feel…"

I looked around. None of their faces seemed to judge me.

"I feel like, oh this is it. This is me. This is what I'm meant to do with my life." Sarah, Jamie, and Carlos smiled.

"That's awesome." Carlos said. "I wish I had something that made me feel like that. Do you want to write books then?"

"I think so, eventually. But this semester in my world history class, I got the idea to be a journalist. It's crazy! During all of these huge world events, it was the journalists that showed the whole world what was going on. You know like, Tiananmen Square or Rwanda…if it weren't for the journalists there, the rest of us wouldn't have known what was even happening. But I'm not sure if I can do it. I don't think I'm tough enough to bust into war zones and everything."

"Well, no one is in the beginning." Sarah said smiling.

"Yeah! No one starts out as a badass. They become one along the way." Jamie replied.

"Yeah and you kinda seem like a badass already, so by the time you're an adult, you'll be a major badass." Carlos laughed.

"Your byline can read, By Grace Park. Parenthesis: Major Badass." Jamie said.

"I like it!" I said. The four of us started to swing freely. I wondered if we were too old to be having this much fun on a swing set, most likely dedicated for elementary school students.

"Alright. Sorry to be a party pooper but I gotta go before my mom gets back from her night shift." Sarah said. We started to let our feet kick the floor and land back on solid ground.

"Yeah, we should get back. Wanna meet up again tomorrow night?" Jamie asked.

"Sorry, I don't think I can make it tomorrow night. I've got my SATs this Sunday, so I have to study." Sarah said.

"Good luck!" Jamie said.

"You've taken yours already, right?" Sarah asked. "What was your score?"

"I'm still waiting on mine."

"Care to make a wager?" Sarah said.

"Someone's competitive." I said with a grin.

"I like it. Do the wager!" Carlos said excitedly.

"Ok. If I get a higher score – you gotta buy us all pizza. Not the cheap stuff like Dominos. The good stuff. I want Mellow Mushroom or above."

"And if *I* get a higher score, *you* have to get Dominos." Jamie said. "I like the cheap stuff. It tastes better."

Carlos and I snickered as Sarah and Jamie shook hands and we agreed to meet again the night after her test. Either way, I was excited to get some free pizza.

I knew we stayed at Blue Haven too long when I referred to this place as home. The first time it happened, I thoroughly freaked myself out. It was simple. Just a "let's go home" after a day of exhausting shopping for Janice's new life in medical school. Binders, outfits, notebooks. We stopped at Walmart, Marshalls, and two different Half Price Books stores to try and find some of Janice's textbooks at a discounted price. Janice and Umma weren't surprised by what I said. It was a simple phrase. But it felt so wrong after I said it. Like I swallowed something immensely bitter.

As soon as Janice found out she got into Hopkins, she got a part-time job as a receptionist at a dermatology clinic to save up money. She was going completely on loans, financial aid, and scholarships. I've been pretending that I don't care she's leaving. But I've already started planning future summer activities for us to make the most out of our remaining time together.

I've also started applying for summer jobs and got an interview at a barbecue joint today. During the car ride over, I started rehearsing for my interview. But what was I supposed to say? It's not like my life's passion is barbecue. Ok, strengths: hardworking, efficient, friendly. Weakness: I'm impatient because I like things to be done straight away and I'm stubborn because I have a lot of conviction. Janice taught me to always disguise my weaknesses as strengths. That should do.

Umma parked at the Rudy's BBQ and I walked through the door, immediately greeted by the scent of smoked meat and sound of energetic chatter. Turns out, I didn't even need to rehearse. The interview took less than 10 minutes. The manager asked me when I could start and what my schedule looked like. He gave me a form to fill out. I paused when I saw the empty space for my address. Eventually, I decided to fill it with my old one. I would be starting on June 5th. I shook hands with the assistant manager and paid him $20 for my uniform.

Afterwards, Janice, Umma, and I ended up eating at Rudy's – my new employer. We shared three pounds of brisket, a pint of cream corn, and a rack of pork ribs.

"Do you know what you want to specialize in?" I asked Janice, who was carefully layering brisket, barbecue sauce, jalapenos, and onions on a slice of soft white bread.

"I think I'd like pediatrics. Or maybe neurology."

"What neuro-new-rol-o-gee?" Umma asked.

"It's like a brain doctor. You treat brain disorders and do surgeries."

"Oh but brain, very hard. You should try something easy. Maybe general doctor. Better hours." Umma said. Janice shrugged.

"If you do neurology you'd be like McDreamy on Grey's Anatomy." I told Janice. We both smiled at the thought of Patrick Dempsey.

"Dude. But I was talking to my friend – she's already in medical school, she said hospitals are nothing like that show." Janice responded.

"Really? I guess that's a good thing. Less shootings and plane crashes and ex-wives randomly appearing." Janice laughed.

"What this show?" Umma asked wanting to be part of the inside joke.

"It's that doctor show!" I told her.

"Oh yeah. That one ok. I like the one in Hawaii better." Umma said.

"Lost?" Janice asked.

"Yeah! It has the Korean nam-ja. Handsome!"

"Yeah, that show's good too." I agreed and took a bite of the brisket sandwich Janice put on my plate.

After barbecue, we went to the outlet mall and walked around hoping to digest. Umma bought Janice a pair of professional-looking shoes and a blazer on clearance at Banana Republic. I started feeling excited for Janice, and just a tad bit jealous. I think Umma could tell because she bought me a frappuccino at Starbucks to make me feel better.

Back at Blue Haven, I fell asleep swiftly and dreamt of our family vacation to Hawaii we took when I was four. I was playing in the sand with Umma. Appa was somewhere far away, I could only see the back of his head as he faded into the sandy distance. Then I was in the water. I was in the middle of a crystal blue ocean, the most beautiful shade of blue I've ever seen. I wasn't scared.

The water was still. Then a ginormous blue wave came towards me. I didn't try to swim away. I didn't panic. The wave, so tall it touched the sky, came and carried me. I rose up in the water and floated over it. There was no chaos, it just passed under me and I was propelled up into the blue sky then gently carried back to the still ocean. Then, another wave was coming, as big as the first. Before I could be carried again, my alarm shook me awake.

Crap! My 3 a.m. alarm was set on repeat. I turned it off as quickly as I could hoping it wouldn't wake anyone up. Janice sat up abruptly, looked around, then went back to sleep. After a few minutes, I left our room to get a glass of water. Normally, I would be afraid to step out into the dark empty shelter alone. But lately, the fondness of our hangouts made it feel less scary. The kitchen was empty as I snagged a Capri Sun from the fridge and slurped on the tiny yellow straw. Suddenly, my skin itched for the night air to wrap around me again. I headed towards the patio door and stepped outside. The lamp post flickered, as if announcing my arrival. I passed by the slide and headed towards the swings – this time on my own.

"Grace?" A voice said. I whipped my head around, alarmed. It was Jamie. He was sitting at the edge of the slide. "Didn't think I'd see any of you guys tonight." Jamie said quietly.

"I didn't either. But my alarm, I guess it was set on repeat." I said and sat on the ground in front of him. "Whenever, I'm out here. It weirdly feels like I'm at camp or something."

"Me too. It's so strange." Jamie said. "Time feels strange here. I'm not sure if it's moving fast or slow."

"I think sometimes it's so fast it's a blur. Sometimes it's painfully slow." Jamie nodded. We looked at each other and Jamie came down from the slide and sat on the grass with me.

"It's nice being here…just the two of us." Jamie said. I didn't know how to respond. "It's quieter, I mean. I can think more." Jamie straightened out his legs in front of him and leaned back with his hands on the grass, staring up at the sky.

"What are you thinking about?" I asked. "I mean, why did you come out here again? We weren't supposed to meet up."

"I just needed to blow off some steam." Jamie said. I admired the smooth profile of Jamie's face. He didn't say anything for a while.

"Do you miss your dad?" I asked. Jamie sighed. Maybe I should've stayed quiet.

"I don't know…I mean, I do miss him. But lately, I just feel so angry. I feel mad all the time. It-It's exhausting."

"Who are you mad at?"

"God…for taking away my dad." Jamie said to the stars. I copied his posture and looked up. It was nice sitting in the silence. The quiet was almost comforting.

"I think it's ok, for you to be angry. God can take it." Jamie looked at me and smiled. "I've been angry too, at God. Sometimes, I still get angry but then…"

"Then what?" I looked back at Jamie, wondering just how close we really were. Maybe our shared circumstance fooled us into thinking we actually cared for each other, even though we'd part ways sooner than later.

"Then I feel, just this overwhelming sense of God's love for me. It just kind of covers me like a warm blanket. And I can't help but think…"

Jamie waited for me to finish. His face looked serene yet tired.

"I can't help but think, God is still a good God. He's good. Even in all of this. I've never felt like the love that he has for me changed. Even after coming here. The world may look at me differently, but God doesn't." I said. Jamie let out a long exhale. I couldn't tell yet if it was one of relief or sadness.

"You're gonna make a great journalist one day." Jamie said, changing the subject. I obliged.

"You think so?" I asked.

"Yes. You're not afraid to ask questions. Ones I would never think to ask." I smiled. No one ever told me that before. Most of the time, people got tired of my questions. "Ask me another one." Jamie said.

"Ok, let me think…Do you want a happy one or a deep one?" I asked.

"Anything. The first thing that comes to your mind."

"What's your greatest fear?"

"Pffffffffttttt." Jamie said, then fell on his back as if he fainted. I laughed and joined him, my hair getting tangled in the grass.

"And don't give me a cop-out answer like ghosts. Something real." I said.

"My greatest fear. Let's see." I waited patiently, not minding the silence. "I'd say my greatest fear, would be losing another person. But the more I think about it, the more inevitable it is. All of us die one day."

I nodded at the night sky.

"But I think other than that, sometimes I fear that I won't make it…That I won't ever reach my dreams. That I won't be smart enough for college or medical school. Or that I won't make enough money to support my family."

"I think…that's a noble fear."

"Nah. Not really. Ok your turn." Jamie said, turning his face towards me.

"My greatest fear. Hmm. Let's see. I think…I fear not living a big life. That things just won't ever work out for me. And…" I let out a long sigh. The air was too warm tonight to show me proof I was breathing.

"Sometimes I'm scared I'll turn out exactly like my dad." Jamie leaned up a little, putting his weight on his elbows, turning towards me.

"Grace. You're nothing like him. Why would you worry about that?"

"You never know what can happen in life. People change." I said looking back at him.

"You won't. You won't turn into him. You're good inside. That kind of thing doesn't change." I smiled at Jamie and he started leaning in closer to me. I didn't move. He came in closer. I could feel his breath on my face. I closed my eyes. Then Jamie kissed me. His lips moved softly on mine.

After what felt like too short a time, Jamie laid back down not looking at me, his hands covering his face. What happened?

"I'm sorry." Jamie said. "I shouldn't have…"

"It's alright." I said. Did he regret kissing me?

"It's just that. I can't. I can't right now. My ma, I have to take care of her. I have to figure out a way to get us out of here. I have to focus on getting into school. Then there's Aisha and Quinn. They need me. They don't even have a dad anymore." Jamie looked panicked and upset. His smooth face contorted in pain and tears started forming in his eyes.

"Jamie! Jamie!" I said, putting my hand on his shoulder. "I'm not asking for anything. I know what this is. I'm not asking for us to be in a relationship…I know this isn't going to become anything." Jamie's conflicted face started to soften. "I don't need any more than this."

Both of us laid silently next to each other on the patchy grass. I could smell the scent of lilacs. They had bloomed on the bushes chained to the fence surrounding us.

"I'm sorry, Grace." Jamie said softly.

"You have nothing to be sorry for."

We kept silent, wrapping ourselves in security and distance. We both knew this wasn't going to evolve into anything more than a secret kiss at a secret place during a secret time in our lives.

"…You want to know what I really fear?" He asked.

"Yes."

"My greatest fear is that I'll never be ok again. My dad is dead. Even saying that feels like a lie. I don't feel the same. Sometimes I worry that this is how I'll always feel. Sometimes I'm scared I'll never not feel sad anymore."

Jamie's words hovered all around me. I started to feel the depth of his sorrow travel through me.

"That's not gonna be your story." I said.

"How do you know?" I turned my head towards him, he was already facing me.

"Because you're not broken."

Chapter 34
Carlos

    Abuelo and Abuela's words still sting. Every time I think about what they said, it makes my heart ache for Tía. I always thought they loved Tía like a daughter. But after Tío died, they changed. They needed someone to blame.

    They came to visit us at the hospital after the surgery was finished. But by the time they arrived, it was already too late. They thought they were coming to see if Tía had recovered, instead they got blindsided by their son's death.

    "Ay, dios míos! How could this be? How could this be? We just talked to him on the phone." Abuela said in tears.

    "My son! My boy. What's happened? How could this happen?" Abuelo said sobbing. Tía's monitor started beeping rapidly and a nurse came in and injected something in her IV.

    "Mom! Mom!" Benny shouted. Tía passed out to a room filled with crying people.

Soon after, Abuelo and Abuela started making plans for Tío's funeral while Benny talked to the doctor about Tía's discharge. Meanwhile, I felt paralyzed. None of it felt real. It was like I was stuck in a dream.

Tía left the hospital earlier than planned. She didn't want to stay any longer with all the bills piling up. We moved into Abuelo and Abuela's house after Tía accepted an offer to sell our old home. The plan was for Abuelo and Abuela to help Tía during the recovery process until we could save up enough to move out. Before I could even unpack, we went to a Catholic church and stood next to an open casket.

I don't understand why people agree to an open casket. It's sad enough knowing someone you love died. But this, this was something else. Tío's face had turned a gray color. He was wearing his only suit. He wasn't smiling. But Tío always smiled. This man didn't feel like Tío at all.

The three of us sat on the front row as the priest recited some prayer I vaguely remembered from my childhood. Then my family stood up and made our way towards the open casket. Abuelo and Abuela walked up first. Abuela started crying and gently touched Tío's hair. Abuelo tried hard not to cry and held onto the edge of the casket, as if balancing at the edge of a cliff.

Next was Tía. She held a white handkerchief over her nose and carefully placed a letter inside with Tío. Then, Benny. He walked up to Tío with tears in his eyes – so full they looked like they were about to flood Tío's casket. But as he looked over

Tío's body, he wiped his eyes, then turned and went back to his seat like everyone else in the procession line.

Then it was my turn. A long line of people stood waiting behind me. I was scared to move closer to Tío – or whatever was in the casket. This person wasn't him. This wasn't his face. This wasn't his body. The Tío I knew was warm and smiley. This was just a corpse. I approached the casket slowly as the dramatic cries behind me got louder. I looked at Tío. Tears started falling down my cheeks. I wiped my drippy nose. I'm sorry Tío. I'm sorry. I'm sorry I wasn't a better son to you. I'm sorry about Mom. I'm sorry you had to suffer so much and work so hard. It isn't fair. None of this is fair. You deserved to live a long life with Tía. You deserved better. I hoped Tío could hear what I was telling him from heaven.

We drove back to Abuelo and Abuela's house in silence. After Tío's death at the hospital, Abuelo and Abuela acted cold towards us. But I thought it was because they were sad, in pain. None of us said much to each other the first few days we were there. But we still ate dinner at the table together, as a family.

But after the funeral, things changed. Abuela and Abuelo were angry. When Tía parked the car, Abuela was standing on the front lawn throwing Tía's clothes on the grass. I couldn't believe my eyes. How could this be the gentle Abuela that used to sit on our rocking chair and pet our old dog CeCe on her lap?

Tía told us to stay put and ran out of the car. Abuela was shouting and Tía was trying to calm her down. But then Abuelo came out of the house and started shouting at Tía too.

"He should have never met you!" Abuela screamed. "If he never met you, he wouldn't have had to go through so much. He worked so hard to provide for you. All you could manage was be a low life cook at a cheap restaurant. My son could've been somebody great if he didn't have to take care of you. You two never should have married!"

"Mamá, please." Tía said in tears.

"You, get out!" Abuelo interjected, pointing his arm out to Tía like he was hailing Hitler. "Leave! I don't want you here. If it weren't for your stupid cancer, my son would've been ok. It was you! He was so stressed because of you. All he ever did was work, non-stop, every day! You gave him that stroke!"

I couldn't believe it. Abuelo and Abuela were kind people. What were they saying? Benny got out of the car and ran to Tía, standing in front of her trying to block some of the onslaught.

"You shut your mouth!" Benny yelled at them. Tía tried to stop him. "You think this is Mom's fault? Do you have any idea how fucked up that is? Dad died. He had a stroke and he died. That's it!"

Upon seeing Benny, Abuela motioned towards him, her face melting from anger to sadness with Benny around.

"Benny. You stay here. You and Carlos, you're staying with us." Abuela said.

"Are you insane! I'm not staying with you people." Benny shouted.

"No. You and Carlos are staying here. This is your home now. Julia you can go somewhere else." Abuelo said.

Benny stormed back into the house and Tía fell to the ground. I got out of my car and rushed towards her, trying to protect her from any more evil words Abuelo and Abuela spat out. How could Benny take their side? I helped Tía get back on her feet. But then Benny came back out of the house with our suitcases.

"Come on." He said with confidence, leading us back into the car.

We ended up driving to Tío's best friend's house. Ali, his wife Michelle, and two daughters lived in a one-bedroom apartment. His daughters shared a bunk bed in the only bedroom and Ali and Michelle slept on a pull-out in the living room.

When I stepped into the apartment, I knew there wouldn't be enough room for us. But Ali's face was so kind and Michelle had dinner waiting for us. We ate piping hot enchiladas, fresh out of the oven.

"Sorry, we couldn't offer you more. I haven't done the grocery shopping for this week yet." Michelle said as she looked in the fridge. It was nearly empty. There were two Chinese takeaway boxes, a jar of sour cream, a couple eggs, and a plastic bag of peaches. She took out the peaches and a box of vanilla ice cream from the freezer for dessert.

"No, this was so much! Gracias!" Tía said with a forced smile. Her face looked exhausted. "And I promise, we'll only stay a little while. Just until we get back on our feet." Tía said.

"Nonsense! You are family!" Ali said. His warmness reminded me of Tío.

That night, the three of us shared the bunkbed in the girls' room while Ali and Michelle slept on a blow-up mattress in the living room and their daughters slept on the pull-out. Tía wanted to sleep on the ground, but Benny got a blanket and laid on the floor before she could. I climbed up the top bunk and Tía slept on the bottom.

I woke up to use the bathroom in the middle of the night. Climbing off the top bunk was a nuisance but it still felt better than being in the same house as Abuelo and Abuela. I blindly searched the wall for the light switch. When I turned it on, Tía was already awake and sitting upright on her bunk, staring at the wall. I jumped back a little. She looked like a ghost. What was she looking at?

The door was creaked open and a thin sliver of sound was invading our little room. I could hear Michelle and Ali's hushed voices.

"Do they have nowhere else to stay?" Michelle whispered to Ali.

"It seems so. They were staying at Juan's parents' house before but that must have ended. Did you see how cold they were to Julia at the funeral?" Ali asked.

"Yes – it was so strange." Michelle said. They paused for a moment. "Ali. I know Juan was like a brother to you. I loved him too! But right now, we barely have enough to feed the four of us. You had to take a pay cut. Remember?" Silence again. It seemed like Ali was thinking.

"We will think of something. God will provide. Don't you worry Shelly." Ali said.

"How can I not worry, Ali!" Michelle said a little louder. Ali shushed her gently.

I turned to look at Tía who was staring blankly at the pillar of light. I don't think she even noticed me. She didn't move.

"Tía?" I asked. Tía didn't respond and laid back down to sleep.

The next morning when I woke up, our things were packed and in the corner of our room. I could hear Tía's voice in the kitchen. As I walked out, I noticed paper bags on the table covered with the McDonald's logo. My mouth started to water.

"Good morning everyone!" Tía said cheerfully. Her mood didn't seem right for the situation. Ali and Michelle looked surprised.

"You didn't have to do this." Michelle said taken aback and still in her pjs.

"Está bien, no te preocupes!" Tía said. "Come girls. Sit!" Tía motioned to Sophia and Isabella. They ran to the dinner table and started chowing down on McMuffins and hash browns. Tía passed Michelle and Ali iced coffees.

"This will be our last meal together." Tía said. Benny appeared behind me. I stared at Tía's fake happy face.

"Qué?" Ali asked.

"Yes! Good news! Charlotte – a friend of mine from work said we could stay with her. They're empty nesters so she said there's an extra room for us. I don't want to be a burden to you all anymore."

"You're not a burden." Ali said with genuine kindness. "You can stay with us for as long as you want. You don't have to rush out of here."

"Thank you – but we're ok. Really!" Tía said unwrapping an egg and cheese biscuit and handing it over to me. I ate the whole thing in less than a minute. Tía unwrapped another one and handed it to Benny but he turned it down saying he wasn't hungry and that she should eat it. Tía smiled. Ali and Michelle sat down and started eating their pancakes.

After breakfast, Benny and I carried our bags back to the car. I wondered who this friend was. I never heard of a Charlotte before. Tía dropped us off at school. The day was a total blur. I kept on seeing Tío. Tío waiting for me in class, passing by me in the hall, sitting in the office. He was standing at the urinal next to me in the bathroom. It scared me so much I jumped and almost pissed on the floor.

After school, Tía picked us up and we drove back to the restaurant. It was a colorful place that served Tex-Mex food. In the afternoon, it was popular for kid's birthday parties. In the evening, it was popular for middle-aged professionals in search of cheap happy hours and large margaritas.

Benny left at 8 p.m. out of boredom and came back at midnight smelling like weed and alcohol. I didn't say anything. Tía didn't either. I tried to do my homework but my mind was stuck. None of the answers were coming. I kept on having to reread paragraphs to remember what I just read. But I couldn't stop. Whenever I let go of my pencil, my hands started to shake.

The restaurant closed at 1 a.m., that's when Tía started mopping the floor. Benny passed out on one of the empty booths. I sat at a table watching Tía clean. How much longer did we have to stay here? Tía finished then looked at me without saying a thing. She wheeled the mop and bucket to a closet behind the kitchen. She came back with a couple of pillows and blankets.

"I'm sorry, mijo. But I think we'll have to sleep here tonight." Tía placed a blanket over Benny and gently tucked a pillow under his head. "There's a couch in the manager's office." She said and gave me a blanket. She then laid out another blanket on a booth across from Benny and laid down. I went to the office and fell asleep to the smell of grease, flour, and salt.

The next day, Tía picked us up after school. It looked like Benny actually went to class today. He came out of the school's front doors rather than getting dropped off on the curb by a stranger. Tía said we were going on a road trip to San

Antonio. Benny and I were surprised. Was Tía losing her mind? Why would we go to San Antonio right now? We got in the car and Tía drove without stopping as we listened to an old mixed CD Tío made. It had songs from Selena, Ray Charles, Aerosmith, and Gloria Estefan.

    About two hours later, Benny, Tía, and I strolled along the River Walk. We stopped to look closer at some paintings, then some jewelry. Boats filled with people floated by. We ate inside the RiverCenter Mall and walked around the air-conditioned shops. We walked into a Nike store where Tía tried to buy me a pair of sneakers.

    "No! It's ok. I don't need them."

    "Carlos. Look at your feet. Your shoes are too small now." I stared down at my swollen, blistered feet and let Tía buy me a pair. After leaving the store, I sat on a bench switching into the new sneakers and Tía threw out the old ones. Then we went back outside and walked some more not saying a word to each other. Tía took my hand and smiled at me.

    We got back in our car around 10 p.m. Tía told us to sleep. I wondered if we were ever going to her friend's house, the empty nesters. I fell asleep somewhere in between Ray Charles' Hit the Road Jack and Aerosmith's Cryin.

    Hours later, a bump in the road woke me up. It was night outside and the clock on the dashboard said 1:11. Benny had his passenger seat reclined all the way back. It looked like he was sleeping. Tía was still driving. We should be back in

Austin by now. I leaned up to see where we were. It was downtown. I noticed the graffiti walls.

We passed Waterloo Records and a Whole Foods across the street. Then we passed the University of Texas tower. Tía drove back onto the highway heading north. Then she did a U-turn and took the Lake Austin exit. We passed Magnolia Café and drove back towards UT again. Tía was driving in circles. She really must have lost her mind.

What was going on? She turned the volume up on the CD, which was now on its seventh rotation. Tía was crying underneath the music. Her hand was held under her nose as tears kept falling. I looked at Benny who I thought was sleeping. His hands were resting behind his head. There were tears falling from his closed eyes.

I didn't know what to do. I didn't know how to comfort them. I didn't know if I even had the right to comfort them. I closed my eyes again and let the soft movement of Tía's car rock me back to sleep.

I woke up again at 6 a.m. feeling groggy and thirsty. Through my blurred morning vision, I spotted the hospital where Tía had her surgery and Tío died. Oh no! Something's wrong! Was Tía sick again? A million thoughts raced through my mind, but before I could panic I spotted Tía walking towards us with a manila folder in her hand.

Tía got into the car and looked at us. Benny was fully awake already with his chair back up and his feet resting on the dashboard.

"Mijos. I've found a place for us to stay." Tía said as soon as she got in and sat down.

"What about Charlotte?" I asked, but Benny shushed me immediately.

"What did the social worker say?" Benny said. I was jealous of Benny. It felt like he grew into a man after Tía got sick and I reverted into a scared child.

"She says there's a place we can go and stay for free." Tía made eye contact with me on the rearview mirror. "Now I know you guys deserve better and it will get better soon. But right now, you just have to trust me until we can afford a place of our own. This will only be temporary. You understand, sí?"

Benny nodded. Tía turned around to me. I nodded as well. If Tía said this was our only option, then I believed her. Forty minutes later, we arrived at Blue Haven.

Chapter 35

Sarah

 I've started to notice Tyler's absence. I didn't think it would hit me this hard. I've gone through much worse before. But it keeps eating away at me. I worked the next day at the diner without Tyler around. By the end of my shift, I quit. Now I just feel weak for quitting. I gave up my apron and nametag to Beck, who had tears in her eyes. "Are you sure?" She asked. I gave her a weak hug and told her I'd keep in touch.

 My mind keeps on jumping back to Tyler's face, seeing his smile disappear as I callously rejected him. I know I did wrong by him, but no matter how much I think about it, there's no other way. I wonder if I could call Grace. But before I could reach for my phone, it vibrated in my pocket. David.

 "Hey, David."

 "Could you come pick me up?" David asked in a monotone voice.

 "Yeah, sure. Where are you?"

"I'll text you the address."

I entered the address into my car's GPS and drove. I assumed he was at a friend's house, but I arrived at a Game Stop. What the fuck? I called David again.

"Are you sure the address you sent is correct? I'm at a Game Stop right now."

"Yeah. Could you come inside?"

"David! Did you make me drive all the way over here to buy you a stupid game?" I asked exhausted.

"Just come inside." This kid, he thinks he can walk all over me. I got out of my car and angrily entered the Game Stop that was filled with teenagers and older men who needed to stop playing video games. I never understood the gaming hype – shooting people until your mind went numb was never an attractive pastime to me.

"Excuse me, miss?" A middle-aged employee approached me. I spotted David and his friend sitting behind the cash register.

"What did you do!" I yelled, locking eyes with David who then quickly looked down at his palms, avoiding my vicious glare.

"Are you his guardian?"

"Yes." I said fuming. David shoplifted once before, only he never got caught when he swiped a comic book out of a second-hand bookstore. I made him return it the next day and apologize to the manager.

"Yeah, your son here."

"She's not my mom." David grunted. I glared at him. Now was not the time.

"I'm his older sister."

"Oh, well. I think I should be talking to his mom." The middle-aged man with a receding hairline said.

"You can talk, to me." I said with a face so angry, he started getting scared as well.

"Ok. Well, this kid tried to steal one of our games, the new Grand Theft Auto. Now if it were months ago, I wouldn't be making a big deal out of it and calling you over. But our new boss is making us crack down on thefts so…"

"David. Apologize!"

"Sorry." David said, still looking down.

"Are you kidding me? Stand up and apologize for real." David got up slowly and made eye contact with the store clerk.

"I'm sorry, sir. I won't do it ever again. Please accept my apology." It looked like David was about to fall asleep.

"Um…yeah. Ok. I accept your apology." The clerk looked at me, not knowing what to do. "If it happens again, I'm afraid I'll have to call the cops."

"D'you hear that?" I asked David, reaching out my hand to grab him. He dodged me and walked towards the exit. This guy's about to get an ass whooping.

"I'm so sorry, sir. I promise this will never happen again."

"Yeah, no problem. Hey if you wanna leave your number…in case-in case I catch him in the act again." David's friend snickered. That shithead was always getting David in trouble.

"Uh, sure." I scribbled down a number that wasn't mine on the back of a receipt.

"What should I do about this guy?" The clerk asked me, pointing to David's friend Isaac. "Can you take him too?" Isaac smiled all wide, I wanted to slap the immaturity off his stupid little face.

"No. Call his mom. She should know what a screw-up he is."

"Bitch!" Isaac said.

"Shut up, Isaac!" David said. I thought he left, but he was waiting by the exit doors for me. We got in the car and David started pressing my radio buttons, switching channels one after the other.

"Stop that! What the hell were you thinking, David?" I said angrily as I got into reverse and backed out of the parking spot. David shrugged. He seemed over it already.

"You seriously have nothing to say?" I asked, switching my car into drive. I made my way towards the outer edge of the enormous parking lot. This complex was so big it included a Game Stop, Barnes & Noble, super-sized HEB, Charming Charlie, and Sally's Beauty store.

"It doesn't matter what I do." David said looking down. Before exiting the lot, I parked in one of the empty spots. David looked at me confused. "What are you doing?" David asked.

"It does matter, David. What you do matters." I said desperately trying to get David out of this weird pre-teen angst that didn't suit him at all. David was strong. David is strong, I thought he handled Curt leaving like a champ. He never seemed to cry or get sad about it. Then again, I haven't spoken to him in days.

"No, it doesn't! Nobody cares about me. You're always gone. Mom is always working. And Dad…Dad left because of me." David's eyes started to fill with tears before he turned his head away from me. I felt an ache in my soul and tried to give him a hug. He pushed my arms away.

"David. What Curt did wasn't your fault. That was his own, stupid decision. It had nothing to do with you."

"Then why did he leave?" David asked, looking out his window. I sat, wondering for the first time why Curt left, why he didn't even think about taking David with him. He never even fought for him.

"Sometimes, people leave because they're not able to love people yet. They don't know how to love people…usually because no one ever loved them." David stayed silent. "Is that why you stole the game? So, Curt would find out?" I asked, trying to be patient.

"I freaking called him! I called him first to come get me. But he said he was busy. He didn't even care." David said crying. I didn't know what to say. That asshole Curt.

"I'm sorry, David." It seemed like sorry was the word I was saying the most lately. "And I'm sorry I haven't been around. You know me and Mom have to save up money so we can get a real place to live." David didn't say anything. He avoided eye contact and started picking at his thumbs, working up the courage to say something.

"…Are we poor?" David asked. His question caught me by surprise. David never asked questions like that before.

"What?"

"That's what Isaac said. He made fun of me because we're poor and I didn't have money to buy the new Grand Theft Auto."

"That mother fucker!" I wanted to drive back to the Game Stop and beat that kid. Before I could put the car back in drive, David pulled my arm and shook his head, knowing what I was planning to do.

"Are we though?"

I looked back at David. Growing up I never considered him my half-brother. How could someone be half family? David was my brother – my very own flesh and blood. His face looked older now, but his eyes still look so young and innocent. For that, I was thankful.

"David…have you ever missed a meal? Have you ever gone to bed hungry?" David thought to himself and shook his head.

"We don't have a lot. But we have enough…more than a lot of people." Poor. The word never crossed my mind before. I'm not sure why it took me so long to realize, we were poor. "It's best not to think about labels. Once you decide something or cross someone off in your mind…you can end up losing them forever." Suddenly, I thought about my own dad.

"I'm sorry…about the game." David said. I rubbed my fingers in David's shaggy hair then put him in a headlock. "Hey, get off!" David yelled with a smile. "You're such a boy! Why don't you act like a girl for once!"

"Why don't *you* act like a boy, ya little siss-ay!" I said, squeezing him even more.

We got back to Blue Haven in time to see Mom before her shift. I decided not to tell her about the Game Stop incident.

"Kids!" Mom said excitedly. David smiled then immediately sat next to Mom. "Did you guys have fun?"

"Yup." David said, eyeing me. I smiled to let him know it was our secret.

"What did you guys do?"

"We just shopped around." I said, taking a seat at the tiny desk.

"That sounds fun. Listen, Sarah – I packed your breakfast for your big day tomorrow. It's a green juice and some pita bread and hummus. Apparently, it's supposed to help your brain. So don't forget to eat it tomorrow before the SATs." I nodded. "Also, I have some very good news!"

"What?" David asked excitedly, looking like a 12-year-old again.

"It looks like we won't have to stay here much longer!" Mom said energetically.

"Really? How? Where are we gonna go?" I asked hesitantly.

"You remember Kim?"

"Aunt Kim?" I asked.

"Yes! My friend from college. We used to be so close before she moved to Boston. But she and her husband are planning on moving back to Austin! She gave me a call a few nights ago and I vented to her everything that's been going on, and she said we could stay with her."

"You told her?" I asked, feeling like our secret life had been exposed.

"Well, she had to hound it out of me. But, I told her we were staying at a motel. She said that they already made an offer and are waiting to close on a house not too far from here. It's a four-bedroom. She said we can stay with her!" It seemed too good to be true.

"Really, Mom? Really?" David asked smiling.

"Yes sweetie!" Mom said, hugging David.

"But when is she coming? Are you sure she's really moving down here?" I asked again.

"Kim said they still have to finalize a few things. But once it's finished, she said they're coming down to Texas. Isn't that great Sarah?"

"So they're still in Boston?" Mom could sense my apprehension.

"I know it's hard to believe, Sarah. But don't worry! This is it. I have a good feeling about this – a great feeling! We'll get to leave this place soon. I promise."

Mom was so convinced it was happening, I wanted to let my heart believe what she said. But Mom hasn't seen Kim in years. How could she offer such a thing to us? It seemed too good to be true. But they both looked so happy. I haven't seen David and Mom smile like this since before Curt left.

"I'll start packing." I said with a smile. Maybe it was real. Maybe we'll get to leave soon.

I woke up the next morning and chugged the green juice Mom made me. It tasted grossly of celery. I tried to get out the odd taste with the hummus, which wasn't half bad. I poured David some cereal and we ate breakfast together in the empty kitchen. He caught me up with everything at school. Teachers he liked. Teachers he hated. Friends, none of which sounded like people I wanted David to hang around. He also talked about a girl, who he claims he didn't have a crush on, for a good 15 minutes. It was nice seeing David be David. He's been so quiet lately. I'd forgotten how vivacious he was.

I drove to school and walked into an over air-conditioned room. The cold blast worked to my advantage. I was alert. My mind was ready. My body felt ready. I went through each time section with minutes to spare so I could look over my answers. I felt good. It felt much better than the last time.

I reached the last section and read over my essay. Damn. I analyzed the hell out of that anecdote. Symbolism, metaphors, and all. The instructor's watch beeped. "Pencils down." That's it. I'm done. I did it!

Walking out of the testing center felt like walking out of bondage into freedom. I never felt so relieved for something to be over. Man, I wish I could talk to Grace but I think she's still volunteering at the library.

I turned on my phone and opened up our group chat, which I named the 3AM Club, and sent a text.

"Wanna meet at 3 a.m. tonight? Jamie, get your pizza money ready. I just dominated the SATs."

"We'll see. 🙂 "-Jamie.

"Ahhhh yessss! You go girl!" -Grace.

"I'm down. Ya boy wants pizza. 🍕 " -Carlos

Chapter 36
Grace

My heart leapt when I got Sarah's text. It was happening again, our 3 a.m. club! After our second group hangout, I started anticipating it. My body would wake up on its own around 3, but then I'd force myself to go back to sleep. It was only at 3 a.m. when each of our families fell asleep, when we could be naïve together, when it felt like our lives were normal. When it felt like we were being rebellious teenagers by sneaking out to see friends. It was like we were in a different place – a hideaway, our secret place.

During the day, we each lived different lives. Other than stats class or in the halls, I rarely saw Sarah or Jamie at school. After school, Sarah was working, Jamie was tutoring, and Carlos was helping out at his aunt's restaurant. And I was at school or the public library trying to get more volunteer hours. I was also working on my applications for the National Honor Society and Newspaper Club at school. After this summer, I'll be a junior. The most important year for a high schooler. I needed to get serious.

The past few days have been an awakening. I never knew how much I wanted to write until I said it aloud at our last 3 a.m. hangout. Tonight, I've been reading articles and watching news reports online. I've also researched reporters I admired to see how they got to The New York Times or became anchors. I ferociously watched clips of Lisa Ling and read through her biography. Both her parents were immigrants and divorced. Her grandfather owned a restaurant. It sounded so similar to my story. I wondered if I could be like her one day.

Then, I started researching different colleges and landed on a ranking list of Best Liberal Art Schools in America. I clicked on the first three schools – Williams College, Amherst College, Wellesley College. All of them, back on the East Coast. My mind rushed to the changing autumn leaves I used to gaze at as a child in my hometown. Me and Umma would take walks down our hidden lane and crunch the leaves under our feet, that dropped from trees as tall as skyscrapers. I felt a surge of nostalgia and desire to go back home. I bookmarked each school's website on my laptop.

I Googled famous alumni from each of the schools. Elia Kazan, David Foster Wallace, Diane Sawyer. My God, this is it. I need to go to one of these schools. This feels right. The dual excitement of a great future and rapidly approaching 3 a.m. hangout was pumping through my veins. After finishing my research, it was only 1 a.m. I decided to read Ernest Hemingway's The Old Man and The Sea to pass the time.

"The old man was thin and gaunt with deep wrinkles in the back of his neck. The brown blotches of the benevolent skin cancer the sun brings from its reflection on the tropic sea were on his cheeks. The blotches ran well down the sides of his face and his hands had the deep-creased scars from handling heavy fish on the cords. But none of these scars were fresh. They were as old as erosions in a fishless desert." Damn, Hemingway. You're a fucking genius!

At 2:57 I nearly finished Hemingway's masterpiece. I wondered if I could ever get this good at writing. *"Up the road, in his shack, the old man was sleeping again. He was still sleeping on his face and the boy was sitting by him watching him. The old man was dreaming about the lions."* Finished. Round of applause for Hemingway!

My alarm vibrated. The time was finally here! Before slipping out of my family's room, I looked behind me to check that Janice and Umma were still asleep. Their chests moved lightly up and down with the rhythm of the night. I closed the door and made a dash for the kitchen, followed by a gentle sliding of the patio door. Outside, night had mixed with day. Maybe, it was my excitement, or maybe it was because the days were getting warmer and nights made a much shorter appearance than usual, but I could see Carlos and Jamie clearly. The dark blue sky had hues of pink that made me feel like God was painting a portrait just for us.

I waved at them. Jamie's eyes met mine and he smiled. I loved when he smiled. Without it, his face always seemed a bit too serious. Carlos waved back at me as well. His eyes looked tired. They seemed to be knee-deep in conversation already. I wanted to hear what they were saying. Were they talking about me? Did Carlos know Jamie and I kissed?

"Hey!" I said in nervous excitement.

"Hey! How you been?" Carlos asked.

"Same old. Same old. Just fantasizing about my future." I laughed. Ever since coming to Blue Haven, all I could think about was my future. The past and present felt like a mass of darkness I wanted to avoid.

"Any new plans?" Jamie asked.

"Kinda. I've been researching colleges and I think I want to go to a liberal arts school for writing."

"Well, that's exciting!" Jamie said.

"Liberal arts?" Carlos asked.

"Yup. It's basically college that is more focused on the arts. So, literature, philosophy, music, history – things like that." I explained.

"That sounds like you." Carlos said smiling optimistically.

"It does, doesn't it?" I laughed. "Where's Sarah?"

"She went to get the pizza." Jamie said.

"Did you beat her score?"

"Well, she hasn't found out her score yet. But she offered to buy it…I let her get the fancy stuff."

"That's very generous of you." I grinned sarcastically. "What was your score by the way? Did you find out?"

"Yeah, I wanna know too!" Carlos said.

"I did well, I think." Jamie said quietly, avoiding eye contact.

"Come on. I want a number!" I said louder.

"Yes! Tell us! Tell us Jamie!" Carlos said imitating my dramatic tone.

"Come on, Jamie. Give into peer pressure." I said.

"Alright. I got a high score." Carlos and I looked at him unimpressed. "I got a…" Jamie muttered something incomprehensible.

"Que?" Carlos asked.

"I got a 1600." My jaw dropped.

"Jamie. That's a perfect score! How is that even possible?" I asked in amazement.

"Seriously dude!" Carlos exclaimed. "I didn't know you were a genius."

"It's not a big deal. The test isn't about how smart you are, it's about understanding the test itself and how to beat it. After that, it's not so hard."

"Damn son." Carlos said.

"What did Sarah say when you told her?"

"Well, she said she'd buy the pizza." Carlos and I laughed.

"What'd I miss?" Sarah appeared out of nowhere, holding a box of extra-large pizza from a place I never heard of.

"Jamie was just telling us his SAT score." I said. Sarah sighed dramatically then sat on the bare grass with us.

"If Jamie told me his score before I started tooting my own horn, I wouldn't have made a fool of myself." Sarah said with a smirk.

"Who knows though! You might get a perfect score too." I said.

"I highly doubt that." Sarah said as she opened the grease stained pizza box. The inside was glorious. A steam rose from a cheesy pizza that was covered with flecks of green spices, pepperoni, sausage, peppers, and olives.

"Wow!" Carlos said. The four of us looked at the pizza in admiration. My mouth started salivating. Sarah got a slice first and we quickly followed – not speaking for several minutes as we each downed a slice or two.

"Man, I wish I had an ice-cold beer. That would make this perfect." Carlos said to no one in particular.

"Oh yeah! I almost forgot." Sarah dug through her bag, taking out a six pack of canned Coors Light.

"No way!" Carlos said.

"How did you get that?" I asked.

"The owners like me. I order from them all the time."

"But you're not 21." I said in confusion. Sarah smiled.

"I know." She said. Carlos and Sarah took a can each, tapped their tin cans together and gulped down a giant sip.

"You guys drink?" I asked in shock. Carlos laughed.

"Only occasionally." Sarah said. I looked to Carlos.

"Yeah, whenever my family had Friday fiestas. My friend Luis and I would swipe some beer. We thought we were so sneaky but I think Tío knew…" Carlos's mind traveled somewhere else as he took another sip. I must have looked concerned because Sarah patted my knee.

"It's alright, Grace. You don't have to drink if you don't want to." I was unsure. I suddenly remembered the time I chugged vodka from a water bottle as a kid, thinking it was water, and hating it. Before I could decide, Jamie reached for a can.

"Ayyyy." Carlos said as Jamie took his first sip. He looked at me and shrugged. "Dad and I used to drink a beer or two together whenever he came back home after getting deployed."

"Crap, ok. Let me try." I said, motioning to Sarah who had the last three cans sitting on her lap.

"Are you sure? Have you ever had alcohol before?" She asked.

"Not really. I tried a sip of wine from my mom once when I was a kid." Sarah chuckled and passed me a can. I opened it carefully and took a small sip. It tasted like sewer water.

"Ugh. This stuff is nasty. Why do you guys like it?" They all laughed and looked at me like a child, which made me try some more. "Nope. Still gross."

"You get used to the taste after a while." Sarah said.

"Yeah. Then it starts tasting better." Carlos agreed. I had another sip. It still tasted like sewer water.

"So, what's new with everyone. Give me the drama. I want all the stories!" I said before eating another slice of pizza to get the taste of beer out of my mouth.

"Aw man. You want drama? My little brother almost got arrested." Sarah said exasperated.

"What!" I gasped.

"No way!" Carlos said.

"Yeah, he tried to steal a video game."

"Which one?" Carlos asked.

"The new Grand Theft Auto."

"Aw. I see. That's a hot game nowadays." Carlos replied.

"That's not too bad." Jamie said, to my surprise. "How old is he?"

"He's 12, I think. Ugh. This isn't the first time he tried to steal either. I'm worried he's going to turn into a delinquent."

"Did they call the police on him?" I asked.

"Thankfully, no. He was with his friend. The employee at Game Stop called me and I had to pick him up."

"He's lucky they didn't call the cops on him." Carlos said.

"Seriously. I had to give the assistant manager my number just so he would shut up about it."

"Did you tell your mom?" I asked.

"No. I think I'm just gonnna keep it between me and him. He's going through a hard time. I think he's learned his lesson." We all nodded.

"This kind of thing happens when they go through that age." Jamie said. "The same thing happened with my younger sister, Aisha."

"Really?" I asked, still surprised he seemed so nonchalant over David's theft.

"Yeah. When she was 10, she tried to steal some clothes at the mall. We were both there to hang out with friends. I let her go with her own friends and me and my friends were at the movies. I got a call in the middle of watching Spiderman. She didn't even try to take off the security tags! She just tried to leave the store with it stuffed in her backpack." Jamie said laughing.

"So, what did you do?" I asked.

"Well, I got out of the movie and went to the Limited Too store. I apologized profusely to the manager and made Aisha apologize as well. But she was already crying so I think he felt bad."

"Did you tell your parents about it?" Sarah asked.

"No. My ma was busy working and my dad…he was supposed to be back home but his deployment got extended. I think…that's why she did it. She was just lashing out. You do that…when you're a kid. But I did give her a real talking to – and I threatened to throw away all her toys. That's what really did it." Jamie started laughing and we followed. I forgot Jamie was an older brother. At 3 a.m., we all seemed like independent beings.

"I hope David doesn't pull that shit again."

"I don't think he will." Jamie said reassuringly.

"Man, I wish I had a brother who would cover for me like that…" Carlos said.

"What about Benny?" Jamie asked.

"Most of the time, I feel like I'm covering for him. He's always sneaking out and drinking or smoking. And lately…" Carlos shook his head and crinkled the weak metal can in his fist.

"What?" I asked softly.

"Lately, it doesn't feel like we're brothers. We've been growing apart for a while. We used to be so much closer. But I never see him after Tío…he's always out with his friends – they all pretty much suck. I'm kinda worried about him."

"Have you told him?" Sarah asked. "I mean, have you told him you're worried about him?"

"Nah man. I don't think he'd care. Plus, he's always gone."

"I think he'd care man. If you told him you were worried." Jamie said resolutely. Carlos looked towards the empty pizza box then took another can of beer. I tried to drink mine again. This sip didn't seem as bad as the last.

"I know how you feel. Janice and I used to be super close when we were kids. But then, somewhere along the line we grew apart. She started acting like a mom. God, I hated that.

I wish she was just my sister." Carlos nodded. "She got into medical school recently."

"That's great!" Carlos said. I nodded.

"I bet you'll miss her though." Jamie said. I shrugged.

"I don't know. Sometimes it feels like…she's already left." I stopped to comprehend the moment. I'd never spoken so openly with friends before. With Angela and Tabitha, something always felt missing. But I found that missing piece here, surrounded by new friends that felt like old ones.

"Anyways, tell me something happy!" I said clapping my hands. Sarah, Jamie, and Carlos looked at each other, trying to think of an uplifting story.

"I think…I have good news…" Sarah said. I looked back at her in great expectation. "Well, it could be too soon to tell."

"You can tell us." Carlos said with a smile. Carlos was growing on me. At first, I felt like he was too different from me. But maybe the problem was that we were too similar. He was easily excitable while also deeply sad. I don't think I wanted to be reminded of that part of me, the part lurking in the shadows.

"I think my mom found us a place to stay." My heart sank.

"That's fantastic!" Jamie said. Sarah smiled hesitantly.

"It's my mom's old friend. They used to be super close. She was like an aunt to me when I was growing up. But she moved to Boston a long time ago. My mom said she's coming back with her husband and they're getting a house with room for us to stay, temporarily."

"That's amazing!" Carlos said happily. I stayed silent, unsure of what to say. I was happy for her. My mind was happy for her. But my heart was disappointed. Sarah's leaving. Sarah's leaving me. And I'm still here. I mustered up a smile.

"I'm so happy for you!" I said, trying to move my voice the way it usually did. Sarah looked back at me, catching my disappointment. How were we going to remain friends now?

"We're still going to be friends, Grace." Did she just read my mind?

"Of course." I said.

"No really. Y'all…" She looked back at all of us. "I want us all to stay friends even after we leave this place. I'm serious. I know we've only known each other for a short time but…I don't know. It feels like we've been friends for ages." Carlos and Jamie nodded. Sarah was right.

"I mean, we'll still be going to the same school. So it won't be too hard." I said optimistically.

"Well…" Sarah fiddled with the grass around her, pulling blades out of the ground. "I looked it up, and her house would be in a different school district, down south."

"Like downtown?" I asked.

"Not quite all the way downtown. A little closer than that. It's in Westlake area."

"Oh." Westlake was where the rich people lived.

"But it's not decided for sure. They haven't moved to Austin yet." Sarah said, trying to cover her tracks. I hated myself for feeling bitter. Why couldn't I just be happy for her?

"I hope it works out." Carlos said smiling.

"I actually have similar news." Jamie said. Oh no. Not you too. "My ma got a second interview for a job…It's at a senior home. She has the interview this week. So, it's not set in stone yet. But, I don't know. I'm trying not to get my hopes up. But she seems to think it's gonna happen. So…"

"I hope it works out." I said to Jamie, forcing a smile. He smiled back. Silence settled in the middle of our little circle. Jamie and Sarah seemed to wait to see if Carlos and I had any similar news. Carlos stayed silent. So did I. Umma and Janice haven't told me anything new over the past month. Umma was still trying to find a job she could do with her limited English speaking and arthritis. I suddenly hated the idea of me being the first one here and the last to leave.

Sarah passed me the last beer as a metaphorical peace offering. I couldn't help but smile at the gesture. I opened the can, the crisp popping sound felt good to hear. I moved the can up to my lips.

"Chug. Chug. Chug." Sarah, Jamie, and Carlos chanted in unison. I lifted the can and chugged it all at once. They clapped as quietly as they could at my success.

"You know. It actually doesn't taste too bad." I said laughing.

"Told ya." Sarah said.

"Alright. It's time." Carlos said. "Give us one of your questions." I tilted my head and scratched it as if I was contemplating the solution to E=mc².

"Alrighty. Now, tonight. What category shall it be? Here we have your light-hearted and funny questions, or your deep and heartfelt, or your super deep only thought about at 3 a.m. question." I said like a gameshow host, pointing to imaginary categories in the air. Everyone's faces started looking fuzzy.

"I like the super deep questions." Jamie said to me. The thought of him kissing me entered my mind and I quickly tried to shake it off.

"Ok! Deep. 3 a.m. Let me think." Carlos rubbed his hands together in anticipation. Sarah smiled with her cheeks rosy in the moonlight. A feeling of heavy sadness started to seep into my mind. An image of Appa flashed before me. "How do you know if you've forgiven someone?"

"Aw man." Jamie said.

"Damn. How do you think of this stuff?" Sarah asked.

"I don't know. Just stuff I think about."

"You really do need to be a writer." Sarah said. I smiled. Carlos seemed deep in thought already. But Jamie stepped in first.

"I think – as cliché as it sounds, forgiveness becomes real, or I'd say complete, when you forget about the issue itself. Forgive and forget, you know. If you forgive someone, but later, say you get mad at them again, and you bring up the old issue again – then it's like you haven't actually forgiven them. But when you forgive someone, you gradually forget the wrong they did to you and move on…But I don't know. That's just what I think."

"I like that idea." Sarah said. "But if that's true, I'm not sure if I've forgiven anyone yet. I seem to remember everything. I can't stop remembering things."

"For me, it's the opposite." I said. "I forget so many things. It's like I block it out of my memory. So in my mind, I believe that I've forgiven him. But I've only just forgotten things temporarily. But not thinking about someone doesn't mean I've forgiven them, does it?" I asked, confused by my own thoughts.

"I think, maybe it's a step in the right direction." Carlos said. "I've forgotten a lot of the things my real mom did to me. But just because I've forgotten doesn't mean I forgave her. There's still – I dunno, feelings, that I can't get past."

"Do you feel angry when you think of those things?" I asked.

"Sometimes, I still do get angry." Carlos said staring at the ground.

"See that's the thing." I said. "I'm not even angry anymore. I feel like I've spent so much energy being angry, it's just too tiring now. Now, it's kind of like I don't even care."

"That can be easier." Sarah chimed in. "Not caring takes a lot of weight off you. For me, I just can't seem to stop putting the blame on people. Why I'm here. Why my family's here. It all comes down to my dad and my stepdad. I thought I forgave my real dad a long time ago. But seeing him again made me realize I haven't forgiven him yet." Sarah said, taking a sip of her beer.

Jamie stayed silent. I could see in his face, he was absorbing what we were all saying.

"I think…" Jamie paused and straightened up from his crouched position. "Forgiveness takes a very long time." He hesitated again. "This may make me seem like a terrible person…"

"What is it?" Sarah asked. Jamie looked apprehensive, then let out a deep sigh.

"I know my dad was a great man. He did more than most people will ever accomplish in life. He always wanted to do the right thing, the honorable thing. He protected me, he protected everyone. But…" Jamie looked absently at the lightening sky above him. "But I think I'm angry at him. He's done nothing wrong. I know this. But I still can't seem to forgive him."

None of us seemed surprised by what Jamie said. Carlos patted Jamie's shoulder letting him know it was ok. "Sometimes, I get mad my dad left at all. I wish he quit the Army years ago. I don't know why he stayed. He could've gotten a normal job. Sometimes I feel like he loved being in the Army more than he loved me. If he just had a normal life…he would still be alive."

I was unsure of what to say. Jamie's world seemed so foreign to me. Army. War. Death. My daily life consisted of thoughts about college and making a name for myself. I suddenly felt foolish for worrying about such frivolous things.

"But if your dad had a normal life, do you think you would respect him as much?" Sarah asked unapologetically. I looked at her, taken aback. How could she say something so insensitive? Jamie's eyes met Sarah's. He seemed taken aback as well.

"I'm just saying, the way you talk about your dad Jamie – it's beautiful. You admire him so much. You see him as a hero, and he is a hero." Jamie's surprised face relaxed a little. "I would love to think about my dad in that way. Your dad was a soldier, and I think you love that part of him. He was a defender. I think deep down, that's something you wouldn't want to change."

I was scared to see Jamie's reaction. But something new appeared on his face, he tilted his head to the side and lifted the right side of his mouth into a crooked smile. I could see his dimple.

"Maybe, you're right." Jamie said simply. "Maybe, you're right."

"Damn, Sarah! You've got some balls." Carlos said, relieving the tension. Jamie and I laughed. Things were steady again. Sarah hit her inner thighs with her hands in a V shape that made all of us laugh louder than we were supposed to outside the shelter.

"I've probably got bigger balls than the both of you guys combined." Sarah said. I admired her, in the moment. She spoke her mind, even at the risk of consequence. Carlos downed the last of his beer and we all agreed to wait until the next weekend to meet again. Final exams were coming up. We made a pact to study hard. School seemed much more important to us than it did before coming to Blue Haven. School used to feel like an obstacle. Now, it became a necessity, a way out of ending up at a place like this again.

Night left the sky and we watched in silence as the sun started to rise above the metal chained fence wrapped in thick green leaves and fragile flower petals.

Chapter 37
Jamie

    Sarah's words echoed in my mind that night. Maybe, she was right. Maybe, I wouldn't have respected Dad as much if it weren't for his job. Maybe, I wouldn't have loved him as much either if he weren't fighting the bad guys in whatever country he was in. I tried not to think about Dad too often throughout the day. Thinking about him put my mind and body on pause. I only let myself think about him late at night, when my mind had the time to rest in memories.

    Dad taking Aisha to a father-daughter dance. Dad taking Quinn to the playground. Dad fighting with Ma. Dad trying to win Ma's affections back with a bouquet of yellow daffodils. Dad playing football with me in the backyard.

    Come to think of it, I don't think the love would have changed. My dream was to see Dad retire. Growing up I felt so possessive of him. He had to serve his country, but what about us? What about me? Why did he have to leave me? My heart feels heavy and tired. Tonight, I let the tears fall as I laid in bed.

Sarah's gonna leave soon. Hopefully, I'll get to leave too. But what about Carlos? Grace? Grace. Her sad eyes, when Sarah said she was leaving, are burned in my memory. The way her gaze dropped after I followed Sarah with my own confession. She has to get out of here. God, please. Please help her.

It's been a couple days since our last 3 a.m. meeting. I miss them. It's nice having people I can let it all out with. Jamal has been great, but he can't understand like they do. He's been trying to make things feel normal again, since Dad's funeral. But things don't seem normal still. I wonder how long this feeling of emptiness will last.

After I felt more settled at Blue Haven, I started tutoring again. We needed the money now more than ever. I loved teaching every day after school. Each time I had a lesson, it felt like I got to learn something all over again.

I always tried to hide my love for all things academia – especially around Jamal and DeShawn. They were never all that interested in school. But I've loved learning ever since I was able to help Aisha and Quinn with their schoolwork. Dad always liked it when I helped.

After school, I walked to the Starbucks across the street to tutor several students. My afternoon was fully booked. As I tutored my third student of the evening, Jamal walked in. He winked at me and ordered a Venti Iced Mocha Frappuccino with extra whipped cream and sat in the corner waiting for me.

I finished up an algebra lesson with a confused freshman who was so stressed out he kept on pulling his hair. At the end of the lesson, I showed him how to plug numbers into the calculator to get the right answers. He smiled in relief. As he left, Jamal walked up and took his seat.

"Jamie!" Jamal smiled in a way that made everyone around him instantly happy.

"Sup, Jamal."

"Well, you'd know if you been around! Where the hell have you been?" I reminded myself, he still didn't know about the shelter. To him, it's only been a month or two. To me, the past few months have felt like a lifetime.

"Sorry man. I've been busy." Not revealing anymore. Jamal waited for me to continue.

"Listen. I've been to your house a couple times. Nobody ever answers…" Jamal eyed me, letting me know he knew something was up.

"Oh…yeah. I'm not home much." Jamal was unconvinced yet again. How the hell did he always see right through me?

"You wanna shoot some hoops?" I looked down at my watch. It was almost 8 p.m. I forgot to eat dinner. "Come on man." Jamal looked at me hopefully. I nodded and he drove us to the courts by my old house in my old car. The inside smelt different now. It no longer reminded me of Dad.

We played until both of us were sweating. He won the first game and I won the second. It was the final match. I jumped for a final three-pointer and Jamal slapped the ball out of my hands before I could even land. He dove towards the ball and shot it from the other end of the court, beating me a final time. I sat down completely out of breath and Jamal did a short victory dance moon walk. I smiled in happy exhaustion.

"Alright, since you lost you have to pay a penalty." Jamal said. I stared at him defensively. "Come on man, you know nothing aint free." I smiled. He was right about that.

"Ok. What do I owe you?" I asked. Jamal sat down and rolled the basketball between his legs.

"I want you to tell me the truth." Jamal looked back at me. "How come you're never home? You or your ma, or Aisha and Quinn. What happened?"

I looked at Jamal for a long time. Jamal was a good-looking guy. Far too handsome and charismatic to be hanging out with a guy like me. But he never made me feel inferior. With basketball, with girls, with friends, with money. Jamal was always by my side. Whenever I felt sad or worried about Dad, whenever I got frustrated with Aisha or Quinn, he invited me to play ball. Sometimes he snuck out of his house and came over to mine, just so I could vent to him. Jamal was one of the few people in life, I trusted completely.

"We don't live there anymore." I said.

"What?"

"We moved out…a while back – after the funeral. They

foreclosed our house."

"Who did?"

"I guess…the government? Or real estate people. I'm not really sure how it works. But we had to move out."

"The fuck, Jamie! Why didn't you say anything? Where are y'all staying now?" Jamal asked becoming increasingly worried.

"We're staying somewhere temporarily…" It's not that I didn't trust Jamie. I just didn't want him to know. I didn't want the inevitable pity or concern.

"Where?" Jamal demanded. "You can tell me Jamie. I'm your best friend, right?"

"Of course you are."

"Then why won't you tell me?" Jamal asked, now completely frustrated.

"Because I don't want to be a burden anymore!" I yelled. Jamal looked shocked.

"Burden? What the hell are you talking about Jamie! You're not a burden. And you never were!"

"I am though. I'm always the one with the problem. Whether it was with Dad or money. Your life is always so good and easy. I feel like I'm dragging you down with all of my problems." I couldn't look him in the eye anymore.

"Jamie…" Jamal waited for me to meet his gaze. "Jamie – Do you know why I try so hard with basketball? Why

I'm at the court every single day? Why I'm the first and last one at practice at school?" I nodded resolutely.

"Because you love basketball."

"Hell no! That's not the reason. It's because I have nothing else." I looked back at Jamal confused. "Jamie, you're smart. You get the grades. The respect. Learning comes easy to you. I don't have that. Shit! There's no subject that I'm good at or even love. My parents know that. They see you, or they see my sister Tasha and they bein' proud. But they look at me and basketball, and they just see a no good kid who's got nothing better to do…Jamie I have nothing else to offer…I can't believe you think that *you're* the loser in our friendship. I'm the loser. I've always wanted what you have."

I looked back at Jamal completely stunned. This whole time I was envious of Jamal, he's been envious of me.

"I had no idea…you thought that." Jamal smiled.

"It's alright though. Imma make it to the NBA, then they'll be proud of me." Jamal said back to his enthusiastic smile.

"I've been living in a shelter." Jamal stopped rolling the ball and looked at me. His smile disappeared.

"What?"

"It's not really a shelter. I mean, they call it that but…basically it's a place where people can live temporarily, for free." I was unsure of how to explain Blue Haven to Jamal. It was a shelter, yes. But it wasn't the image everyone, including myself, had already conceived in their mind. "It's kind of like a halfway house." That seemed like better terminology.

"Like for addicts?" Jamal asked.

"No! Not like that. It's a shelter but we each get separate rooms. It's for single moms and their kids…when they're stuck in a bad place financially or physically and have nowhere else to go." I tried to remember Pamela's wording when Ma and I first checked in. I looked back at Jamal. He had tears in his eyes.

"Stop man! See this is why I didn't want to tell you." I said angrily to Jamal. He wiped his face quickly.

"But why didn't…why didn't you ask me for a place to stay?" Jamal's genuine sadness warmed my heart.

"Jamal. When things like this happen, you don't want to tell anyone. You don't want anyone else to know. Plus, my ma thought we'd be staying with our uncle. But that didn't work out and…things just happened."

"What about your grandparents?"

"Ma didn't want to move far away." A few tears fell from Jamal's eyes.

"It's alright man, really! Ma is gonna get a job soon and we'll be able to leave. It's only for a little while."

"But still. Y'all stay at my house!" Jamal said adamantly. "We have room! Tasha's going back to Rice soon. Yo' mom and Quinn and Aisha can stay there. And you can sleep with me in my room." The tears fell freely on Jamal's face, which he tried to wipe away as quickly as possible. I rolled the basketball back to his side with a laugh. He looked at me, angry again. "How could you laugh at a time like this?"

"I've never seen you cry before." I said laughing. Jamal chuckled, wiping his face once more. I stood up and reached my hand towards him. "I promise we're fine. Blue Haven really isn't that bad. And we're gonna leave soon. I promise." Jamal looked back at me, filled with worry.

We parted ways after I made Jamal promise not to tell his parents. He wanted to save us out of the situation. He didn't understand that staying at his place would've made me feel even worse.

"You can't tell anyone. This place is confidential. We're not actually supposed to tell anyone about it. I've only told you because…because you're my best friend."

"Ok man." Jamal finally said reluctantly.

The semester was gearing towards the end. I've finished three of my finals now and I just have my English exam left. We planned to meet up tomorrow night at 3 a.m. to celebrate the end of exam week. In between studying, I couldn't help but want to see Grace. I wish I could call her. I wish I could do more. Mostly, I wish I could just see her outside Blue Haven. A place where things weren't veiled in secrets. Some place normal.

At the shelter, her door was always closed. Everyone's was. Our families had no idea how close we've gotten. If we ever did pass each other in the halls, there was nothing more than a courteous nod since parents and siblings were also around. It was strange. At 3 a.m., we were all friends. But in the afternoon, we were strangers again. There was this unspoken barrier we all carried with us. We knew not to cross it. I've seen Janice once. Aisha said she saw another boy around her age, that must be David. I think I spotted Benny once too.

  I decided to text Sarah for some insider info, hoping I could see Grace outside of Blue Haven, where things could be normal. I found out Grace volunteered at the city library. This was my way in! Ditching Starbucks, I took to the city bus to the library and texted today's students to meet me in the teen section. I wondered if I could run into Grace, casually.

  I scoped the first floor for Grace, but she was nowhere to be seen. I resigned to a private study room with a clear door where I tutored a sixth grader who had problems with reading and writing. Eva and I went over the fundamentals. English was her second language. She grew up speaking Spanish before moving to Texas a year ago. I tried to help her the best I could. Then I managed to explain a few bits in Spanish, after remembering pieces from my 8th grade textbook. Her face lit up for the first time.

  After I finished my lesson with Eva, I waited for my second student. I looked behind me. A mom and her daughter were looking at the teen literature section. A little to the right, a few elderly women were using the public computers. Come on. Grace, where are you? Maybe I should text her. I looked down at my phone, then decided not to.

When I looked back up, the mom and teenager left the aisle in front of me. A cart stacked with books appeared. Behind it, someone was waving at me. I squinted my eyes to see better. It was Grace! She was waving at me. I smiled back and waved, not knowing if I should get up and go greet her. Grace looked around to see if the coast was clear. She rolled her cart in my direction and left it behind as she discreetly entered my study room.

"What are you doing here?" Grace asked excitedly.

"I'm tutoring kids here today." I said, trying not to get too giddy. Remember Jamie, act casual. Play it cool, like Jamal said.

"Oh nice! I volunteer here." Grace said.

"Wow, what a coincidence!" I tried to act surprised.

"Oh my God, Jamie." Grace let out a dramatic sigh. "I'm so sick of repeating the alphabet in my mind." She laughed pointing at the pile of books left outside.

"Yeah, I bet that sucks."

"At a certain point you think I wouldn't have to." Grace laughed at herself. "But all the books are mixed up like all the time so I keep having to remind myself."

"Hey, if you need stuff for your resume, you should do tutoring instead!" I suggested.

"Man, I don't have the patience for it. Plus, I need volunteer hours and everywhere else is full of volunteers already." I nodded. Grace's face was bright. Her hair was tied up in a messy bun. She blew a few stray strands away from her eyes and my heart almost stopped beating. "So when's your next student coming?"

"He should be here in about 10 minutes."

"Good! That gives us some time." Grace said with a smile. "How are you doing on finals?"

"I think I did alright."

"That probably means you did great." Grace laughed.

"No, no." I shook my head. "I think I really did just – mediocre. I'm sure *you* did great though."

"Aw man, that chemistry final shook me to my very core. My very core!" Grace said lifting a fist into the air dramatically. "It was so freaking hard! I'll never understand it. But I think I did well on my english and history exams."

"Do you just have math left then?"

"I took my statistics exam yesterday so I just have a few electives left. But those are easy. I just have to sight read something in choir and orchestra."

"I didn't know you were in orchestra!" I said. Grace never even mentioned it.

"Oh yeah. I play cello, guitar too, sometimes the piano, but I'm really not that good."

"I want to hear you play!" I said, feeling the giddiness take over.

Grace played an imaginary piano in front of her. I didn't realize how goofy she could be. It made me happy to see her this way, like a normal teenager.

"What do you think?" She asked.

"Amazing!" I smiled. Suddenly, my phone rang. It was Ma. Grace motioned for me to take it.

"Don't leave! This'll just be a sec." Grace smiled and waited. "Ma?"

"Jamie! Jamie! You won't believe it Jamie!" Ma said, her voice high-pitched and loud.

"Ma, what is it? Is something wrong?"

"No nothing's wrong baby. Things are right! I got the job!" Ma screamed.

"What! No way! Are you serious! Ma! That's great!" I said, my voice now becoming as loud and ecstatic as hers.

"Isn't it! Praise the Lord, Jamie. He's heard our prayers. We'll get to leave the shelter soon baby. I promise! I'm going to apply for a new apartment today. I'm gonna go right now. Just you wait Jamie. Things are looking up again!" I tried to hold in tears of joy. Grace was waiting for me with a great big smile.

"That's great! Hey! I'll talk to you later Ma, I'm with a – a student."

"Ok baby. I'll see you tonight. Hallelujah!" Ma hung up and my soul was still singing.

"Did your mom get the job?" Grace asked.

"She did!" Grace squealed and jumped on me with a hug. I wrapped my arms around her too. My heart started pounding. Grace moved back a little and we looked into each other's eyes. I wondered if I should kiss her again. But then, someone knocked on the door. It was my next student. You've got to be kidding me! Of all the bad timings in the world.

"I'll see you later, Jamie." Grace said, leaving the room before I could say goodbye.

Chapter 38

Carlos

Sometimes I forget where I am. I wake up thinking I've been kidnapped, but then I realize I'm still at the shelter. It's been weeks now. I've rarely seen Benny. Tía has been taking extra shifts at the restaurant. When I'm not with her, I'm at our room at Blue Haven.

She hasn't talked about Tío since he died. Benny hasn't either. Sometimes, it feels like he never existed. Like we're living in a parallel universe where Benny is no longer someone who smiles easily and Tía is no longer…Tía.

I haven't seen Benny at school for the past few days. I tried to check and see if he was with his crew, but they weren't at school either. I don't know what to do. I can't let Tía know. She's working all the time. Even after the surgery, she never really got time to recover. Sometimes I notice the scar on her chest when she's closing up the restaurant.

She's resorted to doing two people's jobs. She used to be the cook in charge. Now, she mops the floors and cleans all the tables before the restaurant opens and after the restaurant closes, in addition to cooking food for hundreds of people every day. She doesn't cook for me and Benny anymore. Instead, she sneaks back styrofoam boxes of people's leftovers from the restaurant. I try not to notice the bite marks.

Sometimes I want to talk to her about Tío. I miss him. I think we all do. But I'm worried if I tell her, it'll make her sad again. I miss Tío. I miss his smile. I miss the sound of his voice. I miss working with him at the shop. I miss him teaching me about cars. I miss the way he'd tease me about girls. I just miss Tío. I miss our home, the place I grew up over the last decade. I miss the smell of it and the sound of Friday fiestas.

I miss Luis too. I talked to him on the phone and he kept on telling me how sorry he was. He seemed to feel guilty when I asked him how he was doing. He and his mom were doing well. I haven't called him since moving into Blue Haven.

The first night at the shelter, Benny fell asleep instantly. That, or he laid in bed with his eyes closed. I tried not to cry. This place was better than Tía's car or Abuelo and Abuela's house. I thought Tía would cry, like at the funeral or when Abuelo and Abuela disowned her. But she didn't cry. She didn't even have her eyes closed. I reached over and put my hand on Tía's stiff, cold arm. For a split second, I thought she was dead. But my touch seemed to awake Tía from her stupor.

"Sí, Carlos?" She whispered to me.

"Are you ok?" I wanted to comfort her, or maybe I wanted her to comfort me.

"Sí. Go back to sleep, mijo." Tía said quietly.

"I can't…I keep thinking about…Tío." Saying it out loud filled me with longing.

"…I think about him too." Tía said, lying on her back and looking blankly at the popcorn ceiling.

"Do you miss him?" I asked Tía a little scared. I cried every night at Abuelo's house, but Tía always seemed silent, emotionless.

"I do miss him. So much that if I let myself think about your Tío, I'll die." I looked away from Tía and tried not to cry again. She reached out to me this time and rubbed my cheek.

"I'm sorry I didn't do anything when Abuelo and Abuela yelled at you." I said, trying to hold back my guilty sobs.

"Mijo…you don't have to apologize. That's not your job. You're just a kid."

"I wish I was more like Benny. He stood up for you. He helped."

"You and Benny are different people. I don't expect you to act the same way." Tía's words reassured me, but I could feel the grief in her words.

"Listen, Carlos. I don't want you to hate your abuelo and abuela."

"But I do. I hate them!" I said to the ceiling. Tía waited for my angry breathing to steady before speaking again.

"People handle death differently. Your abuelo and abuela don't actually hate me…they just miss their son. They'll come around one day."

"But what about you?"

"What do you mean?"

"Nothing." I said quickly, trying to cover up my mistake. Tía turned to look at me. I turned my head away to Benny's side of the bed again.

"Mijo, things aren't the same now." I heard the gentleness in Tía's words. "I can't be the woman I was before who could depend on your Tío for things. Right now, my only mission is to make enough money so we can leave this place. I'm sorry I've been distant…I've been a bad mom to you, sí?"

"No. No you haven't." I said.

"If I stop to think of Juan…" Tía sharply inhaled. "I won't be able to work. I won't be able to do a thing. Sadness is a gift I can't afford right now."

Tía's words floated in the space between us. Sadness is a gift. How could sadness be a gift? If it was, I didn't want it.

It's been an exhausting day of exams. But I'm pretty sure I passed my English and geometry tests. Since finals week began, I decided to go back to the shelter after school to study rather than stopping by the restaurant. Maybe if I studied and got good grades, Tía would be happier. Maybe, I could go to college like she wanted.

I started studying for my history final on my bed until a stranger barged into my room. He was reaching for Benny's things in the closet. Without thinking, I tackled the shaggy dude trying to steal Benny's Gameboy and clothes.

"Carlos! Carlos! It's me!"

"How do you know my name?" I shouted.

"It's me Benny!" The dude shouted back at me. But it couldn't be. How could he have changed so much in such a short time? Benny was always on the sturdier side. But now, his muscular frame had shrunk at least three sizes down. His face was so much thinner. I could see the outline of his cheekbones. He'd also grown a beard and had a slightly crazed look in his eyes.

"Hola." Benny said.

"Where the hell have you been?"

"What do you mean. I've been here?"

"No. You haven't." I walked up to Benny and yanked the backpack out of his hand.

"Give me back my bag!" Benny shouted. I could see his jagged collar bone poking out of his yellowed white t-shirt.

"No. Not until you tell me where you've been. I've barely seen you since Tío died! Where the hell have you been!"

"Fine. I've been working." Benny sat on the bed.

"Working? Doing what?"

"None of your business." Benny lunged towards me swinging his fist. I threw the backpack at him in a panic. It fell to the floor and little bulks of marijuana wrapped in plastic wrap spilled out. Benny quickly knelt down and shoved them back into his backpack.

"Are you dealing weed?" I asked Benny.

"No."

"Bullshit. Tell me the truth!" I shouted at him and blocked his thin, boney frame as he tried to leave. Benny stepped back a bit, his face wild and angry.

"Ok. You wanna know the truth, Carlos? I am dealing weed." Benny's bluntness shocked me. "Do you know how much Mom makes at her job?" I shook my head no. "She makes $13 an hour. How much longer do you think it's gonna take for us to get out of here with her salary alone? And since you don't do shit, I've gotta do something to help the family." Benny tried to push me aside and reach for the doorknob.

"The fuck's the matter with you, Benny! Do you know what they'll do if they find out? They'll kick us out! Then we'll really have nowhere else to go."

"It doesn't matter." Benny said, looking back towards me.

"What? Why not?"

"Cause by then I'll have enough money for us to leave."

"…You're gonna get caught Benny. Then they're gonna send you to jail! Do you really wanna ruin Tía's life?"

"No. I'm not gonna get caught. I'm too smart for that."

"You will get caught. And then Tía will have to lose another person in the family." Benny stopped. It seemed like he was going to say something again. But then he pushed me so hard I fell on the bed. I didn't think he had it in him. He got out the door and left.

I punched my fists into the mattress. What the hell was Benny thinking? He was gonna get caught! Then get thrown in jail. How the hell were we gonna bail him out then? What if this is all Benny was now? A drug dealer. I thought he only smoked weed at parties. That's what he said. Now he's dealing. Tío. Tío please. What should I do Tío?

I laid in bed and stared at the ceiling. Benny was right. Not about the drugs, but he was right when he said I don't do shit. I haven't done anything to help Tía. Truth is, I didn't do much for Tío either, back when he was alive. My eyes started to sting with tears. I'm sorry Tío. But what can I do?

Suddenly, the image of mine and Benny's car flashed in my mind. Benny and I first offered to sell it while we were visiting Tía at the hospital during her chemotherapy. Tía smiled, saying we should keep it. I asked Tío about it too. He said since the car was over 12 years old, we wouldn't be able to make much money off of it. But at this point, any money could help. Right, Tío? Benny doesn't even use it anymore. I'm the only one who uses it to drive to school. But I could just take the bus.

But how do I even sell a car? Ebay? Craigslist? Maybe Jamie would know. He's smart. He seems to know a lot. But maybe, we're not close enough yet. I wrote out a text and deleted it. Then I tried again and deleted it again. After a couple minutes, I finally worked up the nerve to press send. Maybe, we were friends now. Maybe, he'd want to help.

I sat up and waited nervously for a reply. Shit. It's not like I'm asking him out on a date. Why am I so nervous? A few minutes passed and my phone buzzed.

"Hey Carlos! Sure I can help you sell your car. Wanna meet me at the library?"

Yes! I left my room at Blue Haven and drove to the city library. Jamie was sitting in a room with a see-through door, his back facing the rows of books out in the main area. I could tell it was him by his buzz cut and wide shoulders. I lightly knocked on the door. Jamie turned towards me with a smile.

"Carlos! My man!" Jamie opened the door and welcomed me into the cramped study space. He seemed happy to see me. Maybe, I wasn't being such a nuisance. Driving over to the library, I thought it would feel uncomfortable, hanging out one-on-one. But Jamie's warm welcome quickly put me at ease.

"Hi, Jamie!"

"So you wanna sell your car, huh?"

"Yeah." Jamie nodded, waiting for more info. I didn't know what to say next.

"So what kinda car is it?" Jamie asked, filling in the looming silence.

"It's uh, a Chrysler. It's silver!" I said nervously.

"Shit. They still make those?" Jamie said leaning back into his chair, relaxed.

"Hey man. It's a good car. She served me well."

"She? Oh, so your car's a girl then?" Jamie smirked.

"Yeah. She's about the only date I can get." Jamie and I laughed.

"You got any pics?"

I took out my phone and showed Jamie some of the photos I took in the library parking lot before walking in. He didn't seem too impressed. Maybe Tío was right.

"You don't think I can sell her, do you?" I asked.

"Nah man. You can but…how old is it?"

"1996." Jamie looked up at me, wide-eyed and amused.

"Damn. How'd you keep her alive this long?"

"You know…" I shrugged. "I got that magic touch." Jamie burst out laughing. It was funny seeing him laugh. At 3 a.m., he seemed much more serious than he did now. Here in the library, Jamie seemed like just a normal dude.

"Could you put it online for me?"

Jamie turned to his laptop. "So I don't think you'll be getting any bids on Ebay. I'll put it up on Craiglist for you. But to be honest, I don't think you'll get more than a couple grand." Jamie said, tilting his head towards me.

"That's fine." I said as Jamie typed something quickly on his computer. He took my phone and sent the images to his email. Within a couple minutes, my car was posted for sale online.

"Now, we wait." Jamie said, leaning back in his chair with his hands resting behind his head.

"How long?"

"It may take a few hours. Maybe a few days. I set the contact number as your phone so once people are interested, they'll text you."

"Great. Thanks Jamie."

"No worries, man. Why'd you want to sell your car anyways?"

I looked at Jamie and blinked a few times. I wondered how much I could share. I didn't want people to know about Benny.

"My aunt…she-uh, has a lot of medical bills from her surgery."

"Oh." Jamie's face turned serious. "I'm sorry, man. She's feeling ok now though, right?"

I nodded and Jamie's face lightened up a bit. Even with him sitting right next to me, I couldn't help but get sucked in by my thoughts. Tía. Benny.

"Hey. How about we take your car on one last ride?" Jamie said.

"Don't you have to study?"

"Nah. I'm pretty much done here."

Jamie and I got in my car. It was the first time having a friend, other than Luis, sit on my passenger side. I started driving randomly through the neighborhood, up and down the suburban pathways. Then I drove by a few random stores, a Ross, a Walmart, a JCPenny.

"Man, this isn't a joyride." Jamie said turning to me.

"Then where should we go?"

"I got an idea. Mind if I drive?" Jamie and I switched spots. He drove to a neighborhood I've never been to. The houses looked a little cleaner than the ones from where I used to live. Jamie was also a much better driver than me. Usually, whenever I stopped at a stop sign, I jerked forward in my seat. But with Jamie driving, it was smooth sailing.

"Where are we?" I asked. Jamie parked in a large, abandoned lot behind what used to be a Target.

"This place closed down years ago, and they never replaced it. So we should be safe."

"Safe for what?" Jamie smiled, then he slammed the gas pedal. My engine made a roaring sound I didn't even know was possible. Then he spun the steering wheel to the right and I felt my body swerve. A few seconds later, he stopped and swerved the wheel to the left and my body flung to the other side. Jamie was driving donuts with a ginormous smile on his face.

"Oh shit! Jamie!" I shouted. He laughed as we flung in circles.

"Wooooooo!" Jamie yelled, opening his car window. Some of the smoke from outside seeped in. For a moment, my body felt lighter.

"Do it again!" This time, Jamie spun in a wider circle and I couldn't help but start laughing. The tires screeched on the cement. After a few more, Jamie slowed down, eventually going into park.

"Man! That was some Fast and Furious type shit." I said, chock-full of adrenaline. "How'd you learn how to drive like that?"

"My friend, Jamal, showed me how once." Jamie said panting. We laughed while trying to catch our breath.

"Man, all this time I thought you was a nerd." He punched my shoulder, laughing. The smoke outside started to dissolve along with the smell of burnt pavement. It was almost night. Suddenly, I dreaded the thought of going back to Blue Haven with nobody in my room but me.

"I'm sorry about your uncle." Jamie said quietly. I turned to look at him. "What was he like?"

Nobody asked me that before. At school, people always just felt bad for me that he died. This time, sitting next to Jamie, I couldn't help but smile at the thought of Tío.

Chapter 39

Sarah

After the SATs, I didn't have much left in me to study for finals. My eyes glazed over Kafka's The Metamorphosis as I tried to finish the book before my essay test. *"As Gregor Samsa awoke one morning from uneasy dreams he found himself transformed in his bed into a gigantic insect."* Shit. I know how you feel Gregor. A giant insect. A bug. In the midst of reading, Mom got a call and her enormously loud ringtone made both of us jump.

"Hello?...Really!...Oh my God! That is so great…Ok. I'll see you tomorrow at the airport." Mom looked at me wide-eyed like a child. I looked back in subdued anticipation. "It's happening Sarah. Kim and her husband are flying to Austin tomorrow! I'm going to pick her up in the morning."

All I could do was nod. While my heart wanted to jump in relief and joy, my mind was telling me to hold it. Hold it in.

Nothing could be this easy. Nothing could be this simple. But I wanted to believe. I wanted to believe that this was real.

Mom started packing David's things. I sat on the bed, motionless. Then, she started packing my things too. Could this be the end? I laid on our bed, unsure if it would be the last time. How long has it been? A month? Two months? Maybe more. The days are sewn together, one after the next, with no distinction in between. But I remember my first moments, feeling totally worn and lifeless. I remember seeing Grace, then Jamie, then Carlos. I remember laughing with Grace on the swings. I remember laughing with all of them. How could I just leave while they were all still here? But leaving was the goal, right? Leaving is the goal. We're leaving tomorrow? We're leaving tomorrow. We are leaving.

I fell asleep to the words of Kafka. *"Was he an animal, that music could move him so? He felt as if the way to the unknown nourishment he longed for were coming to light."* When I woke up, a group of suitcases were piled by the door. Mom was putting on make-up in front of the scratched-up mirror. Was she up all night? Could this be it or was it all a dream?

"Get ready to go, Sarah. I'll have to drop David off at school a little early so I can pick up Kim and her husband."

David was still asleep. I turned to him and gently shook him awake. David sat up as if he just heard a bullhorn. His hair and face were in a disarray upon seeing our things packed.

"Are we leaving?" I nodded slowly. My lack of enthusiasm must have confused him, because he looked to Mom for confirmation.

"Yes, honey! Today's our last day."

"Yes!" David stood up and passed by me. He gave Mom a high five on the way to the bathroom. Mom saw me from the mirror. She came to sit by me in between putting on mascara.

"Sarah. It's gonna be ok. We are leaving. It's a good thing!" Mom said with an energetic smile. I nodded again. My mind was fuzzy. My body felt heavy, unable to move.

"Are we really going?" Mom's face of happiness melted into amused concern.

"Yes, honey. We're leaving." Mom gave me a hug. The warmth of her body seemed to give me some movement. "You should say goodbye to your friends today." Mom said with a wink. I looked back at her confused.

Did she know? Did Mom know this whole time? I tried to hide it from her. I didn't think she would take it well, just like Grace's mom. But it looked like she knew this whole time. Slowly, I got up and got ready for school. I put on a loose-fitting tie dye t-shirt I made during theatre camp, four summers ago, and some light-wash jeans. I tied my tangled hair into a long ponytail.

Mom's words kept repeating in my mind. *You should say goodbye to your friends today.* Goodbye. How does one say goodbye? I sat in my car about to drive to school, then opened up our 3 a.m. group chat.

"Y'all! I know we're not supposed to meet until the end of this week. But could we meet tonight! I've got big news."

I sent the text and waited to the sound of Lady Gaga's Pokerface on the radio.

"Works for me." -Jamie

"Me 🫠." -Carlos

"Let's do it! 3 a.m. tonight. I'll be there!" -Grace

Today at school I managed to complete three out of four of my remaining finals. My literature prompt was an open-ended question, *Did Gregro Sama really turn into an insect or was it purely a symbol?* My response: *There's nothing more real than the feeling of being unworthy of love.* Not sure if I answered the question but I went with it. This was followed by an AP U.S. History final about the founding fathers (none of which were female, of course). Then to finish the day was a brutal AP Human Anatomy exam.

After the school day was over, I debated whether or not I should skip my counselor visit. The last appointment wasn't at all pleasant. But I had to figure out a few things for the sake of UCLA.

"So, what are your top three choices for university?" She asked, wearing a black turtleneck that was too hot for May in Texas.

"Well, nowadays I really just want to go to UCLA."

"You need to widen your search. Not everyone gets into their dream school." She said looking me up and down.

"Yeah. I know. I was just wondering…does it look better to take all AP classes my senior year and get an A- or two, or it is it better for me to take maybe just a couple of AP classes and get straight A's." She blinked a few times then stared down at my record.

"Well, let's see here. It looks like you've taken almost all AP classes this year and have a 3.9 GPA. I don't see why you can't do the same next year?"

"Yeah…it was just, really hard to keep that up this year." She stared back at me and I felt the urge to get up and leave again.

"Colleges don't like seeing students slack off during their senior year. It shows a decline. That you're not a serious student." I couldn't help but scoff.

"I think I did alright."

"Yes, well. You did…good." Who the hell does this woman think she is?

"Ok I think I have my answer. I gotta go now." I stood up and left before I could hear her fake goodbye. As I left the cluster of counselor offices, I caught a glimpse of another student leaving happily from the room across mine. The counselor was patting him on the back and the student was smiling. Shit. I got assigned the wrong counselor. I left in a hurry, after feeling my phone vibrate repeatedly in my pocket. On the way out, I heard the sound of a cold slap on the floor. I turned around to see the student had tripped and dropped a pile of papers. I paused, then decided to head over and hand back a paper that had migrated a few feet away from him. I picked it up and noticed the Harvard logo.

"Here you go."

"Thanks." He said, lifting his eyes in my direction.

"No problem."

"I'll see you tonight, right?" He asked. I looked at him for the first time as we both stood back up. A big smile was on his face.

"Oh shit! Hey Jamie!" I said a bit too loudly. My counselor made a shushing noise and I flicked her off without her seeing. Jamie laughed as we started walking down the crowded hall together.

"Man, you got stuck with Ms. Vickers? She's the Nazi counselor." Jamie said.

"What? No freaking way! Yeah, she's the worst."

"Yeah, I lucked out with Mr. Anders. He's really nice."

"Looks like it. Were you guys working on college apps?" I asked. Jamie nodded. "So you're really gonna be a Harvard man then?"

"Nah. I don't know. I've narrowed it down to eight schools. Most of them are in Texas. But basically, whichever is cheapest I'll end up going to." Jamie explained.

"I bet you'll get into all of them." I said. Jamie shook his head with an embarrassed smile. If it were anyone else, I wouldn't have believed his rebuttal. But with Jamie, I did. He was humble. This whole time of knowing him, I only heard about his grades or class rank from somebody else. Not once did he brag about being ranked second in our entire class. He never even mentioned it.

"Hey! By the way – how'd it go with Grace? Did you end up seeing her at the library the other day?" I decided to leave out the part where I asked whether he confessed his love to her yet. It was clear Jamie was crazy about her. The way he looked at her was completely different from the way he looked at me or Carlos.

"Yeah I did!" Jamie said. "We had a…nice talk." Jamie looked down and I couldn't help but smile at his bashfulness.

"I could ask her, you know." Jamie looked at me a bit befuddled. "How she feels about you-"

"Oh no. Please don't." Jamie said, then coughed. "I mean. I don't, I uh…"

"It's ok." I said patting his shoulder. "I won't say a thing."

"Thanks." Jamie's face looked relieved. "What about you? Are you seeing anyone? Do you have a boyfriend?" The question caught me off guard. I thought about Tyler then quickly pushed the image out of my mind.

"Nope! Just me. Hey, need a ride?" I asked, keys in hand.

"Nah. Thanks though! My boy, Jamal's coming." We waved goodbye as I headed towards my car. It was funny seeing Jamie at school. At Blue Haven, he didn't really seem like another student. Sometimes I forgot we went to the same high school. I guess it was easy to slip pass each other though, our junior class alone had nearly 800 students.

After getting into my car, I took out my phone and was affronted by seven texts from Mom.

"Hey Sarah!

I need you to pick up David from school today.

Then drive to Kim's new house.

I've texted you the address.

Wait, I didn't! Here it is: 4821 New Hope Drive.

Love you!

From Mom."

The last text made me smile. Just in case I couldn't figure it out, Mom always ended the conversation with her signature. So, this was it. It was really happening. I buckled my seat belt and drove to David's school first. He had an enormous smile on his face as he walked towards my car. It looked like he grew three inches. His hair got so long, it was slightly covering his eyes. His shoes looked old and dirty.

"You need a haircut." I told David as he sat in the passenger side.

"Mom can give me one, at Kim's house!" David was buzzing. The life in his voice made me smile despite my apprehensions. I typed in Kim's address. It was 40 minutes away, an hour with traffic. I took Mopac highway down south and we waited for ages, huddled in rush hour traffic like a beehive. David pressed the buttons of my radio, changing the station every few seconds. This time, it didn't bother me. Actually, it was a welcome distraction. David landed on Use Somebody by Kings of Leon.

"I've been roaming around, always looking down at all I see. Painted faces, fill the places I can't reach. You know that I could use somebody."

"How come you're not excited?" David asked during a guitar solo. I looked back at him, he was wearing the same Dallas Cowboys t-shirt he wore yesterday.

"I am."

"...Doesn't seem like it." David said and opened up his window. I pointed my AC fans in his direction and he closed the window.

"I don't know. How do we know if we can trust Kim?" I asked, staring at the endless row of cars in front of us. Where the hell was this exit?

"She's Mom's best friend right?" David asked.

"But they haven't seen each other in years."

"But they're friends."

"Friendships can change."

We drove the rest of the way in silence. I got onto highway 360 and we were transported into another world. Rolling hills. Crystal blue lake. I drove past Lake Austin Prep School. I used to make fun of the rich kids that went there. Turned left. Turned right. Travelled down a few pristine roads. I parked the car outside a house that seemed far too big for just a married couple. It was several stories of white stone topped off with a Spanish-style orange tiled roof. It looked like a house from the movies. The front lawn was as big as a Walmart Supercenter parking lot.

"Holy shit." David said.

"Don't cuss in front of them. They might kick us out if we're not careful." David ran out the car door before I could finish reprimanding him. He rang the doorbell then knocked on the door about seventy times. A woman answered. Her skin was pale and her hair was a striking black. Her eyes were an emerald green that seemed unreal. She was wearing a pearl necklace, a simple grey shirt and black jeans. She was one of the most beautiful people I'd ever seen – a cross between Jennifer Connelly and Angelina Jolie.

"David!" The woman exclaimed.

"Aunt Kim?" David asked.

"Yup, that's me."

"Nice house." David ran inside to look around and Kim laughed. She seemed different than how I remembered her. More refined, less approachable. An image flashed in my mind of when Kim sat me on her lap and showed me how to make shadow puppets with my hands. *They will fight off the monsters at night*," she used to say whenever I got scared to go to sleep.

"Hi Sarah! Long time no see!" Kim greeted me enthusiastically. I recognized her voice – airy, deep, and clear.

"Hi."

"Sarah, come on!" Mom appeared and motioned me inside. Kim's husband started giving David and me a tour. We walked through the spacious living room, a gym, a huge kitchen, and an even bigger dining room. They even had a home theater and another living room on the second and third floors. I tried not to gasp at every turn. How were we allowed to stay here?

Kim's husband, Jonathan, had a friendly aura. He was tall and his hair was highlighted with a few greys. But his face looked young and kind. He looked like the type of guy that went rock climbing and paddle boarding for fun.

Jonathan and Kim showed us our rooms. I was shocked to see we each got our own. David's was already stocked with video games. Mom's had a vase filled with flowers. Mine had some clothes in the closet already.

"Oh, I think you left these here." I told Kim. She shook her head.

"We got those for you. Just a little welcoming present."

"No. I don't want it." I said, quickly releasing my hands from the soft fabrics. Mom's face became stern.

"Sarah, where are your manners?" Mom said.

"No, no! That's fine, Sarah." Kim said. "You don't have to wear them. I wasn't sure what you preferred so I just bought some basic stuff."

"Sorry, I didn't mean to…This just feels like too much."

"Yeah, Kim. This really is too much." Mom talked to Kim while I started touching the clothes again. They were all so soft, delicate. I checked the labels. One was from Philip Lim, another Michael Kors, and another Burberry. Some still had the price tags on. I checked a cashmere cardigan and it was $108. My jaw dropped. I felt unworthy to wear any of it.

"Nonsense." Kim said leaning on the doorway, looking over at me with a smile. "Well, I'll let you guys settle in. Then we can have dinner in a bit."

"Yeah! We made paella!" Jonathan announced happily.

I sat on the queen-sized bed with floral sheets. There were three water bottles waiting for me already on my nightstand, along with an unused Jo Malone candle, and a copy of Steinbeck's Of Mice and Men. I laid down and fell asleep within seconds. I dreamt of swimming, then flying, then falling. I woke up when the sky was still sleeping. I checked my phone. Shit. How was it already 11 p.m.? My stomach grumbled.

I carefully made my way into the hall, walked down a flight of stairs. I passed by Mom's room. She was already asleep. I guess she quit her cleaning job. At Blue Haven she would've been getting ready to go to work right now. I made my way down another staircase and through the living room, around to the kitchen. I opened the gigantic fridge and looked for something I could eat quickly and quietly.

"We saved some paella for you." I gasped and slammed the refrigerator door closed. "Sorry. Didn't mean to scare ya." It was Kim. The glow off her laptop illuminated her striking face.

She was sitting at the dining table, surrounded by a sea of large graph papers and carboard boxes behind her.

"Sorry! I was just hungry." I said, frozen.

"Oh, no worries. Here, I'll get it for you." Kim turned the kitchen light on, then walked up to the fridge in her bare feet and silk pajamas. She filled a plate with food, then put it in the microwave.

"We didn't want to wake you. You were sleeping so deeply – you couldn't even hear us knocking on the door." Kim smiled.

"Sorry."

"No need to be sorry." Kim smiled and her eyes rounded on the bottom like a sunrise. The microwave beeped and I got my plate before Kim could. We sat at the table together and Kim started organizing her giant graph papers.

"What's this for?" I asked.

"My work." I saw a sketch with straight lines and organized boxes.

"What do you do?"

"I'm an architect." Kim sat down and took a sip of coffee from a mug that looked like a prescription pill bottle. "Oh, this is Jonathan's. He's a pharmaceutical rep and got it at a convention. I forget that it looks like I'm swallowing a giant bottle of pills whenever I use it."

"You guys must make a lot of money." I said, before realizing I just announced my thoughts out loud. Kim belted a laugh.

"We do alright. I hear you're applying to colleges in the fall. Do you know what you want to study?"

"Well, I think I want to apply to schools in California and maybe New York and Chicago." Kim shook her head.

"Not where, do you know *what* you want to study?" I looked back at her with a blank stare. All this time, I only thought about going to a city far away. I hadn't thought about what I wanted to study for the next four years and do for the rest of my life. I never had the time.

"I'm not sure. I never gave it a lot of thought…" I carefully gathered a spoonful of paella. The rice was red and it was sprinkled with yellow bell peppers, green peas, scallops, and shrimps that still had the heads attached.

"It's alright. Gosh, when I went to school, I probably changed my major 10 times, at least!" Kim put down a ruler and drew some more lines.

"Are you designing a house?" I asked with food in my mouth. Turns out I was too hungry for table manners. Kim smiled.

"I am. A community of houses actually, I'm trying to see how they can all look nice together." I chowed down more paella. The taste of what I assumed to be a scallop melted in my mouth. It was completely new and delicious.

"Do you like your job?" I liked hearing Kim's voice.

"I do. Except for the times it keeps me up at night. Architecture is not for those who need sleep." Kim jotted numbers and apostrophes in her leather bound notebook.

"What kind of things do you learn if you major in architecture?" Kim stopped writing and looked at me, grinning.

"Well, you learn a lot of things. There's math and engineering, but there's also art and design. I think it's perfect for people who like to think logically but also have a creative side." I nodded and finished the last of my warm meal. I finished eating before the steam even stopped rising from my plate.

"Thank you for letting us stay here." I wanted to give Kim a hug. I wanted to tell her that she saved our lives. Kim looked up from her notebook and a hint of sadness seemed to wash over her.

"I'm just sorry I couldn't come sooner…" I looked back at her in confusion. "Your mom, she told me where y'all were staying." My body transitioned into high alert. We were outed. Mom told her. Kim sensed the panic inside me. "Jonathan doesn't know. Your mom told me a few hours ago while we were catching up in her room."

"Oh." A brief silence took over the dinner table.

"I want you to know Sarah, that you don't have to worry anymore. You, your mom, David. You all can live with us for as long as you need to. Heck! Y'all can move in permanently if you want. I already told your mom to stay with us forever but she's set on saving up for a home for you and David. Your mom is like a sister to me. She's helped me so much through the years. She helped me…after I had a miscarriage. That was such a dark time for me." Kim choked on her words a bit.

"I…I didn't want to live at that point. I got divorced soon after which only made things worse. I felt like I was on the verge of collapsing. But your mom, bless her soul, your mom helped keep me together. She fed me. She let me stay with her when I lost the house in the divorce. You're probably too young to remember. I lived with you guys for a few months when you were young." I suddenly recalled Kim sleeping in a twin bed next to mine in my childhood room.

"Eventually I went back to school – finished my undergraduate degree. Then I got a graduate degree and a new job in Boston – where I met Jonathan. Your mom was the only one who stuck by me that whole time. She believed I could make something of myself. She was the one who was there for me when nobody else was…" I looked back at Kim who had tears in her eyes. Mom never told me what she did for Kim.

"I've already talked to Jonathan. He already loves your mom for what she did for me. And he has absolutely no problem with the three of you living with us. Y'all can stay for as long as you want."

Tears started falling down my cheeks and dropping onto my rice stained plate. I tried to wipe them away before they flooded onto the table. An immense heaviness that was on my shoulders seemed to disappear all at once. We were finally safe. No more worrying about what came next. No more having to figure out a way to survive. We were free.

I wanted to express just how much Kim saved our lives. How much her simple offer changed everything. How much it meant now that we no longer had to dig our way out. But I didn't know how. No combination of words accurately portrayed the gravity of what I was feeling. So, then I just said the only thing I could think of.

"Thank you."

Chapter 40
Carlos

I sat on the bare mattress, still high on excitement from my joyride with Jamie. But as soon as I looked around my empty room, I was quickly reminded of Benny. How could things have changed so quickly? He was a complete and utter stranger to me now.

I turned on the TV trying to drown the thoughts in my head. I landed on a rerun of School of Rock and tried to laugh at Jack Black, he was always my favorite actor. But this time I couldn't. I checked my phone and was reminded of the incoming 3 a.m. hangout. After School of Rock came The Matrix, then National Treasure. Benny and I always loved that movie. Benny.

At 2:30 am, Tía came in and laid on the bed exhausted. She rubbed my back and passed me a to-go box. "Did you have a good day at school?" She asked, her eyes already dozing to sleep. I nodded and left to go eat someone else's leftovers in the kitchen.

After chowing down some baked beans and huevos rancheros, I went into the backyard. I was greeted by the smell of fresh dirt and incoming summer heat. I was the first to arrive and took my pick of the swings. I chose the one farthest from the lamp post. Maybe then, Sarah, Jamie, and Grace wouldn't notice the sadness on my face.

Sarah came next. He hair was in a messy ponytail and she was wearing plaid pink and green pajama bottoms.

"Hola." I said quietly.

"Carlos!" Sarah said and hugged me, to my surprise. She must be in a good mood. Jamie came next and we exchanged nods and smiles. Grace came last. As she walked towards us, she let out a ginormous yawn which made me smile. She reminded me a little bit of Tío for some reason. The way she moved. The way she made me feel, relaxed. There was a warmth and openness to her.

"Someone's interrupting my beauty sleep." Grace said, sitting on the final swing.

"Sorry, my dear." Sarah said still smiling.

"So what's up?" Jamie said. "Why'd you want us to meet early?"

"Yeah, tell us the good news." I said hoping it was good enough to make me forget about Benny.

"Yeah. So…I guess I'll just say it." Sarah said twiddling her fingers.

"Yes, say it!" Grace said widening her eyes, pushing herself awake.

"Tonight's actually my last night here. Well actually, we kinda moved out already. But I wanted to come back and see y'all. My mom got us a place to stay at my aunt's house. She just moved to Austin." Sarah said. A few seconds of silence followed.

"No way!" Jamie said first. "That's great!" Sarah looked around nervously.

"I'm happy for you." Grace said, putting a smile on her face. I wondered if she was truly happy for her. Then the rest of them looked towards me. I wondered why for a moment, then I realized I was the last to congratulate her.

"Yeah. That's – that's really exciting." I said trying to smile.

"I wasn't sure…if I – if it was ok for me to say anything. But I thought it would be best rather than just leaving."

"Of course." Grace said reaching out her hand to Sarah. She must really be happy for her. Sarah smiled gratefully.

"Now that you say that, I guess I should make an announcement too." Jamie chimed in. I turned my head towards him. He seemed taller than I remembered sitting on the swing. Almost, like a man. "My mom got a job."

"That's great." I said, remembering to congratulate him this time around.

"No way!" Sarah said.

"How awesome!" Grace announced. Jamie looked towards Grace. During our joyride, Jamie told me he was into her. By the looks of it, Grace seemed to like him too.

"Yeah, thanks. So, it might be just a short time before...I leave Blue Haven." Jamie said quietly.

"That's good, man." I said. "That's the goal right? Can't stay here forever." Jamie nodded. Grace started to shuffle her feet on the gravel and glide up and down. I followed her lead.

"Yeah...that's the goal." Sarah said in deep thought. "Listen." I tried to slow down my swing as Sarah's voice felt more serious than before. "I know I've said this before. But I really want us to stay friends."

"Yeah, me too." Jamie said, then stopped to think of his words. It was interesting, talking to Jamie. Unlike me, there always seemed to be this gravity with his words. Like none of them were wasted. "Before y'all...I always felt like I had to be *someone* with people. Someone's brother. Someone's son. Someone's friend. But with y'all, I don't know. It's like I don't feel that weight when I talk to you guys. I don't feel like I have to pretend around y'all. I can just be myself with you guys. That's...really rare, I think." Jamie said. I smiled then gave Jamie a nudge, swaying him side to side.

"You going soft on us, Jamie?" I said with a smile.

"I dunno man. Maybe I am." Jamie said with a shrug. Grace laughed.

It made me happy to think of the four of us hanging out one day, out in the real world. But then the thought of inevitability ran into my mind. Before Luis moved away, I thought we'd stay best friends no matter what. But it was harder than either of us imagined. He had a new life in another city across the country. And I was…here. Living this new life I never expected. Staying friends when distance was involved wasn't easy. But maybe this time it would be different. Maybe after we all went our separate ways, the memory of this place would keep us together. But I wondered, after leaving this place would I even want to remember?

"Ok." Sarah clapped her hands together. "It's time. Give us one of your questions." Sarah pointed to Grace, then lifted backwards in the air and raised her feet to propel forwards.

"Hmmmm. Let's see." She said. Jamie and Grace started swinging back and forth as well. I liked the sight of it. Carefree and alive. "I can't seem to think of one today." Grace said.

"Gasp. How is that possible?" Sarah joked.

"I'm gonna leave it to you guys tonight. Does anyone else have a question, make it a good one. Carlos?"

"Me? Oh no, no. I don't have one. One of you guys try." I said, pointing to Jamie and Sarah. I leaned back a bit so I could sway with the rest of them. The warm air felt like someone whispering on my face.

"Do you ever think…" Sarah started. "That there's a life out there, years or maybe decades from now, where our lives today are just a distant memory? Where our future self and future life is just light years better than the ones we have now? Do y'all ever like to imagine a time where we can't even remember Blue Haven?"

"Daaaaamn. Sarah. Way to hit us with a question." Jamie joked.

"I approve!" Grace said.

Each of us started to slow our swing as Sarah's question sunk in. I looked back at Blue Haven. The small window and shallow rooftop. A time where today feels like a distant memory. I wasn't sure. All I ever thought about was today.

"How bout you go first." I said to Sarah, trying to buy myself some time.

"Ok." Sarah swallowed then stared at the sky. There were a few clouds covering the dimming stars. Tío always taught me, if the sky was clear at night, that meant the morning's weather would be good.

"It's hard for me to believe that things will be ok. Sometimes, I try to imagine a future that's completely different from how I'm living now. But then it feels almost dangerous for me to believe that, it could happen. That things will get better." Sarah's face turned sad for the first time tonight.

"I know what you mean." Jamie said. "Sometimes I can't imagine a life where I feel ok again. Where things aren't even better, but just back to normal…"

I nodded looking down at the gravel, my head and shoulders feeling heavy. Suddenly, I didn't feel so far from them. We had the same thought – thinking about the future felt foolish, borderline dangerous.

"I feel the same way." I said. "It's hard to get out of just today's thoughts. It's like there are a million things to worry about to the point where if I think about tomorrow too, I might explode. It's hard to picture a future where things are good, or different. So far it feels like everything's just been a pile of bad." I stopped to let out a deep sigh. Then I looked back at them, feeling a bit self-conscious.

"Keep going." Grace whispered.

"Yeah…I just think sometimes, for a lot of people, life is smooth and steady with just a few bumps in the road that are hard. But for me it feels like the opposite. Life is always so bumpy and hard. And there's only a few moments when things are going smooth. Sometimes I wish it was possible for me to live a normal life." I said.

The air was humming with the sound of cicadas. The scent of lilacs was strong now. And I could see the green glow of the trees and bushes surrounding us. Morning was coming soon. In the airy stillness, Grace spoke.

"I think it is possible." She said looking towards me. "I believe it is possible for life to get better. Right now Carlos…things seem like rock bottom. Everything is kinda, well crap. But that doesn't mean we'll stay here forever. I mean look at Sarah and Jamie. They're leaving. Sooner or later, we'll leave too Carlos. Time always passes. It never stops. Things change. People change. Things will get easier…or we'll just get stronger. Either way, I think that means life will get better."

Sarah and Jamie smiled at her. I couldn't help but also think, things could always get worse. She seemed to read my mind.

"I'm not saying things can't get worse. It most definitely can. What's that saying? When it rains it pours? That seems true, I think. But I also think..."

"What?" I asked fully intrigued.

"I don't know. There's like this, this feeling – almost like a power that comes over you after you've made it through something so hard. You thought you couldn't make it through, but then you do and you realize how much you can take and what you're capable of. You start to see yourself and life differently."

"Yeah, I think I know that feeling." Jamie said. "Like you've gotten harder. But not in a bad way. In a good way. My dad always compared it to a sword. You have to melt the metal with fire, then hammer it until it's strong enough. If you don't hammer it enough, the sword is weak and it'll eventually break during battle."

"I like that." I said. Jamie smiled. "I'm just not sure if I'm strong enough to make it through all that."

"You are." Sarah said resolutely. "You are Carlos."

"Yeah." Grace chimed in. "Plus, things are different now."

"How?" I asked.

"You have us." She said.

"Yeah man." Jamie said patting me on the shoulder. "Do y'all ever think if we didn't meet here how we'd probably never meet each other? I mean, even y'all – Sarah and Grace, we go to the same school but we never really ran in the same circles."

"I think about that all the time!" Sarah said. "It's crazy how we all met. Like if you didn't burn that pizza Jamie, or if I hadn't crashed my car and met you Carlos."

"Yeah, it is crazy." I said with a smile. "Sometimes it feels like..."

"Deeeestiiinyyyyy!" Grace whispered like a mystic fortune teller. We all laughed. God, I'm gonna miss her when this is all over.

The four of us glided on the swing set together for some time. Birds started to chirp and a warmth hit my skin from the rising sun. None of wanted to leave. We savored the final moments where the four of us could be together like this. For a brief second, I dreaded the thought of leaving Blue Haven.

Chapter 41

Jamie

Finals week was finally over. I walked out of class feeling like I could breathe again. I made my way outside, passing the counselor's office which reminded me of Sarah. I took out my phone and texted our group chat – trying to follow through on the promise we made last night.

"Y'all we're free! Finals week is over!"

Ma picked me up with Aisha and Quinn already waiting in the car. "Get in!" Aisha shouted, rolling down the window. I stopped and walked towards them in slow motion to piss Aisha off. Quinn laughed behind her.

"Boy! Get yo' butt in here!" Ma yelled. I went back to a jogging pace and got in the car. "We gotta make a pit stop today, Jamie." Ma said cheerfully.

We arrived at the senior center where Ma got hired as a nurse. It looked like a big colonial home. It had white wooden walls, black shutters, and a front patio that reminded me of a scene from Gone With The Wind. We walked into the senior living center together. It had the faint aroma of fresh cookies, lavender, and moth balls. Quinn and Aisha immediately ran to a checkers table and started playing. There was a row of small tables, each with a checkers or chess board on it. The sight of Quinn and Aisha nestled in between pairs of elderly people made me laugh. Ma walked to the front desk.

"Hi. I'm Jackie Davis. I'm the new head nurse."

"Yes! Looks like we'll be seeing a lot of you." Ma shook hands with the receptionist, who then started organizing a pile of papers. "If you could follow me to Maggie's office. She's the head of HR." Ma nodded and followed.

"Jamie, you stay here and watch Aisha and Quinn." Ma said, following the receptionist.

I leaned over Aisha's chair. Quinn frowned as Aisha beat her at checkers. I always let Quinn beat me, but that wasn't Aisha's style.

"Hey! That's not fair! I always win." Quinn whined.

"Not with me." Aisha snickered.

"But whenever I play with Jamie…I always win." Quinn said, utterly confused at her defeat and looked towards me requesting an explanation. I shrugged and smiled.

"Don't look at me." I said, throwing my hands up in the air.

"He lets you win, dummy." Aisha said.

"No, he doesn't! Do you?" Quinn asked.

"Nope. You beat me every time. Fair and square." I said.

"Does that mean *you're* smarter than Jamie?" Quinn asked Aisha. I walked up to their match and stared at the checkers board. Aisha played the black pieces, Quinn the white.

"Looks like it." I said. Aisha smiled.

"Here son. You can take this seat. We've just finished our game."

An elderly man slowly got up from his seat next to Aisha. He didn't seem to be playing with another person but his chess board looked like it was being played from both sides. As he got up, the gray blanket on his lap fell to the floor.

"Here, let me get that." I picked up his fleece blanket which seemed like it was much better suited for winter.

"Well thank you, young man." The elderly man didn't walk with a cane but it seemed like he needed one. His back was hunched over and it took him almost a minute to take a few steps forward.

"Would you like me to walk you back to your room, sir?"

"Sir? No one has called me sir in a very long time." The man's eyes lit up as I held his arm and took some of his weight, his blanket still resting on my other arm.

"Aisha, y'all stay here."

We started walking towards the corridor. He must have been in his 90s. His blue eyes were overshadowed by his bushy white eyebrows. It took us several minutes to walk no more than

15 feet. Inside his room, I led the man to his bed where he slowly sat down and rested. There was a wheelchair stationed in the corner.

"They try to make me use that thing, but I won't let 'em. My pride gets the best of me. I need to use these legs for as long as I can, until I can't anymore." I nodded. His room had pink curtains hanging over plastic blinds. There was an embroidered pillow on a rocking chair and a candle that had a picture of a beach on it. I wondered if his wife decorated.

On his nightstand were framed black and white photographs. One photo of him holding hands with a beautiful woman. Another of a group of men in Navy uniforms with the sky and ocean behind them.

"That was me and my unit back in my day. A very long time ago." The elderly man tried to pull up his legs to straighten out on his bed and I quickly rushed to help him, so he wouldn't fall over.

"Thank you, young man."

"You're welcome, sir." He chuckled.

"You've got great manners. What's your name?"

"Jamie, sir."

"Well, Jamie. I'm Jeremy." He said with a smile and held out his hand. His handshake felt firmer than I thought it would.

"My dad was in the Army." I said, still looking at the photo.

"Ah. Well that explains it then – why you're so well mannered. Is your father a strict man?"

"Sometimes…"

"I'll tell you. There's nothing quite like serving your country. The camaraderie! My unit, we were like brothers. I'm sure it's the same for your father." I nodded. "I still think about those days. They were some of the best of my entire life…other than when my daughter was born, or when I married my wife."

"Does your wife live here with you?"

"She passed when our daughter was born." I regretted my question instantly. It was foolish to ask about someone's family at a senior home.

"I'm sorry."

"Oh no. No need to be sorry. I like thinking about my wife. She was a firecracker." Jeremy said and lifted the photo of what now appeared to be him and his wife during their twenties.

"I just thought, since the room seems like it was decorated by a girl…"

"Yes, that was my daughter. She's a sweet girl. I guess she's a woman now. She's living in Colorado with her husband and their two kids. I lived with them for a brief time, but the elevation – it wasn't good for my heart. I could barely breathe there. But I can breathe fine in Texas. Plus, I like the heat."

I nodded. Jeremy proceeded to tell me more about his life. He told me about the majestic mountains in Colorado and his daughter, who was also a firecracker just like her mom. Then he told me about his grandkids, Judy and Violet. Jeremy's voice soothed my heart and I found myself wanting to learn more. Outside Jeremy's room, I heard Ma's voice. She and an employee passed right by us. A few seconds later, she did a double take and turned around.

"Jamie? Boy, what are you doing here, bothering this nice man?" Ma said.

"Oh, he wasn't bothering me. Your son was just keeping me company." Jeremy said. Ma smiled and walked towards us.

"Is that so?"

"Are you his mother?"

"I am indeed. I'm also the new nurse here, so it looks like we'll be getting to know each other."

"Well isn't that great!" Jeremy said smiling.

"I'll see you later, Jeremy." I got up to follow Ma out of the room.

"You and your husband did a great job raising your son." Jeremy said. I hoped Ma wouldn't get mad. I forgot to tell Jeremy, Dad died.

"Thank you, Jeremy. We'll be back again soon." Ma said.

Ma and I walked back towards the lobby. She squeezed my arm and smiled at me. Her face looked brighter, more like the face I remember. Quinn and Aisha were talking to an elderly lady and Quinn was putting her fingers in the woman's hair, seemingly amazed by how white it was.

"Come on, girls!" Ma said. Quinn and Aisha bolted out of their chairs and ran towards us. We got in the car, each of us in good spirits.

"Ma. I think you're going the wrong way." Ma was driving straight down the road from the senior center but we arrived from the opposite direction. She didn't say anything and continued driving. After 10 minutes, she pulled into a gated entrance. Ma opened the window and pressed a code, then the gate opened.

"Where are we?" Aisha asked.

"Yeah, where are we?" Quinn repeated.

"Everyone out. I wanna show y'all something."

We dutifully got out of the car and followed Ma. She led us past an outdoor pool, then a green area shaded by trees. We walked on a clean sidewalk through a cluster of six brick buildings. Then we stopped outside a door that had the number 40 on it. Ma took out some keys from her purse, unlocked the door, and pushed it wide open.

"Welcome home." Ma said.

"What?" I asked.

"Yippeeee!" Quinn zipped past us and into the living room. "Look Aisha! Look at our room!" Aisha ran to her. I stepped carefully inside, staying firmly rooted on a little patch of tile by the entrance. The rest of the floor was a sea of carpet. I recognized a clock from our old home hanging on the living room wall.

"It's gonna take a while for me to fill it with furniture. But this is our new place, Jamie. What do ya think?" Ma asked.

"But how did you…" Ma laughed.

"Baby, you look like a deer in headlights. I got approved for an apartment! I applied as soon as I found out I got the job." Ma's words hit a barrier between us. I could hear what she was saying, but I couldn't understand. The words didn't sit cohesively together in my mind. Approved. Apartment.

"This is ours?" I asked, still in a daze.

"Yes, Jamie! Go look at your room."

I walked slowly through the empty living room and turned into the hallway. There was a bathroom. Then two more doors on the right side and one to the left.

"You'll have to share a bathroom with Aisha and Quinn. Sorry, Jamie." I shook my head. I took a few more steps into what appeared to be my room. There was already a bed and my clothes were hung up in the closet. I turned around to Ma.

"What do you think?" Ma asked apprehensively.

"I can't believe it."

"After I start making real money, I'll buy you a desk and a lamp and a bookcase – whatever you need!"

"No, Ma. I mean, I love it!" I gave Ma a hug. I squeezed her tightly and she started laughing.

"Oh baby. I'm glad you like it. You got me worried there."

"I love it, Ma. I love you!"

"I wanna join!" Quinn appeared behind Ma and wrapped around her waist. Ma and I laughed some more.

"Come on Aisha! Get in on this!" Ma shouted behind her. Aisha appeared and tried to squeeze into the center. I stepped back a little to let her fit and the four of us held each other.

Chapter 42
Carlos

Sarah and Jamie went on to new homes. A shiny new house or apartment. I wanted to be happy for them. But I couldn't help asking myself over and over again, why me? Why our family? Why were we still stuck here?

It's just me and Grace at Blue Haven now. A few new people came to stay as well. A Hispanic lady with her infant baby. A black lady with her two daughters. I barely saw them. I barely saw Grace. Without Jamie and Sarah, things were different. The fact that they escaped this place should have brought me hope. But lately, I wondered what the point of it all was.

I haven't seen Benny since the incident. I'm not sure where he sleeps. Tía's working. Every morning. Every night. If I didn't come to help out at the restaurant, I'm not sure I'd ever see her. She comes back to the shelter when I'm already asleep.

I rarely get to hear her voice, except when she shouts out finished orders from the restaurant kitchen.

The manager, Gil, is nice to Tía. He's not even Mexican or speaks a drip of Spanish, but he opened this Tex-Mex restaurant 15 years ago and now there are over 10 locations in Austin. I wish Tía and Tío had done that. If we had the money to start, we'd be rich by now.

Tonight, instead of laying on the grass in view of the stars, I'm wiping tables and Tía is washing dishes. Gil is also closing up at the restaurant. He's been talking to Tía while counting receipts, but she doesn't respond with more than a few words. I wiped away bits of red rice, fallen pieces of tortilla chips, and thin strands of chicken that were thrown about by children and ignored by their neglecting parents.

Tía's moved onto the cooking stations now. I watched as she started wiping down all the metal surfaces with a beige rag that I assume used to be white. Gil is right behind her. He's leaned up on one of the stoves and is watching Tía clean. Tía seems to be ignoring him. I got up to get closer to Tía and tripped over a chair making a loud noise. Gil and Tía turned to look at me, then looked away. Maybe I wasn't wanted. It's bad enough we sleep here sometimes. I think Gil knows.

Gil is too close now. He has his hand on Tía's back, between her shoulders. Is he consoling her about Tío? He did come to the funeral. Tía still had an expressionless face, as she wiped the metal table in a circular motion. Gil's hand dropped a little lower. Tía moved to the opposite side a little bit. The touch seemed to make her uncomfortable. I tried to ignore it and moved to another booth. I'm sure they're just friends. Tía's going through a hard time. She's been working a lot more than usual. They must have gotten closer. I got lost in full cleaning mode and proceeded to wipe down all the booths lined against the wall of the restaurant. Finished!

    I walked to the manager's office to get the mop and bucket. After I clean the floors, Tía and I can go home – well back to the shelter. I walked back out into the dining area ready to begin, until I heard Tía's voice.

    "No. No." Tía said. I rushed to the kitchen. Gil was pushed up against Tía. Their bodies were touching. Gil had his hands pinned to the metal table, with Tía between him and the harsh metal. He was trying to kiss Tía but she had her head turned away.

    "Come on. You're a widow now. You need a strong man to protect you." Gil said. I dropped the mop. Gil turned around. I found myself racing towards him. I clenched my hand into a fist, flung it behind me for momentum, then swung it straight into his face. He stumbled over. Tía moved from her spot, threw her apron on the floor, took my hand and pulled me out of the restaurant.

    "You're finished here, Julia!" Gil yelled. "Finished! Don't come back!"

    We made it to the parking lot where Tía let go of my hand. Her face was furious.

"Carlos! What were you thinking!" Tía yelled out of breath.

"Me? What are you talking about? I saved you!"

"Saved me? Carlos, you just cost me my job!" Tía's face was red and her small frame was heaving up and down.

"Are you kidding me? So, did you *want* Gil to kiss you?"

"Of course not! But I had it handled. He wasn't going to do anything."

"What are you talking about? He was already doing something!" I said fuming. Why the hell was she taking this out on me? I saved her.

"Listen to me, mijo. Gil is a man. He just wanted to feel like he was in control. This is what it takes to be a woman and work here. This job is the only thing that can get us out of the shelter and into a home."

I couldn't believe what Tía was saying. Gil was just a man? No. Gil was a bad person. How could Tía not even care?

"You're acting crazy, Tía! How could you think what Gil did was ok?"

"Of course, I know it is wrong! But this is what it's like to be a woman. And without your Tío, I need this job. Who else will hire a middle-aged woman from Mexico with no other skills? Carlos, I never went to college. I'm not like your friend's parents. I'm not from here. I can't get a better job than this. I've already tried."

I wanted to scream. Tía was acting insane. How could she be defending Gil and blaming me? I was the one who protected her! Wasn't that my duty?

"…You act like Tío dying doesn't even matter to you." I said looking away. "You just let Gil kiss you and touch you. I bet you never even loved Tío."

I could hear Tía's heavy breathing. I turned my eyes back towards her, slightly afraid. She was staring at me. Her dark black hair was falling over her tan and tired face. I tried to remember the woman that held me in her arms and rocked me back and forth surrounded by stuffed animals as a child. I couldn't find her.

"You ungrateful child." Tía said in a low voice. "All you do is complain. You are a burden to me and my family! Tu madre? She was right to leave you."

I looked at Tía incredulously. I started feeling dizzy. Was this moment even real? Maybe it was all a horrible dream and when I wake up Tía will be back to normal and Tío will still be alive. But as I looked at Tía, nothing changed. She still watched me with angry, unrelenting eyes. I took a step backwards. Then another. And another. Then, I started running.

I ran away from Tía through the dark and empty parking lot. I ran across the blackened street, dodging four lanes of cars and honks, making it all the way to the other side. I climbed over a metal side ramp, where a strip of grass swiftly turned into another empty parking lot dimly lit by a Home Depot sign. Then I kept running.

I could hear Tía's voice yelling at me. I didn't look back. I kept on running. Past the Home Depot. Past an empty field. Past an elementary school. Past a darkened neighborhood and into another. This is what I should have done from the beginning. I should have never gone to Tío and Tía's house. I should have been on my own. Sooner or later, they all either die or leave me. Tía doesn't want me. She doesn't want me. Maybe she never wanted me.

I took a break from running, or rather I was stopped by a street that ended up becoming a dead-end roundabout. I sat down on some grass that was shaped in a perfect circle. Maybe I could sleep here. No. I couldn't. Too many houses. Too many people who will call the cops on me. A lone Mexican kid sleeping outside their house. It wouldn't do. Benny. I could text Benny. But Benny never replied. But maybe this time he would, if he thinks it's about Tía.

"Benny. Call me. There's an emergency with Mom."

After a couple seconds, Benny called me. His tone was heightened, urgent. He would have never called me if it was my emergency.

"Carlos! What's the emergency? Is Mom ok?"

"Yeah – I mean, I don't know. She's gone."

"What? Gone where? Where is she?" Benny asked panicked.

"Well, she's not gone. She's back at the restaurant. I'm…I'm gone. I left."

"Left where? Where are you right now?"

"I'm…I'm not sure. I just started running and now I'm in a neighborhood, sitting on a roundabout."

"Rounda-what? Carlos…did you run away?"

"…"

"Carlos!"

"I…I'm on my own right now. I don't know where to go, or where to sleep."

"Ok. Carlos listen to me. I want you to find the nearest street sign. Then pick a house on that street and text me the address. I'll come and pick you up."

"…"

"Carlos!"

"Ok! I'll do it. I'm hanging up now."

I got up from my roundabout and walked back towards a green street sign. Then I texted Benny. I sat on the naked sidewalk and waited.

Benny came in a car I didn't recognize. A black Mercedes. I stood up as the car slowed down near me. Benny was driving. In the back were two of his old bandmates smoking weed. The smell was awful.

"Carlos! Come inside!" Benny said rolling down the window. I opened the door and a cloud of smoke seeped out into the now polluted sidewalk.

"Who's car is this?"

"My boss let me borrow it." Benny said.

"Who's your boss?" Benny didn't answer.

"Ayy Carlos. Long time no see." Antonio said in the back seat.

"Yeah, where you been hanging Carlos?" Miguel asked.

I turned around to see the friends that were also missing from school as soon as Benny stopped showing up. The sight of them smiling and happy made me sick. Benny drove to a neighborhood in East Austin, one I remember driving by before. He parked in front of a rusted red apartment building. We got in the elevator and rode it to the top floor.

Benny took out his keys and opened a door. Inside was an open space with a few bare mattresses, an old couch, an even older TV, a foosball table covered with beer cans, and an empty pizza box sitting like a corpse in the middle of the floor.

"Is this where you live?" I asked Benny.

"It's only for work. As soon as I'm done, we'll all live together again – in a nice place."

Antonio and Miguel passed by me and sat on the hardwood floor in front of the TV. They started playing video games. There were two other people already in the apartment who didn't say hi to me or Benny. I couldn't tell if they were sleeping or awake. Their eyes were open, but nothing was behind them. Benny walked forward to the fridge, got out a cold can of Pepsi and handed it to me.

"You hungry?" I shook my head no. My appetite was gone. Benny took a seat on a sagging gray couch in the back corner of the apartment and I sat on the other end.

"So, what happened with Tía?" He asked. I looked around. The same smell from the car was here too. Everyone's face looked lifeless. Suddenly, the reality of this place clicked in my mind. Everyone here was high. Every single one of them. Was Benny high too?

"Carlos! Hey!" Benny snapped his fingers in front of his face. I looked into Benny's eyes. He still seemed like Benny. It calmed my nerves a bit.

"She…" An image of Tía's enraged face flashed in my mind. "She doesn't want me anymore…"

"What? Did she say that?"

"She told me I'm a burden and that my real mom was right to leave me."

"Holy shit. Were you guys fighting? I'm sure she didn't mean it. She loves you."

"She doesn't though. Not like she loves you." I waited for Benny to argue with me, to prove me wrong, but he didn't. Benny was silent. I wondered what I should say next to fill the silence but the smell of weed clouded my mind.

"Mom loves you." Benny said quietly, staring out the dirt streaked window. "She's just sad right now…"

"Benny. Why are you living here? What are you doing?" Benny turned back to me and hesitated.

"I've moved up the ladder."

"Huh? What ladder?" Benny wasn't like these people. Benny was good. Benny is good.

"After we ended up at the shelter, I asked my dealer who his boss was, he told me and I met him. Then I started dealing weed."

"Ok." Weed wasn't too bad. Weed was for teenagers. It's what people did at parties, at least that's what people told me. It could even be legal one day.

"I did a good job, dealing. I knew who would be an easy target – the rich, bored kids. I started getting into their circles and then making bigger deals at parties and at schools…Carlos, I was great at it."

I nodded my head slowly.

"So, then my boss introduced me to his boss and he put me on a trial run…dealing the harder stuff…cocaine."

My body froze. Cocaine? That's a real drug. That's the stuff people get addicted to and fuck up their lives with. That's how Mom…

"So, then I started dealing cocaine. I went back to the rich kids and sold to them. Then to their friends. Then I got connected with the older adults. The ones with money, in high rises, the big shot jobs. They bought up so much of it, the drugs practically sell themselves. And the crazy thing is…" Benny leaned in closer to me.

"It's the people who look like they're completely normal." Benny's eyes lit up. "You would have never guessed the type of people I sell to now. They're successful! I don't know why they do it, but they do it a lot. They seem like they already have everything. I don't get why they need this stuff.

Anyways, I'm like my own boss now. I'm making my way up the food chain." Benny smiled. "I'm making thousands in a single week. I'm just saving until I can leave the business. I barely get to keep any of the money for myself though. I have to pay my higher ups and then they give me a small cut. But I'm not gonna do this forever. I'm planning on quitting when I have enough saved. My boss said I just have to do a few more jobs, then I'm out."

I couldn't believe what I was hearing. Benny was dealing cocaine. The white powdery stuff you see in movies. The things cartels kill each other for in Colombia or wherever it's from! Benny was a dealer. A real live drug dealer.

"Benny. Have you gone fucking insane! You're dealing cocaine?" I shouted. Benny shushed me.

"Calm down brother. It's not a big deal."

"It is a big deal, Benny! You're a criminal! What in the actual fuck!"

"It's for the family."

"No, Benny. You're doing this for you. Look at this place! You love it here! You've forgotten all about me and Tía. A few more jobs? A few more jobs, Benny? Do you really think your boss will just let you go after all you've done for him – after all the money you've earned for him? Haven't you seen the movies!" I shouted.

"No! He will! I've saved almost enough for a down payment on a house – a pretty nice one. I can buy it for us! Then I'm out."

"No one's gonna give a drug dealer a house!" I stood up shouting. "Down payment? Benny you've gone fucking crazy!"

I stormed out of the apartment and into the deserted hallway. I had no idea where to go or where I really was. I took out my phone. Sixteen missed calls from Tía. I collapsed on the floor and sobbed. I hid my head between my knees. My body felt so heavy. I have no one now. No one. I heard footsteps approach me. I smelled Benny. He put his arm over my shoulders.

"I promise, Carlos. Just a few more jobs, then I'm done. I can pay for us to have a new life once I'm finished." I wiped the tears from my face, no longer embarrassed by the sensation of crying.

"You don't get it. This is your life now. Stuff like this never finishes…until you're in jail or you're dead." Benny shook his head and smiled at me. His attempt at reassuring me did nothing to calm my aching heart. Benny's gone.

With nowhere else to go, I followed Benny back into the apartment. I sat on the lifeless couch, exhausted. Benny went to one of the empty mattresses and laid down. I could hear the faint sound of someone else already snoring along with Mario Kart sound effects from the TV.

I tried to close my eyes. Even though my body ached from tiredness, my mind wouldn't succumb to rest. It was too heavy. I have no one now. No one will care about me if I disappear. Not my real mom. Not Tía. Not even Benny. He says he's doing this for us. But he's doing it for him. I could see the thrill in his eyes when he talked about dealing. The adrenaline, the illusion of control. He'll end up just like Mom.

"Benny?" I stared at the high ceiling. There was a skylight window that showcased the sky. I could see a couple of stars. I wish I was back at the shelter. I wondered if Grace was still there. I wondered if I could go back now. No. Tía would never take me back. Tía doesn't want me.

"Hmm?"

"Have you tried it…the coke?"

"No. If you want to be a good dealer you can't do the drugs. That'll mess you up fast."

"What about weed?"

"Shit, you know I do weed." Benny's response made me laugh. I guess for some reason, I hoped it wasn't real. I hoped Benny would lie to me. "Do you wanna try it?"

"Coke?"

"Hell no! Weed." The stars reminded me of our nights together. The four of us. That time was over now. It was a small window of time that shined brightly. But it's over now.

"Sure." I said.

Benny came and sat next to me. He pulled a joint out of his jeans pocket. I put it between my fingers like how I'd seen Benny do it before.

"Breathe in as I light it." I did as Benny said. It tasted bad. I tried to inhale for as long as I could. As I exhaled, I coughed and Benny laughed.

"How do you feel?" Benny asked.

"I don't know. I don't feel any different."

"Give it a few more drags." I brought the joint to my lips and saw the end glow orange as I inhaled. The second time I coughed less. The third time, I felt it getting easier. My body started feeling lighter. I smoked the joint until it burned my throat and the joint had turned into a tiny nub.

"Damn son. You're a natural." Benny got out a small pipe and put his lighter towards the round part on the bottom.

"I wanna try." I said. Benny shook his head no.

"You've already smoked a lot for your first time. You should take it easy." I held out my hand towards the glass pipe. Benny raised his eyebrow then slowly passed it to me.

"Breath in." I inhaled and felt my surroundings melt. All the problems. All the hurt. They were all put on pause as I smoked. I stopped thinking about Mom abandoning me. Then Tío. Then Tía. I was on my own again. I wasn't happy. But I was no longer sad. My body felt calm. I felt completely still. My mind stopped racing. It wasn't a real peace. I knew that distinctly. But it lifted me out of myself, how I felt, how I was hurting.

"How do you feel?"

"Better."

"Yeah. Weed will do that to you."

"I wanna go."

"Go where?"

"Back to the shelter. I need to talk to someone."

Benny nodded and we got back into his boss's car.

Chapter 43
Grace

    Umma said we're leaving soon – next week even. She finally found a job as a nanny, caring for a family's baby that just immigrated from South Korea. It was a miracle Umma even found this couple through an old friend from church. With Umma's lack of English-speaking skills and spending the last 20 years as a stay-at-home mom, her options were highly limited.

    I was so freaking excited. I couldn't even sleep. Things were going to get better. With Appa gone, things will get better. It doesn't even matter where we go. It doesn't have to be a nice place. Just some place that's not a shelter. For the first time in a long time, I felt excited. My heart felt a sense of relief. Janice is going to medical school. Umma and I will live in a home we aren't ashamed of. Appa is finally gone. This chapter of life will finally be over.

I laid on my cot and stared at the ceiling. I felt lighter. I felt like, good things were coming my way. I started to doze off until my cellphone next to me vibrated, lifting me out of my joyous dreamlike state. Maybe it was Sarah. I asked her to send pics of her new place but she hasn't responded yet. It was a text from Carlos.

"Hey, could you come out? I'm in the backyard."

Maybe Carlos wanted to have a 3 a.m. club with just the two of us? I put on a zipper hoodie to cover my childish pajamas then rushed out. Carlos was standing in the middle of the backyard, staring into the sky. For some reason, his silhouette scared me. He looked like a ghost.

"Grace! You're here! I'm so glad that you're here. You got my text right?" Before I could respond, Carlos started talking again. "It's such a beautiful night. Did you see the stars? I did. I mean, I have. I'm looking at them now. And I saw it at Benny's new place. He's living with a bunch of other people. Look at the stars, Grace!"

I looked straight back at Carlos. I couldn't even get in a word yet. I took a step closer to him. His clothes reeked. Has he not taken a shower? No wait, this smell felt familiar. But I couldn't place it.

"Carlos?" Carlos leaned his head farther back to look at me. He was smiling, his head bent nearly all the way backwards like in The Exorcist. His hair was dirty and matted in the back. His face scared me. It seemed happy, but not at the same time.

"Are you alright?" I asked.

"I've never been better. I feel like my mind is finally clear now. Remember when the four of us were here? That was a fun time. I wish we could all be here again and talk like we used to."

"Well, I'm here now. We can still talk." I took another step towards Carlos, cautiously as if he were a dangerous animal that could at any moment attack me. It was a familiar feeling.

"Are we friends, Grace?"

"Of course we are."

"But what about when you leave this place, or I leave this place? Benny has a new place. I could go stay with him."

"Where is he staying? Did you guys get a house?"

"Not exactly." Something was majorly wrong. This wasn't Carlos. He was not this talkative. He was never this giddy.

"What's wrong? What's wrong with you?"

Carlos stopped looking at the sky and stood normally. His eyes met with mine. There was panic behind his façade of excitement. I could see it simmering like a pot of boiling water inside of him.

"Nothing's wrong with me. I'm free…Well, actually I'm high." Carlos blinked a few times. I didn't know what to say.

"…Are you serious? You're high right now?"

"Yup! I tried it at Benny's place. He's got loads of weed. They all do. And cocaine too. They're all drug dealers." Carlos's words were nonchalant, as if he had just told me he aced his last exam. My mind started spinning. Carlos can't. He's one of the good ones. He can't do this.

"Carlos! Are you insane! You can't be hanging out with a bunch of drug dealers doing drugs!"

"But he's my family. Benny is my only family now. Tía doesn't want me. She said so herself." Carlos's words pierced my heart like knives. The fact that he was so calm made me panic. It was becoming harder to breathe.

"Carlos. Your aunt loves you. I'm sure she didn't mean what she said."

"She did though. I could see it in her face. I saw it in her eyes. It was the same look my real mom had."

"You saw what? What did you see?"

"She doesn't love me anymore." My eyes started to water. I wanted to hug him. I wanted to come closer. But Carlos looked so different to me now. The sight of him high, scared me. I felt a disgust I didn't want to feel towards him. He was becoming like my dad, my Appa. How dare he. How dare he ruin his life like Appa did and ruin his family. No. It's not too late. It's not too late.

"But I love you…" I said. Carlos's intoxicated smile disappeared. His face turned sad again. "I love you, Carlos. You're my friend."

"Do you really love me?"

"I do!" I took a step towards him. Carlos took a step back and his gaze fell downwards.

"You don't. You only love me for what I could do for you. We comforted each other. The four of us. But now it's over and you'll forget all about me. You'll…be ashamed of me eventually."

"I won't. I never forget about my friends. I never forget anyone."

"You forgot about your dad. You hate your dad. You said so yourself. And now you hate me, don't you? The dirty druggie. The orphan nobody cares about."

"No Carlos! Stop!" I shouted. I wanted to shake him awake, shake him back to life again.

"You don't actually care. No one does." Carlos took out a small glass pipe and a lighter. He started moving the lighter under the bowl at the end and it started to bubble. An intense rage came over me. I ran to him and yanked the pipe out of his hand and threw it over the fence. Carlos yelled and pushed my shoulders. I fell to the ground. My hand landed on a sharp rock and it pierced my skin. I stared at the blood, not feeling any pain yet. Carlos was trying to climb over the fence to find his pipe. I stood up again and this time grabbed him back towards the swings and pushed him into one of the seats with all the strength left within me.

"What the hell is wrong with you, Carlos?" I said standing over him. He seemed small now, sitting on the swing like a child. His face was lost. He looked at my hand. I looked at it too. A drop of blood fell and landed on the gravel leaving a red trail on my palm.

"I'm sorry!" Carlos blurted out and started crying. His nose was running. His eyes, red and bloodshot. He started hiding his face in his hands that were covered with grime and dirt. An overwhelming feeling of guilt took over me. I started crying too. Carlos was my friend. Carlos was hurting. I knelt down on my knees and wrapped my arms around him. His back was shaking as he continued to cry. His tears fell onto the back of my shirt.

"Shhhhhhh. Shhhhhhh." I tried to calm him down. "It's going to be ok. It'll be ok."

"I don't know what to do. What do I do now? Nobody wants me."

"I want you. And God wants you. You're not alone." Carlos kept shaking. He tried to wipe away the tears but they kept coming back.

"I don't know what to do. How do I get over all of this? When does it stop hurting?"

"I don't know."

"Does it ever get better?" Carlos sobbed on the swing. His face, his body, looked like a wounded animal, lost and scared. I paused, unsure of what to say, unsure of what I could possibly say to bring back the old Carlos.

"I don't know if it ever gets better, but what I do know is that you get stronger over time. I wish I could lie to you. I wish I could tell you everything will turn out ok and life will work itself out. But sometimes life…is hard. And we can't know the reason why things happen until much later, I think.

But you're not alone. The people around you love you. Your aunt loves you. Benny loves you. I love you too! And Jamie and Sarah!"

"But what should I do now? How can I stop feeling like this…I feel like my world is ending all the time! And I can't stop it. My thoughts never stop. It never stops hurting. I can't breathe."

I looked back at Carlos, wishing I had something profound to tell him. But the brokenness in his eyes reminded me of the cruelty of the world, and people, and how much it hurt to feel abandoned. What could I say that would bring back the Carlos I knew? All I could think of was the words I told myself when I felt like Carlos did right now.

"You just have to keep living." I said feeling defeated. Carlos stared back at me, his shoulders caved in, his head slumped.

"But what if I can't?" He asked. I waited a little longer, hoping the right words would come to me. Instead I felt my mind empty itself. Maybe God wanted to send a message.

"Then you have to fight." Carlos looked at me with sad eyes. "You have to fight back if you want to live."

10 Years Later

My therapist is waiting for me. She's asked me a question, but my mind has wandered back into the corridors of Blue Haven. The smell. The people. The secret nights in the backyard, underneath the stars and blackness of the sky. The soft spring breeze. The sound of laughter. The taste of beer and pizza. My first talk with Sarah. My first kiss with Jamie. My last night with Carlos.

"Sorry, could you repeat the question?"

"What brought you here? After all these years have passed. You said this all happened when you were 16 – leaving your father, ending up at Blue Haven. And the depression happened later in your early 20s, correct?"

"Yes."

"So, why now? What made you want to book a therapy appointment, 10 years after these major life events?"

"I-I don't know. I think it's all just finally caught up with me. Everything that happened before. I never got to process it, until now."

"What's happened now that made you process everything?"

"My friend…he…"

"Sorry, is this one of your friends from Blue Haven?"

"Yes. Carlos."

"What happened to him?"

Chapter 44
Sarah

The first time Carlos asked me for money was when he made a surprise visit to Los Angeles. It was a week after my first role came out. I got a small role in a rom-com TV show that took place in LA. My paycheck was less than $5,000. I didn't know he was high the entire time he talked to me. He told me his aunt relapsed and needed another surgery. I gave him $3,000.

The second time I saw Carlos was after my first leading role. It was an indie drama about a single mom who struggled to support her kids. She goes on a gameshow and wins $1 million but later loses it all to a failed marriage and alcoholism. The movie played at South by South West Festival in Austin and got nominated for a Screen Actors Guild Award.

Grace came to the premiere. We met for drinks afterward when she told me not to give Carlos any more money. He was still an addict and was trying to mooch money from everyone. Grace said she made the mistake of giving him $500, which he used to get high. His aunt, who never relapsed from breast cancer, put him in rehab. He conveniently got out the week I was in Austin.

Carlos came to my hotel room. I tried to give him a meal instead of money. Carlos pushed over the table covered with food, called me a bitch and left. After that, I went back to LA and brought Mom and David with me. David started graduate school at UCLA, where I dropped out after three semesters to pursue my first role. It happened in the most unrealistic and stereotypical way. I got scouted by an agent while biking down the Santa Monica pier.

Carlos called again as soon as the big checks started rolling in. After my first role as a supporting character in a major feature film, he called me. His tone was apologetic. He said he needed a friend. I told him I missed him. Then he brought up money and I said I'd rather he come and stay at my place. He hung up on me.

After that, Grace called again. This time it wasn't to catch up on her journalism career or my acting gigs. It was about Carlos. He showed up on her doorstep in Dallas completely high. I flew back to Texas and got him committed into a rehab center, for the second time.

Once Carlos got out the second time around, I hoped he would be better. In fact, I prayed over it – even after all those years I gave up on praying. I still prayed for Carlos. I wanted with every fiber of me for Carlos to get better, but something inside me told me he wasn't going to get better and that things were only going to get worse.

I tried calling Carlos as soon as he was back in the real world. No response. I texted, emailed, Facebook messaged, Instagram messaged – I even joined Snapchat just to try and contact him. No answer. Nothing. Carlos was a ghost. I did get a voicemail from him once. He sounded incoherent. I think he was crying. But then his voice got happy again. He sounded unwell. I tried calling back but the number was disconnected.

Several years after never hearing from Carlos, I found out he was in Boston. At first, I thought Carlos visited to ask Jamie for money. But that was wishful thinking. Carlos was found unconscious from an overdose and ended up at the hospital where Jamie was a resident. He called me out of the blue. I hadn't seen Jamie since his college graduation ceremony. Hearing his voice, reminded me of home.

I got on a plane from LAX to Boston Logan. My acting skills came in handy. I faked the flu to my director and was able to get a few days off from filming. After landing, I took a taxi to the hospital. Walking through the automatic doors into the tall building made me feel like I was on another set. None of it felt real.

"Sarah!" A man in a white coat approached me. I wondered how he knew my name. As he came closer, his face gave me an intense feeling of déjà vu. It was Jamie! His once short hair grew into dreadlocks that gave him a much friendlier demeanor than I remembered. His face was still soft but he looked older. His eyes though, were exactly the same. Wise and kind.

"Is that you, Jamie? You look like a real doctor!" Jamie laughed as I went in for a hug.

"Well, I'm still trying to be a real doctor. They give us the coat so we can pretend." Jamie smiled which put me at ease. Suddenly I forgot the real reason I flew to Boston. "Do you want some coffee?"

"I'd love some." I followed Jamie to a cramped room with disheveled bunk beds and a tiny round table covered with ramen bowls and piles of emptied to-go boxes. "Oh my God. Is this how you live?" I asked slightly appalled. This wasn't the doctor life I was envisioning on the plane ride over. Jamie laughed.

"It's that residency lifestyle. We run on ramen and 30-minute naps." Jamie pulled a chair out for me and placed a styrofoam cup of coffee on the table. We sat and inspected each other's faces for a little while.

"You look good." I said.

"Thanks. You too. I saw you in that movie, the one with the gameshow. Damn, Sarah. I didn't know you could act like that."

"I didn't either." I laughed. "Turns out acting is a lot easier than architecture. I never really expected everything was going to turn out this way…you though, I knew you'd end up as a doctor one day."

"Aw, thanks. I'm not really a legit doctor yet though. Still have to get through my residency."

"Oh please, I'm sure you'll do great – just like the SATs." Jamie choked on his coffee and laughed.

"Shit. You still remember that? You feelin bitter Sarah?"

"Just a tad." I said with a laugh. This felt good. "God, remember when we first me? We were so young."

"And naïve." Jamie smiled.

"I don't know." I said. "I feel like we were pretty mature for our age."

"Maybe...things were easier back then." I tilted my head and grinned – maybe he forgot we met in a shelter. "Well maybe not *easier*, but...life felt more...I'm not sure what I'm saying."

"Maybe, life felt more limitless?" I asked. "Now everything is much more real."

"Yes, exactly!" Jamie snapped his fingers. "We were so idealistic back then, we had time to think about things, we had each other. Now people just come and go and its work, work, work." I smiled. We both seemed like such adults. The atmosphere between us now, felt slightly different.

"How's Grace?" Jamie asked reverting his eyes away from me just like he used to all those years ago. "Do you know if she's coming to see Carlos? She's always so busy with her job and I'm always so busy at the hospital, I haven't talked to her in a while."

"Yeah, me neither. She seems a lot busier now that she's working for The Dallas Morning News. But she texted me the other day saying she can't make it. She has to stay and cover the midterm elections."

Jamie nodded. His face turned a bit melancholy. I couldn't avoid the thought that he could still have feelings for her. Grace didn't reveal too much to me over the years. She said they met a few times while he was in med school and she was working at The Boston Globe. But I'm not sure if they actually dated. Grace always became reserved when I asked her how she felt about Jamie.

"I see. Well!" Jamie looked back at me with a big smile. "How's David and your mom? They adjusting to LA ok?"

"Ok? They're in love with LA! Mom can't get enough of the city. She's always going to the beach and green juice cafés – she fits right in. And David seems to like UCLA."

"What's he studying?"

"Architecture."

"Following in his sister's footsteps, I see."

"Pah. More like half a footstep. I never even graduated."

"Yeah, but you're a big movie star now."

"Not really." I said with a smile.

Talking to Jamie reminded me of what it felt like to be 17 again. After Blue Haven, it was hard to see each other. But we tried to keep in touch – email, Skype calls, Facebook. The four of us talked to each other a lot, right after Blue Haven. I used to call Grace almost every weekend. But during our 20s, life led each of us down different roads and the calls and emails became farther and fewer in between.

"How's Carlos?" I asked.

Chapter 45
Jamie

Before Boston, I hadn't spoken to Carlos in years. I ran into him once during my college days. I was drinking at a bar with some friends on Sixth Street. He was dealing in an alleyway around the corner. His voice sounded familiar, even from afar. When I approached him, he started running. I think he thought I was a cop. But then I yelled out his name.

"Carlos! It's me, Jamie!" He stopped and turned around. As he got closer, he looked so different. He was at least 20 pounds thinner. His hair was oily and stuck to his forehead. He wore a black hoodie and couldn't stop moving as he talked. He scratched his head and then his arms. Then he swayed back and forth like a metronome.

"Jamie? My man! How you been? You still in Austin?" Carlos hugged me. I could feel all his bones. I tried to remind myself of the Carlos I knew. But the image didn't match up with the man in front of me.

"Uh. Yeah! I go to UT."

"UT? Damn, I thought you would've gone to Harvard or Yale – one of those New England preppy schools like the one Grace went to."

"Oh yeah. I got into Harvard but I got a full ride at UT. Plus it's closer to family."

"I see. A family man, that's right!"

"How you been man? I tried calling and texting but…"

"Yeah man. Sorry about that. I've just been trying to make money – you know how it is."

"Are you dealing now? Carlos, I thought you said you would stop all of this." I said starting to get angry.

"Man! That was when we were teenagers and I still had options. I don't have any options now." Carlos shouted angrily. His once optimistic face had darkened. There was a new energy to him that felt threatening and unsettling, like standing on top of a tall building looking down.

"Listen, Carlos. I can help you. My mom's a nurse – she can help you get off…"

"Man. Who the hell do you think you are? You think you're better than me?"

"No! I just wanna help."

"Help! Man, no one wants to help me. Not you. Not Grace. Not Sarah. None of you guys care about me anymore. Because I'm trash now."

"No! Carlos, we want to help."

"Screw you man!" Carlos shoved me backwards and disappeared behind the alleyway. I thought about chasing after him. Instead, I went back into the bar.

"Carlos is in…bad shape." I told Sarah, snapping out of my last memory of Carlos.

"How bad?" Sarah didn't move. Her hair was the same. Her face looked the same. But something about the way she moved and spoke, felt older – like time really did pass since we met as high schoolers.

"If he ever uses again…it could be over for him. He has to get clean."

"I don't know how much more I can help him. To be honest, I think Grace just didn't want to see him again. He said some horrible things to her last time. He even came to see her in Dallas and tried to take money from her. He made a big mess in her apartment. Actually – she told me he trashed the place."

"Fuck. Is she ok?"

"Yeah. But I don't think she wants anything to do with him now. And I'm starting to give up hope too…what more can we do?"

"I think it's best he goes back to rehab."

"This would be the third time."

"But it's either rehab or…"

We caught up some more. Sarah asked me about Aisha and Quinn. She remembered their names. I told her Aisha was in college doing well, except for the times she liked to get in fist fights with people twice her size – she never did get much taller after middle school. Quinn was in high school. She was dependable and kind to everyone around her. She's become much more soft spoken. Sometimes I worried she got bullied, but she never complained. Ma was doing great. The seniors still loved her and she liked working at the center more than her old job at the hospital. Easier patients, easier hours. The only time she got sad now was when a patient passed away due to old age or when I caught her thinking about Dad. I could tell she still missed him. We all did.

Sarah never asked about Dad. I hoped she would. Whenever people found out he died, they turned silent and never mentioned it again. But I missed talking about him. I didn't want the memories to die too. Sometimes I like to think he's still alive – still waiting to be saved. They never did find a full body.

"It looks like he'll wake up soon." Sarah and I stood over Carlos who was unconscious and attached to an oxygen mask and an IV. He was stick thin. There were dark blue bruises and cuts all over his forearms. His cheekbones jutted out on his sunken pale face. Sarah started to cry quietly.

"I can't believe this is him." I put my hand on Sarah's shoulder and tried to comfort her, the way professors recommended we should treat patient's families when they hear bad news.

"We're lucky he's still alive." I said. Sarah nodded, wiping away her tears. I brought up a chair for her and she sat next to Carlos. She took his hand and closed her eyes. I brought another chair for myself, and we waited for Carlos to wake up.

A few minutes later, Carlos's eyelids started to flutter. I got out my flashlight and shined the light in his eyes. His pupils shrunk and then returned back to normal. He was hazy at first. His eyes darted back and forth between the two of us, then they started to fill with tears. He took off his oxygen mask.

"What are you two doing here?" Carlos asked crying.

"We came to see if you were ok." Sarah said gently.

"Yeah buddy. Lucky you came to my hospital…I mean." Crap. What am I saying? Carlos looked around the room, tears fell steadily down his face.

"I'm sorry." He said with a rasp in his voice. "You should just leave me. I don't want y'all to see me like this."

"No." Sarah said. "We came to see you because we care about you. We're your friends." Carlos's face moved from sadness to anxiety. It seemed like he suddenly remembered something.

"Could you tell Grace, I'm sorry?" Carlos said sitting up. "Oh my God. I don't deserve to live. The shit I've done."

"It's ok, Carlos." I said.

"No! I'm a monster! Grace was right. I've turned into a monster."

"No, you're not!" Sarah said, her voice becoming more desperate. "You're gonna get better!" Carlos laid back down. He covered his eyes with his bluish arm.

"Does Tía know where I am?" Carlos asked me.

"Yes. I called her and she's on a flight to Boston with Benny." I said, not knowing how to comfort the stranger who used to be my friend.

"Boston? I was in New York yesterday. How did I…" Carlos's face scrunched up with tears again.

"Listen." I said, putting my hand on Carlos's shoulder. "You need some rest. It's going to be tough with your withdrawal symptoms. You need to regain your strength." Carlos wiped his face with his long boney fingers. I took Carlos's blood pressure, temperature, and checked his IV. I told him I'd check up on him again after he got some sleep. Then Sarah and I left the room.

"My God. I didn't expect this." Sarah said.

"Yeah. Me neither. I didn't recognize him when he came in. I had to check his ID and then I realized."

"He doesn't even look like Carlos. Who was that?"

"This can happen with addicts…they change." I wished I could do more to comfort Sarah. In fact, the realization still hadn't sunk in that Carlos was one of the people I studied about, an addict – cocaine, heroin, Vicodin. Carlos had more than one type of drug in his system when they found him.

"What are the chances, Jamie?" Sarah looked up at me, her eyes in search of some hope. "What are the chances he can get better? Sober?" In medical school they taught us not to give patient's families false hope, especially in the terminal cases. We have to be straight forward yet compassionate. Direct but not cold. Carlos got addicted to drugs after leaving Blue

Haven…his chances of recovering to full health were not optimal. In fact, it was nearly impossible.

"I'm not sure." I couldn't bare to give her a real answer. "But I think if he gives rehab another try…he could get better. His health could return, somewhat." I think Sarah could tell I wasn't telling the truth. She looked away as we stood in an empty hall.

"Ok. I'll give Grace a call. I think she'd at least want to know how he's doing."

"Hey, let me. You've gone through a lot today."

"Thanks Jamie."

Chapter 46
Grace

Sometimes I wonder, how different things could have been if it weren't for the choices I've made. If Carlos would have gotten better if I chose to forgive him for the way he acted while high. If I made the choice to stay in Massachusetts with The Boston Globe instead of taking the job at The Dallas Morning News. If I had tried to get help after I fell into depression instead of slowly enduring it all. If I gave Jamie the chance to love me and gave myself the chance to love him back. But then I go back to my resounding belief that everything happened for a reason.

I try not to live with regret. I try to tell myself that everything that's happened, was destined to occur that way. That it was all somehow part of God's master plan. I've reached so many of my goals. Janice and I bought a house for Umma. It was really Janice who paid for most of it though. She's become a total badass as a neurosurgeon. I'm living paycheck to paycheck with my reporter's salary. But I feel like I'm slowly changing things, like I have a role in making the world a better place. I'm happy again, well almost. Umma is happy too. She finally got legally divorced after living apart for 10 years. I've made friends in Dallas, mostly the other reporters and photographers. I even try to date – well so far it's been four bad dates, but who's counting?

    I feel better. I feel good. Almost normal. I try to tell myself this, but then I think of Carlos. I underline and highlight his name in my mind, unable to check the box. I should've forgiven him. I should have gone to see him. But I wasn't in the state to. He started reminding me too much of Appa. I couldn't go through it all again. I didn't have the capacity to. But what if I responded differently? Could it really have helped him get sober? I still remember Jamie's voice when he called after Carlos arrived at the hospital unconscious months ago.

    "Hey, Grace."

    "Jamie?"

    "Yeah. How are you?" Jamie's voice gave me a feeling of warmth mixed with longing. When he got into Harvard Medical School, we met up a couple of times. We always had fun when we were together. We went to a Red Sox game once. We also went on a bunch of foodie adventures, stuffing ourselves with lobster rolls and clam chowder. It felt great having a friend nearby. But then he confessed that he was still in love with me. I told him I loved him too, but the way friends love each other. He stopped calling after that and it felt weird for me to call him. Over time, losing touch was natural.

"I'm fine...how's Carlos? Sarah said he's at your hospital."

"He's...he's doing alright..." There was a hesitation in Jamie's voice. "Actually, Grace. He's in really bad shape. He could use a friend right now...I could too."

"I...he's got you and Sarah. I think he'll be ok with you two."

"Ok. I understand..." Jamie's kind voice filled me with guilt. "How are things at the paper? I read your articles. They're great!"

"Really? You read them!" The thought of Jamie reading my articles filled me with gratitude. I thought he hated me.

"Of course! You're one of my oldest friends. Now you're a big shot journalist. I'm happy for you. Plus, it's good to stay current with what's going on in the world and all."

"Thanks, Jamie. I'm happy for you too." Suddenly, I heard a rushing commotion on Jamie's end. "Is everything ok?"

"I'll have to call you back, Grace." Jamie hung up abruptly. Maybe it was a different patient. Please let it not be Carlos. Please let it not be about him. Please God, keep him alive for just a little while longer. Give him the second chance that I couldn't. I paced around my reporter cubicle. My coworkers must have thought I was anxious for the electoral results. Half an hour later, I got another call from Jamie.

"Hello? What's happened? Was it Carlos?"

"He's missing..."

"What? What do you mean?"

"He left. He went out the window."

"Oh my God. Listen, I can get the next flight to Boston and help y'all search for him."

"No...no, it's ok. They've already called the cops. His aunt and cousin just got here and are talking to the police. We just have to wait. I'll call you when we find him Grace. Don't worry!"

It was too late. I made the wrong choice. In that moment, I knew. I tried to make up for my wrong. I contacted an old friend for help at The Boston Globe, an investigative journalist. A few hours later she called me. She found out Carlos owed a lot of important people in the drug business a lot of money. He's been in several different states over the past year. He was on the run.

Seven months after the incident in Boston, I got a call from Sarah. I always admired her. Even moreso, as we got older. She was the only one who vowed never to give up on Carlos – even after he robbed her apartment and even after I told her to give up on him. Sarah was also the one who tried to keep all of us connected as we ventured into our mid-twenties. She worked hard to keep the friendships alive – just like she promised all those years ago at Blue Haven.

"Carlos was found dead in Chicago. They're having the funeral in Austin this weekend." Sarah's voice sounded lifeless.

My mind started to race and my palms began to sweat. I couldn't steady myself. I felt myself lose control.

"I...how? I thought...he was doing...I thought he would get better."

"Me too." Sarah said with a total lack of emotion in her voice. Suddenly, my body went numb.

I was covering the March For Our Lives protest in D.C. when I got the call. I was surrounded by a sea of people – some holding signs, most chanting. It was a historic day, but then I dropped to the pavement. The sea of people started moving around me like a river around a rock. Some bystanders checked to see if I was ok. I must have looked like I cared immensely about gun control. My camera was still in my hand. I was supposed to be taking photos, covering the scene, interviewing protestors.

But instead, I sat on the pavement and cried. A policeman helped me to a sidewalk asking if I was ok. I didn't have it in me to respond. I cried for Carlos. I cried for his life, for his addiction, for the kind soul that yearned for companionship at Blue Haven. I cried for his aunt and his cousin. I cried for the family that would never be the same again. Then I cried for Appa. His story still didn't have a happy ending. It was constantly stuck and revolving in the same unrelenting pattern.

Then, I cried for myself. I cried for my memories. I cried for Blue Haven. I cried for seeing Appa with the needle and Umma collapsed on the kitchen floor. I cried for not being able to shake the pain from a decade ago. And I cried for my mistakes, for not giving Carlos another chance back when I had the chance to change things.

Chapter 47
Sarah

After moving to LA, I tried to be there for Carlos. But he was always bouncing from city to city. And I was grounded, surrounded by people that were always expecting something from me. Expecting me to be skinny and beautiful. Expecting me to keep my mouth shut when a director paid me less than I was promised. Expecting me to blush when asked about my relationship status by the press. Expecting me to be calm, demure, mysterious – because that's the image my agency chose for me.

It should have made me happy, the success. But soon the people around me became faces I could never trust. They all loved me when the critics did, but their love seemed to stop as soon as a bad review was released or I wasn't the "It Girl" for a day or two. The only times that made me happy were when I was acting for the sake of a good story or when I was with the people I loved.

Before the drugs took him completely, Carlos was my biggest supporter. He had nothing but excitement and joy for me. He always told me I would make it big. After spending years in LA, I got used to being surrounded by a sea of artificiality. Sometimes I got lost in it. But Carlos, he reminded me of the old me. Even when he stole from me, I still remembered the old Carlos – bright eyed and compassionate. He needed more from life. But life kept taking from him. Now he's gone. And I'll never get the chance to tell him that I loved him.

Benny was the one to call me about Carlos. Even though he was the one who brought Carlos into the drug world, Benny eventually got out of it. He bought a house for him and his mom and opened an auto shop, naming it after his dad. But Carlos got stuck. There was too much pain he tried to cover by getting high. The wounds never healed for him.

"Sarah, this is Benny." His voice seemed to whimper like a scared dog. Over the years, Benny and I became friends. We called each other about Carlos – helping each other keep track of where he was or if he was sober.

"Hey, Benny."

"It's about Carlos. The cops found him in an empty apartment in downtown Chicago where he was squatting…"

"Is he alright?"

"No…he's dead. It was an overdose." Benny's voice broke. He started crying. I felt frozen. This couldn't be real. "The new tenants found him when they were about to move in.

The cops said he had been dead for weeks…Sarah he's gone. How could this happen?"

My sadness quickly turned into rage. This was Benny's fault. It was all Benny's fault.

"This happened…because you brought him into this world. You had him try drugs. You made him a dealer. This is all your fault."

"Sarah, please." Benny begged.

"You should be ashamed of yourself. You did this." I spat out the words like venom.

"I-I'm sorry. I didn't mean to – I didn't think it would go this far." Benny said through sobs.

"But it did. And now Carlos's dead body is on your hands. I hope it haunts you for the rest of your life."

I hung up the phone and paced around my trailer. Tears stung my eyes and I felt an aching sensation in my chest. But soon the tears dried up and I felt a hollow emptiness. Life shouldn't be like this. It shouldn't have been Carlos. It should have been someone else who had to die. Why do I keep getting this false hope from people? Things never change! They never get better!

I sat at my vanity and tried to cover my swollen face with make-up, but it only made me look worse. My head was pulsing. I lied down on my sofa, closed my eyes, and tried to sleep until it was my turn to film. This was too much to process. My body felt like it was just hit by a car. Before I could sleep away the pain, I heard a knock at my door.

"Yeah, come in." The person hesitated. "Come in!" No movement. I got up from my sofa and whipped open the door in frustration.

"Dad?" I stared back at the man I hadn't seen in years. Why the hell was he here? Of all the times and places, he chose right now to show up at my door?

"Hi Sarah." He said. I felt a restless energy. I didn't know what to do. I stepped back without a word and briefly thought about slamming the door in his face. Instead, I turned and sat back on the sofa in burning silence.

"You can sit." I finally said, pointing to my vanity chair. He sat down cautiously. Dad's hair was completely white now. His face aged and was fuller than before. He had a new belly. I always imagined Dad stuck in the same age. But he's gotten older. Time didn't stop for him either.

"Do you want something to drink?" I asked breaking the silence.

"No, no. That's fine. Thank you."

"Why are you here?" I asked, feeling something bubble up inside me.

"Madeline and I got here yesterday…We flew in from-"

"-Not when…Why? Why are you here?" I asked. The bubble was at a boiling point now.

"I…I missed you." I scoffed. Dad seemed to cower. "And I wanted to tell you how sorry I am."

"For what?"

"For everything."

"No." A deep hate started to rise from my stomach. "That's not enough. You don't get to do that. What are you sorry for?" Dad fidgeted in his seat.

"I'm sorry for leaving you as a kid. I'm sorry for ignoring you after that. And I'm sorry for telling you, you should give up your family and come live with me instead. I was wrong. With everything. I did everything wrong by you. I treated you so badly. I was never a good father to you. I'm so sorry, Sarah."

"It's too late." Dad's fragile eyes met mine then turned away. He nodded his head slowly, understanding his defeat. "You're too late. Why are you coming to see me now? Now that I'm successful. What is it you want? Do you want money?"

"No! No Sarah. That's not it at all. Seeing you on TV helped me realize something."

"What?"

"I screwed up. Sarah you've grown up to be this amazing person and I had nothing to do with that. You grew up great in spite of me…it made me finally see, how much of an asshole I've been to you."

"Yes, you were an asshole." It felt good to tell him. Dad nodded in agreement which only made me angrier. I stood up in a rage. "You were never there for me! I don't need you anymore! I grew up fine on my own. You don't get to be in my life now! What gives you the right to come back here – after all this time?" I shouted.

My eyes started to tear up. I tried for the life of me, to hold it in. But the tears started to fall. One after the other – despite my efforts, they just kept falling. I thought my tears had dried out already. But it felt like the flood gates were finally opened. I was weeping, in front of the man I haven't spoken to in over 10 years. At first, he watched me from his chair, not knowing what to do. Then he came and sat by me. He put his arm around me and I continued weeping. Soon, I was crying into Dad's shoulder as he embraced me.

"I'm so sorry, Sarah. I'm so sorry. It's all my fault. I'm so sorry." I continued crying as an ocean was released. An ocean I wasn't aware still existed. After a long while, the tears finally ceased. Dad looked at me with eyes of repentance.

"I missed you too." I said. Then Dad started crying, not as much as I did. But enough for his walls to come tumbling down as well. The sight of both of us crying like hurt, frightened children made me smile. It's a scene I never envisioned happening. The unexpectedness of our childlike vulnerability led me to laugh. We laughed together as we wiped away each other's snot and teardrops. Dad pet my hair and moved it out of my face like he did when I was a child.

"Oh Sarah. I'm so proud of you. The woman you've become. Getting into UCLA. Acting. How much you've cared for your mom and David. Getting a house – a place for them to live. You're such a strong person. Sarah, you're amazing."

"How did you…how did you know about the house?"

"I uh. I've kept up with you…through your mom."

"You did?"

"Yes. We've kept in contact for the past several years."

"Why didn't you call me?"

"...I did." Dad smiled. "I tried. And I left messages. But after a while I got the picture you weren't interested."

My mind flooded to seeing Dad's number light up my phone at least once a week during my senior year of high school, then again during college. Swiping left to reject his call then deleting his voicemail without even listening to it.

"Oh yeah..."

"Listen. I know I don't deserve another chance. I don't deserve you at all. I know it's too late for me. I've been the absolute worst father. When I think about how poorly I treated you...it. It makes me so ashamed of myself. But Sarah, I've really changed this time. I...I'm not running from my mistakes or my past anymore. I want to be better for you. I want to be the Dad that you deserve. But I'm not expecting you to forget the past. I know you're angry at me and that you hate me. And you should. You should hate me. I deserve it. But Sarah...Do you think you could ever let me be a part of your life again? Do you think you could ever forgive me?"

Dad's eyes looked worn and tired. He looked fragile, not like the middle-aged man I remembered. He seemed, almost like a child that needed to be cared for, powerless.

"I'll try."

Chapter 48
Grace

I left the therapist's office feeling worse than when I first came in. All the memories of Blue Haven were still swirling in my mind. As soon as I sat down, Misty asked me questions about my life. I'm not sure what else I was expecting, especially from a therapist named Misty. Might as well call her fog. I laughed at my own bad joke as I sat in my car.

Everything I had been holding in, burying deep inside of me was released in a single session. I haven't thought about Blue Haven in years. To be honest, I shut the thought of Carlos out of my mind ever since I got the call from Sarah. I didn't want to think about him. I couldn't. It was like my life began after leaving Blue Haven. My life started with Umma and I moving from apartment to apartment, switching every couple months until my senior year when we were financially stable enough to stay in a tiny two-bedroom apartment that I lovingly remember as home. That's when my life started. Everything before felt like the story of someone else's life. Until today.

That girl was me. The scared and desensitized 16-year-old who found herself in a shelter and befriending the other inmates. The girl who so beautifully and naively believed that life would magically become better upon graduation and had unadulterated dreams of improving the world. That was me.

Tomorrow is the funeral. I drove back to my one-bedroom apartment in Dallas, packed a tiny suitcase and got ready to go to Austin. I haven't visited since Christmas last year. Umma hounds me for not visiting enough. She doesn't seem to understand that news never stops to take a break, so I can't either. But somehow, I managed to get a few days off from my editor.

The drive home was long. I passed open fields of green that made me feel like I was transported to the English countryside – until I saw truck stops and gas stations attached to Subways and Burger Kings. I passed by the outlets where Umma, Janice, and I used to shop. I passed by the IHOP we used to frequent that gave me a burst of nostalgia. I decided to pass the exit that would've led me to Blue Haven. I thought about making a pit stop there to relive the memories. But then I decided not to and drove all the way home.

Umma was waiting for me with a steaming hot pot of kimchi jigae and bowl of steamy white rice already set on the dining table. I inhaled the food that reminded me of my childhood and Umma talked to me as I satisfied my hunger.

"How was the drive?...You look skinnier...How is job?...You like boss?...You should be careful...I don't like the dangerous news...you write safe stories...you talk to Janice?...She's always busy...You always busy too...What time is funeral?"

I nodded and reacted as she told me stories of the new church she visited and road trips she's taken with her new friends. After I finished eating, we watched Die Hard 5 together which Umma rented from the library.

"This one not good. First one much better." Umma said. I nodded in agreement. After the movie was over, I changed into a black dress and got in my car. My heart started to race and my palms were sweaty against the steering wheel.

I haven't seen Sarah, in person, for over a year and Jamie for longer. The last time I saw Carlos...I tried to shake the memory out of my mind but the reality of Carlos's death confronted me as I parked outside the Catholic church.

There were people already seated in the first three rows. I didn't see Sarah or Jamie. There was an older lady that I think was Carlos's aunt. I wondered if his real mom knew Carlos died, or if she was here. I sat in the back row, behind everyone. A man in a robe arose at the altar. He spoke of God's love and grace, how loved Carlos was by his aunt and cousin that welcomed Carlos as a son. Then a man, I assumed was Benny, stood at the altar and gave a speech – first in English, then in

Spanish. He started crying, then he went back to his seat. We stood up together in unison and sung a hymn. I could see the large photograph of Carlos. I could tell it was from many years ago, back when Carlos still looked like Carlos. I had to avert my eyes, knowing I would start crying if I stopped to think deeply about the Carlos from my teenage years.

The funeral was a blur. We were ushered outside to a crisp field of green interrupted by gravestones. Carlos's aunt and cousin tossed a pile of soil onto Carlos's lowered casket. I started to feel like I was floating. Was Carlos's body really inside? Was this really not just all a dream? Please God, would you make this a dream, and when I wake up, could you have Carlos appear? I want to talk to him. I want to hear his voice. I want to tell him it's not too late. It's not too late.

But it wasn't a dream. Carlos's casket was lowered all the way to the ground. People started leaving the cemetery and walking back towards their cars. I stood motionless to it all. God, please. Is it too late for a miracle? I tried to turn around, go back home. But it was like I was stuck. Until, I heard the sound of someone speaking to me.

"Grace?" I blinked a few times, trying to process the person standing right in front of me. It was Sarah. Suddenly, it felt like I could move again.

"Sarah!" I hugged her immediately. She was taken aback by my show of affection.

"Oh my God. I can't believe you're hugging me." Sarah laughed, wiping a stray tear.

"It's only cause I haven't seen you in a long time. Don't get used to it!" I said with a laugh, taking in her face. Back during our teenage years, I always complained when Sarah hugged me. I was not a hugger. In fact, hugging was a foreign thing to me until I met Sarah. After a while, I realized another person was standing next to her. Jamie! My God, he's become a man. The sight of his strong and towering frame surprised me.

"Jamie!" I squealed and moved in for another hug.

"Grace! Hi!" Time did Jamie well. Before today, I often wondered how it would feel to see him after all these years. I'm not sure why I worried. As soon as I recognized his face, my heart rejoiced.

"It's so good to see you guys. I can't believe it."

"So good to see you too!" Jamie said. "This is my girlfriend, Ellen." Jamie turned to the woman to his left. She was tall and slender. Her face looked kind.

"I'm so glad I get to meet you." Ellen said. "Jamie's told me wonderful things about his friend, the famous reporter."

"Jamie likes to exaggerate." I chuckled. "It's great to meet you too. How did you two meet?"

"Oh, we met during our residency in Boston." Ellen said with a smile.

"Yeah, we bonded over neurons and electrons." Jamie said elbowing Ellen. The two of them together made me smile.

"Tell me. Is Jamie a good doctor?" I asked eagerly. "I can't imagine him with a white coat and a stethoscope."

"He's a great doctor! Although, probably not as good as me." Ellen said. We laughed and Jamie nodded in agreement.

"It's true!" Jamie said.

"I'll let the three of you catch up." Ellen said and waved goodbye.

Sarah, Jamie, and I started walking down a strangely serene pathway which cut through the cemetery. The setting sun warmed me like a hug. The soft, sweet breeze reminded me of the day we first met.

"Remember when we ate pizza and drank beer together at Blue Haven?" I said, as we walked together amidst the evening glow.

"Yeah, I remember how shocked you were when you found out I brought beer." Sarah said smiling.

"Yeah! And your cheeks got all red after a few sips." Jamie laughed.

"They did not!"

"They did! I think you got drunk." Jamie said.

"Well, I've gotten better at drinking since then." I smirked.

"Are you sure?" Sarah asked.

"Just kidding. I lied. I still can't drink for shit." The three of us laughed together. We stopped at a bench tucked under a giant tree. Sarah took a seat first, Jamie and I followed.

"God, we were so young back then. Now we're old and our bodies are falling apart." Sarah said.

"Nah. You still look great." I told Sarah.

"It's all a façade. I've started getting acupuncture. All my bones are clicking." Sarah replied.

"Tell me about it." Jamie agreed. "I can't even comprehend thoughts until I've had at least two cups of coffee."

"Y'all are old! I still feel young." I said.

"Trust me. As soon as you reach 27, you'll start to feel it." Sarah said. Jamie chuckled to himself. The three of us sat together and watched as the sun set through the leaves and made dancing shadows on the pavement in front of us.

"Do you guys think…if I had come to Boston to see Carlos, none of this would have happened?" I asked, breathing in the warm air around us.

"No." Sarah said as soon as I finished. "It's not your fault."

"Yeah, Carlos was on his own path." Jamie said. "I go back to that time in Boston too. I try to figure out if I had done things differently, if it would have saved him. No matter how much I think about it…Carlos was already so far gone."

"I used to wonder if Carlos would have lived if I went after him back in LA, after he left and disappeared." Sarah stared into the rows of gravestones. In the light, they didn't feel so ominous. "I tried to be there for him but…" Sarah sighed in sadness.

"You were there for him. I just wish I didn't give up on him." I said, turning away to hide my tears.

"Carlos gave up on himself." Sarah whispered, her eyes glistening.

"Carlos…he had a kind soul." Jamie said. "He sent me a letter once. It was when he was in rehab the first time. He told me…" Jamie cleared his throat, trying to hold back tears. "He told me he was proud of me. He was proud of me that I got into Harvard med school. He told me that he wanted me to have a good life."

Sarah and I wiped our tears as Jamie spoke.

"I talked to him once, on the phone while I was at Amherst College." I remembered. "It was when I was going through a hard time. He sounded good on the phone, it was when he was sober for six months. I told him how depressed I felt, how alone I was. And he told me he loved me. He told me he would come visit me…but he never…"

I remembered Carlos's voice that day over the phone. It was filled with concern and care for how I was doing. But I was too blind to see how much he was suffering too. I didn't bother to ask.

"Carlos mailed a letter to me too." Sarah said leaning forward, letting her pale face catch the sunlight. "It was after I put him into rehab, his second time around. He told me how sorry he was about…about the robbery. That he wished he were a better man. How he wished he could get over his past, but couldn't. I wish…I wish I had sent a letter back, but I was still angry at him then." Sarah turned her face away from us.

"It's alright, Sarah. It's not your fault either." Jamie said. Sarah turned back towards us. We let the wind whistle through the trees. A bird started singing above us. "I remember the first time I saw Carlos. He appeared out of nowhere at our – what did we call ourselves?"

"The 3 a.m. club." I said.

"Oh yeah! The 3 a.m. club." Jamie said smiling to himself.

"We thought we were so cool." Sarah scoffed.

"He came storming out because I burned something. What was it?" Jamie asked.

"Pizza?" Sarah and I said in unison.

"Yes! The pizza." Jamie belted a laugh that made me smile. "I was so freaking scared when he appeared out of nowhere, yelling at me because I almost burnt down the whole place. But then he sat with us and we started talking. God. I don't know if I've ever gotten so close with someone as quickly as we did, as the four of us did." Jamie looked at us, his face full of memories.

"Me neither." I said.

"It's strange." Jamie said. "So much time has passed since the four of us met, but at the same time, it feels like time hasn't passed at all."

"I know what you mean." I said. "At times it feels like a long time ago, but then sometimes it feels like we were there yesterday."

"Yeah…I used to get this heavy feeling when I thought about it." Jamie said. "But over the past few years, I don't know. It's almost like a happy memory. It's weird, right?"

"No, I feel the same way." Sarah said.

"Me too." I said. "It's like on one side, it was the darkest time in all our lives. But on the other side, we had each other. It made things easier."

"It really did." Sarah said. "Things didn't feel as bad when we were together…I've missed you guys."

"I missed you guys too." I said.

"Me too." Jamie smiled.

"Let's make a deal." I said. "We'll try harder to keep up with each other. Less missed phone calls and unreplied messages. And let's try to meet in person, the three of us, at least once a year."

"That seems doable. We can take turns every year – Boston, Dallas, and LA." Jamie said with a smile.

"And whenever we visit family in Austin, we should try to go at the same time and meet up!" I said excitedly.

"We're not gonna do one of those blood pacts, are we?" Sarah said grinning.

"Let's just shake on it." I said. The three of us shook hands with each other, one arm over the other. We laughed at how childlike it felt. For a moment, I forgot the sadness I felt this morning.

A man appeared out of the corner of my eye. He was walking toward the three of us. He looked like he was in his early 30s. Tall, thin, amiable.

"Benny." Sarah whispered.

"Hey." Benny said. "I just wanted to give you guys something – from Carlos."

"What is it?" Jamie asked eagerly.

"He wrote the three of you a letter. They found it in his apartment in Chicago. He never mailed it." Benny held out an envelope to me. The edges were frayed and it was covered with dirty smudge marks. It was still unopened. "Carlos really loved you guys." Benny's face looked worn and tired. Sarah stood up and walked towards him. She hugged him and whispered something to his ear. Benny nodded and smiled a little before walking away.

"Should I open it?" I asked. Jamie and Sarah nodded.

Chapter 49

Carlos

Dear 3 a.m. Club,

I am writing this in an apartment that doesn't belong to me. I've been living here for the past several months. I know that I am close to dying, and I've come to the realization that I don't want to die. I want to live. I am trying to live, but it is very very hard.

When I am not getting high, all I can feel is a mountain of pain inside of me. So then I get high to feel nothing at all. I know that I hurt each of you. I'm sorry for the things I've said and the things I've done to you. There are too many things to apologize for and to write down. There are things I've said while I was high and while I was sober that still haunt me and remind me that I've become a monster. But please know that my heart still aches over all of those things and I wish I could take it all back.

But I know, that I can't. I hope you all can forgive me, one day. And I hope I will still be alive when you do.

I have been sober for the past 13 days. I am trying to get to 14. Lately, the only time I feel a pause from the pain is when I think about our time at Blue Haven. It's strange for such a hopeless place to bring me hope. You three were such good friends to me. Even after, when we all grew up, the three of you tried to help me. You were my family. I'm sorry I wasn't family to you.

It's taking everything out of me to not get high, to try not to escape the pain. I am trying to give this over to God. I'm trying to ask for help. But sometimes I feel like I am in too deep. Maybe it's too late for me. Other times, I think there's still a chance I could live a normal life.

I hope that one day I will be able to send this letter. I hope that one day I can undo the wrongs I did to each of you. I hope that one day, I will become the kind of man that deserves all of your friendship and trust. I am sorry. I love you all. Thank you for loving me when I didn't deserve it.

I am trying to live. With everything left in me, I want to live.

Love,
Carlos

Chapter 50
Jamie

The three of us read Carlos's letter with tears streaming down our faces. I could hear Carlos's sweet and gentle voice reading the words aloud to me. He was trying to live. He was fighting. My dear, dear friend. I hope you are alive in heaven. I hope the pain is gone. I hope you and my dad got to meet and became friends. Carlos, I hope you are free.

We sat there for a while. Reading and rereading. Crying and crying some more. I could feel a release happening for each of us. We all had regrets with Carlos. We all wish we had done more. But Carlos felt the same way. He still loved us, until the end. I could have sat there all night, reading and rereading Carlos's letter. But then my phone rang.

"Ma?"

"Jamie. You have to come home."

"I will Ma. I'm just with my friends. Ellen and I will come over tonight."

"No baby. You gotta come right now."

"Is something wrong?"

"No. You just gotta come home right now."

"Ok."

I hung up the phone confused.

"Was that your mom?" Grace asked. I nodded.

"Sorry guys. It looks like she needs me."

"It's alright. We'll see each other soon." Sarah said, smiling. We took turns hugging goodbye and promised to see each other again before leaving Austin.

Ellen and I drove to Ma's new house. She moved in six months ago after saving up her paychecks and the little bits I was able to send her since starting my residency. Ma was in a decorating frenzy now. She seemed to go with a watering can and seashell theme. Aisha hated it, of course. Quinn was amused by it.

I opened the front door, which was unlocked, and was welcomed by the smell of Ma's roasted chicken. Ma, Aisha, and Quinn were gathered together in the living room. A sense of excitement hovered around them.

"Ma?" I asked. She turned around, her face covered in tears. Aisha and Quinn turned around too. Their faces were joyful. They were smiling. "What's going on?" Slowly, the three of them backed away from each other revealing someone behind them. A man in a wheelchair. He looked elderly. His hair was white. Who was this stranger in our house? I walked a bit closer and tried to inspect him. As he became clearer, I noticed his legs were missing. He had a deep scar on his left arm and on his cheek. We locked eyes.

"Hi Jamie." The man said.

"Hello…" I said politely. I wondered if Ma kidnapped a patient from the senior home. No one was saying a thing. I took another step closer. His face became clearer. His eyes were dark. His cheek bones were strong and his skin was smooth, despite the scars. There was something about him that I couldn't place, a feeling of familiarity. Then the man smiled. There was a sparkle in his eyes. His forehead had the faintness of steady lines that never quite disappeared. I spotted a widow's peak pointing out of his hairline. There was something vaguely familiar in his scent. Then, my heart dropped. This couldn't be real. This must be a dream.

"It's me, son." The breath was stolen out of my lungs. I ran to him. I ran to my father. I knelt on the floor and looked deeply into his face. It was him! My dad! My dad is alive. He's in front of me. He's real!

"Is this a dream?"

"It's not a dream, son. I'm your dad. I'm alive. I'm sorry it took me so long to get back to you."

I threw my arms around him. I felt Dad's warmth. His scent. It was him. He was real! I pulled my face back to check if he was still real. It was really was my dad. He laughed, tears streaming down his face. Then we embraced each other again.

"My son. My son. I've missed you so much."

"I knew you were alive. I knew it. I just knew it."

My heart was bursting. Everything I've been wanting, everything I was waiting for was in front of me now. Could this be real? Could this be happening?

"I'm so sorry I was gone for so long." Dad said.

"Your daddy has had quite the journey." Ma said. Aisha and Quinn joined me as we hugged Dad.

"Where were you? Where have you been all this time?" I asked eagerly.

"It's quite a long story." Dad said. The very sound of his voice lifted my soul to the ceiling.

Dad proceeded to tell us what happened to him in Afghanistan. How he was caught in the bombing and lost one of his legs in the process. How he woke up and crawled into a cave for cover. How he tried to survive in that cave after making a tourniquet and lived off of bugs and plants. How he fell from a small cliff after trying to find a way back and woke up in a remote village where some locals took care of him. How he couldn't remember things after the fall. How he lost his second leg to an infection. How the villagers nursed him to health. How he tried to remember who he was and where he came from, year after year. And how piece by piece, he started to remember. How at first, he only got flashbacks of bombings and gunshots. Then, how the sound of a Stevie Wonder song played at a villager's house triggered a memory of eating ice cream in the car with me, Aisha, and Quinn. How he managed to signal for help. And how he was able to come back home.

Ma, Quinn, Aisha, Ellen, and I sat on the couch lined up in a row, listening in complete awe.

"I'm sorry I couldn't come in better condition." Dad said jokingly, looking at his amputated legs which disappeared above the knees.

"Are you kidding?" I said. "I just can't believe you're alive."

Ma got up and headed to the kitchen on her own. She tried to save face, but was still crying at the sight of seeing Dad for the first time in 10 years. Dad rolled in his wheelchair to be with her.

"You're not avoiding me, are ya? Don't tell me you found some other honey while I was gone." Ma laughed through the tears. She bent down and kissed him. They looked at each other in pure adoration.

We all ate dinner together. We talked about the last 10 years. Each of us tried to remember everything that happened and update Dad. Aisha and Quinn fought for Dad's attention. He smiled and laughed through it all.

Later that night, each of us went to bed. But my heart was so full – I couldn't keep my eyes closed for more than a few minutes. I wanted to go back to Ma's room and check to see that Dad was still there. I wanted to make sure that it wasn't all a dream. That Dad was still alive and here with us. At 3 a.m., I finally succumbed to my restlessness and got out of bed. I tiptoed towards the living room. It reminded me of when I was a teenager and used to sneak out to see Jamal.

Halfway through my journey across the darkened living room, a light turned on. Ma was sat down with a cup of tea at the kitchen table. Her eyes were still bright with joy.

"Couldn't sleep?" Ma asked.

"No. I'm too excited." I said grinning.

"Me too." I sat down at the table across from Ma.

"Did you get a chance to see Jamal? He came by earlier asking for ya."

"Yeah, I'm planning to see him tomorrow."

"Oh, Jamie. When I opened the door and saw your daddy, I thought I had just died and gone to heaven. I just couldn't believe it…I keep on checking to see that I'm awake."

"Me too. It doesn't feel real. It doesn't feel like something this good could happen to us." Ma tilted her head to the side, confused.

"What do you mean, baby?"

"It's just…God kept on taking things from us. One after the other, again and again and again. I just couldn't believe something so good could be real. I can't believe that God would give us something I've wanted so much. It doesn't feel possible."

Ma reached out and took my hand, the warmth of her fingers radiated through me.

"Oh baby. It's true. God took a lot from us. He took your daddy. He took our home. He took our finances, stability, you name it. But Jamie, look at your life now. You're a doctor. You're saving lives. You have a girlfriend – who by the way is so out of your league. I don't know how you got her here." Ma laughed patting my hand. "Now, you have your daddy again. What God took away he redeemed. You can look at your life thinking of all the things you've lost. Or…you can choose to see what was given. The moments in life that turned you into the man you are today."

Ma's words sunk deep into my soul. The things that were given. I tried to see it. Ellen, I found the love of my life in her. The white coat. Treating patients and seeing their pain go away, the joy that gave me. Grace, Sarah, and even the memory of Carlos. The love I felt from them. The sense of belonging. And now Dad.

Ma finished her tea, kissed my cheek, then went back to her room. I sat for a while longer, trying to process everything that happened. A feeling of gratitude coursed through my veins. I walked up to Ma's room. I needed to see him one more time.

I opened the door carefully and peeked inside. He was still there. My dad was breathing, alive. Ma was nestled into his arms. They were sleeping. Their faces, still smiling.

~The End~

About the Author

SYLVIA KIM has dreamed of writing books since she was a child. After graduating from the University of Texas, she worked in journalism and marketing for several years. Dissatisfied with corporate life, she quit her job and wrote her very first novel.